Time's Up is R. A. Jordan's debut novel, although he has written four more to complete a pentalogy following the fortunes of the Wall family during the first decade of the new millennium.

Jordan is a chartered surveyor and has practiced in the north west of England for the last forty-five years. With a vast knowledge of the property sector, his dealings have equipped him well to tell stories about his world.

He is a family man, businessman, sailor and classic car owner, and these experiences in business and life have added authenticity to the plots.

To Matthew

Time's Up

[signature]

Nov-2015

R.A. JORDAN

Time's Up

Vanguard Press

VANGUARD PAPERBACK

© Copyright 2015
R.A. Jordan

The right of R.A. Jordan to be identified as author of
this work has been asserted by him in accordance with the
Copyright, Designs and Patents Act 1988.

All Rights Reserved

No reproduction, copy or transmission of this publication
may be made without written permission.
No paragraph of this publication may be reproduced,
copied or transmitted save with the written permission of the publisher, or in
accordance with the provisions
of the Copyright Act 1956 (as amended).

Any person who commits any unauthorised act in relation to
this publication may be liable to criminal
prosecution and civil claims for damages.

A CIP catalogue record for this title is
available from the British Library.

ISBN 978 178465 008 7

All characters in this book are fictitious,
and any resemblance to actual persons
living or dead is purely coincidental.

Vanguard Press is an imprint of
Pegasus Elliot MacKenzie Publishers Ltd.
www.pegasuspublishers.com

First Published in 2015

Vanguard Press
Sheraton House Castle Park
Cambridge England

Printed and bound in Great Britain

Acknowledgements

The author acknowledges the help of the following people whose input to this novel have been invaluable – thank you, all.

Carol, Helen, Sarah and the local vet, and Jon.

To Caro

'Murder, like talent, seems occasionally to run in families'

G H Lewes 1817–1878

1.1.2000 Saturday

It was late for New Year's Eve and far too early for New Year's Day. New Year's Eve had been a real bash. The whole family – Ann, Peter's wife, and his two daughters, Sandy and Si and their boyfriends – all lived it up at the Portal Golf Club New Year's Eve Party.

Ann and Peter had got home at gone two a.m. and the girls and the rest of the gang had gone on into Chester to a club.

"God knows what time the girls will be back," muttered Peter as he slid into the passenger seat of his Range Rover whilst Ann, who had also had a few drinks, drove home. The thinking was that if Ann got stopped and lost her licence it would not be half as bad as if Peter lost his.

It wasn't a long journey back to their converted farm and outbuildings with about twenty acres of land. It was, however, Peter and Ann's dream home. They had bought it some three years earlier at auction when the farmer retired. There was the potential of buying a lot more land but Peter, whilst he wanted some land, did not want the responsibility of over a hundred acres. Peter and Ann bought the main lot which was the house and outbuildings and the twenty acres of land surrounding the house.

It was a wreck and the place needed gutting and sorting out. There was stiff competition at the auction as the developer boys could see the opportunity to do a barn conversion and make at least two houses out of the outbuildings and then modernise the house. At eight hundred and fifty thousand pounds for a wreck of a house, it was a tidy sum and more than the developers could pay and see a good profit at the end.

Peter had some advantage over the normal house buyer as he owned Walls Civil Engineering based on the Sealand Industrial Estate in Chester. That would be the source of labour and money for the conversion.

Peter had started his company some ten years previously in 1989 and he had built up a successful civil engineering business by concentrating on ground works for new residential estates and industrial estates. Peter had been the manager of a similar business which hit hard times. He left with Roger Whiteside and they set up Walls Civil Engineering together.

Like all new businesses hard work from the owners was the order of the day. The firm carried Peter's name as he was a qualified surveyor, a profession he was proud of and one his youngest daughter had decided to follow, although in the estate agency world.

The company needed some cash to get going and Peter was more of a businessman whilst Roger was the hands-on administrator and organiser of the work. Peter had agreed to a second mortgage on his house and raised some funds from the bank to get them started. Luckily in the ground works business most things needed can be hired, so there was no commitment to spending large sums of capital. The company had gone from strength to strength and obtained a number of good and regular customers as the property development boom continued. The Walls team were in constant demand.

They purchased Long Acre Farm in Tarporley, about nine miles from Chester and the firm's headquarters. Life had been stressful at work in the last year of the millennium due to a VAT inspection and now an Inland Revenue investigation. It all surrounded the cost of modernising the farm. This had not only put Peter under immense strain but the relationship with Roger, his business partner, was at an all-time low.

"How lucky we are to live in such a lovely home in this idyllic setting," said Ann as she swung the Range Rover off the main road into a narrow lane, which eventually gave way to a gravel driveway, once over the cattle grid to the farm.

"God, I nearly hit that," she exclaimed as she swerved to avoid a black Vauxhall Astra car with two wheels on the road and two on the grass verge. "What on earth are they doing at this time of night in our lane?"

"It's not 'our' lane Ann. It's a public highway. It's a couple of lovers who have stopped for a cuddle."

"I could only see one person in the car," Ann said.

"Well the girlfriend has probably got her head on his lap doing what young people do nowadays."

"What on earth do you mean?"

"I mean she is probably giving him a blow job."

"Oh, Peter, you do say the most awful things sometimes."

Rattle, rattle went the cattle grid as the car crossed over.

"What a noise that thing makes," said Peter, feeling a little worse for wear.

"It's easier than getting out to open the gate, and you say that almost every time we go over it, why don't you get it fixed?"

Peter didn't reply, he was not getting involved in the cattle grid debate now.

As Ann neared the house and courtyard, surrounded on three sides by buildings, she pressed a button on the remote to open the garage door and went straight in with the Range Rover.

"No lights on above," she said. "I don't know what time the girls will get back."

The two girls had independent flats over the outbuildings with separate entrances.

"It's probable we will not see them until tomorrow; they went off with the boys and will probably stay the night or what's left of it, in Chester."

"Ah yes, those were the days – no they weren't," recalled Ann. "When were we allowed by parents to sleep around? Back by midnight I seem to recall my father insisting. My God how things have changed."

"It's really mild for January," Peter remarked as they walked across the yard to the house.

As they entered the utility room through the back door Purdy the black Labrador didn't move. She was fast asleep. They had given her a sedative to calm her down because there were going to be lots of fireworks to bring in the new millennium, and she was terrified of fireworks. Strange really, as a trained gun dog she had no problem with gunfire but fireworks were a different noise altogether and really spooked her.

Having crept by the dog and secured the back door, they were in bed in no time and Ann was snoring. Too much red wine, Peter thought to himself as he drifted into sleep.

1.1.2000 0700hrs

It's a body clock thing. When you are used to getting up at the same time every day of your life, there is nothing on God's earth that will stop your internal clock from waking you at your normal time.

Peter slipped out of bed; Ann was well away and so he went into the dressing room, quietly closed the door and put on, as he did every day, his old farming clothes for a walk with Purdy. In the utility room Peter pulled on his Musto shooting jacket and green gumboots and noted Purdy was less than anxious to join him this morning, indeed she was virtually asleep and not for waking. There was a twitch of the tail and that was that. The tranquilisers I gave her last night must still be working, he thought.

Leaving Purdy to her slumbers Peter went out across the yard to the machinery shed and got into Jumbo, the 1955 Series Two Land Rover that they had used on the farm for years. It wasn't taxed but it was used for running around the farm taking fodder and mending fences. The canvas top had been removed many a long year ago, as it had got torn. The vehicle was now stripped down to the basics but was very drivable.

Peter liked to drive it first thing in the morning out of the machinery shed and up to the highest point on the farm, where a solitary oak tree stood on top of a mound, and allowed him to view the house and outbuildings one way and, on a clear day, over a small copse to the west and in the distance the Welsh mountains.

He was feeling bad this morning; the alcohol had really left him with a bad head. He was also very concerned that he could lose all this if the Inland Revenue carried out their threat to sue him for the tax and unpaid VAT on the farm improvements. He was also heavily in debt to the bank with the business and personally and unbeknown to the family, he had used all the credit on his various credit cards.

Peter was in a very dark mood this morning, just like the weather as it was taking some time for the sun to spread some light from the east. The sky was lightening but it still would be called dark, although when you are outside the gloom doesn't seem as dark as it does when viewed from inside the house. Peter was really gloomy with a thumping head as he bent down to switch on the ignition and press the start button.

Jumbo puffed out her usual delivery of grey smoke and then rumbled across the yard up the Long Meadow to the top of the rise to the old oak tree, which sat on the very apex of the mound.

The wire cable that was used on the winch on the front of the Jumbo was untied from its drum and the hook end of the cable run round the tree, and the hook connected back on to the cable. The other end of the cable made off with a swaged splice was tied into a loop, the run of cable passed through the loop, so creating a noose.

Whilst in Jumbo's driver's seat Peter had the noose over his head and then Jumbo started down the hill using the hand throttle to keep the vehicle going, ever gaining speed. As it ran down the slope the wheels stayed in the ruts Jumbo had made by going up and down the hill to the very same spot over the last three years.

This was the end. As Jumbo roared off down the hill the cable became tight. At a point the noose tightened, the wire rope stretched and with one last desperate tug on the rope, and with Jumbo running down the hill, the noose closed shut in a second. The cable bit into Peter's neck, through flesh and bone, it had decapitated Peter. His head cut cleanly off his shoulders as if it were a piece of cheese cut with cheese wire. His head rolled into the back of Jumbo and his torso and body slumped to the passenger side of the car. The cable was strung out down the hill with the noose now half way down the slope.

Jumbo, with her gruesome load, came to a stop at the bottom and ran hard up against a stone gatepost, not going anywhere. Peter's time was up.

At about half past eight Ann got up, put on her dressing gown and went to the kitchen to make a cup of tea. Her head was thumping and when she bent down the world swung around violently. After putting the kettle on she heard some rustling in the utility room. Opening the door she was surprised to see Purdy.

"Hello, old girl, not gone for a walk this morning?" asked Ann, who then noticed Purdy had been sick in her bed and was unstable on her feet.

Ann realised that Peter had done his usual trick and gone up to the top of the farm and obviously had found Purdy unwilling to go with him so left her alone, not realising at that time she was ill. Ann soon cleared up the mess and gave Purdy some clean water. "Best not to eat anything just now old girl until your sickness has gone."

Ann took her cup of tea upstairs and showered and changed ready for the day ahead, which would consist of a running buffet as people came and went at all hours of the day. It was always open house at the Walls' on New Year's Day.

It was nearly half past nine and Peter had not returned to the house. Where on earth could he be? Thought Ann.

Ann and Purdy, both still a little the worse for wear, Ann with her big Barbour jacket and wellies on, strode out of the yard towards the top of the farm. There was another cattle grid to go over, and Purdy never liked this obstacle, so Ann opened the side gate and walked round the grid, and then around the back of the outbuildings towards the top of the farm. She could see the old oak in the distance, and she thought she could see Jumbo next to the field gate to the top field. The gate was open but Jumbo didn't seem to be in the gate opening but just to the side.

Peter must have got out to fix a bit of fencing whilst there, she thought, and walked on.

"Peter, Peter!" she shouted, but no response and as she neared Jumbo she could just make out Peter and his mustard-coloured shooting jacket in the front of Jumbo.

Something is not right! She broke into a trot and then, as she was only a few yards from Jumbo, she could see Peter's headless body slumped over on to the passenger seat.

"Oh my God!" she screamed and collapsed on the ground and was immediately sick.

1.1.2000 10.30 hrs

Ann was in a terrible state, she could hardly walk back to the house. She had collapsed yards from Jumbo and Peter, and Purdy, sensing something was wrong, came to her and licked her face.

Ann recovered slightly with this wet warm lick. She staggered back to the house ashen of face and nearly doubled up in distress. What on earth has happened, how could this have occurred? She just couldn't get the sight of Peter's torso out of her mind. His head, she knew, must be nearby but she had not got the stomach or strength to go and look. She was totally devastated.

In the house she dialled 999 immediately.

"I don't know, my husband has died and I just don't know."

"What is your name please?"

"Ann. Ann Wall," she whispered.

"Stay right there madam I am connecting you to the police now."

"Police," came an efficient and yet cold voice.

"I need help. My husband's died. It's awful, can you help me please?" she said, crying down the phone.

"What is your address please?"

"Long Acre Farm, Tarporley."

"And your name please?"

"Ann – Ann Wall," she stuttered out.

"Are you on your own Mrs Wall?"

"Yes."

"Don't worry, we will have someone with you very shortly."

Ann struggled to the toilet in the utility room and was sick again. She just couldn't think straight. What had happened to her husband, her life, everything?

Last night everything seemed so perfect, not a care in the world, the party was really great fun and the girls...

"Oh my God the girls! I must wake them, no they are not there, oh my God where are they?" Ann got her mobile out of her handbag and phoned Sandy, the older of the two sisters.

"Hello?" came a slow and clearly very drowsy voice.

"Sandy?"

"Yes Mum, are you okay?"

"No darling, can you find Si and both of you come home quickly. There has been a terrible accident. It's Daddy, come home please," and with that Ann had to switch the phone off as she burst into tears once again.

She just sat in the kitchen like a zombie, not knowing what to do or who to call. She was numb. She couldn't think about anything other than the terrible sight that greeted her at the entrance to the Long Meadow.

Her inner turmoil was rudely interrupted by a loud knock on the back door. Purdy gave a bark and ran out through the dog flap in the door.

Ann dragged herself to the back door to find a police constable standing there, his panda car in the yard.

"You called the police, madam?" He could immediately see that Ann was in a desperate state and clearly in shock. "Shall we go in, madam, out of the cold?" Ann just stood there with a glazed look over her ashen face.

"Tell me what the problem is, madam."

"It's Peter, my husband, he's dead."

"I see, where is he now?"

"He's in Jumbo."

"Oh?"

"That's our Land Rover, at the entrance to the Long Meadow," she began to cry again uncontrollably this time. The young PC was not sure what to do next but his training clicked in to make him want to inspect the body.

"Are you sure he is dead madam? Do we need an ambulance?"

Ann couldn't reply. She just shook her head whilst the tears streamed down her cheek.

"Where is the Land Rover from here?"

Ann just pointed in the appropriate direction for Long Meadow. The PC went over the cattle grid and out towards the field.

It didn't take him too long to see the Land Rover at the side of the gateway. As he drew nearer he could clearly see the torso of a man in a mustard jacket slumped across the passenger side of the car. From a few steps away he suddenly realised that he was looking at a headless body and there was blood everywhere. He couldn't help himself, he just turned to the hedge and threw up. He hadn't seen such an event before and he certainly never wanted to again.

Oh my God, he thought to himself. What now?

He phoned on his radio to Control.

"Sarge?"

"Yes?"

"It's PC368, I am at Long Acre Farm in Tarporley. We have a very gruesome death. I assume it is suicide but we will need lots of help. I need help, the sight here is horrendous."

"All right lad, don't get carried away, this sort of thing happens."

"He's had his head cut off."

"My God. We will need all the troops, you stay there lad and comfort the wife as best you can. I will get the ball rolling."

1.1.2000 Noon

Geoff, Sandra's latest, had kindly driven both Sandra and Sienna from Chester back to the farm. They thanked him and, still in their party frocks from the night before, ran to the back door and into the kitchen.

"Mum, what on earth has happened?" they said almost as one.

Ann, with tears still streaming down her face, explained it was Peter, their father who had had some form of accident whilst in Jumbo and had died.

"Ooh, no!" They shouted, and in turn started to weep with both of them hugging their mother so they formed one large, sobbing mass of humanity.

Their grief was shaken by another loud knock on the door. It was the PC again, to say that more police had arrived and the forensic team were on their way and a Home Office pathologist would be here soon.

The yard within the hour was filled with police cars, vans and a private ambulance. A private car arrived and the two male occupants, ignoring the possibility of speaking to the occupants of the house, made straight for the field.

"What a muddy mess this is."

"It's what you get on a farm, lad. Didn't you have any Wellingtons?"

"No sir," said the junior detective. "But I will next time."

DS Evans, being an old hand at policing in Cheshire, knew that a farm address would mean mud and so he had come prepared with wellingtons. He was pleasantly surprised to find the yard beautifully paved and was very clean and tidy, but the walk to Long Meadow was a different issue.

The field gate area was already surrounded by police vehicles. As he approached Evans could see the Land Rover and the body slumped across the passenger side of the vehicle.

"Hello Hugh, happy New Year," he said to the pathologist. "What have we got?"

"Thanks, same to you. We have a mess; this guy would appear to have committed suicide in a very bizarre way. He has decapitated himself with his own Land Rover.

That's a new one on me, and a pretty gruesome mess it has made."

"How did he do it?" enquired Evans.

"Well as far as I can tell he used the wire rope off the winch on the front of the vehicle and passed the end with a hook around the trunk of the oak tree at the top of the hill," he pointed to the oak as he spoke. "It would seem that he then made a noose and put it round his neck, drove off down here and about halfway down the noose would have tightened and took his head off, which has landed in the back of the vehicle. The Land Rover continued down the hill until it came to rest here."

"Oh what a mess! What on earth made him think to do such a thing? There must be something behind his desire to end it all."

"I agree," said the pathologist. "It is a suicide, it could hardly be anything else."

"Any idea of time of death and can you confirm the MO?"

"I can't say for sure until I have done the PM," said Hugh, "which will not be until tomorrow."

"Okay, let me have as much as you can as soon as possible and then we can move on."

Turning to the sole forensic officer on site Evans asked if the Land Rover would be taken back to the station for examination, together with the cable.

"Yes, I have that in hand already sir."

"We need a side-loading truck with a crane to get this out of here and there is one on its way from Warrington."

"Okay, let me know what you have as soon as you can." Evans and DC Tarrant, who had been struck dumb by the sight that confronted him, walked back down to the house.

Changing into clean shoes, he looked at Tarrant's feet and suggested he stay in the car and advise control what was happening.

Evans knocked quietly on the partly opened door to the utility room and walked in to find the two girls, who were dressed for a night out, and their mother all huddled together looking ashen and with tear-streaked cheeks.

"DS Evans, madam. I am sorry to bother you at this terrible time. I just need a few words if I may?"

"Yes I understand," said Ann. "Please sit down."

"No I am all right standing. I won't be long but I will need to come back in a day or two to have a further chat."

Evans noted down the very basic information he needed, like names and addresses of everyone in the kitchen and the name of the father. He also got the approximate time the body was discovered.

"Thank you, madam, I will leave a police officer on duty outside for the rest of the day. There will be several police officers here for the best part of the day, and there will be vehicles coming and going. We shall be taking the Land Rover back to the station for a detailed inspection."

"Yes I understand," whispered Ann. Even though she was hearing what was said it seemed like an echo chamber, only hearing snippets of information.

Evans and Tarrant returned to the main police station in Chester to file their report and to notify the coroner's office.

Closed today wasn't it! It would have to be done on Monday without fail.

"I think I should ring Uncle Frank," said Sandy, "he could come and give you something, Mum."

Frank Stringer was the family doctor and by a fluke of timing had been the family doctor for many years. He moved his practice to Tarporley from Chester about the same time as Ann and Peter had purchased the farm. He was not a real uncle but he had been a great family friend and had been Uncle Frank to the girls all the time had known him.

"Uncle Frank?"

"Yes hello Sandy, happy new year darling."

"I am sorry Uncle Frank, it is far from that. There has been a terrible accident, Dad is dead."

"Oh my God, I can't believe it."

"Could you be an angel and pop round? Mum is in a state and I wonder if you could give her something to calm her down."

"Yes of course. Oh, how awful," as Frank was taking in the full horror of what he had heard.

"What happened, Sandy? I was with them both last night I really cannot believe what you have said."

"Can I tell you when you get here? The place is full of police and people and I really don't know what is going on."

"I will be with you in an hour, just some things to finish off here. We were coming over anyway but clearly my visit will be just me, Margaret will stay here. I will get Margaret to phone everyone up to stop them coming."

"Oh would you? Thank you so much. See you soon."

Margaret Stringer had overheard some of the conversation and couldn't believe her ears.

When Frank confirmed her worst fears she burst into tears.

"Come on, Margaret, let's be strong, they need all the help we can give them right now. Can you ring round the gang and stop people turning up at the farm, as that won't be very helpful just now? I need to go to the surgery and get my bag and some drugs and then I need to go and see Ann and the girls."

"Of course," she sobbed, and went to get a tissue to dry her eyes and then get on the phone to many of the people she knew would be turning up at Long Acre Farm today.

Back at the farm there was a really busy yard with all sorts of vehicles and police cars. At the entrance to the lane off the main road was a traffic car stopping all vehicles that wanted to go down the lane. The lane, in fact, went nowhere other than to describe a big "D" so entering the lane at one end would take you through past the entrance to Long Acre Farm and then back out to the main road again. There was not a patrol car at the other end of the lane as anyone who knew the farm would always choose the shorter distance from the main road.

There was a police constable at the farm gate as well so that no visitors were permitted to enter.

There had by now been a number of people wanting to get to the farm but were all turned away politely by the police saying that due to an "incident" it was not possible to go to the farm today. The police would not be drawn so the visitors were sent away guessing what might have happened. A couple of them had rung the farm from their mobiles only to find the phone engaged. In fact, as soon as Sandy had spoken to Uncle Frank they decided to take the phone off the hook. It made an annoying sound but better that than have unwanted and difficult phone calls at this time.

Frank Stringer was successful at breaching the police cordon as the PC on duty could see the sense in the family doctor calling. Frank stayed for an hour and gave all three girls a sedative and some sleeping pills for later and promised to call again the following day.

Whilst there Sandra took him to one side and explained as best she could what had happened and Frank could hardly believe what he was hearing. He left feeling very low, the whole elation of entering a new millennium and the fantastic party last night were gone, replaced by this wretched business. Driving home he wondered how he could make the whole affair more palatable for Margaret.

As the day wore on the police presence began to reduce. Si, practical as ever, decided to make some scrambled egg around four o'clock as none of them had eaten anything all day. The two girls ate it all, but Ann just pushed hers around the plate.

It was dark outside now and the yard lights were on and she could see the lights of vehicles up by the gate of Long Meadow from her bedroom window. As she was looking Ann could see Jumbo lifted on to a special vehicle with a crane, strapped down and brought down to the yard, and away to who knew where.

As the last police vehicle left, the young PC who had been there all day knocked on the door, to say goodbye and that there would probably be some more people back on Monday.

"Thank you for all your help. One last thing; we normally leave the gate open to the lane and rely on the cattle grid, do you mind shutting the gate behind you as you go? We don't want any visitors now." He agreed he would do this and was gone.

The girls went to their respective flats to finally change out of their party frocks, which by now had really lost their sparkle, into something more appropriate – jeans and a favourite sweater. Going across the yard they agreed that it would be best for all of them to stay in the house tonight so they would occupy the two spare bedrooms either side of Mum and Dad's room.

"No," said Sandy. "Just Mum's room now!"

"Oh no I don't think I will ever get used to that."

"It's the way it is sis, but we must be strong for Mum; see you in a minute."

"Oh my goodness," Ann said to herself when the girls went out. "It's six o'clock and I haven't fed Purdy all day. Poor dog what will she think?" Ann poured some dry dog food, the Eukanuba stuff the vet recommended for gun dogs, and whilst Purdy was sniffing at it Ann put some fresh water in her drinking bowl.

Purdy was not really interested in her food, she did have a drink and then went back to her bed near the boiler in the utility room. She knows something is wrong, thought Ann. "You know, don't you girl?"

Purdy flapped her tail which beat the side of the boiler like a drum.

The girls came back, each carrying their night clothes. They locked the back door and turned out the yard lights as they came in.

"Purdy is not eating even though she hasn't eaten all day." The mention of her name got another percussion round on the boiler from her tail, but no movement.

Sandy stroked the dog's head. "Poor old dog, and you're sad, yes? Well never mind, you have a good sleep." Purdy lifted her head. With another noisy wag of the tail she almost admitted that she could clearly understand what had happened.

"Having fed the dog, Mum, would you like a drink or something more to eat?"

"No thanks darling, I'm really not hungry."

"How about a cup of tea or hot chocolate?"

"Yes that would be good. I'll have an Earl Grey."

"Okay I will put the kettle on. What would you like Sandy?"

"Oh, a hot chocolate please."

"Okay that's two hot chocolates and a cup of Earl Grey."

No sooner had the kettle boiled and Si was ready with the cups and bits and pieces to make the drinks.

Sandra went to get the pills Uncle Frank had left and gave Ann her dose, which was two of the large tablet and a small one. The girls were given one large one each.

"I don't know what Frank has given me, they are almost too big to swallow."

"I think you have two sleeping pills, I guess they are diazepam to calm you down, and some paracetamol."

"Si and I have a diazepam each. I am not sure what they will do but if Uncle Frank says we should take them then we must."

"I have boiled some more water, Mum, and I will fill a hot water bottle for your bed." Si took the hot water bottle and put it into Ann's bed, on her side.

They all retired very early, having had one of the most dreadful days imaginable. They had no sleep worth talking about the night before and the events of the day had drained them all.

"Night, Mum. Try and sleep well," came the entreaties almost in sync from the girls, and as Ann kissed them both good night, something she had not done for years since they were children, tears began to stream down her face again.

Ann eventually got into bed, and the hot water bottle was comforting. She was reliving the horrors of the day when sleep overcame her, and she drifted off into drug-induced unconsciousness.

1.1.2000 11.00 Chester

Bleary eyes and a thumping headache were the symptoms that greeted John on the first day of the new millennium. Half rolling over in bed he came to a stop, colliding with a naked female body – Lizzie.

"Uh," moaned Lizzie. "Are you okay?"

"Yes, what a night."

It was possibly just after three a.m. when they both got back to their room on the fourth floor of the Grosvenor Hotel. It was sheer extravagance but there was a deal with the hotel for the millennium. The party with a host of their friends was a huge success, a real bash. The tickets for the night included free drinks all night and champagne at midnight. Not cheap at £150 per head, but the lavish celebrations were typical of this excellent hotel. The Grosvenor was 'the' hotel in Chester, owned by the Duke of Westminster's estate. It was sumptuously decorated, and John and Lizzie's room was no exception.

The gang had met at seven thirty p.m. for pre-party and dinner drinks in the Arkle Bar on the ground floor of the hotel, which had meant the downing of three bottles of champagne between them. The gang were mainly friends of John's but Lizzie knew them all, either through her business in PR or as a friend of John's, or simply because Lizzie was a 'girl about town' who had no steady boyfriend and was more than happy to enjoy the company of a small circle of men friends that she had established. It would be wrong to call her the 'Chester Bicycle' but she did have a reputation and one she enjoyed, teasing her male companions. There was never any jealousy amongst the boys as it was understood that Lizzie had, to say the least, a modern approach to relationships and was a great companion.

"What time is it?"

"Don't know," muttered Lizzie.

John stretched out his arm over Lizzie to the bedside table to look at his watch to see that it was just before eleven a.m. "Oh hell it's getting late, Lizzie, we need to get going."

"Oh no, you don't. You were no use last night John England, let's see how you are this morning."

Lizzie wriggled round so that John ended up on top of her and she pulled him towards her and kissed him a fruity kiss full on the mouth.

Their two naked bodies were inevitably coupled and despite the volume of alcohol consumed by John, he surprised himself that he was able to achieve an erection and have sex, but it didn't last long. After a short encounter they fell away and almost went to sleep again.

"Don't go to sleep, Lizzie. I must get going. I am supposed to be at my parents for lunch. Why I commit myself to this annual lunch thing at home I really don't know, but I have and I promised to be at home by twelve thirty. I must get going."

Lizzie fell over him again and kissed him.

"Okay, off you go."

John slipped out of bed to the bathroom, to shower and shave and get himself ready as best he could for the rest of the day.

"Will you come over to the apartment later, Lizzie? We could send out for a curry and have an early night?"

"That would be a good idea, what sort would you like? If you let me have the keys I will go over there and sort out and order the curry and see you later – what time do you expect to be back?"

"Don't know exactly but I won't be late. I would like to be back by seven o'clock at the latest."

"Great, I will fix up everything. If you would like to leave your case here, I will take it to the apartment."

"That would be great, but in fact all you need to do is to take my DJ in its carrier, I will take the holdall."

Now dressed in a smart pair of trousers, checked shirt and Pringle sweater, John gave Lizzie one more kiss, picked up his holdall and left. John checked out and paid the bill but told the concierge that the room would be occupied until two o'clock. He understood, and that madam would be welcome to stay, at least until two o'clock. "We have very few bookings for tonight, sir."

"Have a good day." John made his way to his car which was parked in the adjoining multi-storey car park. As he approached his Porsche Boxster he pressed the remote button and the indicator lights flashed, the headlights came on. John placed the holdall in the space under the bonnet as the engine in a Boxster is mid-engine.

John slid behind the wheel and roared the engine, driving out to the exit of the car park.

"Oh blast, I need a ticket to get out."

He parked near the automatic ticket machine and inserted the car park ticket. When the machine said it needed eight pounds, he pushed his credit card into the machine, which accepted the payment.

"Blimey, it's twelve fifteen. I need to get going."

Placing the authorised ticket into the machine the barrier went up and John left the car park and around the inner ring road of Chester on to the A49, out towards Tarporley.

John was hoping that he wouldn't meet any police on the way as he was sure he would be over the limit. The day after the night before was always a dangerous time.

John's parents had bought a beautiful Georgian house just on the outskirts of Tarporley, with a sweeping gravel drive to a turning area in front of the house.

"It's half past twelve, I hope John isn't going to be too late," said Audrey, John's mother.

"He will be here. It's a piece of beef, it will keep all right but I guess they had a heavy night last night," retorted George.

A strong mint seemed appropriate as John sped along the A49 just in case a PC plod should want to speak to him. He swung the Porsche off the A49 down the road to Tarporley. After about a mile and a half John could see clearly a police car ahead with a blue light flashing.

Oh blast, he thought to himself. Just my luck, a police check. This could be difficult.

He checked his speed and rolled up to the police car and obeyed the halt signal from the police officer, who came round to the driver's window.

"Good morning, sir."

"Good afternoon, officer," retorted John.

"Oh yes, I've been here too long! Where are you going to, sir?"

"I am just visiting my parents for lunch; they live at the Old Vicarage about a mile further on."

"Did you travel this way last night sir?"

"No I spent the night at the Grosvenor. I didn't drive at all last night," As he said it he realised that he had all but admitted drinking heavily the night before.

"I see, sir. May I have your name and address?"

Here we go, thought John. "Yes, certainly," and John gave the details.

"What's going on here?"

"We are investigating an incident, sir. What's your job?"

"I am a solicitor in Chester."

"I see, sir."

"Is that all, officer?"

"Yes sir, mind how you go. Have a nice lunch and I would recommend no wine and a strong coffee before you drive back to Chester." The PC saluted and stood away from the car to allow John to go on his way.

"Phew, that was a close shave." The PC knew very well he had been drinking but John hoped the fact that he was virtually at his destination and was apparently driving carefully, and the police had clearly other issues to deal with, he got away with it.

It was ten past one as he drove into the Old Vicarage and George, hearing the car come off the road, stood at the front door to welcome his son.

"Dad, I'm so sorry I am late, I would have been on time but there has been some sort of incident down the road and police have a road block and I had to answer a lot of questions."

John was embroidering the issue somewhat as he would have been late even without the police check. It didn't hold him up long, but it was a genuine excuse.

"Hi Mum, I could smell lunch as I came into the drive!"

"You've been drinking John."

"Well yes, Mum. It was millennium eve last night and we did have a party."

"Well it was lucky you weren't stopped by the police. I can smell the drink on your breath." Audrey was obviously feeling somewhat put out as her carefully planned lunch timing had been disrupted.

"Well, as I was just telling Dad, I was in fact stopped by the police, that is why I am late, very sorry."

"Have you been booked?"

"No, it was a police check just down the road. They were investigating what they called an incident and wanted my details – just for the record. They wanted to know if I had driven down there last night."

"Where was this?" Audrey was now curious.

"Just down the road at the entrance to the Long Acre Lane."

"That only goes round and back on itself. The only place down there is Long Acre Farm. Did they say what had happened?"

"No sorry, Mum. You will have to get the rest from the gossip mill in the village tomorrow."

"Cheek! You had better come and sit down and have lunch before it is ruined."

2.1.00 Sunday

It was six thirty a.m. Ann opened her eyes, glimpsed at the digital clock to see the time. She rolled over suddenly realising that Peter was not there – he must have gone for his early morning drive to the top of the field and a walk with Purdy.

"Oh no," Ann suddenly realised that Peter was not there, would never be there ever again. "Oh how could you do this to us, Peter?"

Peter what have you done, my darling? How could you leave us like this? I am sure you must have had your reasons and I guess we will discover what was troubling you as time goes by. I still love you my darling whatever your reason, but why couldn't you just talk to us? I have to face the future without you, what a future. I miss you my darling, I miss you. I love you.

Ann's thoughts caused tears to flow down her cheeks. She rolled over and sobbed uncontrollably into the pillow.

After about half an hour her mind was racing again, turning the events of yesterday over and over in her mind and making no sense of it. She went for a shower and the water fell over her and mingled with the tears that still flowed. The shower was running for some time as the hot water enveloped her whole body and, in a peculiar sort of way, comforted her. Wrapping herself in a big warm fluffy towel she sat on the edge of the bath still sobbing, the towel doing a good job of drying her.

As she was getting dressed in a pair of trousers and sweater – old friends and comfortable but by no means glamorous, and her hair tousled and wet, she was about to dry her hair when there was a quiet knock on the door. Si came in.

"Mum."

"Yes, darling?"

"How are you today?"

"I feel awful. I don't know how many tears anyone has in them but I feel as though I have used them all up, but still want to cry."

"Oh, Mummy, what are we going to do?"

"Darling, I don't know, I really don't know. I am in a total turmoil."

"Why did Daddy do this to us, had he mentioned anything to you?"

"No darling, I have been over everything we talked about again and again. I can find nothing, no clue that he was depressed or stressed or frightened or whatever, no clue at all as to why he should have done this." The tears began to flow again.

"Let's go downstairs and have some breakfast. We have to be strong and get through this. We cannot do that on an empty stomach."

"Mum I've been thinking, we need someone to help us, a solicitor."

"But you are a solicitor, darling," returning Sandy's entreaties.

"Yes I know, but this is different. I'm involved and anyway I really don't want to take my family matters back to the office."

"I understand, darling. Well, who do you suggest?"

"I don't know but someone in Chester would be appropriate as we can go and see them easily."

"I was dealing with a firm who seemed pretty switched on," piped up Si. "Bennett and Bennett, they are on the Bars, in the middle of the roundabout at Foregate Street, you know the extension of Eastgate Street, the one with the clock over it. Why not try them? We can see what we think and decide once we have met someone from there."

"I will give them a ring on Tuesday if they are open," volunteered Sandy.

"Talking about ringing people, we should ring Roger Whiteside and tell him. What's his number, anyone know?"

"Oh I should," sighed Ann, knowing that she really did not like this man very much although Peter seemed to think the sun shone out of him. "I will have a look in my diary."

"No sorry, I don't seem to have his home number, just the firm."

"I will ring them as well on Tuesday, but I am not sure they will be open."

4.1.2000 Tuesday

With New Year's Day being a Saturday, the government had declared that Monday the 3rd January would be a bank holiday, so it was Tuesday the 4th January before anyone returned to work, unless you worked in the hospitality industry in which case you had been flat out all over the Christmas and New Year holiday.

Given a bank holiday tacked on to a weekend the majority of British workers always seem to take the other four days off and use it as part of their holiday. All travel over the holiday period was chaotic. The West Coast main line was dug up in great chunks as there was a long period when Railtrack felt they could disrupt the nation. So bus travel, motorways and airports were busier than they would normally be. Families travelling to the North West of England got caught up in monumental snarl-ups and journeys that took in the normal course of events a couple of hours or so were taking more than twice as long.

The exception to the snarl-up, however, was the business quarter in most towns and cities around the country. They were as quiet as the grave, yet the shopping centres at midday on the days following New Year's Day, Chester Shopping Centre was crowded to capacity. The herd mentality had started, people were buying anything and everything as the January sales had started and bargains galore were to be had in most high streets and out-of-town shopping centres.

Businesses around the country were all delighted. They had escaped the Millennium Bug. Since the middle of 1998 when some computer guru, presumably at Microsoft, had spotted that when the year 2000 came into force there could be a catastrophic collapse of major computer systems in business, in airlines, national security, the NHS and anywhere in fact that relied on computers. What had apparently happened is that when the original PC operating system was developed the system used was MS-DOS and that was programmed using a two-digit year, i.e. for 1996 the digits 96 were sufficient. It seemed that no one had foreseen that the year 2000 would ever come!

For about eighteen months before New Year's Eve on the 31st December 1999 there had grown up a computer engineer's bonanza where they would come, for a fee, and check your computer system would not crash due to this "Millennium Bug".

Bennett and Bennett, a long-established firm of solicitors in Chester, had such a complex system for everything they did; it tracked work, held a vast array of standard documents leases, wills agreements, sale and purchase contracts for property and business, in fact everything that a solicitor needed. The system was linked to a Law Society-approved document drafting company who would email any document so even the smallest solicitors practice could keep up to date with what was going on and have correct documents formulated to meet current legislation.

The most important thing the computer did as far as the partners of Bennett and Bennett were concerned was that it logged all the time taken by partners and clerks working on any job, and would allow the accounts department to create monthly invoices to clients for work done to date. This had revolutionised the cash flow of the firm and put the accounts department into a much better shape. It was not very often clients didn't pay, because what would you do if you were sued by your own solicitor for fees? Not an easy one to deal with!

John England, being one of the newer partners of the firm, but a great fee earner and business getter, had drawn the short straw and was on duty for the rest of the week. There was always the possibility that a client had got locked up by the police or there had been a death or some other event which needed urgent attention. The general work of the office was on hold as the conveyancing and general litigation work required communication with other solicitors, estate agents, insurance and mortgage brokers and barristers, most of whom were not at work, so it was futile to even try and get any response. No, the day-to-day business of the law would have to wait until the following week.

It was about nine thirty on the 4th January when John unlocked the front door of the office. It was a three-storey terraced building, and despite its traditional outward appearance was in fact only a few years old. It was not far from the city centre and the courts and was close to other firms of solicitors. The office was very modern inside and quite a surprise for many who visited for the first time. Quite different from the archetypal piles of files and dusty offices so often associated with solicitors' offices.

John did a quick tour of the building leaving the front door locked behind him. The alarm was off now and John just wanted to check that everything was as it should be. His most urgent task was to power up the computer system. The main servers were housed in a special room on the first floor, which was locked by a key as well as a digital combination lock. The door was substantial and would give protection to the computer servers in case of a fire. The whole firm's future and past was held on the files of these servers. They always held copies of the data off site and partners took it in turns to take tapes of the data home with them, so if the offices did go up in smoke they could at least be back in business with the data on the tape.

John pressed the power buttons on the computers. They normally were never shut down and allowed to run non-stop. However, due to the Millennium and the anticipated Millennium Bug they had been advised to shut down the system over the change of date.

"Eureka!" John whispered to himself as the system burst into life and the server screen held the correct date.

So what was all the fuss about? John thought to himself.

It's as though the computer industry had manufactured fear amongst all computer users to enable computer engineers to earn extra fees to fix a problem which apparently was not there.

Nice work if you can get it, John thought.

Getting back to his office on the first floor at the rear John switched on his computer to make sure the functionality of the system remained, and all appeared well.

That's great, he thought. We are lost without this thing.

John returned to the ground floor and met Donna who looked as though she had really danced the night away and had hardly slept.

"Happy new year, Mr England," she said.

"Thanks, Donna, a very happy new year to you. I hope you had a good time."

"Oh, yes, thanks. Me and my mates we just got pissed and didn't go to bed on New Year's Eve. We were in the city centre with the crowd and dance sung and drank the night away, it was fantastic."

"Oh good, I am glad you had a great time. We are very much a skeleton staff this week. There is only me in all week, you and, I can't remember who else."

"Mr Jackson from accounts said he would come in at some point and Jane is due in today, and tomorrow and Pam is then coming in on Thursday and Friday."

"Okay that's fine, I will be in my office if anyone calls. I am going to try and get on top of a lot of back filing and sorting out stuff that I never have time for."

"Okay dokey!"

He had just started to put papers in their relevant piles from jobs that had just got to be finished before Christmas. 'There is always this rush before holidays and I still don't know why,' he mused to himself.

Then his phone rang.

"There's a call for you, Mr England."

"Who is it, Donna?"

"Oh I forgot to ask, silly me. I'll find out and buzz you back."

How do we employ these people? John thought for a moment. However, she must have been with us for nearly three years now and she was reliable and hard-working, but not the greatest intellect.

The phone went again.

"She says it's Lizzie, you will know her."

"Okay put her through. Hi sunshine," John said, "Did you manage to wake up in time to go to work, now you are back at your home?"

"It was difficult, but I made it. Have you heard the news?"

"No, what news?"

"About Peter Wall."

"Who?"

"Peter Wall, you know, they live at Long Acre Farm in Tarporley and he runs Wall's Civil Engineering. You were stopped by the police near his home on New Year's Day!"

"Oh, okay. What about him?"

"Well," Lizzie was now in full flow at her journalistic best, and some of the information was always colourful and not one hundred per cent reliable. "I was chatting to a friendly reporter on *The Chester Chronicle* who has just syndicated his first major scoop, isn't that exciting!"

"Not to me."

"Oh, John, don't be such a spoilsport."

"What did you want to tell me?"

"Well there was a gruesome suicide apparently at the farm and it's Peter Wall. I understand that he has hung himself, on New Year's Day morning of all times."

"That's very sad to hear, but why does it affect me?"

"I thought you would be interested, having been involved and everything."

"I was not involved Lizzie. I happened to be driving down a road off which lies the lane to the farm now apparently the scene of a suicide. Thanks for letting me know."

"You're a bit of a cold fish this morning."

"Well I am in business mode and I have lots to do to get straight before the start of the rush next week. It's interesting but nothing to do with me."

"Okay, just keeping you in the loop."

"Thanks Lizzie. See you soon, bye."

"Bye," and she was gone.

"Mr England, I have a call for you."

"Who is it, Donna?"

"Sorry, Mr England. I forgot to ask."

"Can you find out please?" John hung up.

A few moments later the phone went again. "Yes?"

"It's a Miss Sandra Wall, she says she knows of you but you haven't met and is potentially a new client."

"Put her through. Hello, John England speaking."

A rather tired voice lacking any colour began to speak. "I am Sandra Wall and I am a solicitor, but my speciality is commercial law and I work in Liverpool. I work for Spencer's, you probably know them?"

"Yes, very well."

"I wonder if you would act for our family in a very difficult matter? I really don't want to take it into the office as this is immensely private and I just want Mum, my sister and me to have a local firm representing us in what is likely to be a very difficult and emotional time for us, and in some way we all agreed it would be easier to talk to someone we didn't know rather than people I know and work with, if that makes sense?"

John, of course, had realised that this was the Wall family of Long Acre Farm in Tarporley and this was one of the daughters.

"I will do whatever I can to help. What can I do for you?"

"Frankly I don't know but we do need some help and someone to hold our hands as our emotions are topsy turvey and very ragged at the moment. You see there was a terrible accident on New Year's Day, my father died in very difficult circumstances." As she uttered the last words, the tears began to flow as Sandra had a mental picture of her father and all he meant to her.

"Please don't upset yourself. I will be pleased to be of any help I can. Would it be helpful if I came round this afternoon and had a chat with you and the family?"

"Oh would you? That would be really helpful."

"I will be there at two o'clock, if that's okay?"

"Yes that's fine. Let me give you the address."

"I know where you live, it's Long Acre Farm in Tarporley isn't it?"

"Yes, how on earth did you know that?"

"I was visiting my parents on New Year's Day and I was stopped by a police officer at the entrance to your lane. It never occurred to me then what had happened, so that's how I know where you are."

"Oh good, look forward to seeing you and thank you."

Sandra was relieved when she put the phone down. It was as though someone had taken a weight off her shoulders, even though nothing had happened yet.

"He's coming at two o'clock this afternoon," Sandra announced to her mother and sister Sienna.

John pressed the intercom button on his desk phone for reception.

"Yes, Mr England?"

"Donna, I have to go out this afternoon to see a client so I will be leaving at about twelve thirty and it is unlikely I will be back today. Can you put me through to Caroline?"

"She's just popped out for a minute, Mr England. I will get her to call you when she gets back."

John began to think of the things he needed to consider when he got to Long Acre Farm, and he thought a list would be a good idea:

Full names of clients and dates of birth.

Full name and date of birth of the deceased.

Name and address of insurance brokers with details of relevant policies.

Business connections, shareholdings etc.

Funeral arrangements.

Death certificate.

A will, and who has it.

Trust information if any.

These headings just came to John's mind as he sat in his office, they were in no particular order but it was necessary these days to get a Law Society-approved letter of appointment. This information would enable John to set that in motion when he got back to the office, tomorrow.

The intercom bell on his phone rang. It was Caroline.

"Sorry I wasn't here when you rang, John."

They had a closer working relationship and in fact operated as a team. Caroline knew almost as much as he did on the matters he was dealing with and most of the legal processes as well, which was a great help to John and to clients as Caroline was always able to give clients comfort by knowing where everything was up to.

"I had to go out for some coffee and I needed some paracetamol as headaches seem to be the order of the day down here."

"No worries, it's just that it looks as though we have a new client, the Wall family in Tarporley. I'm going to see them this afternoon. It is unlikely I will be back today as we close at four o'clock, so can you please ensure everything is locked up? The computers are all on, just leave them running, there is no need for a backup today as we haven't really done anything to record."

"No problem, John. I look forward to hearing all about it. Donna tells me Mr Wall has committed suicide."

"Ah, I think that might be correct. But remind Donna that matters in this office are confidential."

How on earth did Donna know that? John thought to himself.

Then he returned to the rather more mundane task of sorting out some of his files.

Sandra was just telling Ann and Si of the appointment she had made with John England of Bennett and Bennett solicitors, and the call she had made to Walls Civil Engineers to try and contact Roger Wallwork, when the phone rang.

"Hello?"

"Is that Mrs Wall?"

"No, it's Sandra Wall speaking. Who is that?"

"It's DS Evans of the Chester Police."

"Ah, how can I help you, Mr Evans?"

"Miss Wall, I would like to come back and see you to discuss a few things and ask some more questions, particularly of your mother. I need to come over this afternoon; would two o'clock be convenient?"

"That might be a bit difficult. You see, we have our solicitor coming over then."

"That will be fine, it might be a good idea for him to be present."

"Oh, why, is there a problem?"

"No, miss, but in suspicious deaths there are procedures to follow."

"Suspicious, what do you mean?"

"It's a phrase which refers to any death which is out of the ordinary. I will see you at two."

"Very well."

So there was even more to tell the family now and they were to expect two visitors at once. Just as Sandra was relaying the information she saw Uncle Frank's car roll into the yard. The police tape across the cattle grid to the fields was still in place and there was a gap Sandra could see in the machinery shed where Jumbo should be. It would be difficult to remain attached to Jumbo now, with her having played such an important role in her father's death.

"Stupid though," she said to herself and waved to Uncle Frank as he walked towards the back door.

"Come in, Uncle Frank."

"One day you girls will get round to calling me Frank, you make me feel ancient."

"Old habits die hard. Come in, we are all in the kitchen."

Frank was carrying his doctor's bag and was keen to see how his patients were. Stress and bereavement could cause all sorts of unexpected side effects and he was keen to make sure that these were minimised as in the next few days and weeks things would, in his experience, get worse not better as the realisation of what had occurred sank in and the details are laid bare of Peter's life, both private and business.

Frank took Ann into the lounge and examined her, checked her blood pressure and generally gave her the once-over. She was exhibiting signs of higher than normal blood pressure, so he decided to prescribe some beta blockers to help get that under control. He also decided that the time was right to let Ann have a supply of sleeping pills, so he wrote out the appropriate prescriptions and volunteered to drop them into the chemist in Tarporley on his way back to the surgery.

The doctors and the chemist in Tarporley had an excellent system working between them, a repeat prescription could be ordered on the phone from the doctor's surgery or the chemists, and the prescriptions would be picked up by the chemist and have everything waiting to be collected the following day.

On this occasion, despite the fact that they could all drive, no one had ventured out to the village or anywhere for that matter and Frank promised to get the chemist in this instance to deliver the pills as soon as they were ready.

"Now, Ann, you must promise to take these pills as prescribed just the correct amount and also take the sleeping pills, as they will help you and give you the rest you need."

"Yes I promise, but they only work for part of the night, my mind is still racing around."

"I know, but it will get better I promise. You need the sleep, so you must take the pills."

As Frank was talking he was aware of another car coming into the yard, one he didn't recognise, but it was a rather smart Jaguar saloon, and a very professional-looking mature man got out wearing a dark blue overcoat.

I wonder who that is, thought Frank to himself, and as his mind was distracted by this thought Ann said she was finding it hard to eat anything. The consultation continued as the knock came on the back door.

Si went to the door as Sandra had just popped upstairs.

"Good morning, can I help you?"

"Yes, I am the Coroner for Cheshire, Dr Prescott, and I have come to look at the scene where Mr Wall died."

He knew as soon as he uttered these words he should have been a little more tactful as he saw Si's eyes well up and a tear fell down each cheek.

"Oh," was Si's rather croaky response. "You had better come in."

It is a strange thing about farmhouses that most people come to the back door. Whilst there is a front door, they are never positioned in the correct place for an obvious entrance to the house.

As the Coroner entered the kitchen Dr Frank Stringer, preceded by Ann Wall, came in from the hall.

"Hello," said Frank, "I am Dr Stringer, the family doctor. Can we help?"

Ann was pleased that Frank had taken control of the conversation as she was beginning to feel overwhelmed by events.

"This is Dr Prescott, the coroner," said Si.

"Ah yes, I am glad you are here, Dr Stringer. It's much better if we have a chat I think. Shall we go outside?" Frank Stringer and the Coroner went out into the yard.

"I have seen a preliminary pathologist's report indicating death by strangulation that was so violent it in fact decapitated Mr Wall. Are you aware of this, Dr Stringer?"

"I had been given an indication that is what had happened by Mrs Wall, but she has not been able to tell much of the detail and I have not wanted to press the point. She is in a fragile condition just now."

"I understand. I gather from what the police have told me the incident took place in a field behind the outbuildings and a cable was secured to a tree and the other end made into a noose and placed over Mr Wall's head so that, when he drove off down the hill in the old Land Rover, the inertia caused the noose to close and the force was so great he was decapitated, with his head falling to the back of the Land Rover, which ultimately came to rest in front of the gatepost to the field."

"Yes, that is essentially what I had heard but not so succinctly put."

"Where is this field, Dr Stringer?"

"It's just over there."

"Would you mind showing me and accompanying me to the scene?"

"Not at all, I will just tell them where we are going and I will get some boots out of my car. Have you any boots, Dr Prescott?"

"Yes, I will put mine on too."

The two doctors, deep in conversation, made their way slowly up the incline to the old oak tree at the top of the mound in Long Meadow. On inspecting the tree they could clearly see the mark that the wire rope had made in the trunk of this ancient and rather beautiful old oak, bare now in the midst of winter, but the gnarled shape and the latticework of large and small branches silhouetted against the winter sky, still made an impressive sight.

As the two doctors retraced their steps down the hill vehicle tracks were evident, quite a lot of them making to all intents and purposes a rutted track with clearly defined wheel tracks.

"This is presumably the route that the Land Rover took," remarked Prescott.

"Yes, Peter Wall was a creature of habit and most mornings he would drive the old Land Rover up here to survey his farm of which he was justifiably proud. He would then walk on to the copse at the bottom, usually with his dog, and then back again taking Jumbo – sorry, that's the family's name of endearment for the old Land Rover – back down again. Peter was very attached to the vehicle and he said a daily outing would ensure it would never stop running."

At the field gate the old stone gatepost was still in position but the gate was now hung on a new oak post. On the opposite side of the opening the gate came to rest on the original stone gatepost. The old stone posts couldn't be pressed into use for hanging the gate as they were too badly damaged, but as a keep for the gate there was no problem. The posts must have been there as long as the farm itself which was probably two hundred and fifty years. A deep scar showing new flakes of the stone was evident where the metal bumper bar of the old Land Rover had impacted the stone post and brought the vehicle to a shuddering stop. The ruts made by the Land Rover's tyres were also clearly visible in the mud.

"It must have taken quite a lot of courage to decide to end it all in this way," said the Coroner.

"I think that's right. Peter was a very private man in many ways, you only knew what he wanted you to know and the spin he wanted to put on it. We just do not know the full explanation of what's driven him to this desperate end, but for sure once the process was under way there was no going back. As you say, he lost his head, so death must have been instantaneous."

"Yes, I guess that's right. It wouldn't really be possible for someone else to do this to Mr Wall, it surely is a suicide."

"Yes and I regret that suicide is the cause of death. If he was of unsound mind at the time it is one for you, I think."

"Yes, but it is not normal behaviour for a human being to want to take their own life, so the chances are almost in all cases that the balance of their mind is disturbed, even for a few minutes, sufficient to lead to this sort of drastic action. I find the real victims of a suicide are the relatives. The person who has killed themselves has in some way abdicated their responsibility for whatever it was that was troubling them, but the issues still remain to be faced by those left behind. Who very often discover the most ridiculous reasons behind the suicide that, if only communication of the problem by the deceased had been forthcoming, could have been sorted out. It's very often a situation where the suicide victim doesn't want to lose face by having to admit to a shortcoming. It is very sad."

"I am sure you are right, after all you see much more of this sort of thing than I do."

"Dr Stringer, we need to have a formal identification of the body, and the police will organise that. Is this something you would be prepared to do?"

"Yes, of course."

"I will get my office to phone the reporting officer in charge of the case at the police headquarters in Chester for him to arrange that with you."

They were now back in the yard.

"Good Lord, it's quarter to one. I really must be going," exclaimed Frank Stringer. "I have other patients to go and see and I promised my wife that we would go into Chester this afternoon to the sales. I don't mind missing the sales but I can't miss my patients."

"If I were you, Dr Stringer, I wouldn't miss the sales either."

Frank Stringer slipped his boots off and placed them in the specially designed welly boot holder in the back of his car. He was used to needing boots on his patient visits as his was a rural practice, many of his patients were farmers, usually with farmyards that were really muddy, not as clean and tidy as Long Acre Farm.

"I must go, Ann, Si, Sandra. So sorry to have to rush but things to do. I will try and pop in tomorrow and don't forget take the pills."

As Frank was passing through Tarporley village to visit an elderly patient in a nursing home on the outskirts, he double parked and trotted into the chemist. Spotting who it was, the pharmacist came from round the back of the dispensary to see him.

"Here is the script for Mrs Wall and her two daughters. They have had a tragedy as you may have heard."

"Yes I have, it's all over the village, Is it true that..."

"I'm sorry I really cannot discuss the issues as I am sure you will understand," Frank was conscious of two other customers in the shop and the shop assistant, all listening intently to this conversation. "But if you could kindly deliver these to the farm before the end of today that would help them greatly."

"No problem, Dr Stringer, thank you."

"Thanks for the lunch, Si. It was just what I needed. I hadn't realised how hungry I have become and I think I will need all my strength this afternoon."

"It's okay, Mum. It's the least we can do, it wasn't much and I will need to go to the supermarket if not this evening certainly in the morning to stock up."

"That would be really kind, Si. I am so sorry that your holiday is spoilt, darling," Ann burst into tears followed only moments later by Si. Sandra came to join them in the kitchen.

"I have tidied up the lounge and put some lights on and lit the fire, as I think it would be easier and more comfortable to speak to people in there. Do you think we should have tea ready?"

"I guess we should. I will lay a tray and get the teapot and bits and pieces ready. Why don't you go and have a tidy up, Mum, so you feel refreshed, whilst Sandra and I finish up here?"

"You are good, thank you so much. Yes I think I would feel better for a spruce up." With a laboured walk and no hint of Ann's usual spark and enthusiasm for life, she left the kitchen and went upstairs.

"Oh we have a Porsche in the yard now, things are looking up."

"Well, that will not be the police for sure. It looks as though it is probably John England who I spoke to this morning from the solicitors in Chester."

"Okay, you go and welcome him in then."

Sandra, standing at the back door to the house, spoke first.

"I guess you are John England?"

"Yes that's right, and you are Sandra Wall?"

"Yes, thank you so much for coming, please come in. Forgive the back door entrance but everyone ends up in the kitchen and the front door is really on the wrong side of the house."

"So often the case with farmhouses," agreed John, trying to make as much light-hearted conversation as possible.

"This is my sister, Sienna."

"Hello, John England."

"Yes I know, we have corresponded."

"Oh really?" John was now really on the back foot as he couldn't recall this at all and, at that moment, he felt sure that if he had met this delightful, blonde-haired beauty he would not have forgotten.

"Yes, you were acting for the purchaser of The Grange in Tattenhall and I was acting for the vendor."

"Ah I see, I hadn't realised that both of you were solicitors."

"No we are not. I am a surveyor working for Dents in Chester."

"Ah that's you. Yes I do recall now. Despite my client's delays it all went through in the end."

"Yes, sorry if you felt I was hounding you but the church commissioners were keen to see their cash as soon as possible."

Dents was probably the oldest firm of chartered surveyors in Chester, and whilst they had an active and profitable estate agency section it was not as sexy or as forward-looking as some of the newer entrants into estate agency in the city.

"Anyway that's enough of work talk, let's go into the lounge. Mum will be with us very shortly."

"It's very good of you to come out and see us so promptly, many firms are shut at the moment," Sandra remarked.

"Well we are only operating on a skeleton staff as most people are away."

"You didn't fancy going away then?"

"No, I will leave this time of year to families. I go skiing with a group of us in February when the schools have gone back."

Ann returned downstairs. "Hello, I'm Ann Wall, very good of you to come."

"John England, but please call me John."

Ann thought to herself what a very nice young man he was and how comfortable she felt already that he was here to help her and the girls. Just then Ann saw another car come into the yard, so she asked Sandra if she would go and see who it was.

"It's probably the police. They said they would be here at this time."

"Oh yes I remember you saying something about that, or was it you, Si? It doesn't matter anyway, they are here now. I am sorry," addressing her remarks to John. "The police want to ask us some questions and rather demanded that they came now."

"It doesn't matter at all, would you rather that I waited outside?"

"No, not at all. In fact I, no we, would all prefer it if you would be kind enough to stay, as we don't know what they are going to ask and if they try and get difficult your assistance would be much appreciated."

John knew with the police here the questions they ask would give him greater insight into the events on New Year's Day. Lizzie's information was a useful start but from experience John knew he could not rely on it.

"I'm DS Evans and this is DC Tarrant from Chester CID," He introduced himself and his partner as he came into the lounge.

"This is John England our solicitor," Ann informed the two detectives. "Please sit down anywhere you feel comfortable."

"Is there a reason for having your solicitor here madam?" Evans enquired.

"No, there is nothing sinister in John's attendance. He was coming anyway, as we have a great deal to sort out and we felt it would be easier if we had a local firm acting for us. Sandra is also a solicitor but she works for a large firm in Liverpool."

"I see. If I may, there are a number of issues we need to ask about to clear up some anomalies in our investigations. I think you have probably already had a visit from the Coroner, Dr Prescott, he always likes to come to site when there is an unusual death as he finds it helps him in understanding evidence."

"Evidence, what evidence?" retorted Ann.

"There is nothing to worry about, madam. It is the due process of law. It is a requirement that all unusual or suspicious deaths are reported to the Coroner and he will hold an inquest, and that is exactly what will happen here."

"Oh, I see."

"Yes," said John. "There is nothing to worry about, it is a normal process."

"I just want to go through the events of New Year's Eve and New Year's Day if I may Mrs Wall, and for the purposes of elimination we would like to take some DNA swabs from each of you to eliminate you from the results that we get from the detailed examination of the Land Rover. Is there anyone else who could have driven or touched the Land Rover in the last two weeks or so?"

"Oh I see, well I suppose there is Fred, who comes in three days a week to do odd jobs around the place, I don't think anyone else will have driven Jumbo otherwise."

"Is Fred on the farm today?"

"No he isn't, he has this week off, but he will be here next Tuesday."

"Do you have his address?"

"No I'm sorry I don't. My husband dealt with all that sort of thing," and as Ann said it she suddenly had a desperate feeling that here she was and would have to sort all this business out herself, something Peter had always done. He obviously has records but where they are, and how to find the appropriate information, she had no idea, and another tear ran down each cheek.

"I'm sorry to have to ask you these questions Mrs Wall, but we do have to try and finalise this matter."

"Yes I understand, I'm sorry it's silly of me. Please continue."

"DC Tarrant will come here next Tuesday to take a swab from Fred."

"Oh it's Fred Appleyard."

"Fred Appleyard, is he here first thing and works all day?"

"Yes Fred is as reliable as a clock, he will be here at eight a.m. sharp."

"Has he worked for you long?"

"Fred started to work for us when we bought the farm in 1997 and was involved in much of the renovation work. He was nearing retirement but needed some extra work so he asked Peter if he could stay on after the major works had finished and help run the place and repair and renovate some of the outbuildings and fences. He was a godsend as we're all very busy and Fred is mainly responsible for the way the farm looks today. We really couldn't do without him."

With that information tucked away about a new name in the investigation DS Evans then continued with his detailed questions about the events of New Year's Day. This was all useful to John who sat quietly and listened and took lots of notes.

It was gone three o'clock when Evans and Tarrant had finished and went on their way.

"Well that was a bit of a grilling" Sandra said. "Shall I go and make some tea?"

"Oh yes please, Sandy. That would be good."

"Mrs Wall, I can see that you have had the most traumatic time, if that is not an underestimate of what has happened. There are clearly a number of things I need to know from you if I am to be of some help. As to the inquest, I will attend that but I think the Coroner will require you to be there as well as it was you who found your husband on New Year's Day."

"I see."

"I have prepared a list of information I need and perhaps if I leave that with you in the next day or two you could let me have the information I need? I have also prepared a letter of instruction." At that moment Sandy came in with the tray of tea. "I am sure, Miss Wall."

"Oh please call me Sandy."

"...And call me Si," chipped in Sienna who had been sitting quietly in a corner taking in everything that had happened and listening to the dreadful events of New Year's Day once again through the mouth of the police.

"Sandy, I was just saying to your mother—"

"Do you take sugar and milk?"

"Yes please. Both."

"—that it is necessary under Law Society rules that I have to explain in writing who we are, what we do and how we charge for our work, and I have prepared that letter and I will leave it with the list."

"Thanks," said Sandy.

John collected the cup of tea and put it on the small table at the side of his chair, whilst Sandy distributed the other cups to her sister and mother, knowing automatically how they took their tea.

"One other thing I will need is a letter, in fact a number of letters depending on how many firms and insurers are involved so I can get all the papers from them with your authority. Of course I will not be able to make any claims on insurance policies until we have a death certificate and it is the Coroner who will issue that after the inquest, as the cause of death has to be indicated on the death certificate. In cases like this it is only the Coroner who can do that."

After further conversation which revolved around practical steps and what-happens-next-type questions, John took his leave as it was already gone four o'clock and it was just about dark, and went straight back to his apartment.

Driving back to Chester he couldn't help thinking about everything he had heard, and along with the face of Sienna that was etched on his mind, what a lovely girl! But as he said to himself, quite inappropriate to make a move in that direction at the moment.

"So what did you think?" asked Sandy.

"Yes he is a very nice man," Ann replied. "I am sure he will look after our interests very well and help us with all the problems we have to face."

"I agree," Si said, thinking that he was quite a dish and would be very happy to have him around again. "I must shoot off to the supermarket, we are short of a lot of stuff. We have finger food for a party, but it's not exactly what we need now. Let's make a list and I will go to Sainsbury's now."

"Oh thank you, darling, what would I do without you, without both of you? We must stick together and be strong, it's what Daddy would have wanted." Another tear trickled down Ann's cheek.

The phone rang and Sandy answered, "Okay, that's fine. Many thanks."

"That was Wall's," she announced. "That nice Christine, she had picked up the message I had left on the answerphone as she had just popped into the office to make sure everything was all right, as no one was working it's often a time for burglaries, especially in isolated offices on industrial estates when the burglars know there is no one around. Everything was just fine in the office, but she was devastated to hear about Dad. She said Roger was away on holiday, he went before Christmas and was due back in the office on Monday 10th January. Christine thinks she knows the travel agent that will have handled the booking and has left a message for them to call her at home. As soon as she knows something, she will get in touch."

5.1.2000 Wednesday

"Hello?" the caller said on the end of the phone. "Who is that?"

"It's Sandy. Sandra Wall."

"Oh good, I was hoping I would get through to you, it's Christine from Walls."

"Hello, Christine, thanks for getting back to me. Have you any news?"

"Well I was right, Roger had booked his winter sports holiday through Regent Travel, and he is in Austria. He is not due back until Saturday. Fortunately the agent who booked the holiday was in today, and he, Michael that is, has faxed the hotel in Austria and asked them to leave an urgent message for Roger to call you as soon as he gets the message."

"Thank you very much, Christine, that's very helpful."

"I need some fresh air," remarked Sandy. "I think we have been inside since New Year's Day, and I need to get some air in my lungs."

"Good idea," said Si. "Let's all go and have a walk and take Purdy. Mum, will you come too?"

"Yes, darling, I will. It's a good idea."

Purdy didn't need asking twice; she had been outside a number of times as she was able to do at will through the dog flap, a contraption installed in the back door to enable Purdy to come and go as she pleased but her range was restricted by the cattle grids as she hated them and would never walk over one.

"Come on, old girl," said Si as she opened the back door and the three of them, looking more like triplets than mother and two daughters, went out across the yard wearing Barbour jackets and green Wellington boots. Ann opened the gate at the side of the cattle grid as she had done on that fateful morning of New Year's Day when she found Peter's body. She wasn't sure that she could manage to go that way, but the support and encouragement of her two daughters was sufficient to persuade her to do so. Through the gate at the bottom of Long Meadow they went, past the stone gatepost where Jumbo had come to rest and up the rutted track that Jumbo had made over countless trips with Peter on his early morning excursions with Purdy, up to the old oak tree at the top.

They could all see the damage to the tree trunk the wire cable had made, but no one had anything to say. They just observed and walked on to the copse to let Purdy have a run. The copse was Purdy's favourite hunting ground. Very often she would put up a pheasant or a rabbit, and if Peter had his gun with him, he would collect it for the pot. Ann had a freezer full of pheasant, fortunately the local butcher in Tarporley was very willing to draw the birds and dress them, so avoiding doing it herself, and she was thankful for that.

"What's the matter with Purdy?"

"I don't know what's wrong with her," said Si.

"She doesn't seem herself. She would have been in the copse by now. As it is she is just wandering along beside us and looking very lethargic."

"She hasn't been well. That tranquiliser that Peter gave her before the fireworks on New Year's Eve seems to have had a bad effect on her."

"Well I will see how she is in the morning, and if she doesn't seem to be any better I will take her to the vet's."

"Oh would you, Si? That would be a kind thing to do. We don't want her going to get poorly now."

Back at the house Ann was refreshed by having had a good dose of fresh air, but filled with grief having been reminded of the dreadful events of New Year's Day. She said she was going to have a rest for an hour, while the girls made a light lunch. They decided to have a glass of wine with it – why not? Dad would expect it, wouldn't he?

Just as the food was on the table ready to eat the phone went.

"Hello?"

"Is that you, Sandra?"

"Yes. Who is this?"

"Roger Whiteside. Sorry the line's not great. I am in Austria."

"Oh, Roger, thank you for calling. I have some bad news for you," and Sandra began to tell Roger, her father's business partner, that Peter had died and what was happening.

"When's the funeral?"

"Oh we haven't even got to that, but not long probably."

"I see. I'm so sorry to hear this. Give my condolences to your mother and sister, I will be back from my holiday on Saturday so I will give you a ring at the weekend when I am back. Thank you so much for letting me know and I am very sorry to hear your news."

"Funny man that," remarked Sandra. "Never quite seemed to click with him. He is on his own; apparently he was married for a short time but then got divorced and never married again. The good thing is that there are no children. Dad used to say he was a very hard worker but kept himself to himself."

"Yes, we never saw him here. Dad mustn't have liked socialising with him."

"Nice wine, Si. Where did you get it from?"

"It was on special offer at Sainsbury's and I decided we needed a treat after the week we have had... and possibly going to have for many more weeks to come."

"I agree."

"Let's go and have a look in Dad's study; there may be some information we might need. We must be able to find documents and agreements, bank statements and so on to help us build a picture of what went on."

"Okay, Sandy, but we should ask Mum first."

"She is probably asleep at the moment."

"Yes okay, but don't let's bring anything out before we have spoken to her."

Just at that moment the phone went again and they rushed to answer it before Ann could hear it.

"Long Acre Farm."

"It's Detective Evans. Is Mrs Wall available, please?"

"Sorry, Mr Evans, she is asleep at the moment and as she's had such little sleep recently we don't really want to disturb her."

"I understand, can you ask her to phone me when she can? I will be leaving shortly and won't be back at the station until tomorrow."

"Is there nothing we can do for you, Mr Evans?"

"Well I suppose you're next of kin so there is no harm done. It's just that the post mortem has been completed successfully and there is no further reason for us to hold the body, we can release it now for burial."

"Oh, right, thank you. How do we do that?"

"Well the best advice is to speak to your solicitor and he will arrange an undertaker to collect the body from the mortuary."

"Very well, we will start to make the arrangements, thank you for your call."

"Well," said Si, "that's good news I suppose, in that we should be able to answer all those relatives and friends who have been pestering us for the date of the funeral."

"Shall I ring John England, Sandy?"

"Why not? We can get things moving then."

"Hello, John England please."

There was a pause and the girl on the other end with a tinge of a Liverpool accent asked, "Who is calling please?"

"Sienna Wall."

"Oh I was very sorry to hear about your loss."

"Thank you. Can you put me through?"

"Just a moment."

"John England."

"Hello, John, it's Sienna Wall."

"Oh, hello, how nice to hear from you. Can I help?"

"Well yes you can, the police have just phoned to say that the post mortem has been held and they have seen the report and they can now release the body. I gather that means we can get an undertaker to collect the body and organise the funeral?"

"Yes that's right. I don't have your father's will yet, I have asked for it from Frobisher's, the solicitors your father used in Manchester. The problem is that so many people are on holiday it seems to be taking an age for anything to happen. Do you have a funeral director in mind that you would like to use?"

"No, I have no idea."

"Well if you want a local firm there is Cartwright's in Tarporley – they seem to do most of the funerals in the village. Do you have any idea about your father's wishes?"

"Oh, John," and she started to sob slightly as she had not, until that moment, ever thought she would need to think of such a thing.

"I'm sorry. I didn't mean to upset you."

"No it's all right. It's the thought of a funeral that's set me off, sorry."

"No don't you worry, I will give Cartwright's a ring and when she is ready I would like to speak to your mother. Perhaps I can come back to the farm with a copy of the will to advise on your father's wishes and bequests?"

"That's very kind of you – as soon as Mum is awake I will let her know."

Si put the phone on the hook, with a shiver of expectation.

"Let me know what?" Ann said as she came into the kitchen from the hall, "I just caught the last few words. Who was on the phone?"

"It was John England, in fact I rang him as we had a call from the police a few moments ago and they are ready to release Daddy's body for a funeral. I thought it would be a good idea to tell John so he could help us do whatever it is we have to do now."

"Thanks, darling, that was very considerate of you. Perhaps we should tell Frank."

"Yes okay, I will phone him. John said most funerals in Tarporley are carried out by Cartwright's and he was going to ring them for us."

"Cartwright's? I thought they were builders?"

"Well so did I, but apparently they are builders and funeral directors, funny that isn't it?"

"Yes but it would perhaps be best to use someone local."

The phone rang again,

"Hello, Long Acre Farm."

"Sienna this is John, John England."

"Oh hi, that didn't take you long."

"No. I've phoned Cartwright's and Mr Cartwright is in the office doing some paperwork. He is waiting for your call so he can make an appointment to come round and discuss arrangements. I would suggest that you make the appointment for Friday as I hope to get a copy of the will tomorrow and I would like to come and see you – there may be instructions regarding the funeral in the will."

"Thanks so much John, I'll tell Mum."

"Okay – see you tomorrow."

Si was inwardly excited simply by the phone call and she was keenly awaiting John's return to Long Acre Farm.

Ann phoned Mr Cartwright and made an arrangement for him to come at eleven thirty on Friday.

"Mum?"

"Yes, darling."

"Sandy and I thought we should make a start on having a look through Dad's study to see if there are any papers that might be of use to John, what do you think?"

"Well, darling, I see what you mean and I would like to do it with you, but not just now. I'm not sure that I could face looking around Dad's study just yet."

"Okay, no problem. We will leave it for a little while and probably do it in a week or two."

"Yes that would be best."

"Sergeant Evans?"

"Yes."

DC Tarrant placed a report folder on Sargent Evans' desk. "This is the PM report on Mr Wall."

"Thanks, any issues?"

"No I don't think so, Sarge. It is more or less what we had expected. No obvious signs of any outside attack. It all points to suicide as we had expected."

"Any news from the Forensic team?"

"Not yet, Sarge, but I phoned them before I came up with this, and they said they would have something for us just after lunch."

"Good, you have told the morgue that the body can be released? Have you obtained the signatures on the release docket?"

"Yes all the paperwork is in place and I have had a Mr Cartwright on the phone to make arrangements to collect the body, which he expects to do within the hour."

"Don't waste time, do they? Let me know when the forensic report is available."

Time seemed to fly in the police station. It seemed no time at all when Tarrant appeared with the forensic report.

"Here it is. Interesting, just a few small issues we may need to clear up."

"What do you mean?"

"There are some anomalies we hadn't picked up, but they don't amount to much."

In this report we have highlighted some issues we discovered during our detailed examination of the site and the Land Rover. The unexplained points are in conclusion:

- *There is some unexplained DNA which might be explained by further swabs from the farm worker.*

- *There was a very indistinct bloodstain which, due to contamination with other substances. It has not been possible to get a reliable DNA signature from.*
- *There is a sharpening stone in the rear of the Land Rover which is contaminated with blood and hair from the deceased. This is not exceptional considering the volume of blood and the movement of the head around the back of the Land Rover during its journey.*
- *The Land Rover does not have a conventional ignition key starting mechanism; instead it has an ignition activated by a switch. We could not ascertain by whom the ignition was turned off. Our forensic photographs just miss this switch as it did not appear to be an issue to the SOCO team on site at the time.*
- *The wire rope used as the noose had been on the winch of the Land Rover. The noose at the opposite end to the hook had been formed by a loop in the wire made by a bowline knot, and the body of the wire fed through the loop the bowline made.*

CONCLUSIONS

We expect the DNA of the farm worker to be matched by numerous unexplained yet similar or same contacts on the vehicle. The contaminated blood sample of the front bumper of the vehicle is only very small and cannot be identified. This identification might be possible but it would be necessary to send the sample away for further specialist analysis, which has a time and cost implication. We think the blood and hair contamination of the sharpening stone is as a result of contact with the head and being subject to blood and other body fluids being present in the rear of the vehicle. We are unable say with any certainty how or when the ignition switch was put in the off position, however this switch is upside down so anything striking the switch from above would turn it to the off position. This is the most likely scenario. Finally, the choice of a bowline for the noose indicates an automatic reaction on behalf of the person tying the knot and could indicate previous experience in scouting, sailing climbing or any other pastime with rope involved.

We consider that the overall picture displayed to us, despite the anomalies highlighted, leads to the conclusion Mr Wall committed suicide.

"I see what you mean, Tarrant. But frankly I think this is Forensics being their usual fastidious selves, and just covering their backs. That Land Rover would have stalled as soon as it hit the gatepost, turning off the switch would have made no difference. I guess we should ask the collection crew if they did switch it off. It is always possible Mrs Wall turned it off, but I don't see why if the engine had stopped – assuming it had."

"I will be back at the farm to get the farm worker's DNA swab next Tuesday, so I could ask Mrs Wall about the ignition switch. I will ask the farm worker about the sharpening stone in the rear. I am not sure what anyone can tell us about the blood on the front bumper, but it might be worth knowing where it has come from."

"Well go and tell Forensics the report doesn't tell us, we should know where the blood comes from."

"Okay, Sarge."

"Don't forget – keep me posted."

"I will."

"Hi, Lizzie, how's things?"

"John! Good to hear from you."

"I was just wondering if you had decided to come on the skiing trip, and if so did you speak to the others?"

"Yes, we are all up for it. Have you thought of exactly where we are going?"

"Well, the reason for my call was to find out if we had all eight coming so I can pop into Regent Travel whilst it's quiet here. I intend to get the details now as promised – Austria seems a good bet."

"Great, can't wait to hear it's booked, it will be a fantastic week."

"I'll get back to you as soon as I have been to Regent Travel."

Regent Travel was only a short walk from John's office and Caroline was in so John felt quite confident to leave the office for an hour, to get his week's skiing sorted out.

"Can I help you?"

"Ah, yes please, I spoke to someone called Michael just before Christmas about a skiing holiday in February for eight people."

"That was me. Is it Mr England?"

"Yes, full marks for remembering my name. Are we too late to get this sorted?"

"No, I don't think so. The good thing is that you have chosen to go out of school holidays so let's have a look on the computer and see what I can fix up for you. How many rooms do you need? There are mainly doubles available."

"I guess we need four doubles."

"Think we were looking at the Active Spa Hotel at Seefeld, which is not far from the centre of the village, but has lots of facilities in the hotel. It is extremely popular with our clients, we are always sending people to the hotel. I have just checked and Inghams can provide the accommodation. I need to do some paperwork and check flights but I am sure I can make the arrangements."

"What date can you fix it for?"

"The flights are from Manchester and I think I can arrange it so you are there for Valentine's night if that would be good?"

"That would be excellent."

"Can you leave me a deposit of £100 per person, and your contact details and I will do the rest?"

"No problem," John presented his credit card and completed his details on a booking form, thanked Michael, and returned to his office.

"That couldn't have been easier, they are really good at Regent Travel," he remarked to Caroline as he entered the office.

"We are off to Austria in February for a week, can't wait."

"It's all right for some! That's great, hope you have a great time."

"Thanks. I had better get the rest of the team updated with the details."

"Hi, Lizzie, we are off! And we are off to the hotel I mentioned, the Active Spa Hotel in Seefeld, hopefully the holiday will include Valentine's night, how's that?"

"Fantastic, you are a real treasure John. Thank you so much, I can't wait to tell everyone else. Are you in tonight John?"

"Yes, I don't think I have anything on."

"How about I bring an Indian takeaway and we can look at the brochure and plan the holiday?"

"That would be great. See you about what, half seven?"

"Great, see you then. Bye."

John had just about given up on sorting out the filing in his office, so he decided to go and get a sandwich for lunch.

"Caroline?"

"Yes, John."

"Could you spare me an hour or two this afternoon? I really need to get my papers and files in order and every time I started sorting things out this week something cropped up."

"Yes, sure, John, I should be back from lunch around two."

"Great, thanks."

John was really pleased to have Caroline's help, as she was a very orderly person and he just wanted the chance to run over the Wall case as he needed to talk it through with someone just so he could get another point of view .

"It's gone four thirty, John, time we shut up shop."

"Yes, sorry, Caroline, I hadn't realised. Off you go, I will lock up."

"Thanks, John. Goodnight."

When Caroline had gone, John sat at his desk and made some notes of the conversation he had had with Caroline over the last couple of hours whilst they were tidying up his office.

6.01.2000 Thursday

"How are we all feeling this morning?" Frank Stringer remarked as he came into the kitchen.

"Not too bad thanks, Uncle. Sorry Frank, would you like a cup of tea?"

"Oh yes please, Si, I have been on the go since very early today. I had an early morning emergency at the care home, unfortunately one of my elderly patients died."

"Oh dear, it's all bad news at the moment. I have to take Purdy to the vet's later, she isn't at all well. Ever since Daddy died," Si's voice cracked and she found it difficult to continue as a few tears appeared.

Frank gave her a big hug as any father or favourite uncle might do. He knew they were all going through a lot just now and it was not easy to find words on any subject that didn't have some other meaning and recall Peter, their beloved father who doted on his daughters.

"Hello, Frank, how good of you to call," said Ann as she came into the kitchen.

"One lump or two, Frank?"

"No sugar for me Si, just milk thanks."

"Is Sandy okay?"

"Yes she is fine, we haven't seen her today. She wanted to go back to stay in her flat. She will be over soon."

"I must go and get Purdy to the vet's, Mum, she is still not well and she's off her food."

"Okay, darling, are you going now?"

"Yes I thought I would. You and Unc... sorry, Frank, can have a chat just the two of you whilst I am gone. Can I take the Range Rover? It's got the dog guard in the back and much easier for me and Purdy."

"Yes of course, the keys are on the hook." Si left, but not before giving Ann and Frank a kiss.

"She's a good girl that one, Ann."

"Yes I am very lucky, Frank, but I am also frightened and I feel very alone, even though the girls are with me."

"I know, it's called grief, there is no way of hurrying the process. The important thing is to get the funeral and then the inquest out of the way and then we'll have a degree of closure."

"Do you think so? I am not sure that I will ever be right again, I miss him so," tears welled up in Ann's eyes as she spoke.

"How are you sleeping?"

"Not bad. I don't wake in the night but it takes ages to go to sleep and I seem to be waking at six thirty every morning."

"That's fairly normal, try reading a book or watching some TV when you get to bed. That will give your mind something else to think about and the sleeping pills I prescribed will do the rest. As you begin to settle down we can cut the pills down a bit, but don't be afraid to take them."

"Thanks, Frank, you are so kind."

"Well I must be going I will try and pop in tomorrow. Bye."

Sandra was either having a monumental lie-in or was busy tidying the flat. Ann decided to walk over to see how she was.

"Sandy, it's Mum."

No response, no sound at all. Ann went up the stairs from the lobby to find the flat lights on and music playing on the iPod speakers, but no sign of Sandy.

"Sandy, it's Mum."

No response. Where on earth could she be?

"Sandy, Sandy!" With ever increasing volume. Still no response, at this point Ann was beginning to get very worried.

She went outside and shouted, "Sandy ... Sandy....Sandy!" for all her worth. No reply.

Ann went back to the farmhouse to get her boots and Barbour jacket and started off across the fields to see if she could find Sandy. As she got to the gateway to Long Acre and looked to the top of the field to the old oak she could see a crumpled figure at the bottom of the tree.

"Oh my God, no, no, no!" She screamed, running up the incline to the tree, half way there she had to stop and walk as she was out of breath. As she neared the figure of Sandy sitting on the ground with her back to the tree and facing away from the farm, Ann saw movement. Thank goodness for that, she was alive.

"Sandy, darling are you all right?"

Sandy, with an ashen face and tears streaking down her cheeks, looked up at her mother.

"Why did Daddy do this? Why, why, why?"

"Oh, darling," Tears streamed down Ann's face. She fell to the ground next to her daughter and they hugged one another.

There was of course no explanation, no reason any of them could think of why Peter had ended it all, and in such a dramatic way. The method of his departing was as painful to endure as was the suddenness of it. It would never be possible to look forward to New Year's Eve again.

"Mummy, I feel so alone. I just feel empty. How can we ever replace Daddy? Oh, Daddy, why did you do this to us?"

"Darling, we must be strong, it is not easy but Daddy would not have wanted us to suffer. I am sure he made up his mind to leave us so that we could enjoy life as we have known it, my fear is that he did this because of money or lack of it, and he felt he would be letting us all down if he had to sell the house or lose the business. That is all I can think of."

"Why would he kill himself though? We could have sorted things out. It doesn't matter where we live or how much money we have, just so long as we all have one another and now we don't have Daddy."

Another torrent of tears descended from both of them and they just sobbed and sobbed. When it seemed that they had no more tears to shed Ann stood up, "Come on, let's go home."

The pair of them slowly walked down the hill to the farm in silence.

As they neared the stone gatepost Sandy turned to her mother,

"You won't let them bring Jumbo back again, will you?"

"I really hadn't given any thought to the matter darling, why?"

"It was Jumbo who did the killing."

Ann realised that Sandy was in a very delicate state and Ann didn't want to argue the point now,

"Of course, darling, we don't need to have Jumbo back, there are too many bad memories attached to her. I will ask the police if they can dispose of her for us."

Sandy didn't reply and the pair carried on to the farmhouse.

The Range Rover rattled across the cattle grid and navigated its way into the garage which had been left open by Si when she had taken Purdy to the vet's.

Si opened the tailgate and Purdy flopped out of the car, her tail slightly wagging, walked behind Si across the yard to the house.

"Hi, are you two all right?" immediately detecting an atmosphere as soon as she entered into the kitchen.

"Sandy has been upset as we all have, darling. We all just need some time and space to try and get our lives back together. How is Purdy?"

"Oh, Sandy, don't cry, darling. We must be strong for Mum, as well as ourselves. The vet said Purdy had effectively been poisoned. They have taken some blood tests and given her some vitamins to help her recover. They don't think it was the tranquiliser that Dad gave her, as it would have needed a considerable dose of the tranquiliser to poison her to the extent she has been. They say she will recover but it will take a few days yet. If there is anything else they discover from the blood sample they will let us know."

"Thanks darling, poor old Purdy, maybe you just don't like the tranquiliser and it doesn't suit you? We mustn't give you that again."

Purdy wandered around the kitchen drumming her tail on the kitchen cupboard doors as her name was mentioned.

"Look at the time, it's nearly a quarter to one and John England will be here at two," said Si. "Shall I knock up some lunch?"

"That would be good, do you mind if I don't help you? I don't think I need much to eat, maybe just some soup."

"Okay, no problem are you going over to the flat to get changed for when John comes?"

"Well yes, I will go over now. Will you be coming over when you have done lunch, Si?"

"Yes, I will just help Mum with the lunch, and have something to eat. I will leave some soup in a mug for you so it only needs microwaving when you come back over."

Sandy ran a shower and stood under the torrent of water for what seemed to her an absolute age. She washed her hair and stepped out of the shower and put on her towelling robe, and wrapped her hair in a towel like a turban. Whilst the moisture was being absorbed by the towel she tidied up all her clothes and made her bed, and felt considerably better.

It was about ten to two when Sandy reappeared into the kitchen and heated her soup.

Neither Ann nor Si were around but Sandy could hear noises upstairs so she knew there was activity. Sandy sipped her mug of soup and Purdy came and sat on her feet under the kitchen table.

Sandy glanced into the yard to see John England arrive in his sports car but with the hood up against the January cold. As he arrived in the yard and was getting out of the car, Si appeared at the entrance to her flat and almost skipped across the yard to shake John's hand.

I recognise the symptoms here, thought Sandy. Someone is rather taken with our solicitor.

Si and John entered the kitchen, John, forever the perfect gentleman, allowing Si to enter first.

"Hello, John, good of you to come, I was just supping a mug of soup, can I get you anything?"

"No, I'm fine thank you," and he bent down to pat Purdy who was now rubbing up against his leg.

"Come into your bed, Purdy," ordered Si, and as obedient as ever she went to her bed in the utility room, and Si shut the kitchen door. "Let's go through to the lounge."

Si led the way with John following. Sandy called upstairs to Ann and shortly they were all assembled in the lounge.

"Well here we are again. I am pleased to advise you I have been able to obtain a copy of Mr Wall's will which Frobisher's in Manchester assure me is the latest will Mr Wall made with the firm. I am obliged to ask again if you are aware of any other will Mr Wall may have made?"

"No I'm not," said Ann, and the girls nodded in agreement.

"Then let me tell you of the contents of this will. I have made some copies to leave with you, so there is no need for you to take notes. I have also prepared a brief summary of the main points of the will which I shall also leave with you today."

John pulled a bundle of papers from his briefcase and selected one document which seemed to comprise of about ten pages and a single piece of A4. Before he started to read from either document John opened his 'address' with some preliminary statements:

"This is the last will and testament of Peter Wall, it is as far as wills go a fairly standard will taking into account the current way of looking at estate planning and has been formulated to ensure that the minimum Inheritance Tax is payable. In fact I think there will be no tax to pay but that is a question I would like to put to your accountants. Do you have some accountants?"

"I'm sure we have but they will be the firm's, I think my husband got them to do his personal tax matters at the same time as they were doing the company audit and the company paid."

"Not unusual, but I shall need to know who they are."

"When Roger Whiteside returns from his holiday I will ask him. I assume he will come and see me, possibly on Monday. He doesn't get back from Austria until Saturday."

John was tempted to make a comment about Austria and holidays but thought better of it. Stick to the task in hand, he thought. "Good. As soon as you know who it is I would be grateful if you could let me know.

"As with all wills it has a standard format, and every deceased person who leaves a will has to nominate executors. In this instance there are two, you Mrs Wall and Dr Frank Stringer. I am not sure if either of you knew that?"

"Well the will leaves to you, Sandra, and you, Sienna, the sum of £175,000 each – a sum of £350,000 in all which is bequeathed to you as the maximum amount that can be bequeathed tax free.

"The balance of the estate – that is the house and any monies from deposits shares in Wall's and insurance – comes to Ann.

"Have you been able to find any insurance policies, or other documents relating to either personal arrangements or the business?"

"We haven't wanted to rummage about Dad's study, but I guess we need to now. Sandy and I are more than willing to get stuck in and make a list of documents and let you have them."

"Good, that will be excellent. I will need as much as you can give me so I can make claims on life assurance policies."

"Will that be possible?" interrupted Ann, "I thought if someone had committed suicide then they couldn't claim on their insurance?"

"That used to be the case but the rules changed a short while ago so that any policy entered into twelve months or more before the death was capable of being claimed against."

"Oh, that's a relief, I thought we would be penniless. I am sure John had a number of policies, I do know he put another one in place last year as I recall him going for the medical, and he was advised to exercise more."

"I think that is a common piece of advice, but if that policy was not in force before the 31st December 1998 then I regret that one will not be possible to claim against."

"Did you make contact with the undertaker?"

"Yes, he's coming tomorrow John, we are not sure when we are allowed to hold the funeral. Sandy and I need to make some arrangements but we just don't know when."

"The body has been released with what they call a temporary death certificate, this is all that is required for the burial or cremation. By the way, there are no special instructions in the will as to funeral arrangements, so you can make whatever arrangements you like with Mr Cartwright."

"Oh good, we will be able to make a little progress and Sandy and I both feel that there will be a degree of closure once the funeral is over."

At that moment the phone rang and Si went to answer it in the kitchen. She was back in no time.

"It was the vet, they have had the blood sample tests back and it is as they had thought – Purdy has ingested far too much tranquiliser for her own goo-d, that is why she was so sleepy and sick. They say she should be as right as rain in a few days."

"I am pleased to hear that. You have enough on your plates without Purdy becoming ill. I don't think there is much more to tell now, I will need the accountant's contact details and as many of Mr Wall's papers as you can find. Please let me know when you have them and I can easily pick them up. Also please let me know the date of the funeral."

Almost as one they all thanked John and Si escorted him out to his car. Despite the cold snap Si was not wearing a coat, just a light sweater and skirt.

"Thank you so much, John, for all your help. It is a great relief to have you sorting things out for us."

John drove off, but he could not help realising that there was more than a normal client relationship here with Si. He said to himself, "Be professional, don't let personal relationships interfere with the job."

"What a great day skiing," remarked Roger as he came into the foyer of the hotel where he was staying. Helga the receptionist and party host was out from behind the reception desk to greet the skiers as they returned.

"I am glad about that. How about some Glühwein on the terrace or in the lounge or, if you like, in the sauna?"

Helga was not Austrian but Norwegian; she had an excellent grasp of English and also spoke fluent German. On top of all that she was a very good skier and quite pretty.

"That's an offer almost too good to refuse, I will go to my room and leave all my ski clothes there and go to the sauna. Yes thank you, I will have a Glühwein then."

He's cheered up since the New Year. Obviously his friends in Innsbruck have cheered him up, thought Helga.

"I will arrange for that straight away, Roger," and she left and went to speak to room service on the house phone.

Roger was nearing the end of his two week winter holiday. It was not easy going on holiday on your own, but this hotel was very good at making sure no one was left out and that everyone had a good time.

Helga was one of the team whose job it was to make sure everyone enjoyed themselves. The accommodation up on the fourth floor was fine, in the eaves of the chalet-style hotel. The room was equipped with the basics and had an en-suite bathroom. There was a balcony with fantastic views of the mountains and ski runs and the ski lift was only minutes away from the hotel. The entertainment was all thrown in with special dinner nights and of course a special gala dinner for New Year's Eve.

Helga had organised a large table for ten people who were either singles or couples who wanted to party on Millennium

Eve, and Helga had found a seat for herself at this table, so she could join in the fun at the same time act as hostess to everyone else. In fact Roger was the only person on his own at the table so Helga positioned herself next to him.

Roger was a lonely man, he did his best to get into the swing of things but, since his divorce from Judy eight years earlier, he had not been very good at socialising and he was very bitter generally towards women.

Judy had been well advised and despite the fact they had only been married for four years, she managed to get the house, the car and the majority of savings such as they were. The issue was that Roger had not been earning very much and Judy had been able to show that she was the main wage earner working for M&S Financial Services in Chester, where she still worked. Roger was starting the company with Peter Wall and the two of them had to keep their income low as the firm was just starting out and needed every penny, so the proprietors really had very little.

Two years into the building of the business and Judy had had enough and sought a divorce. This was a bitter blow to Roger who was left with very little. In fact he had to rent a flat in Handbridge, just outside the city walls of Chester. Luckily for Roger it was owned by a buy-to-let landlord and so he had been able to secure a long lease. He was still living there. He was settled, he had no outgoings and despite house prices rising he had little appetite for taking on a mortgage.

The best bit as far as Roger was concerned about the settlement was that there was no order for him to pay maintenance, and as there were no children it was a straight settlement based on assets and money. Roger felt aggrieved that he didn't take more out of the business but he recognised that his 49% shareholding really didn't amount to much as he had no majority stake to get his own way, unlike Peter Wall.

As the business grew Peter was good enough to make sure Roger had a good wage and he always got a good dividend at the end of the year. Despite this, Roger never felt that he was a joint owner of the company, it did after all bear Peter's name and it was Peter who was wined and dined by banks and customers, Roger was the backroom boy who ensured the jobs got done. He hardly had an expenses claim whereas Peter was taking literally thousands a month in expenses.

Roger felt particularly angry inside when Peter announced that he had bought a farm at auction. Angry because the farm, Long Acre Farm, was in need of substantial renovation and Peter had announced that the firm would be doing all the work. Roger knew what that meant, the firm and Roger would be getting all the work done and the firm would be paying for it.

It was a real surprise to Helga as Roger told her, walking through reception with a small holdall, that he would not be back until New Year's Day, as his friends in Innsbruck had invited him down to their home for the New Year celebrations.

"I have left all my stuff in my room and I will be back possibly late on New Year's Day, so I will see you then. Happy New Year, Helga."

Blast, thought Helga All my planning has been undone. Not being used to people pulling out of celebrations at the last moment Helga had to set about reorganising the table, and in doing so found another couple who wanted to join in. So Helga removed herself from the seating plan and the table of ten was re-established.

Roger took the bus to Innsbruck, it was quite early in the day, but Helga had assumed that his friends in Innsbruck were going to entertain him for the festivities and perhaps he wanted to do some shopping before he got to their house.

Roger asked Helga to the disco. They had a great night albeit not New Year's Eve, Helga was tired but she played along and, to her surprise and Roger's, ended up a little drunk in Roger's room. This she knew was strictly against hotel rules and she hoped no one would find out. They were both well away on wine and schnapps. It didn't take long before Roger and Helga were enjoying one another so much that it ended with both of them naked on the single bed. It was not easy and the wooden sides of the bed really hurt Rogers's knees.

They both passed out in one another's arms and then woke again in about an hour feeling cold as their hot and steamy bodies had cooled quickly without any bed covers. They decided to have a bath, after which Helga crept out of the room at about three a.m. She hoped she would not be discovered.

The rest of Roger's time in Austria he was light hearted and jovial and enjoyed Helga's company on more than one occasion. If the management knew of this liaison they were not for letting on, perhaps they thought that Helga was fulfilling her role and, anyway, this guest was a single mature male.

7.1.2000 Friday

On the dot of two o'clock a darkly coloured Ford Mondeo estate entered the yard, rattling the cattle grid as it did so. Out got a man who was clearly Mr Cartwright, and clearly in funeral director's mode. He had a dark long overcoat, black suit and black tie with a white shirt.

Sandy went to the back door to let him in. Purdy looked up out of her basket with curiosity, but made no attempt to greet this new visitor.

"Please come in, Mr Cartwright," said Ann, as she stretched out a hand in greeting.

"Oh, Mrs Wall, please accept my sincere condolences."

"Thank you, Mr Cartwright, shall we go into the lounge?"

"These are my two daughters, Sandra and Sienna, Mr Cartwright."

He nodded in acknowledgement of their presence.

"I am not sure if you are aware that we have collected Mr Wall's body and he is now lying in our Chapel of Rest next to my office in Tarporley. You are all most welcome to visit at any time, please just give me a ring to indicate when that might be." He handed out a business card, one to each of his female audience.

"The position is that we will need to have some forms signing not just by you Mrs Wall but also by the family doctor. Would I be right in assuming that might be Dr Stringer?"

"You would."

"Very well, that's excellent. Now have you seen your late husband's will and are there any special requests regarding his funeral?"

"Yes, we have all seen the will and no there is nothing my late husband requested regarding funeral arrangements."

"Good, then may I make some suggestions?" Mr Cartwright went into the full script which he must have given a hundred or more times. By the end they had finalised just about everything the funeral required. Mr Cartwright bade farewell to the ladies. He promised he would phone later with a proposed date and time for the funeral, having checked with the vicar of Tarporley about the Church service and also the availability of the crematorium.

"Phew, I am glad that's over. Shall we have a cup of tea?"

"That would be good, do you mind if Si and I have a rummage around Dad's study this afternoon Mum, to see what we can discover that would be of help to John?"

"Yes of course, but don't throw anything away until I've seen it."

"Okay we will get cracking and take our tea into the study."

"Blimey, where do we start?"

"Si, you make some piles of documents, let's have some blank paper and put labels on each pile. I guess we shall need bills, credit cards, insurance and other documents. That should be good for a start."

Peter Wall's desk in his study was a kneehole partners desk, possibly not antique but certainly old. The drawers ran smoothly and were full of paper, documents and other office paraphernalia. The desk top had two filing trays, but no filing had been done for some time as they were full of invoices, letters and so on. Sitting at the desk the occupant had a view of the fields through the bay window in the study. Peter's large green leather chair, currently occupied by Sienna, swung all the way round and faced back into the room where there was a green leather Chesterfield on one side and a small table opposite on which were piles of magazines. Next to the table was a four drawer filing cabinet.

"I bet there is some interesting stuff in here," she said as Si swung the chair round and leapt out to the filing cabinet and pulled at a drawer.

"Bugger, it's locked!"

"See if there are any keys in the top drawers of the desk."

"No, can't see any."

"I will go and ask Mum if Dad's keys are around as the key is bound to be on there."

Sandra was back in a moment with a bunch of keys, some looked possible.

One small key did the trick. "Open sesame," she exclaimed.

The filing cabinet drawers were almost as untidy as the desk top. Nothing much was labelled other than one or two files, the ones the girls found first were: - Wall's Civil Engineering Limited, Inland Revenue, Buy to let Property, and Long Acre Farm. These files were without doubt the thickest and they parcelled them out between them. Sandra took Wall's Civil Engineering Limited, as she felt she would know most about the content, and also the one marked Inland Revenue. Si took Buy to let property and Long Acre Farm as those sounded as though the contents were more directed to her specialism.

Silence fell on the study for nearly an hour with just the odd "Good heavens" and "I didn't know that" and "what did he think he was doing buying that" and so on. The tea didn't get finished. By the time the two of them had extracted sufficient documents they thought would be useful from the files, they both looked up from their task almost at the same time.

"Well what do you think of your pile?"

"It seems as though Dad was up to more property speculation that I ever thought. I knew about the two buy to let properties at Squirrels Chase. I have let them both. I had no idea of the other two or the development land. I am sure they were never put through the company's books... it must have been personal. What I haven't found is the financing arrangements but they may still be in the filing cabinet."

"What do you mean, Si?"

"Well it seems that Dad had bought four buy to let properties in Chester, and also has bought an option to buy ten acres of land subject to planning consent for residential development."

"Blimey, I dint know that! Do you suppose he was planning to move into development in addition to civil engineering?"

"It would seem so, he was looking to set up a development company and to secure about two million pounds of development funding."

"Is there any suggestion that he would do this through the company?"

"Not as I can see."

"Mm, well my search of the company file has produced some interesting documentation. The most interesting of which I have been reading for the last quarter of an hour is a Shareholder Agreement."

"Oh, and what does that tell us?"

"Well for one thing, Mum gets the shares in the company. Dad is, sorry was, responsible for the financing of the business. It also makes clear that any of the companies' money used for the personal benefit of a shareholder will be repayable in full including VAT by that shareholder. It also makes provision for key man insurance. It is quite interesting that the insurance is to be paid for by the company and half of the total premium is to be debited to the capital account of each shareholder, the benefit of the key man insurance is to go personally to the surviving shareholder. They are to use the money by way of a capital injection into the business to enable the business to take on any additional staff in the event of the loss of a key worker, but primarily it is to recompense the surviving shareholder for the additional work they will have to do, and pay them a salary so the company is not denuded of cash at a difficult time."

"That sounds quire a sensible arrangement, Sandy."

"It does on the face of it, but it is most unusual, normally the company pays the premium and gets the benefit of the insurance. I guess it was done this way as there were only the two of them in the company."

"Is there any information about insurances in your folders? I have found nothing in mine."

"No, it's odd. I am sure there are some policies, but there appears to be nothing in the filing cabinet."

"How are you two getting on?"

"We are doing fine, Mum. Sandy has just found the Shareholders Agreement which helps the firm should one of the shareholders die. What we can't find is any insurance policies."

"No, you won't find them in the filing cabinet. Your dad was always concerned about fire, so they are in the fireproof safe."

"Where is that?" asked Si who was sitting on the floor in front of the filing cabinet.

"It's under your bottom Si, just move to the side a bit and roll the rug back, then lift the square section of floorboard and you will find the safe."

"So it is. Sling the keys across, Sandy, and let's see if there is a key that will fit."

Si tried the keys that looked most appropriate, and the last one did the job. Off came the top of the safe.

"How exciting," exclaimed Si.

"I don't think that is quite appropriate under the circumstances," said Ann, as Si fished out a bundle of papers, some small cloth pouches and a tough brown envelope.

"The cloth pouches are my jewellery so you can keep your paws off those."

"I wonder what is in the envelope."

"If you open it, Si, you will find the answer."

"Wow, there must be thousands here," the envelope had revealed its secret and contained two large bundles of fifty-pound notes. In fact, on counting them, the amount was ten thousand pounds.

"I think we can put the money and the jewels back in the safe and lock it up now and I will take the key thanks, but you two can keep searching the papers for John so he can get underway."

"Okay, let's split the bundle, Sandy, and see what we find."

Si handed half of the bundle of papers to her sister and she started to look carefully at what she had discovered.

"Whilst you two are doing that I will go and make some food. I am feeling a bit peckish this evening." With that, Ann retired to the kitchen.

"That's good news. Mum needs to eat and the fact she is getting her appetite back is great."

Ann hadn't been gone long when she returned with Frank in tow. "Hello, girls. I see you are hard at it sorting out the papers. Well done, it is a frightful job."

At that moment the phone rang and it was only a short step for Si to pick it up from Peter's desk, "Hello, Long Acre Farm."

"Is Mrs Wall free please? It's Cartwright, the undertaker."

"Mr Cartwright! Yes, Mum is just here can you please hang on?"

With her hand over the mouth piece Si announced to the assembled company that it was Mr Cartwright who wanted to speak to her mother.

"Mr Cartwright, thank you for coming back to me. What news have you?"

"Mrs Wall, I am pleased to say that I have been able to arrange for a service at St Helen's Church on Friday 13th

January at eleven in the morning and then afterwards at twelve thirty p.m. at the Chester Crematorium, I hope you will find that acceptable?"

"Thank you very much, Mr Cartwright, that would be fine. We just need to make some arrangements now."

"Well Mrs Wall, I have taken the liberty of asking the vicar to arrange to come and see you, he has your phone number. Also I enquired at the Swan in the village if they had the function room available for a funeral gathering at about one thirty and they have. Once again I have given your number to the manager who will ring you and discuss any arrangements you may wish to make. You are not of course obliged to accept this suggestion, but I felt it would be one less thing for you to think about."

"Thank you, Mr Cartwright. How very kind, is there anything further we need to do?"

"Well, if I may, I would like to come and see you on Monday morning just to run over a few last minute things. The vicar will need to know about hymns, and I will need the details of the service for the service sheet... also whether you want flowers or donations, and if you wish to place an announcement in the paper? However all that can wait until Monday, I think that is all."

"Thank you Mr Cartwright."

"My pleasure, Mrs Wall. Goodbye."

8.1.2000 Saturday

The Monarch Airways flight from Innsbruck touched down at Manchester Airport only a few minutes behind the scheduled time. Roger Whiteside was in good heart having enjoyed his winter sporting holiday. It must be the Helga influence, he thought to himself.

Having made his way through passport control and baggage claim he phoned the car parking service who delivered his car to him outside the terminal building. It wasn't a flash car, not like Peter's. Roger was content to drive a BMW 3 series, the smallest in the range, but as he was on his own and didn't have much to carry this was an ideal car. Peter was always trying to get Roger to change his car saying, "It's four years old now that car of yours. Time it was changed." He won't be saying anything any more, thought Roger as he mused about the death of his business partner.

Peter and Roger had set up Wall's Civil Engineering Limited in 1989, and it had run from the back bedroom of Peter's house to begin with until they had managed to get suitable office premises in Blacon in Chester in 1990. Christine Franks had come to work for them firstly part time and then full time as secretary and book-keeper. As Peter was always customer facing and visiting their offices he always had a smart car and dressed the part. Roger didn't mind this, although as time went by it began to irritate him.

As the business grew they moved to an office and yard that they were able to buy with a twenty-year mortgage from the bank. The premises were ideal as they provided parking and servicing facilities for some of the vehicles they now owned.

There was suitable storage for a small plant they had purchased and excellent offices for the six staff employed in the offices.

The accountants, Berry and Berry of Chester had advised that really the property should be purchased in a pension fund, but as Peter's pension pot was not big enough, nor was Roger's, they then had to go for a straight mortgage of the property. However what did come out of this was that both partners bought the premises together outside the company and let the property to the company which paid the mortgage on it. That seemed to be a sensible approach and left the possibility open to put the property in one or both pension funds in the future. The advice from the accountants was that they should get a Shareholders Agreement to make it clear how the shareholders should behave in given circumstances. One of the issues was that if something ever happened to one or both of the partners whereby they could no longer work or were dead, the company would be in difficulties and would need to spend money on employing additional people to fulfil the role that was vacant.

The other cost that would have to be covered was the cost of the mortgage, which was personal to the individual shareholders, and if anything should happen to a shareholder it could adversely affect the income available from the company to pay the rent, so leaving the remaining shareholder exposed. The mortgage was half a million pounds, and that needed to be dealt with. Peter and Roger were advised to get this all written into the Shareholders Agreement and that there should be key man insurance taken out by the company for the personal benefit of the survivor. A firm of solicitors in Manchester was chosen, Frobisher's, and there was a budding young corporate lawyer there called Sally Moulton who they went to see, explaining what they were doing and what they wanted. Sally was up to the task and fully understood the issues. She needed to speak to the accountants and to their insurance brokers so that everything could be tied in.

Unusually, it didn't take Sally very long at all in letting them have a draft of the document. With the permission of the shareholders Sally had also copied the document to the insurance brokers Birch and Co., and the accountants for their opinions. All in all it took about a month to put this document together and get the insurance in place which was to last as long as the mortgage – twenty years. Peter had to go for a medical, but all that was okay. The deal was done and the two shareholders had celebrated with their wives at a night out at the Grosvenor, "A treat for the girls," as Peter put it.

Roger had been detached from reality in Austria so he had not really given any thought to the practical issues of taking over running the business. He had also the difficult business of speaking with Ann Wall, dealing with the funeral and whatever came after all that.

The traffic was quite busy on the M56 from Manchester Airport to Chester; it was all this holiday traffic and the closure of the West Coast main line for renovation works that had caused all this. Roger was able to unlock his front door at just after five o'clock; it was dark and starting to rain. Welcome home, he thought to himself as he pushed open the door and squeezed through the open section, as the door would not open fully due to the mound of mail that had fallen through the box while he had been away.

The apartment was on the first floor of a converted house. He had his own front door which made the place, somehow, feel more like home. First job was to clear the post so he could open the door fully and get his luggage inside. All the lights were now on and the heating turned up. There appeared to be no issues with bursts or anything of that sort. The flat was fairly spartan – Roger had not bothered with Christmas decorations due to the fact he was away all Christmas and New Year.

He looked at the soft bag with all his now dirty clothes in it and decided tomorrow was the day to deal with that. As soon as hot water was available he would have a shower and go out for something to eat. He was just starting to look through the post when the phone rang.

"Hello, Roger Whiteside."

No sound, just the fact he knew that there was someone on the other end.

"Hello, who's that?"

Nothing, and then the phone went dead. If only he had one of those machines which gave the number people had rung from. Then he recalled you can find out what number it was by dialling 1471.

"The number that called is not available," came the disembodied voice of a recording.

"Blast," he said out loud to himself. "Who on earth could that be?"

After he had separated the mail into three piles – junk not worth opening straight for the bin pile, bills, and others – he opened the letters. There was one from the letting agent advising that the tenancy was up in two months, and did he want to extend?

There was a letter from the bank saying that his credit card had been used a lot in Austria and did he know, "Yes I bloody well do know, it was me!"

Fed up with opening crap, he went to the bedroom and stripped off his travel-weary clothes which always seem to attract certain sweatiness about them no matter how hot or cold it has been. In the hot shower he let the water cascade over his body for quite some time.

"Is that the bloody phone again?" he said out loud. "Oh, let it ring."

Eventually it went off.

He changed into a clean set of togs ready to sort the rest of the post out and opened a can of beer from the fridge to help make the task easier.

Roger, now with the holiday firmly behind him, was feeling a bit low realising what he had to do. Swallowing the last of the beer he put on his coat and went out to get a pizza.

Back at the flat, having devoured the pizza and leaving the cold crust rattling around in the box, he decided it was time to phone the Walls.

"Hello, it's Roger, Roger Whiteside, who is that?"

"Hello Roger, Sandra here, is it Mum you would like to speak to?"

"Yes, please."

"Roger, Ann Wall."

"Ann, I am so dreadfully sorry to hear of your loss. I am also sorry that there was nothing I could do as I was away in Austria."

"Roger, it's good of you to phone as soon as you got back. We are still in total shock, it's hard to know where to start."

"Well I guess I could come over tomorrow and help sort out some of Peter's papers and get insurance and stuff going if that would be a help."

"Well that's awfully kind of you, but the girls have been fantastic and we have engaged a solicitor in Chester, John

England of Bennett and Bennett, who is helping us and he will be arranging the insurance claims and so on."

"Oh I see."

"Well, you were away and we were uncertain what to do and Frank Stringer, our doctor and friend, thought that an independent person would be a good idea. The funeral is at St Helen's Church here in Tarporley on Friday next week. There will have to be an inquest, you know."

"No I didn't know. Why was that?"

"Well Roger, Peter's death was unusual and the police are making enquiries and then the law requires an inquest."

"What have the police been saying?"

"Nothing much. They have been asking questions more than saying anything, I think they have confided in John England more than us."

"I assume from what little I have heard that Peter committed suicide?"

"Yes," Ann's voice cracked at this point. "Sorry Roger, I just cannot get the events of this week out of my mind."

"Please don't upset yourself on my account, would you find it useful if I came over tomorrow?"

"It's very kind but we are all okay, thanks."

"Very well, I will be in the office on Monday to see what has arrived while I have been away. See you soon then, goodbye."

"Bye."

"I don't know what it is about that man but I never feel comfortable with him even on the phone. He wanted to come over and help with Dad's papers but I told him we had a solicitor on the job, and he was a bit taken aback by that. He's not coming anyway."

"That's good, we will be okay, Mum. I am sure John will look after us."

The phone rang again and Ann answered.

"Yes that will be fine, look forward to seeing you at about three o'clock tomorrow then, goodbye.

"That was the vicar, he's coming at three tomorrow, I was surprised he chose Sunday. I would have thought he was busy on other matters, but he said it fitted in well."

9.1.2000 Sunday

The day dawned bright, too bright, too early, the forecast was for rain. By lunchtime it was chucking it down. Purdy was looking much better and back to her old self, she had enjoyed her walk this morning up to the old oak and beyond to the copse, and she had managed to put up a rabbit.

It was a day now for inside jobs and the girls were back in the study looking at all the paperwork they had unearthed. Ann joined them midmorning with a cup of coffee for all of them.

"It's looking like Dad owed quite a lot of money, Mum," Sandra informed her mother. "There are credit card bills, bills from the garage for service on the Range Rover and your Freelander subscriptions for the AA and a huge bill from the Inland Revenue. It is a demand for payment and there is no explanation, just an amount."

"How much is it?"

"It's two hundred and eighty thousand pounds!"

"There must be some mistake."

"I guess it is the accountants we need to speak to. Oh dammit, I knew there was something – I had to ask Roger who the accountants were. Let me go and put a note by the phone so that I will remember tomorrow and I can ring the office."

At three o'clock on the dot the vicar arrived and they spent nearly two hours talking about Peter, and what he had achieved. They also chose some hymns and the vicar went through the order of service. He also indicated that he would be at the crematorium.

When he had gone Ann allowed herself another cry.

"I must phone the Swan tomorrow to see if they can do a funeral tea on Friday, another note by the phone for Monday."

Roger was getting on with all the holiday washing and had it all done by six o'clock. The phone went, which he thought unusual, as he rarely received calls on a Sunday.

"Is that you, Whiteside?"

"Yes who is this?"

"Never you mind, but we both know what we are talking about. I hope you are going to be a rich man as I will need some of the spoils." And with that the caller rang off.

11.1.01 Monday

"Long Acre Farm," Si answered in quite a cheery voice for a Monday morning, especially after the events of the last seven days.

"It's Cartwright, the undertaker. Is Mrs Wall available?"

"She isn't here right now but she will be back shortly."

"Oh I see. I just wondered if it would be convenient for me to call about ten a.m. to see if you had chosen the hymns and the order of service as I will need to get the details to the printers today as soon as I can."

"I am sure that will be fine Mr Cartwright, I will tell Mum as soon as she returns."

Ann had taken Purdy up the fields to the old oak and then over to the copse. She needed the exercise, as did Purdy, and Ann felt that if she continued to make the journey Peter had taken almost every day of his life she would eventually come to terms with what had happened.

"Mr Cartwright called, Mum. He's coming about ten to go over what we discussed with the vicar."

"Oh, all right. I'd better make myself presentable."

"There is no need, Mum, you will do just fine as you are."

"Well I've been outside and I'm a bit dishevelled."

No sooner were the words out of her mouth than Frank's car came into the yard, for his daily check-up.

When Frank had left Mr Cartwright appeared. He took down all the details for the service and rushed off to get to the printers so that the order of service sheets could be printed in time.

One of the jobs Sandra had agreed to do was to arrange for an announcement in the local paper and she phoned them to place the announcement and paid by credit card over the phone. "The papers are out on Wednesday so everyone will be able to read it before Friday," the helpful but slightly unfriendly voice informed her, on the other end of the phone.

Sandra phoned her senior partner at Spencer's in Liverpool to advise him what was happening and that she hoped to be back at work in a week. He was very understanding and passed messages of sympathy to the family.

"Do you think you could please pass me through to the commercial department as I need to update them on some jobs that are in train?"

"Certainly." What a dedicated young woman he thought. Sandra got through to her department and advised colleagues of what had happened and then went on to update them on some matters she had been dealing with.

Si had done much the same for Dents, the surveyors in Chester, they were very sympathetic but said that there wasn't much going on at the moment so there was no problem with the time off.

After lunch, who should arrive at the back door but Fred Appleyard.

"Hello, Fred. We weren't expecting to see you until tomorrow."

"No, Mrs Wall." As he said it he touched the brim of his cap, no one could recall seeing Fred without his cap on, it seemed moulded to his head. "I have just been to the village and I heard the terrible news about Mr Wall, and as I was passing the end of the lane I felt I should come in and offer condolences, Mrs Wall."

"Well, that's very kind of you, Fred. We all appreciate it very much." By this time Fred had arrived in the kitchen and had acknowledged the girls.

"Fred, since you're here I wondered if you knew the police are involved now, and they want everybody for one of those new DNA tests."

"Oh why? I had nothing to do with it!" he sounded frightened all of a sudden.

Sandra entered into the conversation "There's nothing to be worried about, Fred, we have all given samples, it's because you used Jumbo and Jumbo was involved in Dad's death you see." As she finished her voice cracked, as the mere mention of the words brought a flashback of the events of New Year's Day.

"Oh I see, so it will be all right then, Mrs Wall?"

"Yes, Fred, it will be fine, there is nothing to worry about at all."

"Very well, Mrs Wall, I will be here at eight o'clock as usual tomorrow, good day."

Fred left on his trusty bike.

"It's difficult for some older people who are not aware of modern techniques to grasp what is going on."

"Oh, he will be fine."

Roger was at the office early today as he needed to see what was in the mail and if any issues had cropped up with jobs over the holidays.

There were no calls on the answerphone, which he thought was a bit odd, but there was plenty of post to open. A brown envelope from HM Customs caught his eye and he decided to open it first. It was the result of the VAT inspection. The VAT people carried out checks periodically on all companies that were VAT registered. In Wall's case they hadn't had an inspection for four years. During the inspection they asked all the usual questions and picked up on directors' expenses and the VAT claimed and on petrol claims which, he knew, would lead to a claim for back VAT and a fine.

When they were doing the inspection they also discovered that Roger had all the work done at Long Acre Farm by the firm and hadn't paid for it, neither had any VAT been charged on it. "This is a very serious matter," Roger was advised by the VAT inspector. "There will be a hefty bill to pay. We have calculated that the VAT unpaid on the totality of the work which we estimate to be worth £350,000 is £61,250. The fact it has not been declared and we have had to find it will mean an automatic penalty of the same again."

Wall's had claimed back the VAT they had paid to sub-contractors and equipment hire companies and builders merchants, but they had never raised an invoice for the work to Peter Wall.

Roger had been very angry about the work they had done at Long Acre Farm, it got in the way of the normal work flow, it wasn't the sort of work they normally did so they were spending a lot of time finding subcontractors to do specialist work, electricians, plumbers, roofers, brickies, plasterers and so on. The job had cost a lot and the firm had run up an overdraft as a result. It made Roger very cross, and here was the living proof of his anger – a bill from the VAT people for £122,500. Roger knew how big it was going to be before he went on holiday, but knowing the amount and seeing it in black and white were quite different.

"Bugger," he exclaimed, "this is fucking ridiculous, what the fucking hell did Peter think he was doing?" Calming down, Roger recalled the benefits that would come his way now Peter was gone. In fact he felt he should phone the brokers this morning to get matters rolling.

"Morning, Roger," Christine Franks said as she came into the office "Did you have a good holiday?"

"Yes I did, thanks."

"Terrible news about Peter."

"Oh yes it was dreadful, I spoke to Ann Wall on Saturday when I got back. Thanks for getting a message to me in Austria, there wasn't much I could do."

"No, I expect we shall hear when the funeral is."

"It's on Friday in Tarporley."

"What are you going to do, close the office so we can all go?"

"I hadn't thought what to do actually; do you think that would be the right thing to do?"

"Yes I do, Roger, he was the boss of the firm after all, I am surprised you even had to think twice."

"Well we have work to catch up."

"Well whilst you are on about work there was a message from the bank. They want you to call them," said Christine in a very cross and frosty voice. She returned to her desk and started to get organised for the week ahead.

Roger continued with the post, he knew what the bank wanted; Wall had exceeded their overdraft limit again!

Roger returned to his apartment at about six thirty and he realised that he was out of his normal routine as he had failed to call at the supermarket to get a food shop. As he was preparing a list of the things he wanted the phone rang.

"Is that you, Roger?"

"Yes, who is this?"

"Had a bad day at work?"

"Never you mind. Who are you?"

"Don't forget I need a slice of the action, bye bye."

These phone calls were beginning to get on Rogers nerves. "Who the hell is this? What do they want?"

11.1.2000 Tuesday

At eight o'clock on the dot Fred Appleyard cycled in to the yard, parked his bike at the side of the machinery shed, and went to his little store at the back where he had a kettle and a tap and brew up facilities. He kept his precious tools and bits and pieces in there and he always kept it locked. There probably was a key in the house for Fred's Shed as it was called but no one ever thought of going in there if Fred was not around.

By half past eight Fred was hard at work in the yard with broom and shovel trying to tidy the place up after all the vehicles that had been in and out. There was a considerable amount of mud, especially near the cattle grid to the fields as the vehicles that had been up there had cleaned their wheels on the paved yard as they left the fields. What a mess, Fred thought to himself, this stuff is really compacted and the paving stones are really stained with the mud. I will have to get the pressure jet on them, later.

Just after nine, Ann came into the yard to speak to Fred.

"Hello, Fred, good to see you again."

"Hello, Mrs Wall, I'm just trying to tidy the place up."

"Yes good idea, it has become rather muddy with all the vehicles."

"That's the problem these days – too many vehicles, I was only saying in the pub last night that...." And he was about to get into one of his long rambling discussions that only Fred could, so Ann made her excuses and left.

Around ten o'clock a new car arrived in the yard and parked just where Fred was going to sweep.

"Can you park over there please sir? I will be sweeping that bit in a minute."

"I don't think you will. I hope you will be speaking to me."

"Oh, and who might you be sir?"

"I'm DC Tarrant of Chester CID, I assume you are Fred Appleyard."

"Yes that's right. Ah! Mrs Wall said something about you coming, you want to take some of my spit."

"Well not quite, it is a simple process using a swab in the mouth. If you are free now I would like to go into the house and talk to you," They both walked over to the back door.

"Mrs Wall?" shouted Fred as he walked into the utility room,

Ann Wall came into the kitchen and could see them both standing in the utility room, "Come in both of you. Fred can you leave your boots in the utility room, please?"

"Right you are ma'am."

"Mrs Wall, would you mind if I had a few words with Fred on our own?"

"Not at all." Ann left the kitchen. "Just give me a shout when you need me," she called back, "I'll be upstairs."

"Very well, thank you."

"Have a seat Fred; I have the swab here. Let's do that first."

"Well what's it for? I've done nothing!"

"No I understand that, it's just that we have the old Land Rover and we are testing all the contacts that there have been on the vehicle and we need your DNA to enable us to identify you and eliminate you from our enquiries."

"Oh I see," he said, not really seeing at all. He co-operated with Tarrant in giving the sample.

"Good, now I have a few questions I need clearing up."

Tarrant went slowly through the whole routine of name and address, age and where Fred was on the night of the 31st December and the morning of the 1st January.

"So on January 1ˢᵗ you were doing your odd jobs around the church yard in Tarporley?"

"Yes that's right."

"The first of January is a holiday."

"Not to me it isn't, the place has to be kept tidy and I only have Mondays and Fridays to do it because I work here the rest of the week you see."

"The first of January was a Saturday?"

"Yes well, you see I hadn't been to the church since before Christmas, Christmas Eve was a Friday my usual day, but I hadn't been near since because I spent Christmas with my sister in Mold, that's in Wales, and I didn't get back home here until the afternoon of the thirty first, so Saturday was my first day. It was a real mess that churchyard, it had been busy with people over Christmas and they walk all over things and drop litter you should have seen it, it's much better now. It's the younger generation they…"

"Yes, yes," interrupted Tarrant as he could see that Fred was off on one. "Where were you on New Year's Eve?"

"I was at home."

"I've got your address but how far is that from here?"

"About two miles. It takes me only about twenty minutes to get here and half an hour to the church in the village, my bike could do it on its own now."

"Do you live alone?"

"Yes, my missus left me some years back now, couldn't stand the construction business which took me all over the country."

"I see. So did anyone see you at home on New Year's Eve?"

"I guess my neighbour saw me or heard me, but I was in on my own. I watched the TV until after midnight then went to bed. I don't go to bed that late normally, because I am up at half past six every morning."

"What time did you get to the church on New Year's Day then?"

"Eight o'clock as always."

"Did you cycle down the road past the end of the lane to this farm?"

"Yes, it's the only way to go."

"Did you see any traffic or anyone coming in or going out of this lane?"

"Can't say. I really don't recall. There is always the odd car about but I don't take a lot of notice of them unless they get too close."

"I see. Now your tools, where do you keep them?"

"In the machine shed, locked up."

"Locked up?"

"Well it depends on what you mean by tools, but all my small tools and nails, screws, trowels, hammers and so on are all locked up, yes."

"In the back of the Land Rover we found an object that looked like it was made of carborundum and about a foot or so long, and it is round like a broom handle but tapers a bit to each end, is that one of your 'tools'?"

"It is, it's a sharpening stone I use with the scythe, I need that back before the spring and the grass starts to grow."

"Where was it when you last saw it? Would it have been in your shed?"

"No, that's not a tool as such, I leave it with the scythe which is hung up on the wall in the machinery shed and the sharpening stone is kept on top of the scythe so I always know where it is."

"Could you have put it in the Land Rover for any reason?"

"Not as I recall, but Mr Wall may have used it for something and not put it away."

"Mm, the winch on the front of the Land Rover has a wire cable; did you ever take the cable off the winch?"

"Once or twice, why?"

"I just need to know if you may have taken it off the winch in the last week or so?"

"I did as a matter of fact. I didn't use the cable on the winch, I needed something to pull some tree branches and logs out of the copse. The winch was not strong enough to do that so I took the cable off and used it tied to the tow bar. If you are taking it off be careful. The wire as it runs around the winch at the end has lots of sharp little bits sticking out, like needles they are, didn't half hurt my fingers when I got stabbed by one."

"Did you cut your finger then?"

"Yes, as I said it's like getting stuck by a needle."

"Did you put the cable back when you had finished?"

"Yes and I gave the winch a good oiling as it was looking a bit rusty around the drum and the bearings. You don't take the cable off very often, you see."

"Right, well thanks, Mr Appleyard, you have been most helpful."

"Mrs Wall?"

Ann Wall reappeared into the kitchen as Fred was putting his boots back on.

"Mrs Wall, can I just ask you one question?"

"Yes, by all means."

"I am sorry to take you back to that awful morning of New Year's Day, but can you recall if the engine of the Land Rover was running when you got to it?"

"No I don't think so," she replied in a shaky and croaky voice, the very fact of having to throw her mind back to that fateful morning was enough of a trigger to set her off again.

"Very well, I am sorry to trouble you, thank you for your help," Tarrant departed, although he had to wait at the yard side of the cattle grid whilst Frank Stringer entered the yard.

"Hello, doctor," called out Fred.

"Morning, Fred," replied Frank in a cheery way.

"Hello, Ann, how are you doing?"

"Thank you for coming, Frank. I have been fine but that policeman took me back to New Year's Day and it all came back to me, just like it does some nights even with your pills. I still get flashbacks to the morning when I found Peter."

"I am afraid that is something that will be with you for some time to come."

"Yes, I suppose so. I just hope they become less prominent."

"They will, time is the only healer in these circumstances."

"The girls all right are they?"

"Yes they appear to be. Sandy had a big crying session the other day, but Si seems to be coping very well. They have both gone to the village to organise the funeral tea and also organise some flowers."

"I have heard that there will be an inquest possibly before the end of the month. The police are the main witnesses and they have just about finished their reports, so I expect you will be hearing any day now when the inquest will be. Let me know as soon as you hear as I will come along and support you and the girls."

"You are good to us, Frank. What would we do without you?"

"I'm on my rounds so I must go, just popped in to check you were okay."

"Thanks again, Frank".

"Bye."

As Ann was at the back door she shouted over to Fred, "Cup of tea, Fred?"

"Yes please, Mrs Wall."

Back at the station Tarrant updated Evans with the latest information. He indicated that it all pointed to suicide and there seemed no doubt about it.

"I will send Appleyard's sample for DNA testing to make sure forensics have eliminated every find they have made on the Land Rover. Appleyard was at home on New Year's Eve but he is one of these country folk who go to bed early and get up early. I cannot see any motive or reason why he should want Peter Wall dead. Furthermore consider the way he died. If it was murder, surely the murderer would have needed the co-operation of the victim to despatch them the way Mr Wall was killed?"

"Yes, I agree, it seems an open and shut case. While you were out the Coroner's office was on and asked if we were ready to have the inquest, the coroner was trying to avoid opening the inquest and then suspending it until we had made all our enquiries. I told him we were satisfied that it was suicide and would be ready at any point from now on. The date has been set for Thursday 27th January at ten a.m. Can you phone the Walls' solicitor and advise him? Also, just for completeness, check if he has received the will and who the main beneficiaries are."

"Okay, Sarge."

John England was pleased to hear that the police had just about completed their enquiries, and as he had the will he was able to advise them who the major beneficiaries are. The police seemed satisfied with what they heard and confirmed that they were of the firm opinion that this was a suicide and would be giving evidence to that effect.

As soon as he had heard this he phoned Ann Wall and advised her of the date and time of the hearing. Surprisingly there was not a coroner's court in Chester, the coroner's court for west Cheshire was in Warrington.

"We can make more detailed arrangements later when the funeral is out of the way."

"Thank you for your help and support John, you are very kind."

Fred put his head around the kitchen door "I'm off, Mrs Wall – me time's up!"

"Okay, Fred, thanks. See you next week."

Ann smiled to herself as Fred always left with his little comment 'Time's up' he was a stickler for timekeeping, good old Fred!

14.1.00 Friday

It was half past ten, and the girls and Ann were all ready and dressed in sombre clothes. Ann wore a black suit but no hat, where as Si had a dark grey suit and Sandra, being in the legal profession, had opted for a black suit with stripes.

It had been agreed that the cortege would leave at ten past eleven and that Frank would join them with Margaret. All three members of the Wall family were having a last cup of tea in the kitchen. Conversation was sparse, and nothing left to say, really.

"Have you got a handkerchief, Mum?"

"Yes, darling, don't fuss. I am fine"

"I had better get one, good thinking." Sandra left the group and went over to her flat to get a spare hanky. She had one already but she knew she would be the worst at the funeral, and anyway it occupied a few more minutes of what seemed like an age.

"What are we going to do?" she uttered to herself as she had a little weep whilst on her own in her own flat. "It looks as though Dad has ended it all because he had run out of ideas as to how to pay back all the money he owes. I don't know how we will pay it back, either. We need to get some idea of the amount we shall get from the insurance. It was good of Dad to make a bequest to us, but it seems that there might not be any money left over."

She heard the cattle grid rattle and looked out of her kitchen window to see Uncle Frank and Aunty Margaret drive into the yard.

I had better go and join the others, she thought.

"Hello, Uncle Frank, Aunty Margaret, thank you so much for coming."

"I will never get you off this Uncle and Aunt thing, will I? I am sorry we have to be here, it is most distressing, how are you all?"

"We are as good as you could expect, I think this morning is going to be really painful for us all, but it has to happen Frank, and we are so grateful you could be here."

"Don't mention it, shall we go in and see your mum and Si?"

They all greeted one another again in the kitchen, and Purdy was weaving in and out of legs and drumming her tail on the kitchen cupboards. Shortly afterwards two large black cars emerged and swung round in the yard. The lead car was a black hearse with a light oak coffin and brass handles on display at the back. On top of the coffin was a wreath of white lilies, as the girls had instructed, no other flowers. The second car was a black shining limousine with seats enough for six.

There were four men involved, three in the hearse and the driver of the big car, plus a passenger, Mr Cartwright. He got out and came into the kitchen, head bowed and wearing all black.

"Good morning, Mrs Wall."

"Hello, Mr Cartwright, is everything organised?"

"Yes, madam, we are all set. I have checked with the Swan the refreshments are ready. We will collect names of people attending, and as you have requested no flowers, there will be envelopes provided so mourners may make a donation to the local hospice as you requested."

"Thank you, Mr Cartwright."

"I shall wait outside in the car, madam, until you are ready to go. It's just gone eleven o'clock and I suggest we get underway at ten past."

"Very well. We shall just finish here and we shall be out shortly."

On the dot of ten past eleven the hearse with Peter Wall's coffin, the limousine carrying his widow Ann and his two daughters Sandra and Sienna, followed closely behind with Doctor Frank Stinger and his wife Margaret behind that, made the journey to St Helen's Church.

They passed over the cattle grid. "That's the last time Daddy will go over that noisy thing," said Si.

"He never fixed it so it was quiet, did he?" Ann responded.

The cortege swung out now onto the road to the village and St Helen's Church, slowly down the road at not much more than twenty-five miles an hour down an essentially country road. With limited opportunity to overtake, it didn't take long for a queue of cars vans and a lorry to build up behind. The hearse pulled up outside the gate and, as a small knot of mourners saw the hearse arrive, they all filed into the church. Mr Cartwright organised his men to unload the coffin and place it on a small collapsible trolley, this was a bit of a surprise to Ann as she had thought Peter's coffin would be carried into church.

Ann and the two girls filed in after the coffin and took their places in the front pew which had been reserved for them. They were conscious of a large number of people being there but, as their heads were bowed, they were unable to see the full enormity of the congregation. Ann wept a little tear, she suddenly realised that Peter would not be able to give away his daughters at their weddings, something she had secretly hoped for, but it wasn't to be and couldn't now happen.

"Can I welcome you all to St Helen's Church," boomed out the vicar. "I would like to let you all know what is to happen after this funeral service. There will be a private committal at the Chester Crematorium to which only the immediate family will attend. The congregation of mourners will after this service be most welcome to attend the funeral lunch at The Swan, just a few yards from here, and later Mrs Wall and her two daughters will join you. In the meantime whilst they are at the crematorium, your host will be Dr Frank Stringer. Thank you.

"Our first hymn is Psalm 23, *The Lord is My Shepherd* which is on your order of service sheet." The organ struck up and singing commenced.

Ann and the girls found it almost impossible to sing, their eyes now flooded with tears. The service continued through to the blessing having had a reading from Frank Stringer and a eulogy from the vicar who had certainly done his homework on Peter, as he was able to mention the most interesting things that he had done in his life, despite Peter being only a very infrequent visitor to the church.

After the service, Ann and the girls followed the coffin out again to the hearse. When they got into the limousine they were off to Chester Crematorium, leaving what seemed like a hundred people to be shepherded into The Swan for a buffet lunch.

The crematorium was a cold, bleak place, although the authorities had done their best to make it as comfortable as possible. The rather irreverent queuing for Peter's hearse to get to the door whilst the previous funeral and mourners left seemed rather like a production line to Ann, not what she had expected at all.

The committal was short and to the point. The vicar read a couple of prayers and then committed Peter's body to the flames. Some canned music struck up and the curtains closed and that, as the three of them realised, was definitely the end and the very last contact with a wonderful father and husband. The tears were flowing now and the vicar left the three of them for a few moments before inviting them to leave and get back into the car to Tarporley. The hearse had already left, just Mr Cartwright and a driver were there to escort the three ladies back to The Swan.

There was very little, if any conversation in the car on the way back. All three were deep in thought, and to some extent still in shock.

By the time Ann and the girls arrived back at The Swan, the throng of people had thinned out a bit, but long-lost relatives, friends from the golf club, mainly retired who had nothing much else to do, and all the folk from the office were still in The Swan. There was quite a gaggle of conversation which died to almost nothing as the ladies entered.

Frank met them and gave them all a drink. This broke the ice and the conversations that had been going on resumed. The babble of numerous conversations took hold again. Ann and the two girls suddenly became immersed in the throng and were swept up by the various groups, who immediately included them in their conversations.

John England came over to see how Si was. The small talk really did not interest John, or Si. It seemed people were just talking for the sake of it and doing their utmost to avoid the one subject that joined them all this day, the suicide of Peter Wall. John and Si were left on their own. John was keen to talk about his upcoming skiing holiday. He couldn't help thinking all the time whilst he was talking to Si what a beautiful young woman she was and, despite the occasion, she radiated a warmth of character and animated conversation that was very attractive – well, to John, anyway.

Once the clock ticked past four o'clock most of the residual company started to leave and Ann and the girls felt it was time to go. Si went along the High Street to Mr Cartwright's office and asked if he could run them back to the farm as arranged.

"What a day, I'm glad that's over," Ann remarked on the way home.

"John told me the inquest has been set for the 27th January at ten a.m. at the coroner's court in Warrington. John said he would write to you, Mum."

"In Warrington?"

"Yes. Apparently that's the court for our area."

"So be it, let's get that over with and then hopefully we can move on."

Sandy thought she detected a change in attitude in her mother now, a degree of anger rather than remorse. She was clearly feeling angry at being left to pick up the pieces.

15.1.2000 Saturday

Both the girls had spent the night in their own flats last night for the first time since New Year's Day. It was a good feeling, Si had commented over breakfast, to be back in her own place again at the same time recognising that her mother was now alone in a big house with her thoughts and worries.

"John England has invited me out to dinner tonight," Si informed the family over breakfast.

"Blimey, he's a quick worker," exclaimed Sandy.

"He seems a very nice young man, I hope you have a good time darling. Are you going out tonight Sandy?"

"I hadn't thought of it, Mum. I was kind of concerned to stay and look after you."

"Now look here. Let's get one thing straight from the start, your father has left us and he has left us with what looks like a real mess. I will need all the help I can get from the two of you to help me sort it out, but I fail to see why your lives should be ruined by your father's actions. It seems he had not got the guts to sort out the problems himself and left us to do it for him."

Si and Sandy were dumbstruck. Ann had clearly had a change of heart on the situation and had overcome her grief very quickly and her grief had now turned to anger.

"Okay, Mum, Si and I will live our lives but you mustn't get too angry at Dad. He probably had a breakdown or something and was not really aware of what he was doing."

"Yes, Mum, Sandy is right, we want to support you all we can, and we still love you both but we can only kiss and cuddle you."

"Oh, stop it you two. You have got me going now. I am sorry to have lost my temper with your father, I just saw the other side of the issue and feel that it is so unfair on us all."

"Mum, we know your emotions must be all over the place at the moment, don't cry. How about you and I going out somewhere tonight, if Si is already going out?"

"No, darling, you must not worry about me, I don't feel like going out anyway. I will stay in and watch TV. I am going to take Purdy a long walk this morning so don't expect me back till early afternoon at the soonest."

"Okay, Mum, whatever you say. Where are you going on your walk?"

"I haven't decided yet, it will just happen, I guess."

Roger was having a lie-in after a busy week catching up after his holiday. He was in no hurry to get up, but the phone rang so he had to get out of bed.

"It's me again, how's your conscience today?"

"My conscience is clear how about yours?"

"I know you were involved in the death of Peter Wall."

"That's ridiculous. I was in Austria."

"No you weren't."

"Yes I was and I can prove it."

"Oh, well I was sure it was you."

"Who was me?"

"The person I saw coming out of Long Acre Farm on New Year's Day morning."

"I know your, voice I'm sure I do."

As soon as Roger said that the phone went dead.

It had been a funny week; it was strange not having Peter around the place. Roger had taken a number of calls from customers who expressed their shock and sympathy in equal measure. It was good, however, for Roger to hear that they would continue to support the firm. They had all recognised that Roger was the person who got the jobs done, Peter was the man who got the jobs in the first place.

I guess we are going to need a sales person to keep in touch with customers, he thought. I need to look into that as soon as possible. I think I will have to make quite a few changes. We have too many people in the office and we are strapped for cash, and the bank is breathing down my neck so I will have to make savings and soon.

The restaurant John had chosen was 'Paparazzi', an Italian restaurant near the outer edges of the city and, as the name would suggest, full of the movers and shakers of Chester.

"Good evening, sir, do you have a reservation?"

"Yes, the name is England."

"Very well, sir. Would you like to go to your table now or would you prefer to have a drink at the bar?"

"Shall we have a drink first?"

"Yes please, that sounds great."

"What would you like? Choose anything you fancy."

"I would really like a Kir Royale."

"No problem."

The barman, on overhearing the conversation, was already on with the task of blending champagne and Kir in a champagne flute for Si.

"I will have an alcohol-free lager please. I just don't like drinking too much and then driving a long way afterwards. Apart from the fact I might break the law, which isn't good for me, I just think it's silly."

"No, that's good. Will you have a glass of wine with your meal?"

"Yes, but just the one. Tarporley is a good drive and I could get caught. I think that is why I chose to buy an apartment in the city, to avoid any driving. It's not that I'm an alcoholic, it just makes sense to be able to walk everywhere."

"Certainly your apartment is very convenient."

They parked the Porsche in the basement car park and walked along to the Paparazzi.

"Hello, John, how great to see you," said this rather busty and flamboyant girl with plenty of cleavage on show.

"Hi, Lizzie. Fancy seeing you here. Have you met Sienna Wall?"

"Oh no, I haven't. I was so sorry to hear about your father. It was your father who, err, died on New Year's Day?"

"Yes, that's kind of you. It has been a difficult period for us."

"Yes I am sure, what a terrible thing to happen."

"Well you never know the day."

"Are you based in Chester?"

"Yes. I work for Dents as a chartered surveyor," Si said, thinking sticking some qualifications on the end might just show this rather flashy woman that she was more than a pretty face but had a brain also.

"I know them; they are a bit old fashioned. I my own PR company so if you have any great houses you need writing up in the press or you sell to a celebrity, just let me know and I will see what I can do for you."

"That's very kind, we find our celebrity clients like to be very discreet when it comes to where they live."

"Oh I understand, but they love the publicity really. It's what they live for."

"Well if it is ever appropriate to make an address public I will remember you."

"Are you eating, John?"

"Yes we are Lizzie. In fact we were just about to go to our table."

"Okay, it's just I need to have a chat about transport to Manchester Airport on February 12th. I think we should have a minibus possibly for fourteen people. I know there are only eight of us, but with all the gear and everything."

"Yes, you are right I am sure, Lizzie. Why don't you get some prices and chat to the others and I will go along with whatever everyone else wants to do?"

"Okay, I will let you know. Have a good meal, I'm sure you will."

Si and John moved to their table, which was situated in a corner of the restaurant in a discreet area and well away from the bar.

"Sorry about that, Lizzie is very upfront."

"Oh I could tell that, in fact I could see most of her front."

John laughed and Si had broken the ice. Si smiled back.

"You are going skiing then?"

"Yes we always go as a group after all the school holidays are over and have a great week. This year we are going to Austria, Seefeld in fact."

"That's a coincidence, that's the place my father's business partner has been to and he was there when... when Daddy died."

John could tell that Si still had not fully come to terms with the fact her father had committed suicide.

"We have booked into a hotel on the fringes of the town so as to be close to the ski lifts and yet within a few minutes' walk of the bars and clubs. Well, so the brochure says."

"That sounds great. It is good to go away in a group like that."

"Have you decided on your order, sir?"

"Oh no, can you give us a few more minutes? What would you like Si?"

"That was a beautiful meal and the wine was delicious. Thank you, John."

"Would you like to stay here for a coffee, or go to a club or...?"

"I would like a coffee but some fresh air first would be nice. It's still very mild and a walk first would be good."

"Very well then, let's do that."

John paid the bill and retrieved their coats and they walked out onto Grosvenor Street and then down towards John's apartment block. Si involuntarily put her arm through John's and they walked on in silence, except for the odd giggle when they avoided a very large puddle.

"Why don't we go to my apartment for coffee? That would be simplest."

"That would be great."

No sooner said than they were taking the lift to the fourth floor.

"Here we are," said John as he opened the front door.

After the small hallway they were straight into a very large lounge and dining area, with huge panoramic windows looking straight across to the Roodee and lights beyond.

"What a fantastic view."

"Yes it's the reason I bought this flat," John was just putting on his iPod-controlled music system.

"Can you see the racing here on race days?"

"Yes you can, although it is difficult to pick out the horses' numbers. It's also impossible to pick a winner from here or anywhere."

The joke was lost on Si.

"How big is the balcony?"

"Have a look and see," said John. With that John pressed a button and the patio doors slid effortlessly to one side. He only opened them a short way to avoid all the heat being lost.

"Wow, it's fantastic. The view is really breathtaking. You don't realise when you drive past these apartments what a good view they must have."

"Haven't you been in one before?"

"No, we wouldn't be asked to sell anything like this. We are too fuddy duddy to be selling trendy apartments."

They stood arm in arm on the balcony overlooking that part of the city on a strangely balmy January night. No words passed between them; no words were necessary. Si felt so comfortable with this man, and John couldn't believe his luck to be out with this beautiful girl who seemed to be attracted to him as much as he was to her.

After a few moments the spell was broken when the kettle whistled to signal that the water had boiled for the coffee. On his way off the balcony, he enquired:

"Black or white?"

"Just black please, no sugar."

"Same as me."

A few moments later Si came in off the balcony and, having seen which button it was John pushed to open the doors, she pressed the top of the swivel switch and sure enough they closed.

"Here you are – one black coffee as ordered."

"Thanks, that's great. Just beginning to feel the chill out there."

Si now was thinking that she had a dilemma. Should she insist on going home or should she break the habit of a lifetime and stay the night on the first date? The temptation to say yes to an invitation to stay, if it came, was great and one she would really like to accept.

John was having parallel thoughts although he felt he should be the perfect gentleman and take Si home. After coffee they took the lift to the basement car park and drove back to Tarporley.

"I bet this is great with the hood down on a summer's day."

"It is and it is surprising how often the hood comes down, even in the winter. I will give you a ride with the hood down the next fine day we have."

John turned on the stereo, and Si drifted in and out of semi-consciousness as she was transported home by this handsome man in his sports car. It's what dreams were made of.

Ann knew Si was back as the cattle grid gave its usual rattle. She returned to reading her book. Despite the fact it was nearly one o'clock in the morning, she was not able to sleep.

"Would you like to come in for another coffee or drink?"

"That's kind. No more coffee for me, but I would like to come in and use the loo, I've drunk too much coffee already."

16.1.2000 Sunday

Ann had eventually drifted off but woke early, unable to sustain sleep for very long. She had so many jumbled-up things in her mind. All she could see were problems and no solutions. She dressed in her old outdoor clothes and decided to take Purdy for a walk up the fields. She couldn't help noticing that John England's Porsche sports car was parked in the yard near the entrance to Si's flat.

Good for her, she thought to herself. She needs all the solace she can get, and what a nice man John is. It's Sandra that worries me more. She has taken her father's death really hard and she appears not to have any male friends, or indeed a circle of friends at all.

It's going to be difficult to get all this sorted out, she thought to herself, as she and Purdy started the long walk up Long Meadow. Peter, what have you done? Why have you left us in such a mess?

Ann was turning things over in her head. There was this massive bill from the revenue, there were unpaid and large credit card bills, the issue of the mortgage on the house and the mortgages on the buy to let property and the bank loan on the land which he had bought. God knows how much all this adds up to and I have no idea how much the insurance is going to pay out. Oh Peter, what have you done?

"Hi, Mum, are you okay?"

"Hello, darling, you are up and about early. Hello John, I thought it was your car in the yard."

"Yes, John stayed the night as he had a lot to drink so it was best not to drive back to Chester."

"Very sensible," Ann said but she knew her gregarious daughter had an ulterior motive in the don't drink and drive routine.

"How about some breakfast? Purdy and I are done out here and we are both hungry."

"That would be very good. Thank you, Mrs Wall."

"Oh, call me Ann please John. We are not in court now."

"Well if it's not too much trouble. A single bloke will always go for the easy option of someone else's breakfast. Thank you."

"John's asked me if I would like to go skiing with him and some friends to Austria in February. Would you mind if I went, Mum?"

"Darling, it's your life. You mustn't think of me all the time. I have plenty to do and I will get used to living a life on my own, I'm sure. You must go, what a wonderful idea."

"Oh, Mum, you are good. Thank you."

"It's only a few weeks Mrs... sorry, Ann, and we shall be in a group so if previous years have been anything to go by, it will be great fun."

"I'm sure you will have a great time, you must tell me about all your plans for it over breakfast."

Sandy had seen John's car in the yard and assumed that he had stayed the night. As she couldn't see any signs of life just now she had assumed they were still in the flat, so she went over to the farmhouse to see her mum.

"Ah, here you are. I thought it was your car I saw in the yard, John."

"Yes, John stayed the night. Too over the top to safely drive back to Chester."

"Would you like some breakfast darling? Sit down and join us."

"Thanks that would be great. Just a coffee and cereal will do just fine."

"Orange juice?"

"Yes please. Thanks."

"What are you guys going to do today?"

"I need to get back to Chester. I have a bit of housework and domestics to attend to. Bachelor life is not all beer and skittles, you know."

"Would you like a hand, John? I have to just tidy up my flat a bit then I could help you do yours."

"Well, if you don't mind, I have to confess it is the bit I least like about living on my own. I thought I would just pop in to see Mum and Dad whilst I am so close."

"Do they live in Tarporley?"

"Yes, in the Old Vicarage at the entrance to the village."

"I know that. It's a lovely house, John. Have they lived there long?"

"About ten years. I think Dad bought it about five years before he retired as their retirement home. They love it and it is so easy to walk into the village from where they are. That's where I was going on New Year's Day when the police stopped me at the end of the lane, here."

John wished he could have recovered the words he had just uttered. How insensitive could you be, he thought to himself.

"Sorry, I didn't mean to cause you any pain."

"John, life has to go on. It's very painful for us all. You must not be frightened to mention Peter or his death, it's happened and we must make the best of life as it is now."

After breakfast John and Si went back to the flat. After about half an hour, they looked in at the back door to say they were off and would be back later in the day.

"Hi, Mum, Dad, anyone at home?"

"Darling," said Audrey as she entered the hall to find son John and Si standing there. "What a lovely surprise."

"Well I was just down the road Mum and as I was so close I thought I should pop in."

"That's very kind of you, and who's this?"

"Oh sorry, how rude of me. This is Sienna Wall."

"Hello, Sienna, how nice to meet you."

"Call me Si, please, everyone does."

They went through to the kitchen where, as the kettle had just boiled, they were entertained to a cup of coffee.

"Your father's just gone down the garden to bring in some more logs. We seem to get through them so quickly and the weather is starting to get cold at night again."

Just as she had finished speaking George came in through the back door with a basket full of logs, and he was struggling a bit.

"Here, Dad, let me help you with those."

"Thanks son, good to see you. You came at just the right moment."

"The lounge?"

"Yes John, the lounge please."

John took the heavy basket of logs to the lounge whilst Audrey introduced Si to George.

"Do you live nearby?"

"Yes I live at Long Acre Farm."

"Oh, I am so sorry to hear of your sad loss."

"Thank you. It has not been an easy New Year and there is a lot to sort out." A tear trickled down Si's face. She hadn't really been exposed to people she didn't know and since the events of New Year's Day it was not easy.

"Oh, I am so sorry. I didn't mean to upset you."

"It's quite all right. I have just not got used to the idea yet."

"Dad, what have you been saying?"

"It's nothing John, it's just me, and I haven't got used to the idea yet."

Audrey started to fuss and the biscuit tin came out and they all sipped their coffees and talked about many things as far away as possible from the events for New Year's Day.

"Si is hoping to come skiing with the team at the beginning of February."

"That will be great. It should take your mind off things dear."

"Mum!"

"Oh, Si, I am so sorry."

"It's okay, Mrs England. My father's death has to be talked about, and it's just that I have tried to shut it out of my mind."

"Is it back to work on Monday for you, Si?"

"Yes, John. Sandra, that's my sister, has some documents she wants you to have so I will bring them to your office."

"We could have picked them up now."

"Well Sandra wanted to put a note with them as she has looked at them. She has some observations to make."

Addressing everyone, Si informed them that Sandra was also a solicitor but she specialised in commercial law. She had come across some documents which were her speciality.

"That will be a help to me, my expertise in commercial matters will not be as extensive as Sandra's."

"Would you two like to stay for lunch?"

Si and John exchanged glances, and they knew instinctively that the answer they should both give was no.

"Kind of you, Mum, but we have had a large breakfast at the farm, and we have some jobs to do in Chester."

John's parents immediately knew that the relationship was clearly a little more than just client/solicitor and it seemed that John had chosen well. Father approved anyway.

On their way back to Chester John and Si sat in silence for a good half of the journey as John negotiated the country lanes of Cheshire in his Porsche.

"I hope Regent Travel can get me in for the skiing."

"Oh I am sure they will. I will see what I can do first thing tomorrow, and when you come in with the documents I should have the answer."

"How exciting, I can't wait."

"When we have finished my flat tidy, how about a walk around the walls?"

"Yes that would be great. I am ready for some fresh air."

It didn't take long for the two of them to get the flat sorted, dirty pots into the dishwasher, a quick whizz round with the Hoover, plumping up cushions and getting rid of old newspapers and the job was done.

On one of his favourite walks around the ancient Roman Walls surrounding the city, Roger was contemplating what was to come. The company owed just over a quarter of a million pounds, and then there was the mortgage on the office building of around two hundred thousand. He was not sure of the actual amount as it was a repayment mortgage and the amount should have reduced a bit since the statement in June the previous year. The shareholders agreement which Roger and Peter had entered into about three years earlier, which was drafted by Frobisher's in Manchester, was a lengthy document. It covered all eventualities. Roger could not recall what would happen to Peter's shares in the event of his death.

"Good morning."

"Oh, good morning," he replied almost automatically as he came out of his trance-like state trying to recall the terms of a complex legal document.

"It's afternoon actually."

"It's Roger, isn't it?"

"Yes, you're Sienna. Sorry I was miles away and not even thinking."

"This is my friend, John England."

"Hello, isn't it a great day for a walk? So mild and a fine day."

"Yes it really is lovely."

"Roger, haven't you just got back from a skiing holiday in Austria?"

"Yes, in Seefeld. Why?"

"Well, John and I and some friends are off there in February."

"To Seefeld?"

"Yes, we are both really looking forward to it."

"Oh, you will really enjoy it. I'm no great skier but I had a good time."

"What made you go there? Did you know anyone who had been there before?"

"No, I didn't have a clue where to go. I think it was on the recommendation of the chap at Regent Travel. I had never been there before and they catered at my hotel very well for single people and I had a really great time."

Roger couldn't help recalling the final week of "entertainment" provided by Helga.

"Where are you planning to stay?"

"It's a hotel on the outskirts, Alpine something or other?"

"Alpen Park?"

"Yes I think that's the name."

"What a coincidence, that's where I stayed."

"Oh, do tell us some more about it. How long were you there?"

"I was there two weeks. Living on your own Christmas and New Year is not great, so I chose this place which seemed to make a special effort for single people and they had special party nights and all that sort of thing. Take your swimming costumes; there is a great swimming pool in the basement."

"Wow, that does sound good."

"That's great, can't wait now. Thanks for the comments, we had best be getting along. See you soon, I have no doubt Roger."

"Yes that's right, there will be a lot to sort out."

John and Si pressed on around the walls in the opposite direction to Roger.

Roger's concentration on his plans was now broken and he thought to himself there was no purpose in trying to work things out now, better to see how the situation unfolds.

"Considering he is, sorry was, your dad's business partner, he isn't very forthcoming. I felt he was keeping something back and just being polite."

"He has never been on the same plain as Dad. He is the man in the business who got the jobs done and organised, he was never customer-facing."

"Back to work tomorrow and I am looking forward to getting back in harness. Christmas and New Year in the years to come will never be the same again, they will always hold bad memories."

"Oh don't be too gloomy. Time is a great healer."

"That's what Uncle Frank said."

"He is right, but the memories remain. The important thing is to remember the good times you had with your dad."

"Yes I am sure you are right, anyway, we have things to look forward to and I can't wait to get to Austria."

The phone rang back in the apartment and it was Lizzie advising John that the rest of the group were happy to go for the minibus option to Manchester.

"Glad you rang, Lizzie, because I want to add another person to the group."

"Oh yes, and who might that be?" said Lizzie, as if she couldn't guess. Her voice was suitably smarmy on the other end of the phone, goading John.

"It's Sienna Wall. I will phone Regent Travel tomorrow and put her on the list if they have accommodation."

"Fine," was the almost casual response from Lizzie, who was boiling inside to find that one of her men had been stolen from her.

"The sleeping arrangements are going to be a bit difficult now with an odd number?"

"I guess the agents and the hotel will be able to sort something out."

"I guess they will, I will let you know how much the minibus is as soon as I find out," she said rather abruptly.

"Lizzie, this is my holiday too, and there is nothing to stop me inviting someone else."

"No, I agree, if that's what you want to do and change all the arrangements then fine, have it your own way."

"Lizzie, you are overreacting to the situation."

"I don't think so John, I thought we were going together."

"No eight of us were going together."

"Yes. Four guys and four girls, where does this new arrangement leave me?"

"Lizzie, you are getting all fired up over nothing, the arrangements will stand. It's just that Si is coming too. She has had a bad time and needs a break."

"Yes I know, however there is nothing more to say. Your mind is made up so that's that."

Lizzie hung up abruptly.

Will I ever understand the female brain, he thought to himself. I know full well if Lizzie found a tall blond ski instructor, whether I was there or not, she would be off like a shot. It's all one way traffic with her.

John and Si spent the rest of the afternoon snuggled up on the settee in the apartment and had a bowl of steaming soup and crusty bread. As the sun was setting, a really orange sunset bathed the apartment in a golden hue. Si explained that she had lots to do back at home and so John drove her back to the farm. He didn't linger, but they did manage a kiss and embrace before Si left the car. This Sunday has been a perfect day, just John and me, she thought.

"What a great day," Si said to herself as she half skipped and ran to the farmhouse's back door as the Porsche rattled the cattle grid on its return to Chester.

"Hi, I'm in the study with Mum."

"Great, I have been chatting with John..."

"Yes, we could guess that."

"Don't be sarcastic, Sandy. Si is perfectly entitled to spend Sunday with whoever she wants."

"I know, Mum. I was only being cheeky to my younger sister."

"I know, I was chatting to John, as I was trying to say, we met Roger on the walls as we were walking round Chester. Roger has been staying in the same hotel in Seefeld in Austria, so we had a brief chat about that. Apparently a swimming costume is a requirement; they have a big pool in the basement."

"Sounds good to me."

"I told John that you had the shareholder agreement and I said that you were making some notes on it. I promised John that I would drop it off to him. Do you have any objection to me dropping off a copy to him tomorrow?"

"No, not at all, darling. Let's see where we put it."

There was a joint rummage through the piles of paper, and Sandy collected up the agreement as well as details of the four buy-to-let properties and the land that had been purchased by Peter. It wasn't clear from the papers who actually owned these properties.

"John will need these as well. He will be able to discover the true ownership and the mortgagees as he will have to advise them of the present situation."

"Is there anything else Si should take with her?"

"Perhaps all these insurance policies not only on Dad's life but accident insurance and house and contents insurance and the details of the mortgage on Long Acre farm. I will draft a note for John on this shareholder agreement so you can take that as well."

"Yes, I told him you were doing that. I will drop this lot off to him tomorrow. It's quite a bundle."

17.1.2000 Monday

It was the first day back at work for the two Wall girls, and there was unanimous sympathy for them both from their employers and colleagues.

"Sienna, I was very sorry to hear of the loss of your father. I am sure this has been a tremendous shock to you and your mother and sister. Please pass on my sympathies. It goes without saying that if there is anything Dents can do to help in sorting out the estate, we should be pleased to help."

"That's very kind of you, Mr Dent."

Si couldn't help thinking that the remark was angled at getting some work for Dents rather than just being happy to help.

"If you need any time off then please do not hesitate to ask."

"Thank you, Mr Dent. That would be really helpful. I would like to have some time off initially today and an extra half-hour for lunch as I have to drop some papers off to Bennett and Bennett who are looking after things. Then there is the inquest which should last no more than a day on January 27th."

"No problem at all, Si."

"Mr Dent, I am sorry to go on with my shopping list of time off but I wondered if I could possibly have a week of my holidays commencing on February 12th."

"Yes, I am sure that will be okay, just check with my PA."

"Thank you, Mr Dent."

James Dent was of the third generation of Dents. Mr Dent was a very old-fashioned but not very old employer. Si thought he was in his mid-forties. The firm, as a firm of chartered surveyors, was highly regarded in Chester but they were not a sexy firm of estate agents, more the land agent professional surveyor variety.

Lunchtime couldn't come soon enough for Si. It was twelve thirty p.m. and she fairly scampered out of her Victorian office in the centre of town around to Eastgate Street, under the famous Chester clock towards the traffic island on which John's, and several other offices in a terrace, were situated.

"Mr England please, he is expecting me."

"Please take a seat. I will let him know you are here. Can I have your name?"

"Sienna Wall."

"Thank you."

"Mr England, there is a Miss Wall to see you in reception."

"Very well."

"Miss Wall, would you please come this way?"

Sienna was ushered into a splendid room just off reception. The centrepiece was a long boardroom table with oval ends and antique-style chairs down each side and carvers with arms at the ends. On one side of the room were three windows overlooking the small garden to the front of the office and the continuous stream of traffic on the other. Opposite the windows were floor-to-ceiling bookcases the whole length of the room, containing a massive number of law books, mostly statutes of the various years all dating back, as far as Si could tell, to the beginning of the century. The twentieth century, that is.

"Please take a seat. Mr England will be with you shortly. Would you like a drink?"

"No thank you, I'm fine."

Si was left in this meeting room of law. She could only imagine the deals and discussions that might have taken place in this room. She couldn't help wondering how often anyone looked at the books. She undid the large brown envelope and spread the contents onto the table. She divided up the various documents into piles that were relevant to one another. There was the shareholders' agreement on its own except for the note from Sandra in an envelope, which Sandra had sealed, the insurance policies of various types and the mortgage details of the buy to let properties and the land.

"Si, good to see you," and in deference to the surroundings a peck on the cheek was the best John could do just now.

"John, here is all the stuff. We were at it for hours last evening, sorting things out. I suspect there is still more to find. Sandra did the note for you which she has put in a sealed envelope. I'm dying to know what it says."

"Well that's just fine. Thanks a lot. I will have a look at all this shortly. I have a bit of a panic on at the moment. I have some clients selling a house in Chester and there has been a hiccup with the purchaser's mortgage and I have to try and sort that out this afternoon."

"Okay, have you time for lunch?"

"Sorry, I would love to but my lunch will be a sandwich at my desk."

"Oh," Si was disappointed and she looked it.

"Hey, don't be so down in the mouth. It's not the end of the world."

"Well I thought we might just get half an hour together."

"Sorry my sweet, I have just not had a moment this morning."

"Did you manage to phone Regent Travel?"

"Well I don't know how I managed it but, yes, I did."

"And what?"

"Well the hotel is really busy, and they didn't have any standard rooms left."

"Oh no, don't say it's off."

"I didn't, just that standard rooms are off the menu."

"So what, don't be a tease, what have you done?"

"I have arranged for us to have a suite on the top floor and I have downgraded one of the rooms we had booked to a single so that no one will be paying more than they had expected, and I will pick up the tab for the extra for this suite."

"Oh, John, how fantastic. You are wonderful."

"I suspect that there will be at least one nose put out of joint, but we can live with that. I paid the full amount so if you are able to let me have a cheque for £525 which is the price we would have paid in a standard room, then we shall be straight."

"Fantastic, I can give you a cheque now."

Si rummaged through her large handbag and found her chequebook and wrote a cheque to John England, recording the payment in the stub. A down payment on my future she thought, as she was signing the cheque.

"Thanks, Si, that's great. Look, I must rush. I will give you a ring this evening, okay?"

"Fine," another peck on the cheek and she was ushered out into reception and then she was on the pavement before she knew it. The extra half-hour for lunch seemed hardly worth asking for. Si thought that the best use of the time would be to grab a sandwich and have a rummage around the shops in the Grosvenor Shopping Centre. She was looking for a new wardrobe for the impending trip, as well as some sexy-looking ski wear to throw anyone else who might have designs on John.

I wonder what Sandy had said to John in that note on the shareholders' agreement, something she didn't want either Mum or I to know about. I must remember to ask Sandy and John, Si thought.

"Mr Birch, please. It's John England of Bennett and Bennett Solicitors speaking."

"Just a moment, please."

"Ian Birch here, how can I help you?" came the cheerful announcement on the other end of the phone.

"Mr Birch, I act for the Wall family–" John was just about to go on and explain the circumstances of what had happened when Mr Birch intervened.

"I guess you will want to make some claims against the various life policies? A very sad situation all round."

"Yes you are correct."

"I have the file on my desk as I have already had Mr Whiteside on the telephone on the very same subject."

"Mr Whiteside?"

"Yes. He was Mr Wall's business partner and there were two key man policies in place. One in favour of the firm, and the other in favour of the survivor of either of the business partners."

"I see. Well I do need to get an assessment as soon as possible as to the total value of the insurance monies so I can start to get the estate sorted out, and some of the debts paid off."

"Yes, I can do that but it will only be an estimate at this time as we need to make a formal claim to get accurate figures. Do you have a death certificate?"

"No, not as yet. That must wait until we have had the inquest."

"An inquest? Is there any doubt as to the cause of death?"

"No, I don't think so. It is just the usual requirement when an unusual death occurs. I am pretty certain the verdict will be suicide."

"Very well. I will need to look very carefully at the policies as suicide can negate a claim in certain situations."

"I would be grateful if you could let me have the estimate as soon as possible. I have written formally to you but, in view of the urgency, I need to get on with advising the bank and other creditors of the situation as soon as I have a rough idea."

"I will let you know in a matter of days. Mr Whiteside is anxious to know as well."

"As there is a common interest in the key man policies, in so much as the shareholders of the company have a right to know, I would be grateful if you would indicate the figures involved in those policies."

"I will, but you understand that I will have to advise Mr Whiteside of the request."

"I fully understand. If there is any resistance to you releasing that information I would be grateful if you would kindly let me know."

"I will, of course. I will be back to you as soon as I can. Goodbye."

As John put the phone down it rang again.

"John England."

"I've got Berry and Berry Accountants on the phone. It's Mr Hirst."

"Mr Hirst, good afternoon, John England speaking. How may I help you?"

"Mr England, I gather you are acting for the Wall family in connection with the estate of the late Mr Peter Wall?"

"That is so."

"Well I am the accountant to Walls Civil Engineering and I have also been involved with Mr Wall's own private tax affairs."

"Ah, just the man I need to speak to."

"Well, yes, I have a lot of questions and there are some unfinished issues regarding taxation and VAT all to do with the refurbishment of the farm. Do you know what value the life policies will have?"

"No I am afraid I don't at this stage. I have in fact just put the phone down to Ian Birch, at Birch & Co Insurance Brokers, asking the very same question."

"Ah right, I have an urgent situation with the Inland Revenue which they are threatening enforcement action, but in view of the circumstances I may be able to delay. Could we meet when you have more facts on the table?"

"Yes, I think that would be a good idea. Can you write to me so I have your contact details on file?"

John proceeded to give Andy Hirst the Bennett and Bennett address and phone and fax numbers.

"Thanks, I'll drop you a line."

Despite the fact we were just into the twenty-first century, the use of email had not yet developed as a universal tool for business communication, but it was coming. The computer system Bennett and Bennett had recently installed with the updates coming on line had a drafting suite for documents that allowed the partners to effectively create their own documents on line. All that was left for typists to do was to add in their dictated amendments and the details of the parties.

Dealing with drafts documents electronically was becoming so much easier with Microsoft Word and its drafting tools. Deletions and additions could be made and tabulated and shown in different colours and emailed back again almost the same day. The older partners of the practice were not so keen as John. His two other partners of similar age to John could see that this was the future. It meant that the number of typists could be reduced or their role altered so that they became the assistant to the solicitor, not just someone who bashed out letters.

There didn't seem much that John could do to rescue the sale of his client's property due to defects discovered by the surveyor for the purchaser's building society. It was up to the agent to sort it out and, when they had finished their negotiations, they would let John know. He had advised his clients, the vendors, of the position, and so they were stuck, looking forward to retirement and hopefully buying a small cottage in North Wales to retire to. That is now on hold and the clients were fearful they might lose that. The old chain situation again, thought John; there must be a better way. People had been saying that for generations but no one had come up with a better solution.

Looking at the pile of papers Si had left just before lunch, John's attention was drawn to the sealed envelope from Sandra on the top of the pile. His curiosity got the better of him, and despite the fact he really did not have the time this afternoon to go into this matter in any depth, he couldn't help himself tearing open the envelope. John had consoled himself that he had a few days to get his thoughts together on the Walls' matter as, until the insurance estimates were in, he couldn't move forward.

John read the note from Sandra Wall which went into a considerable amount of detail and legal views on the validity of the shareholders' agreement. It clearly had been a carefully crafted document containing a number of trigger points as to who could do what and how the business might be sold from one party to another, and what happened on the death of one or the other.

The document also covered the situation between the parties as to what happened on death or dissolution of the business to the joint ownership of the company's property, which was jointly owned by Peter Wall and Roger Whiteside. Sandra then went into what John thought was really a flight of fancy, which was totally out of character for a solicitor, especially one whose days are involved with commercial law.

"Can you please get a Miss Sandra Wall on the phone for me? She works at Spencer's Solicitors in Liverpool."

"Right away, Mr England."

The next time the phone rang it was Sandra, who was on the end of the line after the operator's introductions.

"Sandra, its John England. Sorry to bother you but do you have a moment to discuss your note to me?"

"Yes, but I am in an open office and I would wish to stick to the legal aspects of the agreement."

"Very well, but I think we need a chat and quite urgently. Some of your thoughts may need to be looked at by the police."

"I'm in tonight John if you are able to come over. I am sure you don't need asking twice."

"That was a bit below the belt but yes, I would be pleased to come over. I would rather discuss the contents of your note with you in private, not in front of your mum or Si."

"That's no problem. Just pop up to my flat. Any idea what time?"

"Would seven thirty be all right?"

"That would be fine. See you then."

John decided that a careful look at the shareholders' agreement was called for before he met with Sandy, so he spent the next hour studying the document and looking up precedents for the various options and cross options contained in the agreement.

Sandra would be a great help to him.

The meeting took place at the appointed hour and afterward John popped next door to see Si. They spent a couple of hours together, a most enjoyable and agreeable end to a day, John thought to himself, before he headed back to Chester.

18.1.2000 Tuesday

The morning post brought the expected letter from the Coroner's office. The inquest was to be held at the coroner's court at ten a.m. on Thursday, 27th January 2000. The same letter as John had received was also sent to Ann Wall, Sienna and to Sandra. The police had their copy, as did Frank Stringer and Fred Appleyard. Fred was the most nervous of the lot as he looked on this as a criminal hearing and, because of the fact he had been tested for DNA, he was frightened that they may think that he had something to do with Mr Wall's death.

Fred decided the best thing to do was to speak to Mrs Wall and check that he actually had to attend. The only interested party, as far as the outcome and the production of the death certificate was concerned, was Roger Whiteside, and as he was not even interviewed by the police he had not been included in the witness summons.

John England sent Roger Whiteside a copy of the witness summons so that he was aware of the proceedings, with an invitation to attend if he so wished. He did wish, as he had a keen interest in the outcome and the issue of a death certificate could trigger serious wealth. The shareholders agreement and the key man insurance would all be triggered by Peter's suicide. Roger had thought to himself that this was clearly the way Peter had expected things to work out. Why have the agreement and the insurances if the end result was not what he wished for?

"Si, it's John."

"Oh hi, everything okay?"

"Yes, just to let you know that there will be a letter waiting for you at home to summons you to attend the Coroner's Court for the inquest on 27th January at ten a.m. I will be there. Perhaps you can tell Sandra and your mum they need not be worried about it. It is a normal occurrence and this is how the Coroner's Court works."

"That's fine, John, thanks. I have already told Dents but I will make it formal now."

John had decided that he needed to speak to the accountants, Berry and Berry, that Peter had used not only for the company but also for his personal affairs. There was clearly an issue regarding the recovery of insurance monies and settling debts as well as making sure the Inland Revenue was correct in its attempt to recover tax as a benefit in kind, plus a fine from Peter, or now, Peter's estate. John also needed a valuation of the company as that was going to be a material factor when or if the option agreement in the shareholders' agreement was triggered. There were serious issues to be faced when it came to dealing with the agreement and there was a strict timetable to be followed. John was also anxious to discover the value of the insurance policies, which Ian Birch was trying to sort out for him.

"Andy Hirst? It's John England, Bennett and Bennett Solicitors."

"Oh yes John. Good to hear from you so soon."

"The reason I am phoning is twofold. Firstly the inquest is to be on Thursday 27th January, and I would hope a death certificate can be issued after that. The other issue is one of valuation of Walls."

"Thanks for the information on the inquest. I may try and make that. On the issue of a valuation, I really cannot help you."

"Oh, why is that?"

"Well I have already had Roger Whiteside for the company for whom I act in a primary capacity asking me to do the same thing, and clearly I cannot work for both sides."

"I see. Are you able to carry on acting in connection with Peter Wall's tax matters in respect of the Revenue's attempt to recover tax for the benefit in kind and the fine they are imposing?"

"Yes I don't see a problem with that, but I would not be able to go any further than that."

"Very well, I will contact you again after the inquest and when I know the family's financial position to discuss the tax issue."

"Very well, I look forward to speaking to you."

"Can you get me Roger Whiteside on the phone please?"

"Very well Mr Hirst."

"Roger, its Andy Hirst, Berry and Berry. I thought you should know that I have just put the phone down from John England who is acting for the Wall family, and he asked me if I could provide a valuation of the company."

"Interesting. It looks as though they are considering triggering the option, what do you suggest we do?"

"I would sit tight. There is still lots of time. What we need to try and discover is the amount of funds the family are likely to have and their view as to the future ownership of the company."

"How would you find out the value of the insurance policies that the family can cash?"

"That, Roger, is something we will just have to guess at."

"That could make life a little difficult."

"Yes I agree, but it is something we shall have to work out when you are ready to make an offer under the terms of the option, unless you get an offer first."

"It would be interesting to get an offer. It would clearly indicate which way they want to go. How will they be able to access the value of the company?"

"As shareholders and in accordance with the terms of the shareholders' agreement, as I recall it, they will be entitled to see the last audited accounts and management accounts up to the last month end. In fact, if you have management accounts to 31st December, then that will be the set of accounts they will be entitled to see. They are in effect the year end accounts despite the fact they are unaudited."

"We should be able to have those available in the next week or two," said Roger. "I think I would like you to have a look at them before we release a copy to make sure they show the worst possible trading position."

"Okay I can do that."

"As soon as we have them in draft perhaps you could get someone to come over for a day to have a look at the numbers so you can help me with the accounts finalisation?"

"No problem, speak to you again soon."

"Bye, thanks Andy."

"Si, it's John."

"Hi, twice in a day. This is going to get people talking."

"I suspect they already are."

"And what can I do for you, sir?"

"Blimey, what's come over you?"

"Mr Dent was walking past my desk."

"Ah, it's possibly Mr Dent I need to speak to, you see I need a valuation of the Walls' premises."

"I am sure Mr Dent will be delighted to help, do you want me to put you through?"

"Yes if you could please, darling."

Si liked that she hadn't been called darling by John before or not at least in a semi-public arena.

"Mr Dent, I have John England of Bennett & Bennett on the phone. He would like to discuss with you the valuation of the Walls' office premises in Sealand."

"For the estate to be able to make some intelligent decisions they need to know what the value in the current market might be. The joint owners pay themselves a rent which goes to pay off the mortgage and leaves a small surplus."

"Will I be able to get into the premises?"

"Well not just at the moment as I don't want the other side to be aware that we are considering looking at purchasing their father's partner's share."

"I understand. I will dig the file out. Would you please be good enough to let me have formal instructions and I will try and work something up for you?"

"Many thanks, I will arrange a letter for you straightaway."

John felt he was making some progress but realised he needed an accountant who could value the business. I will need to try and get a cute commercial guy on this. We don't want to be outmanoeuvred here. I had better talk this through with Ann Wall and Sandra.

Leaving his office a bit early for lunch, Roger Whiteside called at the off-licence and purchased a bottle of Glenmorangie Scotch whisky in a very elegant cardboard tube presentation case. Then to Thornton's to get one of their large boxes of chocolates. Having found a parking spot, no easy matter these days in Chester especially when the sales are on, he called into Birch & Co's office at about ten past one.

"Hello is Mr Birch in please?"

"Is he expecting you, sir?"

"Well not exactly. We were talking today about some insurance policies you look after for me and the firm. I'm Roger Whiteside," Roger hesitated for a moment, "Managing director of Walls Civil Engineering." He felt that was an appropriate title as he was the only person running the show now.

"Mr Whiteside, how nice to meet you. We have spoken on the phone often. I'm Christine, Ian Birch's assistant. I am afraid Mr Birch is out at lunch."

"Well, how nice to meet you, Christine, especially as I have something for you."

"For me?"

"Yes I am afraid I was on holiday abroad all over Christmas and New Year and I was unable to call in with my Christmas presents for you before the festive season, so I thought as I was in town I would drop in and see you personally. Sorry to have missed Ian but I am sure you can make sure he gets this," he said, handing over the bottle of whisky.

"This is for you Christine," he said, handing over an almost too big box of chocolates.

"Mr Whiteside, what a wonderful surprise. Thank you so much."

"Did Ian leave me a copy of the insurance schedule we were discussing this morning?"

"I don't know. Were you expecting one?"

"Yes it is quite urgent. Is there any chance there is a spare copy I could take now?"

"I know the schedule you mean as I typed it for Mr Birch only this morning."

"If there is a spare copy it will help me greatly in my thinking about the future arrangements I need to make for the firm."

"The file should be on Mr Birch's desk. Just hold on a moment."

"No he seems to have locked it away, but I can print you a copy off without a problem. It is on my computer, do you mind waiting a moment?"

"No not at all. That's very kind of you. I hope it isn't too much trouble?"

"Not at all, I will do it now."

Christine produced the two page document for Roger within a matter of minutes.

"There we are. I have placed it in an envelope for you, perhaps you would just check it's what you needed?"

Roger extracted the document from the envelope and saw that the schedule included not only the Walls Civil Engineering policies but also the Peter Wall personal policies, which was just what he wanted.

"That's great, Christine. Thank you so much."

"It's no trouble. I am sorry you are having such a sad time."

"Yes, it's awful. I was away when Peter Wall died so I am trying to pick up the pieces."

"Yes I understand and thank you again for the chocolates."

Roger left and returned to his office to study the schedule or those bits of it which were of particular interest to him.

Christine left Birch & Co to go for a late lunch. It was gone half past one already. It was ten to two when Ian Birch arrived back in the office, and it was nearly half past two when Christine reappeared.

"Did you find the bottle of whisky on your desk Ian?"

"Yes I did, that is a very pleasant surprise."

"Roger Whiteside called in just as you had left for lunch, and he gave me a big box of chocolates. He apologised that he had not been able to come in before the holiday but he had been abroad all over Christmas and the New Year."

"It's most unexpected I must say, I have never known Walls to do that before. Did he want anything else?"

"Oh yes he just needed a copy of the insurance schedule you had been discussing with him this morning."

"I haven't spoken to him today; I was talking to John England."

"That's very strange. I am sure he said he had spoken to you and asked for a copy of the schedule. I couldn't see that you had left one out for him, so I produced another copy and gave it to him."

"Oh my God, you haven't?"

"I haven't what?"

"Given Whiteside a copy of the insurance schedule?"

"Well, yes, he said he needed a copy and many of the policies on there concern him."

"Many yes, but not all, and he now knows the funds that will be available to Ann Wall. How very difficult."

"I'm sorry, Ian. I had no idea that I was doing wrong."

"No, you have been taken in and the Christmas gifts I suspect were all part of the plan. I'm not sure what to do. Should I declare this to John England or leave it alone? It is as you say mostly to do with Walls policies anyway, so let's hope no harm has been done, let's forget it."

"I am very sorry Ian I had no idea I was doing wrong."

"Well don't worry, but for the future don't release any document to even a known client without reference to me."

"I will, I promise. Sorry."

Roger saw that the schedule contained details of every insurance policy associated with the business and Peter Wall, including car insurance, which to Roger's further annoyance included the insurance on Sandra and Sienna's cars. There was plant and machinery insurance and a comprehensive contractor's policy with ten million pound third party liability for their contracting activity. A comprehensive office policy and a computer hardware and data policy.

The buildings were insured by the company, noting the joint owners and the National Westminster Bank who had provided the twenty-year commercial mortgage on the property. There was also a policy on four houses which Roger didn't know anything about, the beneficiary being a company called PW Developments. It gave details of their addresses. There was also a list of life policies:

> *Key man insurance on the lives of Peter Wall and Roger Whiteside, payable on death. Sum assured £1m. Premium £500 per month, payable by the insured*
>
> *Key man insurance on Peter Wall and Roger Whiteside for £500,000 payable on the death of one of them. Premium £250 per month, payable by Walls Civil Engineering Limited.*
>
> *Mortgage protection insurance for Long Acre farm. £750,000 on the joint lives of Peter and Ann Wall, payable on second death, premium £180 per month.*
>
> *Two life insurance policies on Peter Wall's life, the first dated 1990 for £500,000 and the second for £1m dated April 1999.*

This was just the information Roger needed. He now had all the ammunition he needed to exercise his option rights. Just how to play, this was the question. He needed to think carefully, check the shareholders agreement again and schedule out the dates and decide how to play any offers he might make.

I think I will use Sally Moulton of Frobisher's solicitors in Manchester, he thought. After all they drew up the document. They cannot be acting for the Walls as they have instructed the local chap, John England, who is all over Sienna anyway, so I will get the best possible advice.

19.01.2000 Wednesday

In the morning's post came the schedule of insurance policies John was waiting for. This should allow him to see how much was likely to come to the family as a result of Peter Wall's death. The issue was to link the value of the policies with the obligations and opportunities laid out in the shareholders' agreement.

John read the agreement to himself. It had numerous clauses, mainly dealing with how voting should be organised and what happened if the parties fell out and how those situations might be resolved. What would happen if one of the parties became mentally ill, and most importantly what would happen to the two main assets of the parties, namely Walls Civil Engineering Limited and the premises they occupied. Whilst it might seem that the two situations were the same, they were far from it. The note Sandra had sent John was very useful to help John fully understand the option arrangements in the agreement.

The business was held by shareholders, and Peter Wall and Roger Whiteside were the two shareholders. As Peter was dead, there was nothing in the agreement indicating a change of the rules in the event of suicide or whatever. The option was clear: either party, in the case of Peter Wall, that was held to mean his executors Ann and the two girls, should make an offer for the shares of Roger Whiteside. This provision was automatically triggered in the event of death of one of the parties. The assumption being that the relatives of the deceased person would not wish to continue running the business, thereby giving them the opportunity to sell the shareholding quickly to the remaining shareholder. The rub came that if one party made a bid which the other party didn't think acceptable they could force the bidder to sell their share at the same price as they had just bid.

The Mexican option, a dangerous and yet effective way of ensuring that each side should think carefully about the offer they might make. The financial strength of each party, of course, if known by the bidder, is of great assistance in setting the bidding price. John England was satisfied that the information on the value of the policies was known to only a very few and not known to the other side. Little did he know that Roger Whiteside had obtained the information on the policies. Ian Birch equally was not aware of the significance of the policy details as he had not been made aware of the terms of the option agreements in the shareholders' agreement.

Continuing his research, John read on. The shareholders' agreement also had a most unusual clause to the effect that, if either party had been charged or convicted of fraud or a criminal offence, then the Mexican option was null and void. The offending party had to sell at open market value as assessed by the company's accountants, taking into account all relevant matters – one of which would be the fact that the company no longer had the services of the offending party. The agreement also gave rights to the remaining party to terminate all key man insurances in this eventuality for the benefit of the offending party, so that they would never get any financial gain from criminal activity.

The Mexican option was also embodied in the agreement to cover the ownership and sale of the premises which were owned outside the business by Peter Wall and Roger Whiteside personally. The trigger point for a sale or purchase under the Mexican option rules in this agreement was the death of one of the parties. It didn't have to be that either party could make an offer under the option at any time, but an automatic trigger was reached as soon as one or the other parties died. Roger expected the estate of Peter Wall to make low offers to buy Roger's share, to tempt Roger to buy the Walls estate share. Now he had the policy details he felt certain that this would occur.

The trigger had to be pulled in this case no later than midnight on the 30th March 2000. Once an offer to buy had been made, the recipient had a further twenty-eight days to exercise their right under the agreement.

Working through the various permutations, it was firstly clear to John that the mortgage on the farm could not be redeemed under the existing mortgage protection policy. It had been written on the basis that the mortgage would be satisfied in full by the policy on the second death of the two insured parties. They were Peter and then Ann Wall, so both had to die to give effect to a claim. This policy was of no help at this stage. John needed to note this as Ann would need income to allow her to go on paying the mortgage and insurance premiums.

The next policy on the schedule that was of interest to John was the £500,000 life insurance on Peter's life taken out in 1990. He must have taken this out just as he had started the company to protect his family against any financial hardship in the event of his premature death. This policy seemed satisfactory and was sure to be available for the benefit of the beneficiaries of the estate.

The key man insurance: this was a whole heap of money, one and a half million pounds in total, and all of it escaped Peter's estate and either went to Roger Whiteside or the Walls company. With this cash sum, Roger Whiteside could put in a significant offer for the business, which would be very useful for the Walls.

There was one other policy which Peter had clearly taken out to protect his family from financial problems in the event of premature death and that was for one million pounds. He had taken this out in April 1999, just about the time of the purchase of the land for development and the two houses on Squirrels Chase. They were all wrapped up in a single purchase. Peter didn't want a formal legal charge on the properties as he was planning on demolishing them to give himself access to the development land at the rear that he had purchased for one million pounds from the farmer who had decided that on principal he would not sell his land to the developer of the adjoining estate who was trying to hold the farmer to ransom as he thought he had the only access. Peter had acquired the two houses to provide access and the plans that had been submitted for planning showed that very clearly. To give the bank additional collateral, Peter had agreed to charging a one million pound insurance policy on his life to the bank until the debt had been satisfied. The charge on the policy was noted on the schedule.

However the policy was not worth the paper it was written on as Peter had committed suicide, and the policy was not one year old when Peter had died, so no claim could be brought against that policy.

John realised they were forced back onto the key man policies and how much they could get for the business and the buildings. This was clearly not going to be an easy situation to manage, because if the offer was too high Roger may decide to chuck in the towel and take the money, requiring the estate to buy him out of the business and the property. That would be disastrous as there would be nowhere near enough money in the pot for that, despite the fact that buying the business meant the £500,000 policy would go into the business. John believed that the company had a large overdraft, so it would be swept up by that.

John decided he needed a meeting with all the Wall family as a whole, to explain the dilemma we have.

"Ann, it's John, John England."

"Hello, John, how are you?"

"I'm just fine thanks, how are you is more to the point?"

"I'm making good progress, thanks, John, but it has not been easy."

"I'm sure, are you free for a moment?"

"Yes of course. There is no one here except for Fred working outside."

"Ah good, I really need to have a business meeting with you and the girls, if that would be possible. We need to discuss the situation regarding the business and the business property so I can work up a strategy to meet your wishes."

"That all sounds very heavy, just up Sandra's street. Would you mind if Frank Stringer sat in as well? I do value his advice."

"No not at all, when do you think it would be convenient?"

"How about six o'clock in the evening on Friday, John? Afterwards you must stay to dinner."

"That would be excellent. That suits me fine."

"Well, I need to check with the girls and Frank, and as soon as I have it settled I will let you know. Just give me your office number again please, John?"

Once the formalities had been satisfied the meeting and dinner were arranged and it was agreed that Frank Stringer would come to dinner with Margaret. Margaret had a book she was well into and would go and sit in the lounge and read until the meeting was finished.

Ann hadn't entertained now for some time and was suddenly all of a jitter as to what to do. She decided to enlist the support of the girls for this; that should ensure the meal at least turned out to be a success.

Ann decided to plan the meal and then dispatch the girls to get the shopping done. I think I will have a bowl of soup and a sandwich for lunch whilst I do the list for the girls, she thought. She was just contemplating the sandwich filling when there came a knock at the door.

"Hello, Fred, have you got a problem?"

"No, Mrs Wall, not at all, but I wonder if I could have a word with you?"

"Yes, Fred, of course. Take your boots off and come into the kitchen. I was just about to make a cup of tea. Would you like one?"

"That would be very kind ma'am."

"Now, whilst that's boiling, what is on your mind?"

"Well I have had this letter see, from that coroner chap, and they want me to go to the court on the 27th January in Warrington. I don't know why they need me in court, I haven't done anything wrong as I told the policeman."

"No, it's not that sort of court, Fred. Hang on just let me make the tea, two sugars isn't it?"

"Yes that's right."

"Now where were we? The Coroner's court is to establish how Mr Wall died and they take evidence from all sorts of people who could know something, or in this case worked on Jumbo and the farm. That's what they want you for, just to help the Coroner establish the cause of death."

"So I'm not in trouble then?"

"No certainly not, how are you thinking of getting there Fred?"

"Well I have no transport and it's too far on me bike so..."

"Don't worry your head about it. We shall be leaving here at eight thirty on that day so if you come at your normal time, you can come with us."

"That would be grand, thank you."

"Is there anything else on your mind?"

"Well I was just wondering if you would still want me to work here, what with Mr Wall gone an' all?"

"Fred, how could we continue without you? Of course we want you to stay. Don't you think otherwise."

Ann hoped this would sound sincere but she had no idea how she would afford to pay for Fred in the future. It was straightforward when Peter was alive. Fred was paid through the business as he had always been, but now, well who knew what the future held?

Ann met his gaze with a faint smile and hoped that would reassure him.

"That's good Mrs Wall, it's important to me this job, without it I don't think I could still pay the rent on my cottage, and I wouldn't like to move to one of those modern flats in Chester run by the social."

"Of course not, Fred. Don't think any more of it."

"Very well Ms Wall, thank you for the tea. I will go and have my lunch and then tidy the yard again. It's all this traffic we have had recently that makes it untidy."

"Thanks, Fred. That would be good. Bye."

Fred replaced his boots and returned to his little workshop at the back of the machinery shed to make another brew and eat his sandwiches, and, as normal, have a short nap.

John set about making up a chart of all the insurances so he could use this on Friday at the meeting. He also created a list of liabilities and their monthly cost. He also drew up a calendar showing the trigger points and the time when the options had to be exercised.

"Si, have you a moment?"

"Yes, Mr Dent, what can I do for you?"

"Well there are two things. Firstly, the simplest of all, is the management inspection due at Squirrels Chase. As you did the letting, it's time for the midterm inspection, would you like to do it? It would be best if you don't mind as you can determine what needs to be done to the property to put it right in the event of any dilapidations."

"That's fine. I have no problem in arranging that. I will give the tenant a ring and arrange the inspection for tomorrow if that suits him."

"Good, that's the easy bit. My problem is that I have to give John England a valuation on the business premises occupied by Walls Civil Engineering in time for the meeting I understand you have with him on Friday evening with your mother and your sister."

"Yes that's correct, we are apparently going to try and decide what to do with everything."

"Well the problem I have is that at the moment I cannot go inside, but John needs an indication of value for Friday. Clearly I will have to go in to prepare a formal valuation. I wondered if you had been in the offices recently and could give me an indication of how the property is presented now?"

"Well it has been a little while since I was in there, but I think I can give you a rough idea of how it is now."

"Good, do you mind just spelling out your recollections and I will make some notes?"

"No problem. As I recall, the whole site has a perimeter fence which I think has been improved since Dad bought it. It has big steel double gates to the road. I am sure Dad had the whole yard concreted. The workshop and plant repair shop is about five thousand square feet, I would guess."

"Good guess, it is shown as six thousand on the particulars of sale."

"Ah that's good. I was just counting the distance in my mind's eye between the portal frames, but if it's six thousand that will be correct. The office building is a typical 1970s-style brick building, rectangular in shape. It used to have a flat roof, and I think Dad had a pitched roof put on it within a few years of buying the place as the flat roof was always leaking. Do the particulars say how big that is, Mr Dent?"

"Yes, they say it is again six thousand square feet on two floors, so that's three thousand feet per floor."

"Yes, and Dad and Roger had a big office each on the first floor with an office for Christine Franks between them. There were a set of toilets and a small kitchen on that floor. I think Dad's office was the biggest as he used it for meetings. There was a boardroom table in there and there was not room for one in Roger's office, as I recall.

"On the ground floor there were two big open-plan offices and one had a sliding window which was used for reception. The staircase to the first floor was in the middle of the building with ladies and gents toilets on the ground floor."

"That's great, thanks for that. Any idea what it might be worth now?"

"Oh, Mr Dent, what a question!"

"Well you are a surveyor, and it's good to get some technical valuation practice in rather than the seat of the pants stuff you do on the estate agency side."

"Yes I am sure you are correct. Well, just as a rule of thumb, the repair workshop would probably be valued at about three to four pounds a square foot per annum in rent, so between twenty-one thousand and twenty-four thousand pounds per annum. The offices on an industrial estate would only be worth about seven or eight pounds a square foot for the net floor area which is probably around five thousand square foot, so I would say £35,000 per annum. So the combined value at the lower end would be £46,000 but say £50,000 per with all the yard area and external storage."

"You certainly don't seem to have lost your knack at doing that, I think you are just about right. The issue is, what is the capital value?"

"Would it be half a million, ten times the annual rent?"

"I think that is very optimistic in the current market. It is unlikely to be attractive to an investment fund and with all due respect to your father's business, it is a dirty business so you don't get the same yield you would expect from a nice tidy office building. No, I think £400,000 is the valuation, which is a yield of twelve and a half percent or eight years purchase of the open market rental value."

"I can't argue with that."

"Please don't say anything on value to your mother. Let John England put it all into context for her."

"No that's fine, no problem. Is that all Mr Dent?"

"Yes thank you, Si."

"Is that Mr McCullock?"

"Yes, who's that?"

"It's Sienna Wall, from Dents, Mr McCullock."

"Oh, is there a problem?"

"No I hope not, Mr McCullock. It's just that we always do a mid-term inspection and I wondered if I could arrange a time to visit to do the inspection?"

"Yes certainly, when had you in mind?"

"Would tomorrow morning be convenient?"

"Yes, what time?"

"Shall we say ten o'clock?"

"Yes, that's okay with me. See you then."

Gary McCullock spent the rest of the day and some of the evening tidying up and making the place look respectable. He had been using the dining table for an office with the computer plugged in and papers all over the table, but in specific piles depending what they were about. The large desk diary also had to be tidied away so there was no evidence of business when Sienna Wall arrived.

"Si, it's Mum."

"Hi, Mum, how are you?"

"Fine, darling, I just wondered if either you or Sandra would go and do a big shop for me at the supermarket tonight as, with the dinner party on Friday, I need to get everything in so I can prepare it all tomorrow?"

"No problem. If you would like to read the list out for me now I can go to Sainsbury's on the bypass before I come home."

"Oh that would be great. Have you got a big piece of paper handy?"

"Yes, fire away."

Ann dictated a long list of groceries and meat and smoked salmon as though Ann was going to cook a feast for some very important dignitary.

"Is that it?"

"Well I thought that would do, what do you think?"

"I think that's just fine, Mum, but you shouldn't go to so much trouble."

"Well there are Frank and Margaret coming and, of course, John."

"Oh Mum, you are not doing all this to impress John are you?"

"No of course not, don't be silly."

Which of course is exactly what she was doing, but would never admit to it.

"I will go there after work."

"Thanks darling, see you later."

The girls were such a support to Ann and she felt that she was so lucky having two such wonderful daughters.

20.01.2000 Thursday

Si rang the doorbell but there was no answer. She knocked on the door, still no answer. There wasn't a car in the drive, but she had hoped it was locked in the garage. She waited in her car for five to ten minutes and still no sign of the occupier. Si decided to do some work whilst she was here so she looked around the front garden and then decided to go to the back garden. The side gate had something blocking it, but after a good hard shove she made it open sufficiently to make a gap she could pass through.

The obstacle was three black bin bags that had been piled up against the gate. The gate had split one open and out had fallen some rubbish. Si thought she had best put the rubbish back as it was mostly paper – it might blow around the lawn. She was just putting the last bit back into the bag when she noticed that one of the opened envelopes was addressed to Peter Wall, 18 Squirrels Chase, Chester. What on earth has this tenant been doing opening mail addressed to Dad? Just then she heard a car come onto the drive so she held on to the envelope.

Exiting from the back garden out on to the drive, she hailed Gary McCullock.

"Mr McCullock, I am glad you have arrived. I have been here for nearly half an hour."

"Have you? I am so sorry, but I thought I was early for our appointment at ten thirty."

"No, it was ten o'clock."

"I'm sorry I had it down as ten thirty. I see you have already been into the back garden."

"Well yes, and I am afraid one of the bin bags split just as I was pushing the gate open. I couldn't help noticing this is an envelope addressed to my father that you seem to have opened."

McCullock could feel the blood coursing through his veins and up into his face. He was certain he was blushing, something he never did.

"Ah, you have found just some of the mountain of junk mail that comes here. I know your family have been in mourning and the last thing I thought you needed was a load of junk mail."

"This doesn't look like a junk mail envelope to me."

"Well I assure you it is and I have had to dispose of loads of the stuff, so it's you who should be thanking me, not getting cross with me for being thoughtful."

"Yes of course. You are quite right. I'm sorry, shall we start again?"

"Very well, please come in."

Si carried out her inspection of the property and had a look at the back garden from the dining room patio window. As the tenancy had been during winter months so far, there was nothing to be done to the simple grass lawn and two borders. It was virtually as it was let, except for a few extra leaves.

"Is everything okay?"

"Yes, Mr McCullock, it is, thank you."

"You are very like your father. Keen to jump to conclusions."

"You've met my father?"

"Yes, it was just before Christmas. He came round and was extremely rude."

"I find that hard to believe. Why was that?"

"He was accusing me of lying about my wife and child and about my comings and goings."

"That's very odd. Dad never mentioned anything to me but, as you have mentioned them, where are your wife and child?"

"They lived here for a month and didn't like Chester, so they have gone back to live with her mother in Coventry."

"Sorry to hear that. Does that mean that you might go there when the tenancy ends?"

"No, I don't think so. It looks as though we might be splitting up."

"I'm sorry to hear that, but it still doesn't really explain why my father called."

"Well apparently the tenants in number 20, which I understand your father also owns, sorry your late father, they complained about noise when I had a party one weekend for some mates from work."

"Oh, I see why Dad was so cross."

"He wasn't really cross, he just was not happy having to deal with a complaint, I think."

McCullock was doing his best to sound plausible, after all Si could never check on his story with her dad being dead now. She seemed satisfied with his explanation anyway. Si then left.

Back in her car she realised that she still had the envelope in her hand. There was no point in going to give it back to McCullock so Si just slipped it into the pocket of her clipboard without further question. McCullock watched her go and she waved back to him as he was standing next to his black Ford Focus car.

Gary McCullock realised that after the visit he was on borrowed time. He hadn't got long and he needed to get the funds from the Halifax transferred to him or his account within Halifax bank as soon as possible. He spent the next hour chasing the money with Halifax online banking. He didn't want to use the local branch in Chester; it was too personal.

At the end of his trawl through the various mortgage departments of the Halifax, he discovered that the advance had been approved and that the money would be transferred into his account on Monday 24th January. That would be £100,000, more money than he had ever had before. The next call was to advise the Halifax online bank that the funds were coming into his account and that he wanted to withdraw the money in cash in two amounts of fifty thousand pounds each.

"This is very unusual sir. May I ask what you need the funds in cash for?"

"Yes, I am setting up my own car sales business and I have to buy some stock. I know a number of traders but being a new business they will only deal in cash to begin with. For security I don't want to draw it out all at once so if I could have the balance on Thursday 27th January that would be fine."

"Well we shall need the request in writing and the address of the branch where you will want to collect the cash. You will have to produce some ID when you go and collect the money."

"No problem at all. I will take my passport along if that's okay?"

"Very well, can you please send us the letter today by first class post?"

"It's as good as done."

Gary set to creating the letter to the Halifax online banking facility requesting to draw out £50,000 on Monday 24th January and the balance, except for £1000 so as to keep the account open, he required in cash on Thursday 27th January. Once typed it was off to the main post office to catch the lunchtime post so the Halifax could put the arrangements into place for this client.

"Mrs Wall."

"Fred, come in, take your boots off. You must know when the kettle is on, what can I do for you?"

"Well I have been thinking about everything concerning the death of Mr Peter."

Fred had caught Ann at a bit of a low ebb because, at the moment he mentioned Peter's name, she flooded with tears and they began to stream down her cheeks.

"I'm so sorry Mrs Wall. I didn't mean to upset you."

"You didn't Fred, it's just that Peter's memory is so raw and, what with everything, I am living life on a knife edge."

"Shall I make the tea? The kettle is boiling."

"Would you? No sugar for me," she sobbed.

As Fred returned to the kitchen table with two mugs of tea he could see that Ann was not crying as much, but he realised that perhaps this was not the moment to say what he had been winding himself up to say for some days now.

"How's the tea?"

"It's just fine. Thank you Fred."

An awkward silence fell between them for quite a few minutes whilst they both sat there, the one not knowing what to do or say, the other being totally distraught by the events since New Year's Eve. It was just one of those moments when there was no stopping the distress Ann felt. Fred had finished his tea, yet he could clearly see Ann was still distressed.

"Mrs Wall, I will pop in another day if I may? There is nothing spoiling and I will have a chat with you next week when you might be feeling a bit better."

"If you would Fred, thanks."

Fred put his boots back on again and left the kitchen with Ann still sobbing to herself, hugging her mug of tea and hardly aware that Fred had left.

It was nearing noon when the cattle grid rattled, and who should drive in but Si? Goodness me, I wonder what's the matter, thought Ann as she rushed to the back door to welcome her youngest daughter.

"Darling, how nice to see you! But, shouldn't you be at work?"

"I am at work Mum."

"Oh, how can that be if you are here?"

"Well I have been doing a few management inspections this morning; one was at Squirrels Chase so when I had finished them all I wasn't far away, so I thought I would just pop in and see if you were all right."

"Yes I'm fine. You really shouldn't worry about me."

"You've been crying, I can tell."

"Yes, Fred came in for a cup of tea and he just mentioned your father and for some reason it set me off."

"Oh, Mum," and Si hugged Ann for some time.

"Did Fred just want a cup of tea? He doesn't usually come here for a cup of tea, he has his own facilities in the machinery shed."

"No, he wanted to talk about something. I assumed it was going to be about the inquest again. He has been requested to go and he thinks that he is guilty of something, but frankly I was not up to having a discussion with him over that."

"Don't worry, Mum. I will go and have a chat to him for you."

"Would you, darling?"

"Yes of course. No problem, I need to go to the loo first and then I might also have a cup of coffee."

"I see why you came now, and I thought it was to see how I was!"

"It was and you know it."

"I'll put the kettle on again, and when you have finished chatting with Fred, come back and have a drink and a biscuit."

"Great."

Si disappeared into the loo in the utility room, and then she crossed the yard to go and see Fred.

"Hello, Miss Wall."

Fred was always the most polite of people, real old-fashioned country respect and a clear understanding of master and servant relationships. A trait that has all but died out now, she thought to herself.

"Fred, you wanted to have a word with my mother about something. As I was here anyway, I thought you might like to speak to me and I will see what I can do for you?"

"That's kind missus. Shall we go into my workshop? There are two chairs there."

"Yes okay." Si realised this was almost an honour. Fred's workshop was his special place and rarely did anyone else get to go there. The doorway to the workshop was clearly on display now that Jumbo was no longer in the machinery shed. She used to occupy the space immediately in front of the door to Fred's workshop.

"I just wanted to mention to your mother something that had been troubling me for some time."

"And what is that, Fred?"

"Well, you see, when I am not working here on Mondays and Fridays I work at the Church in Tarporley – St Helens, you know?"

"No I didn't know that, what do you do there?"

"I do all sorts of odd jobs. I cut the grass between the graves, sweep the churchyard and generally keep the place tidy. I even dig a grave when required, but that isn't often now."

"I see, so what is on your mind?"

"It's just that I was cycling to Tarporley from my cottage on New Year's Day morning. I know it wasn't a normal working day but there was so much to catch up with at the church at about seven o'clock or so, I am not rightly sure of the time as I don't have a watch, but I was nearly knocked off my bike when a car raced out of the lane. I don't know if it has any interest to the police, but I haven't known what to do. I thought I recognised the driver but I think I was wrong about that."

"That's interesting. Who do you think the driver was?"

"I'm not sure I should say, Miss, as it clearly was not him as I have now found out."

"Well just tell me and it will be our little secret."

"Well, miss, it looked, I thought, just like Roger Whiteside but it was dark, and it wasn't his car and it was only a fleeting glance. Now I realise he was in Austria at the time so, you see, I am just being silly. There was a car, though."

"Well I am glad you have told me Fred. I will ask John England, our solicitor, what if anything we should do about this. Don't you worry about it, if John thinks there is something to be done he will be in touch but I think it was possibly a courting couple or something."

"Most likely, miss, thank you."

When Si got back to the kitchen and her coffee and biscuit she related Fred's story to her mother.

"That's very strange, it has just jogged my memory."

"What's strange?"

"Well when I was driving home on New Year's Day, I had to swerve violently in the lane to miss a black car parked half on the verge and half on the lane. It had no lights on and I nearly hit it."

"It is unlikely it stayed there all night but I suppose, as it was about two a.m. when you came home, it wasn't all that long to stay in the car, and it was a mild night as I recall."

"Well your dad made some crude remark about a courting couple, so it wouldn't surprise me if they had been there all night."

"That will be it then."

"Well I am glad we have sorted that out. I was beginning to wonder what Fred wanted to speak to me about."

"Yes. Look, Mum, I must fly, see you later," and with that and a big kiss for her mother, Si fled and raced over the cattle grid which gave its usual farewell.

"Hi Christine, is Mr Roger available?"

"How are you doing, Duggie? Still living on your own?"

"Yes but I'm not lonely. In fact I met Fred Appleyard in Chester last night. I hadn't seen him for ages and he was telling me about Mr Peter."

"Roger, Duggie is in reception and asks if you can spare him a moment."

"Sure Christine, send him up."

"Hi, Duggie, how's things?"

"I am afraid I have come to give you my notice Mr Whiteside."

"Now why would you want to do that?"

"Well it's nothing to do with the firm or the job or anything," he rattled out in his broad Irish accent. The Irish were past masters at civil engineering and are very hard workers. Roger was thinking he would need to be lucky to get anyone as good as Duggie.

"It's me family, you see. They are all now back in Ireland and I'm living here on me own, and me wife wants me back with her."

"I fully understand, Duggie, when do you want to go?"

"Well we are at the end of a contract I have been working on in Crewe, so it would be handy if I could just give you a week's notice and go."

"Okay, Duggie, do you still have the red Escort?"

"Yes, Mr Whiteside, it's a bit knackered now and I think the tax and MOT are up at the end of the month."

"How many miles has it done now?"

"I can't rightly remember but it's over 150,000 miles so it is."

"Mmm, it's probably ready for the scrap."

"Are you saying to me you want to go now?"

"Well, yes. I had not wanted to bother you up to now as you have a lot on your hands just now, what with Mr Peter and all."

"So when do you want to go?"

"I would like to finish tomorrow night."

"Okay, Duggie, we can agree that. In fact, if you go and see Christine she will make up your wages, holiday pay and so on and you can go now and leave the car in the workshop."

"Well Mr Whiteside, that's very good of you. It's a real help. I will be back in Dublin for the weekend and the missus will be really pleased."

"How many children have you now?"

"Four, with another on the way. The missus is finding it hard on her own."

"Yes I can imagine. Anyway, Duggie, thanks for all you have done and good luck in the future."

"Thank you, Mr Whiteside. Bye now."

Duggie left Walls and returned to his wife in Ireland. The Ford Escort, now ten years old and with a lot of miles on the clock, was left in the workshop.

"Christine, can you please let me have the keys to the Escort and I will have a look at it later and decide what to do with it?"

"Colin?" Colin was the workshop manager in charge of vehicles in plant.

"Yes, boss."

"I have had a quick drive in the old Escort, and I think it has probably had its day. I am not prepared to spend any more money on it, tax and MOT. Can you see if you can get a scrapyard to take it away next week?"

"Yes sure boss, leave it with me."

"Thanks. When you need the keys I have them in my office."

"Okay."

"John, it's Si."

"Hello, darling, how are you? Good to hear your voice."

"I'm fine. Are you free early evening? I need a chat with you about some issues that have cropped up."

"Yes, no problem. When would you like to come round?"

"Well I have to go to Sainsbury's for Mum, so when I have finished there. Possibly about seven?"

"That's fine, will you have eaten?"

"No, possibly not."

"Then when you are at Sainsbury's, get one of their excellent Indian meals."

"Okay, sounds good to me. See you later."

"Mum?"

"Yes, darling?"

"I need to pop into John's after I have been to Sainsbury's and we are going to have supper together, but I won't be late."

"That's fine darling, however don't let the frozen stuff go off. Can you stick it in John's deep freeze whilst you are there?"

"Yes, no probs."

"Don't forget to bring it home with you. I will need it for the morning."

"No I won't. See you later."

"Bye, be careful."

After work Si set off for Sainsbury's to do the massive shop her mother had requested. She must think we are having an army for dinner, she thought. When the trolley was full and the list exhausted, Si was making her way to the checkout when she realised she had forgotten the Indian meal. John would be furious, she thought, and a bit hungry too. Loading it into her trolley she turned to go back to the checkout and bumped into Roger Whiteside.

"Hello, Sienna, fancy seeing you here."

"Hello, Roger, yes I do not come here that often, but Mum is having... some people round for dinner tomorrow and I said I would help her."

"That's good. I am glad she is getting back into the swing of things again."

"Yes, she still gets very down but is making good progress."

"I am glad I have seen you. I just wanted to know if Fred Appleyard was still working at the farm?"

"Yes he is, why?"

"Well one of my main men has just handed in their notice and I wondered if he might be available."

"I would doubt it. He is not far off retirement and I think he is happy with his current lot."

"I might just speak to him though. Does he still live in the same cottage?"

"As far as I am aware."

"What are his hours at the farm? I don't want to interfere with his work there."

"I think he works from eight in the morning until four thirty in the afternoons on Tuesday, Wednesday and Thursday."

"Oh, so he isn't full time then?"

"No he never has been. He works for the church in Tarporley on Mondays and Fridays."

"Okay I will try and catch him sometime then. Thanks for your help."

"No problem. Sorry, sorry I must go."

"Okay, thanks again. Bye."

That man gives me the creeps, thought Sienna. He is so insistent on having every last bit of information on any subject when he talks to you. A shudder went down her spine as he walked away.

"Hi it's me, can you let me in?"

"Hi, no problem," John pressed the button on the intercom to allow the lift to be accessed by Si from the basement. Si had left her car in a visitor's bay. She had the box of Indian food in one hand and an insulated bag of frozen food in the other.

"Goodness me, what have you been buying?"

"John, it's not all for us. Well, not tonight anyway."

"I'm glad about that."

"Can I put the frozen stuff in your deep freeze whilst I am here so it doesn't defrost?"

"Of course," and once decanted Si put the freezer bag across the front door to remind her that she had to collect the frozen food before she left.

"Come here. I haven't been able to have a good look at you yet."

John caught Si and pulled her towards him and they embraced and kissed one another for several minutes. John's hand slipped down to caress her bottom and felt her smooth skin.

"Not now, John. I mustn't be late back. I promised Mum I would have all the shopping back this evening. I need to talk to you, I am worried."

"Darling, what are you worried about?"

"No, not like that. I just have a funny feeling about several disconnected events that I just cannot make sense of."

"Well let's get this supper on the go, I will open a bottle of wine and then we can see what all this is about."

A glass in hand and the Indian just being zapped in the microwave, it didn't take many minutes to find them both sitting at the dining table in the apartment.

"It's just that I have been thinking about various unconnected events and I cannot make sense of them."

"Well why don't you spill them out and I promise not to interrupt?"

"Some hopes. Well, the first thing that happened was that Fred – he's the chap that works on the farm three days a week, told me about the time he was cycling to Tarporley on New Year's Day, and as he was passing the end of the lane leading to the farm, he was nearly knocked off his bike by a car. At the time he was convinced it was Roger Whiteside who was driving. He did admit to me that he only had a fleeting glance and cannot be sure. He is sure that it was a black car, however."

"I see. Roger, as I understand it, was skiing in Austria."

"Yes that's right, and Fred now knows that so he knows he was mistaken about the driver, but he is quite clear that the incident occurred."

"Okay, what's next?"

"Well, I was doing management inspections this morning and one of the properties was one of Dad's buy-to-let properties, the ones on Squirrels Chase. It looks as though he bought them to get access to the land he bought at the rear. The tenant was late and so I went around the garden. Pushing my way through the gate at the side of the house to get to the back garden, I burst open a bin bag. The gate was stuck because the tenant had piled the bags up at the back of the gate. A pile of paper and envelopes fell out and I found one addressed to Dad at Squirrels Chase. The envelope was empty, but it was clearly addressed to Dad. When I asked the tenant about it, he got very shirty with me and explained that he had received loads of junk mail and that Dad had agreed that he could destroy stuff like that. When I asked him how he had met Dad he said that Dad had called round to see him as he had received a complaint about noise from the tenant of the adjoining house. I just find that hard to believe. I am sure the tenants would have spoken to Dents first and I would have dealt with it. It just doesn't make sense."

"No, it is a very strange reaction and set of events. Do you still have the envelope with your father's name on it?"

"Yes, oh blast, it's in the car. I will go and get it, won't be a mo."

John topped up the wine glasses whilst Si was getting the envelope, and he cleared away the plates and stuck them in the dishwasher and put all the rubbish in the trash.

"It's me."

"Okay, come in," John said, speaking on the intercom phone.

Si came up in the lift from the basement carrying the envelope.

"Oh, you have cleared up."

"Yes I thought we could sit in something more comfortable."

"Here it is," she said, holding out the A5 white envelope for John to have a look at.

"There is something else I forgot to mention. The tenant of 18 Squirrels Chase drives a black Ford Focus, you know Fred saw a black car coming out of the lane on New Year's Day."

"Now, Si, don't let's get ahead of ourselves. How many black cars do you think there are on the road?"

"No, well I thought I should mention it." She curled up with John on the sofa their bodies entwined and shoes off. John was trying to have a careful look at the envelope between pecks on the cheek from Si.

"Hey, this cannot have been a circular. It's from the Land Registry and it is dated 18th November 1999. I wonder why they were writing to Peter at this address in November?"

"I don't know. Surely they would normally write to the owner at the owner's address?"

"Yes that's right. It is odd, I grant you, but not something we can go to the police with. We need to know a bit more about what is going on, first. I will speak to the Land Registry tomorrow. I know them quite well. They are based in St Annes-on-Sea, not far away."

"Okay, well I guess I had better go. It doesn't sound as though there is much in all this, I just wondered."

"No, you were quite right to wonder."

Having packed up all the frozen food again, Si left John after another amorous snog on the doorstep, and went back to the farm to deliver the food to her mother. It was nearly half past nine when she got home.

"Si, is that you?"

"Yes, Mum."

Ann and Sandra appeared in the kitchen and Sandra came out to Si's car to help unload the numerous plastic bags containing all the shopping Si had acquired.

"How much do I owe you, darling?"

"No that's all right, Mum."

"No, I insist, I am not having you paying for the food."

"It's quite a lot, £63.62."

"Can I give you a cheque? It's just that I haven't been out for ages and certainly not to do shopping or to the bank."

"Yes, Mum, that will be fine."

Ann wrote the cheque and the girls helped stack the food away in its various places and the deep freeze.

"I'm tired. I think I will go over to the flat now if you don't mind, Mum."

"No not at all. Sleep well, Si."

Sandra was a night person but not good at getting up in the morning. Sandra stayed with her mother until gone midnight and then she, too, returned to her flat.

21.01.2000 Friday

"You will never guess what has just happened, Audrey."

"No George, what has happened?"

"They are really cheeky these people. I don't know who they think they are. They seem to think they own the place, these young people these days."

"George, what are you talking about?"

"I was just opening the drive gate when a car reversed hard into our drive, off the lane, and then drove off in the other direction."

"Oh, that? People use our drive on a regular basis to turn round. It's happened to me lots of times before."

"Huh, the cheek of it!"

"Has the paper come yet George?"

"No, not yet. We are earlier this morning because you said you wanted to be in Chester at the shops before the crowds got there."

"Yes I know that, but I just wondered if it had come."

As she was speaking, she heard the sound of a police siren, or possibly an ambulance as the vehicle sped down the lane. A few moments later another one sounded and then another.

"What on earth is going on?"

"How should I know? I have been sitting here eating my breakfast, minding my own business. The only time I have been out was to open the drive gate and that whippersnapper came and backed into our drive."

"Very well, I suppose we shall hear what it is all about in due course."

"Yes, I suppose so."

They tidied the breakfast things away, put on hats and coats, locked the house, started the car and prepared to drive off to Chester. Further down the lane they passed a police car with its blue light flashing, but that was all there was to see. There was nothing to indicate what had happened.

"No. I am not."

"What do you mean?"

"In case you ask, I am not going to stop and ask the police what has happened."

"It never crossed my mind that you would."

"Audrey, how could you be so two-faced? You would love to know."

"Colin?"

"Yes, Mr Whiteside."

"Did you arrange to get the Escort scrapped?"

"Yes, boss, they may be here today for it or possibly Monday."

"Okay, if you can get it shifted today, that would get it out of our way for the weekend. Can you take the plates off and the tax disc and let me have them, please."

"Yes, boss."

Colin decided that he had better do that right now, as when the day got going something else would take priority and the car would disappear to the scrap, with the plates on. Strange, he thought to himself, the engine is warm and the headlamp on the near side is broken. Colin didn't recall that it was broken when it came back from Duggie.

"Here are the plates for the Escort, boss, and the tax disc. Did you drive it this morning?"

"Yes. I took it home last night just to see what it was like. My decision to scrap it is a correct one. It drives like a brick."

Colin decided not to mention the broken headlamp. If the boss had broken it, fine, and it was off to scrap anyway, so what the hell?

John was busy first thing with routine matters, post and general correspondence, when he remembered at about eleven o'clock that he needed to ring the Land Registry. He spoke to a very helpful clerk but he got nowhere, the request had to be in writing. Yes, a fax would do. John sent off a fax explaining he was the solicitor acting for Peter Wall and that he was just checking, if and when, the registered address of the owner of 18 Squirrel Chase, Chester had been changed. Furthermore, were there any charges on the property? If so, when were they registered?

John was quite surprised to receive a fax back by three in the afternoon. The fax did not go into detail, but it did confirm that the address of Mr Peter Wall for the property had changed on November 24th 1999 to the property address, at the personal request of the owner. Also, a charge had been registered online by the Halifax Bank, for a first charge on the property for the sum of £100,000.

Very interesting, thought John. I wonder why Peter did this and what has happened to the £100,000? Perhaps it was the money he used for the deposit on the land, but he managed to persuade the bank to take a charge on the land and not the houses, so he was already the owner of the land by the time this charge was registered. Very strange, what on earth did he do with the money?

"Sarge, I was wondering if you had any further thoughts on that sample of blood and oil Forensics found on the Land Rover from Long Acre Farm. They want to know if they should send it to London for analysis."

"I really can't think why we will need it, but I suppose if we haven't checked as best we can all the evidence we have available, the rule book could be thrown at us at some future date. Have Forensics been on about it?"

"Yes, Sarge they rang me just now."

"Okay, tell them to send it off and let me know when they have it back."

"Very well. Did you hear what happened this morning?"

"No Tarrant, I didn't. What's on your mind now?"

"It's the farm worker from Long Acre Farm, he got knocked off his bike first thing this morning."

"He probably wobbled into the path of a car."

"Traffic says it looks like a hit and run."

"Hit and run? Why didn't you say?"

"Well, I wasn't sure if it would be of interest."

"It most certainly is. Why would anyone want to do him harm?"

"I don't think there is any evidence to suggest that it was deliberate sir, it is probable the driver took fright and drove off."

"Not a very charitable thing to do, to leave someone hurt in the road."

"How's the cyclist?"

"He's in the Countess of Chester Hospital now, apparently not very well."

"Okay, get down to Traffic and see what you can find out. Let me know what you find."

"Okay, Sarge."

"Detective Sergeant Evans speaking, can I help you?"

"Yes. I am the manager of the Halifax Bank, formerly the Halifax Building Society. I am sorry to bother you Sergeant, but I have a rather unusual request."

"And, what is that?"

"Well, a new customer opened an account with the internet bank and has received into his account today £100,000 as the result of getting a mortgage on a house he owns."

"Well, that's what you do isn't it? There is nothing unusual about that, is there?"

"There is when the customer wants to withdraw the money out in cash!"

"Blimey. What is he going to do with all that cash?"

"Exactly. His explanation is that he is starting a car sales business and he has to buy stock. As he is new, his suppliers of second hand cars will only accept cash."

"I suppose that isn't all that unusual."

"No, I suppose not. I just thought the withdrawal of that amount was rather out of the ordinary."

"Well if it's his money and he wants it in cash, then there isn't much we can do."

"Very well. I just thought you should know."

"You really should go through the proper channels and advise SOCA. Well, just give me some details for the record, so if anything goes wrong, we will have some information to go on. What's the customer's name?"

"It's Peter Wall."

Evans nearly fell off his seat at this revelation. This has to be the most amazing coincidence, surely?

"Are you still there, Sergeant?"

"Yes I am. Please continue, I need his age and address."

"His address is 18, Squirrels Chase, Chester. He says he is fifty-six years old."

"How long has he lived at the address given?"

"Sorry, I don't know. That would be something that would have been handled by the mortgage side of Halifax."

"Mm, well what I would like to do is this..."

Evans went on to explain to the manager what he wanted to do, and how the manager was to help in this arrangement. The most important part was that they should use an interview room to hand over the money, half of which was to be handed over on Monday 24th January, the rest on Thursday 27th, and the day of Peter Wall's inquest. Evans explained that he didn't want to apprehend Wall on Monday, as he had no reason to do so, but may very well do so on Thursday. Evans would have a man at the branch of Halifax in Chester on Monday to recover the evidence and the CCTV tape.

DC Tarrant was tasked with attending the Halifax on Monday to carry out the first part of the exercise. Evans had not told the manager of the Halifax why he had suddenly become so interested, but the detective's nose has certainly smelt something very suspicious.

"Caroline, can you get Parry's the accountants on the phone for me, please?"

"Tom Hastie. Can I help you?"

"Yes, it's John England of Bennett and Bennett solicitors in Chester. I am acting in a rather complex estate where it would seem as though the deceased has committed suicide, and there are rather complex option agreements in place in the shareholders' agreement regarding the business and the property. I need someone who knows company accounts well and will be able to help my clients put some valuations on the business. We are already getting the property valued."

"I would be only too pleased to help, what do you want me to do?"

"Well nothing just now, I have a meeting with my clients this evening and I wanted to recommend someone to act for them, so I assume I may put your name forward?"

"Yes of course. That would be very kind of you."

"No problem, I will be back to you probably on Monday."

"Thank you John, look forward to hearing from you."

The afternoon rolled on and, as promised, John left the office early fully prepared for the meeting with his clients at Long Acre Farm. John arrived at about a quarter to six. Si was already there; Sandra was on the last minute.

"The traffic just gets worse, sorry I'm on the last minute everyone."

"Don't worry, Sandy, there really is no time pressure on this meeting, you are the client after all."

"Yes it's easy to forget. I must say, the more I travel to Liverpool every day, the more disenchanted I become with the journey, and the more I keep thinking I should work closer to home."

"Would anyone like a drink, tea, coffee or alcohol?"

"Thanks, Ann, but I will just have a glass of water please."

"Girls, any requests?"

"No thanks, Mum. In fact I will join John with water."

"Good idea, Si, I will too."

"Well, I'm going to have a gin and tonic."

"Mum!" They exclaimed together.

"It's my house, my meeting. I feel like becoming a little more relaxed and this will help."

"Okay. I will get you a G and T."

"Thanks, Sandy. Let's go through to the dining room, we just need Frank now."

They all trooped into the dining room and John brought his rather bulging briefcase in with him.

"I am glad we are here together before Dr Stringer arrives, I just wanted to make sure that you are all content with me discussing some rather personal financial details in front of him."

As one, they all agreed they were happy with that. John was ushered by Ann to the head of the table and started to disgorge the contents of his briefcase and make some neat piles of the paper he had brought with him. He had nearly finished this exercise when there was a knock on the back door.

"That will be Frank now."

Ann had hardly got the words out of her mouth when Sandy was up on her feet to go to the back door. Si had found a seat next to John and Sandy was next to Ann who was sitting at the opposite end of the dining room table to John.

After about five minutes, Frank and Margaret had not yet arrived. Ann thought it strange that they were still talking to Sandy in the kitchen; she decided to go and have a look for herself.

"Frank, Margaret?"

Ann realised as soon as she had uttered their names that Sandy was not speaking to the Doctor and his wife, but a lady who she hadn't met before, but clearly had come in a little car, a Mini she thought, and was chatting to Sandy at the back door. As Ann approached the back door she was conscious that the conversation was not a cheerful one.

"Sandy? What's the matter?"

"Mum, this is Mrs Jackson. She lives next door but one to Fred."

"Yes?"

"Well I think we should go in. Mrs Jackson would you like to come into the kitchen?"

"Thank you, yes please."

Once inside, Mrs Jackson, Sandra and Ann all sat down around the kitchen table.

"I am afraid I have some bad news for you, Mrs Wall, as I was just saying to your daughter."

"What has happened, is it Fred?"

"Yes I am afraid so, he was knocked off his bike early this morning, and was taken to the Countess of Chester Hospital in an ambulance."

"Oh, how awful. How is he?"

"I think he is pretty bad, by all accounts, but I thought I should come and tell you as you would be wondering where he was next week. I am just off to see the vicar and tell him."

"That's terrible. Do you know, I have no idea if Fred has any family, a wife or anything."

"No, he lives on his own in the row of cottages just off the main road. You know, if you turn right out of your lane, and then before the main road turn right again, and about half a mile down there are two terraces of workers' cottages, about twelve in all."

"Yes, I know. Is there anything we can do?"

"No, I don't think so. I just wanted to let you know."

Ann couldn't help having a sob, suddenly all the problems of New Year's Day welled up in her and she thought of Fred being really helpful to her, and now he was lying injured in hospital. He probably didn't have the proper lights on his bike and the car couldn't see him.

Just then Frank and Margaret arrived.

"Frank, Margaret, thanks for coming." Sandra went to the back door to let them in.

"Sorry, Ann, Sandra. I was called away to the Countess for a consultation and I was delayed by traffic. Sorry we're late."

"This is Mrs Jackson, Fred Appleyard's next door neighbour, who works here three days a week."

"Next door but one, actually," she said as she bobbed and shook Frank Stringer's hand.

"I see, are you aware that Fred has met with an accident?"

"Yes, Mrs Jackson kindly came round especially to tell us."

"It's because of Fred that I am late, he was a patient you see and the consultant wanted a word with me in view of the seriousness of the case."

"You said 'was' a patient, Uncle Frank."

"Yes, Sandra. I am afraid he was a patient, but no more. He died about an hour ago whilst I was at the hospital."

"Ooh no." Ann began to cry now, as did Mrs Jackson. The hullabaloo in the kitchen and the fact no one had come to listen to what John had to say by now, prompted Si to go into the kitchen to find out what was going on. Frank and Sandra between them gave Si the bare facts. Si then went back to the dining room, to relay the information.

It was clear to John that this news was going to seriously delay proceedings, and as the kettle was prepared for a cup of soothing tea for Mrs Jackson and Ann, Frank decided to join them in having a cup. It was about seven o'clock when Mrs Jackson eventually left to go and see the vicar in Tarporley.

She wasn't far down the road when she saw a yellow sign asking for witnesses of a serious accident to contact the police.

"Shall we try and have our meeting now, Mum, what do you think?"

"Yes, Sandy, you are quite right. We should try and make progress," but there wasn't a great deal of enthusiasm for the meeting ahead.

Once everyone was sat down, Margaret established herself in the lounge with her book and wiped her tears away. John started with his explanation of the state of the Walls' finances as a result of Peter's death.

"I have prepared some documents for you all to save you making notes. Can I stress that there is no requirement to make any decisions now, or in the immediate future. This is simply a meeting where the facts are laid out. All I need to do now is for you to approve the appointment of a new firm of chartered accountants, so that we have the best tax advice and also get someone to review the request from the revenue regarding the tax bill that is overdue. The first document for you to look at is a schedule of assets. You will see it includes the farm, the shareholding in Wall's Civil Engineering Limited, the development land and the four buy-to-let properties."

"It doesn't include the half share of the business premises."

"No, that's true. It's because I have been unable to get hold of Mr Dent to give me a figure to put in here for the total value of the premises."

"Four hundred thousand pounds," chirped in Si. "I went through the valuation with him yesterday, he wasn't in today. I am not sure where he is today, but that was the figure."

"Great, perhaps you can just add in the business premises at four hundred thousand pounds but note it is only a fifty percent share."

There was a degree of scribbling and then Ann requested that John continue.

"Right, the farm has a mortgage and I have prepared another sheet of liabilities. This also takes into account insurance. The farm, for instance, has a value of one and a half million pounds and a mortgage of seventy five thousand pounds. The mortgage is protected by a mortgage protection policy which, unfortunately, is written on a second death basis which means there is no claim possible against that policy. The development land is valued at one million and the two houses associated with it at one hundred and fifty thousand pounds each, giving a total of one point three million. There is a bank facility on the whole thing of one million pounds, except there is no direct charge against the two buy to let properties at Squirrels Chase. There are two other buy to let properties in Chester valued together at three hundred thousand pounds, and they have a buy-to-let mortgage on them of two hundred and fifty thousand each. So, there are a total of borrowings excluding the farm of just over one and a quarter million. In addition, there are the business premises which as Si has indicated are worth four hundred thousand which had a mortgage initially of two hundred and fifty thousand pounds, but that had a twenty year term and now I guess has a sum outstanding of something in the region of one hundred and fifty thousand pounds."

"Why isn't it half of what was originally borrowed, John?"

"Good question, Dr Stringer."

"Oh, John, call me Frank, please."

"Okay, Frank. The answer is that in the early years of a repayment mortgage, the majority of the repayments are to pay off interest and it is only towards the end of the mortgage that the capital sees any significant reduction."

"Thanks. This is all a bit heavy with all this money being owed. What is there on the insurance side of things to try and deal with some of the debt?"

"Well, there is the mortgage protection I have already mentioned and a life policy worth half a million pounds that Peter took out in 1990, which can be claimed in full. Peter also took out in April 1999, a life policy for one million pounds, but if his death is confirmed as being a suicide, then I regret that this policy will not be in play, as it hadn't lasted for more than a year before death. It is a rule now that life policies will only pay out on suicides if the policy has been in force for at least a year. I must also remind you all of the tax liability of two hundred and eighty thousand pounds. There are credit card debts of about thirty five thousand pounds and a small overdraft. So, you will see that there are significant liabilities. The five hundred thousand pound life policy should satisfy the revenue and the other smaller debts and leave a small surplus."

"It's all very difficult as far as I can tell, John. I will have to continue to pay the mortgage and I am not sure how I can do that without any income?"

"Well, that is the next aspect of the matter. There is, as I think most of you know, an agreement in place called a shareholder's agreement which has a number of provisions, most of it standard stuff and it also makes provision for key man insurance. There are two key man insurance policies, one of half a million, which is paid for by the company and for the benefit of the company. It is intended that these funds should stay within the company and pay for a replacement of the deceased partner that is Peter. There is a second policy which is for the personal benefit of the remaining partner and the premium is paid by the shareholders, although in practice the company paid and debited the director's accounts. This was intended to provide some income for the remaining partner, and to allow them to pay off the mortgage. That is an obligation of the remaining partner, so the business premises are mortgage free."

"That's great, but how does that help me?"

"Well it does mean that the premises are mortgage free and the rent is not required to pay off any loans. The Shareholder Agreement does contain some rather unusual options. I need to explain these."

"Does anyone want another drink before John starts off again?"

"Well, as you all seem to be okay I am going to have another G and T."

"Mother!"

"I have had enough shocks for one day Si, so I need a sedative and I would rather have a G and T than Frank's pills."

"You go ahead, Ann. It will do you no harm."

"See, you can't get better than medical advice."

"Okay, John, you press on whilst I pour myself a drink."

"Fine, the options are a bit complex, but they are both the same. In essence, what they say is that on a given event, for instance on the death of a partner, the remaining partner or the estate of the deceased may make, in effect, a bid to buy out the other side. If the bid is accepted then a sale one to the other takes place at the bid price. However, if the party receiving the bid really does want to buy the other party out, they can by buying the bidder's share out at the same price as the bidder placed on the share. Is that clear?"

"No. Not very."

"Well, I appreciate, Ann, it's not the usual method of going on, but in essence let's use the premises as an example. If you want to keep the premises, and we know, thanks to Si, they are worth four hundred thousand pounds, you may be inclined to make a bid of say one hundred and fifty thousand for half the share or even possibly two hundred thousand pounds. This would then show you a profit on the whole deal, if the one hundred and fifty thousand pound bid were accepted, but no immediate profit if the two hundred thousand pound bid was accepted. There is no guarantee however that Roger would accept the bid and may well say, 'No. I want the premises, so I will match your bid and will pay you the amount you bid,' so he ends up with the whole building. This is a very likely event if you bid one hundred and fifty thousand, not so likely if you bid two hundred thousand and almost certainly wouldn't happen if you bid, say two hundred and twenty five thousand. You have to remember that in this case the obligation to pay off the mortgage is Roger's, so, by paying over the odds you are getting a good deal. From Roger's point of view, it would cost him in this example, say, one hundred and eighty thousand pounds to pay off the mortgage and two hundred and twenty five thousand to buy half the building which would actually cost him in total four hundred and five thousand. Whereas if he accepts your offer of two hundred and twenty five thousand, he is better off by forty five thousand pounds, once he has paid off the mortgage and the company still pays the rent. So, by making a slightly higher bid than half market value, you may well end up owning the property without any mortgage and the return would be fifty thousand pounds rent on a capital outlay of two hundred and twenty five thousand or the equivalent of about twenty-two per cent. This would give you an income, which is what you don't have at the moment."

"I think I understand now, thanks, John."

"Does the same apply to the company, John?"

"Yes, Frank. That is why apart from tax issues and so on, I want to get a new firm of accountants to look at the books of the firm and help us find the correct value so we can make a bid. I suspect as far as the company is concerned there will be a bit of brinkmanship to see who is going to bid first. There is a time limit on this process and the bids have to be in by the 30th of March."

"What happens if no bids are made by the due date?"

"Well, Si, Sandra and I have discussed this and there seems to be no provision for extending the date, and therefore in the absence of anything to the contrary the status quo will remain. But be warned there would be no provision after this to make the other side sell if you wanted all the business, as the options have to be actioned within ninety days of a specified event, which all relate to the health or death of the other shareholder."

"Why would leaving the status quo be a problem?"

"Well it wouldn't really; it's just that my recommendation would be that a member of the family should take a seat on the board. We have to be ready however, as Roger may manage a bid even if we don't."

"Mm, I have been thinking about the business, because if there was a chance to get involved and take over Dad's place, I think I would be really interested. It would stop me having to travel to Liverpool every day, what would everyone else think of that?"

"Well blow me down, I can't believe you would be interested in doing that Sandy, your father was qualified in the business. It's not just sitting in the office you know, and you would have to deal with Roger, would you be happy to do that?"

"Yes, I am quite used to dealing with difficult directors. As for the business, I am sure I will be able to get to grips with the business. It shouldn't be that difficult and there are plenty of people around who know the technicalities, I can check the legal bits in contracts and tenders."

"Wow. That would be fantastic, Sandy. I would love you to do that."

"Yes, I am really keen if the opportunity presented itself."

"Well then, there seems to be a direction of travel. The firm of accountants I would recommend are Parry & Co, Tom Hastie is the chap there. I have already had a chat with him and he would be pleased to act. Are you happy for me to instruct him?"

There were nods all round, although Frank Stringer didn't become involved in this as it wasn't his to vote on.

"Can I suggest we keep Sandy's thoughts on the business very quiet? We really do not want to let Roger know your plans. I am not sure what his view would be, but in the meantime we should let him think he is going to get an offer for the business, and we will string him along to the bitter end. I will get the accountants in to do a due diligence check, because if there is an issue, or some serious liabilities that have not been disclosed, then you may want to change your mind."

"You are quite right, John. I certainly do not want to inherit a can of worms!"

"Well, I think that was an excellent meeting, thank you very much John. I have a casserole cooking on a low setting in the oven. Let's get ready for dinner. Si and Sandy can you lay the table? I will get the food organised. Frank, could you be a dear and rescue Margaret from her book and open some wine? There are a couple of bottles of red on the side and there is a bottle of Chablis in the fridge."

"What would you like me to do, Mrs Wall?"

"It's Ann, and you've really worked for your supper, so I'll let you off, this time."

"Does that mean you will have me back?"

"I think that is quite likely, don't you?"

John smiled and looked at Si as he did so.

"Smoked salmon, my favourite starter."

"Mine too," added John to Si's comment on the first course, which Ann had prepared and left in the pantry, plated up and ready to go.

"It is really sad to think that poor Fred has been killed, I can't get over it. I was only speaking with him in his special little shed earlier in the week."

"Oh, what was that all about?"

"Well, he wanted to speak to Mum, but I happened to be here. He had a rather fanciful idea that Roger was driving a black car that sped out of the lane on New Year's Day morning, but he was clearly mistaken as Roger was on holiday in Seefeld in Austria. For some reason, Fred thought that he was being suspected of something to do with Dad's death."

"He was a very loyal worker, strangely Roger was asking about him only yesterday. I happened to run into him at Sainsbury's and he was asking about Fred."

"Oh, what was all that about then?"

"Well, it seems as though Roger had a long-standing worker hand in his notice and he was wondering if Fred might be available."

"Sadly, he isn't now."

"No, but I doubt that he would have been keen on giving up working here or at the church."

"No, it leaves me with having to find someone else to help here. I don't think I can manage this place without some help."

"No you definitely can't and you mustn't try, or I will be after you. That's advice from a medic and a friend."

"Frank, you are so good, always looking after me. Coffee, anyone?"

"I think it really is time Margaret and I should be away, thanks Ann. We have a busy day tomorrow, I still have a few patients to keep an eye on and I have a golf competition at noon."

"I hadn't realised what time it was, it's quarter to eleven. Time flies."

After Frank and Margaret had departed, Sandy Si, and John helped Ann clear up and stack the dishwasher.

"Listen, you two," said Ann, addressing John and Si, "why don't you shoot off? Sandra and I can finish off all this. Anyway I want a chat with Sandy."

"Okay, Mum, if you're sure."

"I'm sure, off you go." Si and John went out into the cold, damp night. John went to his car and threw in his briefcase and came over to give Si a farewell kiss.

"Where do you think you are going?"

"Back to Chester, it's where I live."

"You've had far too much wine to safely drive home, and anyway you should go and see your mum and dad in the morning."

"So, what do you suggest?" he said with a broad grin on his face, as if he had no idea what was in Si's mind.

"You know very well, the heating is on. Let's go in and be together on our own for a bit."

Si put a CD on the hi-fi and when the kettle boiled made two cups of hot chocolate, which John was not expecting. They kicked their shoes off and snuggled up on the settee.

"Hot chocolate? Long time since I have had one of these."

"I've been checking. It's what all skiers should drink after a day on the slopes."

"Mm, it's very mellow and really great at this time of night."

"What did you think of Sandy's idea of taking over Dad's place in the businesses?"

"Well I didn't expect it, but I see no reason why she wouldn't make an excellent MD."

"No, thinking about it, I'm sure she would do well. She has got me thinking as well."

"Oh yes, and what's that?"

"Well something has got to be done with Dad's land; it's ten acres of residential development land. I could run a company that could develop and sell the houses."

"What are you two like? Budding entrepreneurs."

"There is no reason, John England, why two women cannot turn their hands to running a business."

"No, no I agree. I was just amused at the prospect."

"Well, you will see. I will make you laugh on the other side of your face," as she trailed off, John pulled her closer and they embraced. He still couldn't believe his luck at meeting such a beautiful, intelligent and hard working-girl as Si.

There followed what might reasonably be described as a modern version of the dance of the seven veils, except no veils were in use. They gradually undressed one another, laying a trail of clothing leading to the bedroom where they fell onto the bed in one another's arms with their naked bodies entwined.

They were not affected by the fact it was winter and the heating had turned itself off. Their bodies were on fire, John was in a trance with this wonderful, sexy loving, and seductive girl in his arms. One minute underneath him, the next on top of him, riding him as if she were some international show jumper, except she had no need to remember the course: she knew where she was going.

Eventually, as they were both exhausted, they pulled the bedclothes over the top of them, cocooning themselves in a warm embrace. They both slid effortlessly, like two babies, into a trance-like sleep.

"So, what made you come up with the idea of running Wall's, darling?"

"I really don't know, it was on the spur of the moment. Maybe it was because I was so pissed off with my journey home, but I see a real opportunity to do something for myself rather than working for someone else."

"I think it's great. Your father would be very proud of you, you know that?"

"I would hope so, but I am not thinking of doing it for that reason. It's just that I see a real opportunity and I want to take it, Mum."

"That's great, I hope it works out. You deserve it darling."

"Thanks, Mum, I will try not to let you down."

"I need to try and find someone to help me here on the farm. Without Fred, or someone like him, I just cannot see how I can manage this place."

"Don't worry about that now, Mum, fortunately grass isn't growing just now. We should think of poor Fred, being knocked off his bike. I wonder who did it."

"I don't know, Frank didn't say did he?"

"No, he made no mention of it."

"I will pop in and see the vicar tomorrow to see if we can help in any way with the funeral arrangements."

"That's good of you, Mum. Do you feel up to going into Tarporley now?"

"Yes. I feel as though I need to get out and about a bit and it would be good to go into the village and see the vicar."

"Okay, I'm not sure what I am doing tomorrow. I may in fact go into Chester and have a snoop around the outside of Wall's. It's been ages since I was there, and I need to have a look at the place."

"Yes, good idea. I'm off to bed now, darling. I really do feel tired now."

"That's good, night, Mum."

"Put the Yale on the back door on your way out."

"Yes. Night, night."

22.01.2000 Saturday

"Hi, Mum."

"Hello, Sandy. You are up early."

"Yes, I couldn't sleep very well. I have a lot to think about following the meeting last night. The prospect of running Wall's has made me really excited. I just can't stop thinking about it. I just have very little knowledge of the actual job, so I need to go to Waterstones in Chester to try and find some books on the subject."

"Have you had a look on the internet?"

"No, that's a good idea. I will have a rummage around there to see what I can find."

"Have you had breakfast?"

"Yes, thanks, mum. I see the lovers are still not up and about."

"Yes, I am really pleased for Si. She seems so happy and comfortable with John, he is a really nice chap."

"Yes he is. I think he is a good all round solicitor as well."

"What has happened to your George?"

"I don't know. We spent New Year's Eve together, but I have heard nothing since."

"No spark there then?"

"Sorry, Mum, I don't think so."

"I am going to go to Tarporley village this morning to have a chat with the vicar. I thought I would give him a ring to see if it was convenient for me to call round. I think I had best leave it until nine before I phone him."

"Yes. I don't know what time vicars rise."

"Oh Sandy, you are funny."

"Well if you're sorted, I'll shoot off to Chester before the weekend traffic builds up."

"All right darling, have a good day."

Sandy drove out of the yard and rattled the cattle grid, just as John and Si were half awake. The rattle acted as an alarm clock.

"What time is it?"

"It's just ten to nine, and what's your hurry this fine Saturday morning, Mr Solicitor?"

John was not able to reply. No sooner had Si uttered those words, they were deep in an embrace, which lasted for what seemed like ages.

"Look we have lots to do. I should pop and see Mum and Dad so let's get cracking."

"Very well," said Si, as she stretched her naked body across the covers that John had pulled down over the bed. He couldn't help but admire this beautiful female frame that looked so alluring, and yes, downright sexy as she squirmed to get out of bed.

Standing by the bed, she gave John one last kiss before beating him to the shower.

"Ahh beat you!"

"Mm, so you have, and I wanted a shower."

"Well come and join me."

So, he did. They embraced under the warm running water and soaped one another all over, which inevitably led to them having sex again, but this time standing in the shower.

"God, you are gorgeous, I could eat you."

"I love you too."

They exited the shower, spilling water all over the bathroom floor, dried one another before a degree of common sense took hold, and they dressed. John had dressed down for the meeting the night before, so he was suitably attired with a blazer and grey trousers for a Saturday. Si decided on jeans and a fluffy polo neck sweater, but it didn't seem to matter, John thought she looked fantastic in anything she chose to wear. Come to think of it, he mused to himself, she looks fantastic without clothes as well.

"Penny for your thoughts."

"What makes you so sure I was thinking about anything?"

"It was the way you were looking at me."

"I was thinking how wonderful you look this morning with your sparkling eyes and glowing skin."

"You flatterer. Breakfast?"

"Yes, please. That would be good."

"Fry-up or cereal?"

"No. Just cereal please, I am still digesting your mum's excellent meal last night."

After breakfast and a quick tidy up in the flat, they emerged and went over to the farm.

"Hi, Mum."

"Hello, darling, John. How are you two this morning?"

"We are just fine thanks."

"Have you had breakfast?"

"Yes, thanks, Mum."

"I have just phoned the vicar and I'm going to see him at about eleven this morning. Would you like to come into Tarporley with me?"

"Well, we're going to see my mum and dad anyway," said John. "Can we cadge a lift and then perhaps we could meet up for lunch at The Swan?"

"That would be excellent John, what a good idea."

"My God! Who is this turning in our driveway now?" George England exclaimed as a Range Rover arrived at the front of the Old Rectory and performed a total circle ready to exit the drive. George was on his way to the front door to have a word with the driver but, as he opened the door, he was surprised to see John and Si getting out of the Range Rover, heading for the front door.

"Morning, Dad, did we surprise you?"

John and Si turned to wave goodbye to Ann.

"Who is that?"

"That's my mum."

"Oh, Si, why on earth didn't you invite her in for coffee?"

"She is just off to see the vicar, but we are meeting her for lunch at The Swan. Would you and Mum like to come as well?"

"Hang on, let me have a chat with your mum, she may have something on the go for lunch. Audrey? It's John and Si."

"Hello, you two. How good of you to pop in, ever since John has met you, Si we see more of him than we ever used to!"

"Oh, Mum. That's not fair."

"Audrey, they have asked us if we would like to join them at The Swan for lunch. Mrs Wall will be there as well, she has gone to meet the vicar now."

"That would be lovely, yes please."

Sandy had parked her car round the corner from Wall's premises in Sealand, an industrial estate on the outskirts of Chester. She was walking around the perimeter fence to weigh up the whole complex. As she was approaching the main gate a blue BMW drove up and looked as if it might ram the gates. Instead the driver got out and unlocked the gates and opened one side, just enough to let the car in. The driver was just about to get back in the car when he saw Sandy staring at him, he recognised her immediately.

"Hello. What are you doing here?"

"Well, I was in Chester and it is a long time since I saw Dad's business, so I thought I would stop by and have a look."

"Would you like to come in? It's Sandra, isn't it?"

"Yes, Roger, spot on. Yes I would love to come in, and have a look round if I may?"

"Of course. It's part yours or your family's anyway."

Roger drove his car into the compound and parked it in front of the office building. He got out and unlocked the front door of the office, went inside and turned off the alarm.

"I will just lock the gate in case anyone takes the opportunity to get in."

"Okay. No bother, I will hang on here."

"Go in, it's cold out here and the alarm is off in the office."

Sandra went into the office. The reception area in front of the stairs was a typical man's idea of how a reception should be. A basic desk with a phone and computer screen, dark terrazzo tiles on the floor in that irritating pattern supermarkets have and gloomy decorations darkened by the fumes from the countless cigarette smokers that must come in and waited to be seen. There were some rather uncomfortable-looking chairs for visitors, a small table with a dying, if not already dead plant of indeterminate species, and some out of date trade journals.

"Sorry, I always like to keep the place secure when I am here on my own."

"Oh yes, I fully understand. It makes sense, there are so many people who would take advantage of the opportunity to pinch something if they thought they could get away with it."

"You are quite right, there are too many people on the fiddle or dealing in criminal activity. Many get away with it because the police are not up to full strength and simply cannot deal with everything."

"So, this is where Dad worked?"

"Yes, when he was here. This is the office building, shall I show you round?"

"Yes please."

Roger led the way.

"Let's start at the top," he said and he led the way up the flight of stairs to the landing, pointing out the loos and the kitchen on the way.

"This is my office, and in the middle here is Christine Frank's office, she has been with the firm as long as I have. At the end here, is your dad's office, which also doubled as a boardroom."

"My word! I never expected to be in here this afternoon." A small tear trickled down Sandra's cheek and her voice cracked up.

"Are you all right?"

"Yes. Sorry it's silly of me. It's only an office but it was Dad's and that is very special to me."

"Well, don't upset yourself. Let me show you round the rest of the premises and then perhaps you would like to come back here and have a look at your father's personal things, and you may want to take some home with you?"

"Yes. That might be a good idea."

Down the stairs again, Roger led the way through to the accounts office, pointing out the toilets and small canteen-cum-kitchen, then through estimating and purchase departments, to the outside. "This is the workshop, where we repair and maintain machinery and lorries used in the business."

"I see, and it has big doors to the yard. I see someone is garaging a car in here."

"Yes, ahem! That was used by an employee who has just left, in fact it is about to be scrapped, as it is in a very poor state. It's time is up and it isn't worth spending any more money on it."

"I see, thanks."

They returned to Peter Wall's office and Sandra had a good rummage in the desk drawers and in the cupboard by the boardroom table. There were a few family pictures and her father's diary, which she thought she would take, but the rest was paper work associated with the business. She then opened the filing cabinet behind the desk, strangely there was very little in it. However, a book on the practice and methods employed in civil engineering caught her eye, and it was signed by the author, a fellow chartered surveyor who had at some point clearly given it to Peter Wall.

"Roger?"

"Yes, Sandra, have you finished?"

"Well, I have found these few items. If it's all right with you, I would like to take Dad's diary, the family photos and this book, which seems to have been presented to him."

"No problem. If you ever want to come in again, please just give me a ring. Here is my card, it has my direct line and mobile number on it."

"Thank you Roger, you are very kind."

Sandra decided to drive into the centre of Chester to go to Waterstones, and then get something to eat.

"Hello, Sandy, how are you keeping?"

"Hello, Lizzie. Long time no see."

"Yes, I was at the do at The Grosvenor on New Year's Day but I have not caught up with events since, other than the usual gossip and what has been in the papers. I was so sorry to hear about your father."

"That's kind of you, Lizzie. Yes, it's been a traumatic time and it isn't over with yet. We have the inquest next week and then all the legal stuff that will follow."

"I'm so sorry, Sandy."

"Are you at a loose end, Lizzie?"

"Well, not exactly but what have you in mind?"

"I just fancy having a chat with someone who isn't family, if you know what I mean? How about lunch?"

"No problem, I would be pleased to help if you feel it would be helpful?"

"How about the Bistro at The Grosvenor? We can have a bite to eat, a glass of something and a chat."

"Fantastic. Let's go."

"Much to Sandy's surprise Lizzie linked arms with her and they strolled off down towards The Grosvenor for lunch.

"Hi, Mum, we are over here."

"Oh good, you have got a big table."

"Yes, let me introduce you to Mr and Mrs England," both of whom stood up as Ann approached.

"Please do not stand, sit down everyone, you make me feel like the Queen."

"Please, call me George, and this is Audrey, my wife."

"Yes, and I am Ann."

"Great, what can I get everyone to drink?"

John took the complex order that only changed a couple of times when people decided to join others in wine instead of the multitude of drinks they originally had chosen. Si went to the bar with John to help carry the order back to the table.

"Those two seem to have hit it off."

"They do, Ann. We are very pleased John has found a girlfriend rather than just playing the field, as they do."

"Yes, I have the same feeling about Si. John has been such a tower of strength to us recently and I am sure he has been a real help to Si in dealing with her grief."

"One bottle of Chablis, five glasses and some water are on the way. Here are the menus for lunch."

"Mm, thanks, Si. That looks good."

"There are some specials on the blackboard but they look more appropriate for dinner."

Lunch came and there was much chatter between the assembled company, with Si and John explaining their forthcoming skiing trip.

"How did the visit with the vicar go, Mum?"

"Fine thanks, darling. He will hold a service for Fred and then I gather Fred's wish was to be buried in the churchyard. But, as it was Fred who was the church sexton, they have to find a replacement at short notice, which is not easy. They hope to get someone from Chester to come down to help. I have said that as Fred worked for us for a long time, I would be pleased to help with the cost of the funeral."

"That's really kind of you, Mum."

"Had you heard about this second tragedy, Dad? Fred Appleyard, who worked at Long Acre farm, was knocked off his bike and died on Friday morning."

"No I hadn't. Although I have seen the board out for witnesses, I had no idea what had happened."

"There appears to be more to it than I had first thought. The vicar told me, in confidence, that the police thought Fred had been knocked off his bike and then the car had come back and ran over him again."

"How dreadful, that is clearly not an accident. What happened? Did the car reverse over him or something?"

"No, the police seem to think that the car drove off and then turned round and then, on their way to the A49, drove over Fred again in the opposite direction."

"Good Lord! Why on earth would anyone do that?"

"I don't know, but clearly whoever has done it wanted Fred out of the way because he knew something or had crossed someone. This will be a tricky one for the police, I suspect, and another inquest."

"Do you think there will be an inquest, John?"

"Yes, sure to be. A suspicious death requires that an inquest is held in every case."

"So, the police think a car came down the road towards the village and then turned round, and then went back and ran him over again?"

"Yes, that's what the vicar said."

"Well that's very strange, because first thing on Friday morning, as I was opening the gate to go to Chester with Audrey, a car backed into our drive from the road at high speed, as bold as you like, and sped off. Do you think he could be connected with this?"

"Dad, if that's what happened, you must speak with the police. That could be important evidence for them."

"Do you think so?"

"Yes I do. If you like, we can come home with you and if the police want to send someone round I will stay with you whilst you make a statement."

"Oh goodness. What are we involved with now?"

"Don't worry, Mum. It is essential Dad makes a statement, as the information he has could be vital in trying to catch the person who killed Fred."

"Well whatever next. Look, let me get the bill."

"Under no circumstances, Ann. Si and I will get the bill." John stood up and went to the bar and settled up.

"We will see you at the farm later, Mum, after we have dealt with the police interview, if that is what is to happen."

"Okay, see you later."

Ann left and went back to the farm in her Range Rover, whilst George and Audrey gave John and Si a lift back to the Old Vicarage and George phoned the police.

"Very well, sir, I will have a police constable come and take a statement from you shortly. As it's a Saturday afternoon, we are a bit stretched as Chester is playing at home and I have a lot of officers on football duty."

"Very well then. We shall wait for the constable to appear, we shall not be going out again today."

"It could be ages before the police arrive, I am sure there is no need for you two to stay."

"Well, we are more than happy to hang on if you prefer?"

"No, no. It's only a simple statement after all. All I saw was a dark red car with, what I think was a Welsh CCP registration plate, back into the drive just as I was opening the gate. I am glad I did open the gate as I think he would have run into it had I not done so."

"Okay, Dad. If you are quite happy to be interviewed without me then, so be it. I will be at the farm with Si, so if you want me I am only a few minutes down the road, just give me a ring."

"Okay, son, I will. Thanks you two for a lovely lunch. It was nice meeting your mother Si, I hope she is not too badly affected by the tragedy of Fred's death."

"No, I am sure she will be fine Mr England."

"George."

"Oh yes. Sorry, George and thank you Audrey. See you again soon I suspect."

John and Si set off to walk back to the farm.

"Did you know there was a short cut over the fields and we can get to the farm that way?"

"No I didn't, but let's do it."

"Fine, I am not sure my shoes are up to it, but what the hell."

They climbed over the stile with the wooden finger post buried in the hedge indicating 'Public Footpath'.

They skipped hand in hand over the rather soggy grass towards Long Acre Farm. They went by the copse, up the hill to the old oak, where Si pointed out to John where the cable had been tied around the tree. In a rather less jolly mood they walked down to the farmyard, hand in hand.

"Hello, Mum."

"Hello, darling, John. You two are back sooner than expected, come in."

"No we won't. We have very dirty shoes and wet feet as we have come over the fields."

"I see. You must be daft, don't catch your death of cold. Get some dry shoes and socks on!"

"We will. We'll be in the flat if needed."

"I said I would go back to Dad's if he felt he needed me there. The police do not think they will get an officer there to take a statement for some time. They're all on football duty this afternoon."

"I see. Well, if you are going out just give me a shout will you, before you go? I will be staying in this evening."

"Okay, Mum, will do. See you later."

John and Si went back to the flat and decided that after the walk, they were cold and damp. They decided to have a shower and put John's shoes and socks on the radiator to dry. It seemed irresistible to both of them to avoid a joint shower again. No one was keeping a check of time, but they probably were in the shower for a good twenty minutes. Fluffy towels and a cuddle in the bedroom, and then on the bed seemed to be a suitable place to be whilst socks and shoes dried.

"Mum. It's Sandy."

"Hello, darling, are you all right?"

"Yes I'm just fine. I went to the yard and I met Roger Whiteside there, who kindly showed me round and I have collected some of Dad's things from the office."

"Well what a coincidence, I hope you didn't let on what we were planning?"

"No, of course not."

"Good, and he didn't suspect anything?"

"No, not at all."

"Good. I have some bad news regarding Fred. He has died, as you know, but he was the subject of a hit and run, it's possibly murder."

"Oh no, how awful! Are you okay, Mum?"

"Yes darling, I am fine. The vicar was very nice to me and I have had a lovely lunch with John, Si and John's parents at The Swan."

"That's good, I wasn't planning on coming home tonight. I have met a friend and we thought we might take in the pictures and go for a meal, and then I will stay in Chester and return tomorrow."

"That's fine. Glad you have found some company."

"Yes it's good, see you tomorrow."

"Come on, snoozy, it's time to get going. I really need to go back to the apartment as I'm beginning to get tired of these clothes."

"Oh, you poor old thing."

"Well, it was Friday morning when I left and I really would like a change despite the fact I am well showered!"

"Yes well, do you want me to come or shall I stay here with Mum?"

"No, you sausage! Of course I want you to come, let's go and we shall decide what to do this evening later."

"Okay. I need to change my clothes again, where shall we be going? Do I need to be smart?"

"You could wear anything, and go anywhere without a problem."

"Mm, well I need something other than these old jeans and T-shirt."

"Well yes, some knickers and bra might be a good place to start!"

"Mum. John and I are just going now, we may stay in Chester tonight."

"All right, darling, you might see your sister, she is there with a friend tonight as well."

"Oh. Who?"

"She didn't say."

"Oh great. Well, we will be back tomorrow, I will phone you in the morning."

Purdy wagged a friendly tail and stayed with Ann in the kitchen, as the two of them departed to Chester in John's Porsche.

23.01.00 Sunday

"Lizzie, can I use some shampoo?"

"Yes, of course you can darling."

Sandy disappeared into the shower cubicle of Lizzie's bathroom. Lizzie's flat was not as grand as John's as it was in a converted old house in the city centre. It was full of character and so convenient for everything. You didn't have to try very hard to have a good time in Chester. Lizzie's flat was so close to the centre that you could roll back into it after an evening out. It was an interesting building, made out of red sandstone with a small turret on one corner. It was strictly the top floor of an end terrace, but as it was an end terrace, there were no neighbours on one side, and the bedroom was on that side, so no noise emanated from one property to the other. It was in a quiet back street, yet in minutes you were in the hustle and bustle of the city centre.

Sandy had not realised that she could have feelings for a girl in the same way she had for a boy, but last night was a revelation. She had believed that Lizzie was a man's girl and that she had no feelings for the same sex. In fact, it transpired that she really only egged on the guys when she was unable to find a girl to be with. Her lesbian tendencies had escaped all who knew her. Lesbian tendencies were not something Sandy had recognised in herself, either. However, she had really enjoyed herself and was looking forward to spending some more time with Lizzie.

Ann woke early and made herself a cup of tea, then went for a walk up the fields with Purdy. Both of the girls had spent the night in Chester. Alone with her thoughts, she went over the events of the last twenty days or so as she walked up the now infamous hill to the old oak tree.

On reaching the tree, she sat on the large root that protruded and made a low but quite comfortable seat. What had happened to her well-ordered life? Why had Peter taken his own life and left the family so bereft in this way? The complexities of the business, his development activities that he was looking forward to being involved with, the Inland Revenue inspection, the VAT due and then all the other debts.

What would become of the three of them? The girls had their own lives to lead and this was the first day Ann had woken up alone on the farm. Fred has now gone, so there is no one who will be here as a regular feature of her life and of the home Peter and she had built together. Is this where she wanted to stay? Would she be better somewhere else? Perhaps a smaller place in the village?

I really do not want to be here on my own, but it would be wrong to expect the girls to stay here. The flats had been a great success, but as time passes they inevitably will want to move on.

Oh, Peter will not be here to see them married. How terrible! What a terrible thing not to have your father at your wedding. Perhaps I should stay on here until they have all gone away and flown the nest, but then again, there would be grandchildren, and they would love the farm.

"I don't know Purdy, what shall we do?"

Purdy wagged her tail and nuzzled her face into Ann's lap at the sound of her name.

"You were here on New Year's Eve, and early New Year's Day, what was happening that we didn't know? Can you tell me?"

Purdy looked as though she would like to say something, but her secret would always remain with her.

Ann began to sob, and the tears once again streamed down her face. She made no attempt to wipe them away, she just knew that this was nature's way of letting the pain out. Ann believed she would never ever get over this.

Walking down Long Meadow again she realised that a car had come into the yard whilst she was away. It was Frank.

"Morning, Frank. Sorry, I was just having a walk with Purdy."

"I should have let you know I was coming, but I thought I would just pop in and see how you were."

"Oh, Frank that is good of you, I guess I am all right. It's just that I have these spontaneous fits of crying whenever my thoughts turn to the events of the last few weeks. I just do not know what to do, Frank."

"There, there. Let's go inside and have a magic cup of tea." Again, Ann was sobbing as they went inside with Frank's comforting arm around her shoulders. Purdy stayed in the yard and had a good sniff at Frank's car and then had a patrol around the edge of the yard and the outbuildings.

"Sandy and Si have both been in Chester overnight, and it occurred to me that it was the first time I had been alone in the farm since Peter died," Ann said. The tears flooded again.

"Hey. Now you just take off your coat and boots and I will make the tea."

"Thank you, Frank. You are a gem."

It must have been over an hour that Frank and Ann sat in deep conversation in the kitchen, going over and over what had happened and the issues that faced Ann. She couldn't start to think how she would ever get through it all.

The phone rang.

"I will get it. You stay there."

"Hello? Long Acre farm."

Si was surprised to hear a man's voice on the phone, and then suddenly realised who it was.

"Uncle Frank."

"Frank to you, Si."

"Oh, sorry yes. Frank, it's good to hear you've just popped round to see Mum, how is she?"

"She is all right really, we have just been having a long chat."

"I was ringing to ask if Mum needs anything, as John and I can pop to Sainsbury's before we come back early this afternoon."

"I'll put your mother on."

"Hello darling, did you have a good night?"

"Yes thanks, Mum, it was just the two of us, and I wondered if you needed anything from Sainsbury's? John and I can go that way and pick something up before I come home this afternoon."

"Oh, let me see. Some bacon and half a dozen eggs would be helpful."

"Oh, and a loaf – one of their crusty ones, and a jar of coffee. We are getting through quite a bit just now."

"Okay, Mum. I have all that, see you later. Bye."

"Bye, darling."

"Those two have hit it off like nothing on earth. They seem to be very much in love, it's strange how love can flourish in the face of tragedy."

"Yes, it works in mysterious ways, but it is lovely to see."

"I had lunch with John's parents at The Swan yesterday. They are a delightful couple."

"Yes. I have met them both. They are patients, but I couldn't say I know them really."

"Mm, we shall have to see what develops there."

The phone rang again and Frank answered.

"It's Sandy this time Ann."

"No that's fine, you just come back when it suits. John and Si said they would be back sometime this afternoon, bye."

"I am glad Sandy has found a friend, not sure who but I'm sure all will be revealed in due course."

"Yes that's good. Well my dear friend, I really must be going myself, Margaret will wonder what has happened to me."

"Bye, Frank, thank you again for stopping by."

"Bye. See you on Thursday, if not before."

"Oh heavens yes. Okay, bye."

Frank drove out of the yard over the noisy cattle grid, and back home. He could not help reflecting during the short journey on the conversation he had had with Ann.

"Should she stay or move from the farm? What about the girls? If they got married, what about their grandchildren? I think she should become selfish now and do what Ann Wall wants to do, rather than dedicate herself to her family for the rest of her life.

"Damn! I nearly missed the turn for my own house." Frank turned sharply into his drive, he realised he had driven all the way back from Long Acre Farm and had no recollection of the journey at all, he had been on autopilot whilst his mind was elsewhere.

Was this how Peter felt on New Year's Day morning?

"Hi, Mum," came the cheery voice of Sienna as she came into the kitchen. "How are you?"

"I'm fine, darling. Did you have a good time?"

This was almost a silly question, Ann thought to herself, as clearly her youngest daughter was full of beans and had a glow about her that only someone in love can achieve. It would seem as though Si could take on any challenge right now and deal with it.

"Purdy and I have been for a long walk, we have had lunch and I was going to see what was on TV as the day has gone. The day is getting dark already."

"Good idea, John and I are just taking a few things into the flat and will be back shortly."

"Okay. Oh, here is Sandy."

"Just as I was about to have some peace and quiet and put my feet up, the troops return!"

"Hello, Sandy. Have you had a good time?"

"Yes, fine thanks, Mum. I will be over soon, just need to unpack and throw on some other clothes."

Within half an hour Sandy, Si and John had all arrived at the farmhouse, chatting ten to the dozen about what they had been up to. Sandy managed to stop the conversation in its tracks when she announced she had been out last night with Lizzie and stayed the night at her place. John for one knew she only had one bedroom with a double bed, so he raised his eyebrows thinking about what might have gone on.

"Lizzie has suggested, if you guys don't mind, that I may like to come skiing in Austria with everyone on the 12th February. Would you mind if I tagged along?"

"No of course not," Si and John responded in stereo.

"Lizzie will need to have a chat with Regent Travel first thing tomorrow, but I would think they could possibly fit you in. The minibus to Manchester Airport is a fourteen-seater, so there will still be plenty of room."

"Great. I will give Lizzie a ring later and ask her if she can organise things."

It was eight o'clock and the phone rang. Roger was a little startled; it never rang on a Sunday night.

"Roger Whiteside."

"I know what you have been up to. Fred told me all about it, and now he is dead. It's nothing to me but I worked for Peter Wall, not you, you bastard."

"Who is this?"

"Never you mind, but if you don't recognise my voice, it is a shame. I have some very influential friends who can sort you out if you cause trouble. Listen to me, I will keep my mouth shut, but I need a share of your windfall, shall we say, one hundred thousand pounds? I need it soon, and you need to bring it to me."

"I have no idea what you are going on about. I'm hanging up."

"No, I know what Fred knew, but you are not going to get me, and I am over the water."

"It's Duggie."

"Maybe, but I have some good friends who are short of work here and can easily visit you if necessary, it can hurt, quite a lot."

Roger was beginning to feel decidedly uncomfortable.

"I think you know nothing, but we should meet."

"I need one hundred thousand pounds. Delivered to Belfast."

"You must be fucking joking!"

"No, I am not. I will be after you if you don't cough up."

"Okay, but why Belfast? I thought you were in Dublin?"

"Yes, but we use euros here. Pounds are more use in the north."

"I don't think you know anything, there is nothing to know!"

"I need it next week so you had better get going!"

"Fuck off."

"I will ring you again to remind you, but I want to see this money soon."

"Go away. This is a try on, there is nothing for you to know."

The phone went dead.

24.01.2000 Monday

"Are you all organised for this afternoon at the Halifax, Tarrant?"

"Yes, Sarge. I have the necessary bits and pieces and also half a dozen bags to bring items back in for Forensics."

"Good. What I also must have is a copy of the CCTV tape. Make sure their machine is working and bring it back with you."

"Yes, Sarge."

"What time is Peter Wall due at the Halifax?"

"Two thirty, sir."

"Right, make sure you are there in plenty of time. Check everything twice and be sure to bring a photocopy of his passport."

"Have you heard the latest, Sarge?"

"No, what have you got now?"

"The farm worker Fred Appleyard, from Long Acre farm, who was run over and killed on Friday morning. Traffic thinks it was a hit and run. Well, they are sure it was now, they have retrieved some evidence from the bike and they believe the car that hit him was dark red."

"Well, that narrows the field I suppose," Evans responded sarcastically.

"That's not all, sir. It seems there is a witness, a Mr England who lives at the Old Rectory. He was opening his gate first thing Friday morning when he saw a dark red car come hurtling backwards into his drive and speed off in the opposite direction, away from Tarporley."

"That could be helpful. Let me have a copy of the full witness statement. I may need to call on Mr England, it depends what I get from the statement. When is the PM on Appleyard?"

"This afternoon, sir."

"Hi, is Michael available?"

"Michael speaking. Who is this?"

"Hi, it's Lizzie. I am one of the John England party going to Seefeld on 12th February."

"Oh yes. I know the booking, I have had to change the accommodation already. Strangely, I have received a fax this morning from the hotel in Seefeld to say that they cannot do a single room for the dates, they have only a twin."

"That's fantastic."

"Oh well, I wasn't expecting that reaction, normally that will cost more for single occupancy."

"Well that's the point, it will not be single occupancy. Sandra Wall will be coming as well. Do you think we can get an extra seat on the plane?"

"I don't know. Can you hold whilst I just check the computer?"

"Okay."

Michael started to key in his agency code to get to the Monarch booking screen and checked to see if there was another seat on the plane to Innsbruck on the 12th February, and he was pleased there was. He was also able to confirm that the return sector had availability, so he reserved it on line.

"Are you still there, Lizzie?"

"Yes. Any luck?"

"Yes, I have the flights held. I will fax the hotel back and tell them it will be for two people, just give me the name of the additional passenger."

Lizzie did as requested and she confirmed that she would call in at lunchtime to pay the full amount for Sandy, as it was so close to departure.

"Sandy, it's Lizzie."

"Oh hi. Any luck?"

"Yes! It's all fixed, I will go and pay at lunchtime for you."

"Just let me know what I owe you and I will let you have a cheque. Thanks so much Lizzie."

"No problem. Can't wait, bye."

"Berry Berry Accountants?"

"Is Andy Hirst available, please?"

"Yes, sir. Who should I say is calling?"

"Roger Whiteside."

"Roger, good to hear from you. How are things?"

"Quite well I hope, Andy, thank you. I just wanted to touch base with you regarding the possible acquisition of the business from the Wall family. I am certain, as ever I can be, that they are going to make an offer to buy the business."

"What makes you so sure?"

"Well I met Sandra Wall, the solicitor's daughter, and the oldest of the two having a snoop round the premises on Saturday. I invited her in and she looked all round the premises, but she didn't say much. She took some of her father's personal effects."

"Mm, interesting. It doesn't however mean they will make a bid."

"No, but I bet they will, they have until the 30th March of course, to do so."

"Yes, I think I will need some thoughts from you on how to play any bid I get."

"Yes. We have already had a chat about this, it will not take me long to advise you, we just need to know what they are going to do."

"Should I have a bid in place in case one doesn't come from them?"

"Yes. That would be sensible, but until you have the money in your bank to make a bid you will be a bit stuck, especially if they accept your bid and you are still awaiting the insurance money."

"I suppose you are right, however the inquest is on Thursday. I hope we shall get a death certificate then, which will mean I can make a claim."

"Very well, let's have a chat at the end of February. By then you should have received the money and that will give sufficient time to formulate any plans."

"Thanks, Andy. I will call you then, bye."

"Good afternoon, sir, can I help you?"

"Yes. My name is Peter Wall. I have an arrangement to collect some money."

"Oh yes, sir, just a moment."

"Mr Wall?" McCullock didn't immediately react, as the voice came from behind him and he was not used to answering to the name.

"Mr Wall!" came the second call, suddenly realising they were speaking to him, and he swung round to be met by a small middle-aged man with glasses and slightly greying hair and a dark grey suit.

"Mr Wall, I am the manager of the branch. In view of the nature of this transaction I will be dealing with you today."

"Very well, that's good of you."

"Come this way please. We have a private interview room here. First things first, can I get you a drink of coffee or tea perhaps?"

"Very kind of you. Could I have a glass of water?"

"Of course."

Gary was beginning to feel the pressure of the moment and he needed some lubrication. The water was delivered and the manager explained the process of taking out such a large sum in cash.

"It is quite unusual for anyone to take such a large sum in cash, but of course it is your money and we are here to oblige."

"Thank you."

"Do you have a copy of your passport and a recent utility bill?"

Gary produced the documents.

"Bear with me a moment whilst I get these copied."

The manager left Gary on his own in the interview room and went to the copier in the back office. He made two copies and immediately handed one copy of each document to Tarrant, who was standing right by the copier. Whilst the utility bill was being copied, Tarrant had a very good look at the passport.

"Here we are, Mr Wall, your original documents back. I have kept copies. Can you please read this waiver, please? It means that I have explained to you the risks involved in carrying around such a large amount of cash and that you are fully aware of those risks and that you will not hold the Halifax liable in any way for any loss however caused."

"I see. No, there is no problem in me signing that, do you have a pen?"

The manager handed Gary a Halifax biro and the document was signed.

"Just the withdrawal slip, for £50,000 that's right, isn't it?"

"Yes, that's correct."

"Just sign here please."

Gary was about to pocket the pen when the manager held out his hand for it to be returned.

"Just a moment, I will get the cash."

The manager retrieved the bundles of notes from the back office and 'Peter Wall' placed them carefully in his small suitcase. The majority of notes were fifty pounds each, which made the haul of cash much easier to manage.

"Thank you very much."

"Are you not going to count it?"

"I don't think I need to, do I?"

"It's a matter for you sir, but the money is all there, I understand you will be coming back for the forty-nine thousand pounds on Thursday 27th January, is that correct? Will it be the same time?"

"Yes that's correct I will be here, thank you."

Peter Wall left the interview room and went out of the door to the car park on the other side of the road.

Wall, or McCullock, was not aware that someone had followed him out of the Halifax. The police officer noted that he had the case with him as he got into his car in the multi-storey car park.

I've done it, thought McCullock It was like taking candy from a baby. I will be able to get a load of gear with this and turn this into a pretty pile in no time.

He left the car park with a grin on his face as wide as a Cheshire cat.

"He got in a dark red Astra, registration CCR546H."

"Okay," said Tarrant. "I have just about finished here, I have bagged the glass, emptied the water, and the pen, and I have the copies of the documents. So it's back to the station for us."

The main police station was a short walk from the Halifax branch in Chester. Tarrant took the pen and the glass straight to the forensic team and asked them to deal with them as soon as possible. A DNA match to something or someone for this unknown Peter Wall would be really helpful, Tarrant reflected. Forensics are really good now, I will need to persuade them to put this lot at the top of the queue.

25.01.2000 Tuesday

John England was in the office early to prepare papers for Thursday's inquest. He decided that if Ann was to give evidence, he needed to ensure that he had all the background information he needed. Preparing the detailed schedule with cross-reference to statements and insurance details, it suddenly occurred to John that Peter had not left a suicide note. This struck John as being somewhat odd as every suicide he had heard of the victim usually left a note. Such a note would be helpful here to assist the inquest and to ensure the suicide verdict.

"Could I speak to Dr Stringer, please?"

"I will see if he can speak to you sir, he is holding surgery just now, and may be engaged with a patient. Who shall I say is calling?"

"John England, I am the solicitor for the Wall family."

"Oh I see, I am sure Dr Stringer will speak to you if he can."

"Mr England, do you mind holding for a moment? Dr Stringer is just finishing with a patient."

"No, not at all, thanks."

"John, it's Frank Stringer here."

"Frank, sorry to interrupt surgery."

"No problem. In fact, there seems to be a gap at the moment, so we can have a chat for a few minutes."

"I have been collating papers and information in readiness for the inquest on Thursday, and it has just struck me that Peter Wall never left a suicide note. I don't know if you have much experience of suicides, but would this be unusual?"

"Good question, John. In fact the same thing struck me the other day. I drove from Long Acre Farm to my house and I nearly missed the turn, it was such a familiar journey that I had managed to drive it without any conscious effort or recollection on my part. I thought to myself that is possibly the sort of state Peter was in when he committed suicide on that fateful day."

"I see what you mean, so you think the suicide was a spur of the moment action?"

"Yes I do, in fact I am sure it was."

"Mm, quite a complex method of death though for an off the cuff suicide, wouldn't you say?"

"Yes, I would. But the mind does very strange things John, and who knows what he was thinking when he decided to end it all?"

"I suppose it was suicide, because, as I am talking to you now, I am finding it very hard to believe that someone on the spur of the moment would go to all the trouble he did."

"You are thinking with a rational mind, John, this was clearly an irrational act. He got there possibly on autopilot as he had done so many times, and the winch cable was handy in the back of the Land Rover, so he did what he did. I bet it didn't take him more than a few moments and the whole ghastly thing was over."

"Yes, I'm sure you are right, thank you for your thoughts and advice. The mind certainly plays tricks with us, sometimes."

"Yes, and from what I can gather, your mind has had a few tricks played on it recently thanks to a Miss Sienna Wall."

John laughed. "You're so right. I have loved every moment of it, in fact my mind is totally fogged with thoughts of Si."

"My diagnosis is that you two are in love, and long may it continue. I must go, John, my next patient has now arrived, cheerio!"

"Bye."

"Sorry to butt in, Sarge, but I have just received the forensic report on the articles I brought back from the Halifax, and it is all very interesting."

"Well don't just stand there lad, spill the beans."

"Well, Sarge, the lab was able to get a good match of DNA from the glass as it had residue of saliva on the rim. The pen was fairly good but not as good as the glass."

"Yes, yes. So what?"

"Well, the DNA has been matched on the police computer database and Mr Peter Wall, who came into the Halifax yesterday, is in fact Greg Mason."

"Greg Mason, that name rings a bell. Have you a photo?"

"Yes, here is a photo from the police computer and also the photocopy passport of Peter Wall. Uncanny isn't it?"

"We certainly have a match here, that is really good police work, but what have we got him for?"

"Well, clearly impersonation and identity fraud."

"Yes, but what else? Where has all this money come from?"

"I don't know, sir. The Halifax might be able to help us here."

"Well, get on the blower and see what you can find."

"There is one other thing, sir."

"Come on Tarrant, out with it, you do like to dramatise everything. Let's be having some facts if that is what you have."

"Yes sir. Well, it was Forensics who gave me the clue, I was having a chat with them about this Peter Wall and explained how a Peter Wall had committed suicide and that they had done the forensics on the Land Rover. Well, they told me they were also working on a connected death, that of Fred Appleyard, and as far as they could tell the car that ran him over was a dark red car, possibly a Vauxhall Astra."

"Are you going soft in the head, Tarrant? You've already told me this once."

"Yes, sir, but I haven't told you that the car Peter Wall or, more correctly, Greg Mason drove was a dark red Vauxhall Astra."

"Is that so? Well, well, well! Now that is very interesting. Let me have the file on the Fred Appleyard case, and I need the witness statement from Mr England in Tarporley. I will go myself and have a word with him. It seems as though he may be a key witness in all this."

"Very well, sir. Do you think Mason could have had any connection with the real Peter Wall's death?"

"Not sure yet, lad, but I wouldn't put it past him, as soon as I have the file, I will be off to Tarporley."

"Mr England?"

"DS Evans here, Chester Police."

"Oh yes, DS Evans. I have given a statement to one of your constables."

"Yes, I know. I have it here in front of me. There have been a few developments and I would like to come and see you and have a chat about the car you saw."

"That would be no problem Mr Evans, when did you want to come?"

"I will be there within the hour."

"Oh goodness me, well yes, that's fine."

"Goodbye. I will see you in an hour."

"Could I speak with the manager please?"

"Who is calling?"

"DC Tarrant of Chester Police."

"DC Tarrant, hello. This is the manager speaking, how can we help you now?"

"I need to know where Mr Peter Wall is," Tarrant stuttered and nearly gave the game away. "I need to know where Mr Peter Wall got all his money from, can you help me on that?"

"Well I am afraid not, the funds did come to us from head office into Mr Wall's account but the circumstances that led to that were dealt with on line, by Intelligent Finance, and only they can help you. If you would like me to guess, he has taken out a mortgage on his house and these are the funds. He cannot have had a mortgage on the house before."

"Can you give me the contact for the IF people? This is urgent and very important."

After about an hour of being passed from pillar to post, Tarrant eventually discovered not only the address of Wall's/Mason's house. Tarrant discovered that Wall/Mason had obtained a mortgage on the house he was in fact renting.

The man at IF had said, "Yes, he applied online for a mortgage. He was able to get a mortgage as he self-certified his income."

"What the heck is that?"

"It's where a borrower confirms what he earns and he certifies it as correct. The bank accepts what he says but charges them another half a percent interest for accepting their assessment of their earnings without the bank making any enquiries."

"Good Lord, how amazing!"

"It is normal for the sort of borrower Mr Wall is, as he is in the car trade and his income is very susceptible to fluctuation."

"So that's normal then?"

"Yes, sir, quite normal."

"Okay thanks. That's fine."

"Mr England?"

"Yes. Are you the police officer who phoned?"

"Yes, sir, I am DS Evans, Chester CID."

"Come in, Sergeant Evans."

They went into the sitting room where George introduced Audrey to Evans and they all sat down – George and Audrey in their favourite arm chairs, Evans on the couch.

"I have read your statement Mr England. Am I correct in believing that John England, the solicitor, is your son?"

"Yes, that is correct. He works for Bennett and Bennett in Chester."

"Good. Now in your statement you say you were opening the gate to your drive. I have had a look at the gate as I came in and I assume you are referring to the farm gate that shuts across your driveway?"

"Correct."

"And according to your statement, you were outside opening the gate prior to leaving for a trip to Chester. Is that correct?"

"Yes."

"The time was?"

"As far as I can tell, it was about half past seven, quarter to eight in the morning."

"Are you sure of that?"

"Well, as sure as I can be. We got up early, as we wanted to get to Chester for the opening of the shops, we left here at about eight fifteen to eight twenty and between that time and opening the gate I had some breakfast of cereal, toast and coffee. We didn't do any washing-up, just put the pots in the dishwasher, and then left."

"I see. Can you recall exactly what happened when the car you mentioned backed into your driveway? I assume from your statement that's what happened?"

"Yes, this car with one man at the wheel."

"You are quite sure there was only one person in the car?"

"Absolutely certain."

"Good, please continue."

"He drove down the road towards us at high speed. I could hear him coming before I could see him. He slammed on his brakes, as he was nearly adjacent to the driveway opening, and slewed the front of the car halfway across the road, so the front of the car was in the opposite carriageway. He then reversed at high speed into the driveway, it was a good job I was opening the gate, he would without doubt have hit the gate at the speed he was going if it had been shut. He then sped away in the direction from which he had come."

"Thank you, Mr England, that's excellent. Do you recall anything else about the car or the driver?"

"Well, the car didn't look all that new, it was a bit dirty."

"Do you remember the colour or make?"

"Oh, yes, it was a dark red colour. I can say that as it was so close to me, and if I am not mistaken he scratched his car on the hedge on the outside of the gatepost as he came back."

"Did he? That is interesting. I may need to get Forensics down to have a look to see if there are any traces of the paint. Please do not touch that area until they have been tomorrow."

"No that's easy, no problem."

"You referred to the driver as a male, why was that?"

"Well he looked male. I have to say, I cannot categorically confirm he was male, it was semi-dark at that time, you understand."

"Yes, is there anything else you recall, like the make?"

"No I don't know the make. They all look very alike, these modern cars."

"Yes, registration number?"

"Ah yes, I did notice that. I'm sorry but I didn't get the whole number but I do recall that it was a Welsh plate, it began with CC."

"Excellent. That is very helpful, do you think the driver saw you?"

"I very much doubt it. He seemed too preoccupied in driving the car around and off again to look around."

"Mr England, you have been very helpful, and the additional information you have provided is extremely valuable."

"I was sorry to hear of the death of the cyclist, it is a terrible thing."

"Yes, but the information you have provided is invaluable. I will have the statement added to with what you have said, and I will get a PC to call for your signature if I may, Mr England?"

"No problem, Sergeant."

Evans left to go back to the station.

"Sergeant Evans?" the radio crackled.
"Yes. Evans speaking."
"It's Tarrant here, sir."
"Yes, Tarrant."
"Have you passed the entrance to Long Acre farm yet?"
"I am just passing it now, should I stop?"
"Yes Sarge."
"What is the issue?"
"I wondered if you could call on Mrs Wall and find out if she knew if her husband had called on, or knew, Greg Mason, Gary McCullock or whatever he was calling himself?"
"Yes, I can do that. And the thinking is?"
"Well sir, there may be a connection with the death of Mr Wall. It's just a thought sir, but if this man has killed Appleyard for some reason, maybe he was the driver of the car leaving the lane on the morning of New Year's Day, and Fred Appleyard might be the only person who could identify him."
"Good thinking, what is it specifically that has made your mind run this way?"
"Well, he has effectively stolen one hundred thousand pounds by way of a mortgage on Mr Wall's property. I don't fully understand yet how this could have happened, but if Mr Wall found out about it, he would justifiably be very angry and would confront the man who had done it."
"I think it is a bit of a long shot, but it is worth a try."

"Mrs Wall? DS Evans, Chester CID."
"Sergeant Evans, please come in."
"I was just passing and I wanted to clear one thing up."
"And what is that?"

"The house your husband owned on Squirrel Chase that was let out to a Mr Mcullock. Do you know if your husband ever met the tenant or had any dealings with him at all?"

"No, I am afraid I don't, but my daughter Sienna would know."

"Really? Why is that?"

"Well, she is a chartered surveyor and works for Dents, and lets and manages the two properties my husband bought on Squirrels Chase."

"I see. I will call on her at Dents then. I am sorry to have troubled you."

"Miss Wall, please."

"Who shall I tell her is calling?"

"DS Evans, Chester CID."

"Oh! Yes, please take a seat for a moment."

"Sergeant Evans, Sienna Wall, would you like to come into my office?"

"Thank you, I need to talk to you about your father's house in Squirrels Chase."

"There are two, both or anyone in particular?"

"Yes, number eighteen."

"Ah yes, Mr McCullock."

"Firstly, can you please give me the details of how he came to be living in this property?"

"Yes. He took a six-month tenancy back in November, I believe. He lives there with his wife and child."

"You know that for a fact?"

"Well no, not for a fact. It's what he told me would happen. At the time he took the tenancy, his wife was with her mother in Coventry with the child."

"Did you ever see the child or wife?"

"No."

"Is he up to date with his rent?"

"That is a guaranteed yes."

"You seem very certain."

"Yes, that is easy because he paid six months rent in advance."

"And how much was that?"

"Four thousand, eight hundred."

"That's a lot of money, didn't you question him where he got it from?"

"I didn't see it was any of my business. He had just started a new job at the Ford dealers as a salesman and he said it would be some time before he would have sufficient income, and his employers would not be able to give him a reference as he had just started. He offered the six months in advance, so it seemed a simple solution to the problem."

"Did your father ever meet him?"

"Yes, I believe he did, it was something to do with noise. I was surprised at that, as normally my dad would have referred that sort of thing to me."

"Would McCullock know where your father lived?"

"Oh yes, the landlord's name and address is on the tenancy agreement."

"I see. Don't landlords expect your address to be on the agreement to make them, as it were, at arm's length from the tenant?"

"No it's the law that a name and address for service of notices on the landlord has to be provided in the tenancy agreement or by separate notice. If you don't do that, the tenant can withhold rent until they have that information."

"I see. You live and learn."

"If McCullock tried to get a mortgage on the property would you or your father know about it?"

"Good Lord, I should say so. It has a registered title and the Land Registry would not allow a registered charge on a property by someone who is not the legitimate owner."

"I see, thank you."

"Do you mind telling me the relevance of these questions, Sergeant Evans?"

"We are just making enquiries at the moment, thank you for your help."

"Tarrant?"

"Yes, Sarge?"

"Get on to the Land Registry, wherever they are, and ask them if they have re-registered the ownership of 18 Squirrel Chase to the name of McCullock recently, and be sharp about it."

"Yes, Sarge."

26.01.2000 Wednesday

DS Evans was sitting at his desk in police headquarters in Chester, trying to make a rational story out of the events of the last twenty-six days. He had been asked to keep the Chief Constable closely informed of developments, as there was a growing alarm in Tarporley at the two violent deaths in the village. Nothing like that ever happened there, and the local population were getting somewhat worried. The Chief

Constable had asked for a report, and then to meet Evans at two o'clock this afternoon to discuss the progress that had been made with the case.

Evans started to work things out on a whiteboard. He found it easier to have these connections, and to set them out in a logical format so that he could see where he was up to.

- The Walls return home and nearly hit a black car in their lane at about two a.m.
- In the early morning of New Year's Day a local businessman, Peter Wall, apparently commits suicide in a most unusual way. He is decapitated by a wire strop whilst the old Land Rover he owned ran down the hill.
- Fred Appleyard tells Tarrant that he thought he knew the driver of the black car which came out of the lane at about half past seven on the morning of New Year's Day. He thought it was Roger Whiteside, but he was skiing in Austria.
- The tenant of 18 Squirrels Chase, Greg Mason alias Gary McCullock alias Peter Wall, somehow managed to get a mortgage of £100,000 on the rented property and has already collected half in cash from the Halifax.
- Greg Mason is a known felon with convictions for GBH and burglary and several warnings about using cannabis. He is suspected of being a small-time drug dealer but so far no proof, but he is on the radar.
- Greg Mason collected the money using a maroon car with index letters containing the letters CC – the index letters recalled by Mr England.

- The PM on Appleyard indicates that he was run over twice, once from behind and then again from the opposite direction over his abdomen.
- The pathologist's report indicated that, in their opinion, this was a case of murder.
- The car Mason used in November when he rented the property was a black Ford.

"Can I speak to Miss Wall please, its DS Evans, Chester Police."

"Sergeant Evans, what can I do for you today?"

"Just one question. Can you cast your mind back to November, when you let the property to Mr McCullock? Do you recall what sort of car he was driving at the time and if possible the make?"

"Yes I can, the make is easy, it was a Ford, and it was black."

"Thank you Miss Wall."

Evans could now return to his wall chart and start making some further progress.

"Sarge?"

"Yes, Tarrant, can't you see, I'm busy?"

"Yes, Sarge, but I have just heard back from the Land Registry."

"Yes? Don't just stand there, lad, cough it out."

"They have never changed the registration of the house to a Mr McCullock."

"Oh?"

"They did, however, get a formal request to change the address for correspondence from Mr Peter Wall at Long Acre Farm, Tarporley, to 18, Squirrel Chase, Chester."

"So, how does that help us?"

"Well, sir, what they did was to change the details of the registration so that they would correspond with Mr Wall at Squirrel Chase. They also confirmed back to Mr Wall at Long Acre Farm that they had made the change in the register."

"I see. So, if Peter Wall received a letter telling him about the change he might have confronted the tenant to find out what was going on."

"The chap I spoke to at the Land Registry, which is in St Annes by the way, said he did recall just before Christmas, shortly after the letters went out confirming the alteration in the register, that a person who said he was Mr Wall, saying he had not authorised a change and what the fuck did they think they were doing? He asked them to change it all back again, but they said they could only do that if they received the appropriate form and the fee."

"Mm, that is interesting. So it is quite probable that Mason/McCullock had been confronted by Wall before Christmas, and Mason, thinking his plan to scoop £100,000 in cash was about to be blown apart because the real owner had been alerted to the change of address of ownership, could have decided to top Peter Wall. If he did that there is no reason why he would not stop at killing Appleyard so as to get away with the crime and one hundred thousand pounds in cash."

"Yes, sir, it does leave the issue of how Mr Wall could have been killed in the way he was without his compliance."

"Well, we have Mason on site watching the house, Mr and Mrs Wall return home very late, and then, when they have gone to bed, Mason goes to the machinery shop for cover, and conveniently finds the sharpening stone by the scythe, and uses it as a cosh."

"Yes, and his luck was in when Wall came over to drive the Land Rover. Mason would have hidden in the back, and when it came to rest at the top of the hill he whacked him on the head with the stone, and the rest we know. He then scarpers a bit sharpish, nearly knocking Appleyard off his bike."

"I will take this to the Chief Constable and then run it across the CPS for their view. I mean the man's got form and he wouldn't stop at this sort of thing. If we are right we need a welcome party for him tomorrow at the Halifax."

"What will we do about the inquest, Sarge?"

"I think we should let that run. We don't want any chance of anyone spotting what we are about to do, or give any hint to Mason that we are after him."

Evans did as he had said, and ran through the scenario with the Chief Constable and the CPS. The CC was delighted with the work of his sergeant and said that if he pulled this off and got a conviction, he'll be in line for promotion.

Evans could hardly wipe the grin off his face, but started to make plans and organise the troops for the following day.

"Ann, it's John England."

"Hello, John. How good to hear from you."

"I hope you are keeping well?"

"Yes, but I'm feeling a bit lonely in this big house, I don't even have Fred for company now."

"I understand. I really rang to see if you would like me to take you all to Warrington tomorrow. It's a bit cheeky, as we would have to use the Range Rover but I thought it would be nicer for the three of you to be together?"

"Oh, John, how thoughtful, that would be great. You can drive it there, no problem. What will you do? Come over in the morning or this evening and stay overnight?"

Ann thought to herself for a split second that it was a silly question as she was virtually certain what the answer would be.

"Well, I haven't spoken to Si yet, but I may very well come over later this evening."

"Good, that is excellent. Well, I look forward to seeing you tomorrow."

"Si, it's John."

"Hello, darling, how are things?"

"Fine and busy, I have just spoken to your mum and arranged to drive her, you and Sandra to Warrington to the inquest tomorrow in the Range Rover."

"That's a good idea. Why don't you come over here tonight? That way, we shall all be here in the morning."

"What a great idea! The thought hadn't crossed my mind," replied John with a great big grin on his face.

"Liar. It was a trap you laid, I know you."

"Well, if you don't want me to come…"

"No, no, that's not what I meant."

"Great, see you later."

"Do you want feeding?"

"Well now you are talking."

"Okay, come on when you are ready. I will prepare something for around eight o'clock."

"Thanks. Bye, darling."

"Bye."

"Tarrant?"

"Yes, Sarge?"

"We need to get organised for tomorrow. I need to go to the opening of the inquest on Peter Wall, and I will have a word with the Coroner beforehand and take him a copy of the report I prepared for the CC. You need to get geared up to prepare a welcome party for Greg Mason, alias Gary McCullock, alias Peter Wall."

"Okay Sarge. We will need at least two PCs and a custody van, and a SOCO team to recover his car, I suspect."

"Yes, you will. I think you will need three PCs and SOCO. You need to make sure everyone is out of sight, including the van. Leave a driver in the van, have the two PCs with you in the Halifax, and SOCO can get into action once you have the keys to his car and know its location. Bring him back here, and when I get back from Warrington later tomorrow we can start to interview him."

"Very well, Sarge, I will get this organised."

"Don't cock this up Tarrant, and make sure he has been through all the business of getting the money and he has it in his possession before you arrest him."

"Yes, Sarge."

"Do you know what you are going to arrest him for?"

"I guess it will be for deception, using a false passport, fraud, obtaining money by fraud and deception, just for starters. I assume you want to put the other charges to him at the station?"

"Yes, that will do to be going on with. You're correct, I do not want him to have any idea that we are on to him for the murders, and I would rather he was not told in the Halifax, because it will be all over the papers and on the TV before we have done our job."

"Okay, I will get organised."

"Hi, it's me!"

Si ran over to John and gave him a big hug and a kiss that was eagerly reciprocated.

"Busy day?"

"Yes, I have been preparing all the papers and some notes as a reminder for Ann for tomorrow."

"Ah, do you need to give them to her now?"

"Yes, that would be a good idea. I am just finishing supper, so be back in ten. Okay?"

"Yes, as you instruct madam!"

"Cheek!"

"Ann, it's John."

"John, hi, how are you doing?"

"Fine thanks. I have just popped over with this for you, it's a few notes I've written regarding the process tomorrow, and what you may be asked and what you need to recall. You shouldn't read from this, keep it in your handbag, it is just so that you can be aware of what the Coroner is likely to ask, so you can rehearse the information and it doesn't come as a complete surprise."

"That's very kind John, I confess I am beginning to get a bit nervous."

"Oh you shouldn't be. What I have written down is the procedure and the likely questions you will be asked. Clearly, I cannot tell you what to say. They must be your own words and statements. You have to give your evidence under oath and you will be required to swear on the Bible."

"Very well, I will have a look at this later. Are you staying tonight?"

"Yes, Si is making supper."

"That's great! I have filled the Range Rover up. What time do you think we should go?"

"About eight thirty in the morning will give us ample time to park, find the court and settle in."

"Okay. I will tell Sandy when she comes. She is coming over to me for supper."

"Great, see you in the morning."

"All done, Mr Solicitor?"

"Yes, Miss Chartered Surveyor, how has it gone with you today?"

John stood behind Si as she cut the stones out of a pair of avocados and gave her a squeeze.

"Look here, sexy, if you need something to do, how about opening that bottle of wine?"

"Yes, miss!"

Over dinner they discussed the forthcoming holiday and the plans they had for skiing and partying.

"Oh, I've just remembered, I had a visit from the police today."

"Really, what did they want?"

"It was that DS Evans, and he wanted to know all about the tenant of 18 Squirrels Chase, that's one of the buy to let properties Dad bought, which he hoped would give him access to the development land at the rear."

"Really, I wonder what he wanted to know about all that for?"

"I have no idea and he wasn't for letting on, either. I'll tell you what happened later. He rang and asked what sort of car this tenant guy had when he took the tenancy. Strange question, don't you think?"

"Well now, I wonder why he needed that, what did you tell him?"

"I told him I knew exactly the make – it was a Ford. McCullock, that's the tenant's name, was working for the Ford dealer in Chester. The colour was black, I know that."

"Very interesting, I wonder what's going on? It might of course be to do with Fred Appleyard, but I really don't see the connection as Dad said the car he saw, which we might assume is something to do with Fred's death was dark red, not black. A real mystery, it may be to do with something else altogether. We shall see."

After dinner, they cleared away the pots, snuggled up on the sofa and finished the wine. It seemed like an age but in reality it was less than an hour before they were heavily involved with one another like two love-struck teenagers. They explored each other's bodies and in the process shed most of their clothes. It was only a short step to take to roll off the settee and onto the thick rug in front of the gas log-effect fire which gave the whole room a cosy glow and made it feel snug and warm. Sex was of course the outcome of all this, and despite the temperature outside being low, they were both hot and perspiring. John fell flat on the rug, face down whilst Si massaged his back, his legs and shoulders, first with her hands and then with her naked body. John was in seventh heaven – he could not remember ever feeling like this before, his mind was totally scrambled, and all he could do was groan and moan with pleasure.

"What do you think your mum will do when all this has died down?"

"Are you thinking of my mother whilst I am massaging you?"

"Why not? I have great affection for your mum, she's been through a lot."

"Well, I see. You fancy her then?"

John rolled over and pulled Si to him.

"No you great sausage, it's just that I was in a relaxed mood thinking about us, and then I thought about your mother."

"What were you thinking about us?"

"I was thinking how lucky I am to have met you."

"Is that all?"

"No. I was actually thinking how much I love you."

Si fell on top of John and kissed him so hard he could hardly breathe.

"So," as she pulled away for a breath. "You were really thinking about us?"

"Yes I was."

"So what other thoughts did you have?"

"Just how beautiful you are and what a wonderful body you have."

John felt that ought to suffice for now as he was not ready to declare any further thoughts about their future together.

"Let's have a shower."

And they did, and then fell into bed, not waking until seven o'clock the next morning.

27.01.2000 Thursday

"Morning, Ann, how are we today?"

"Fine thanks, John. Sandy and I are ready albeit a little nervous about what is to come."

"Yes I understand. Shall I get the Range Rover out?"

"Sure, thanks. The keys are hanging on the hook in the utility room."

"Okay."

"Morning, Mum."

"Hello, darling, you okay?"

"Yes. I'm not sure I'm looking forward to this very much, but I guess it has to be done."

"Yes. I'm so glad we have John with us."

"So am I."

"Well I mean to help us through the inquest, nothing else."

"Yes I know, that's what I meant as well, but also... if you know what I mean."

"I think I get your drift. What are you like, Si!"

"Can I say, in love?"

"Oh, darling, I'm delighted for you, your father would have been so proud."

A small tear appeared in the corner of Ann's eye but she brushed it aside with her handkerchief.

"Hi, Mum. Si, are we all ready?"

"Sandy! You look as though you're going to conduct a case."

"Standard court clothes, although I confess to being a little nervous and apprehensive about this inquest. I suppose it's because of the personal involvement."

"I have the car ready, my papers are in the back – shall we go?" said John

"Just let me go to the loo, John and I will be right with you."

"Come on, girls, you can get in and be ready."

Just after eight thirty, they rattled over the cattle grid into the lane and then onto the main road on their way to Warrington.

"Have you got everything you need, Sarge?"

"Yes, I think so, Tarrant, if I get through this one early I'll try and get to the Halifax in time for the arrest."

"Okay Sarge, I've heard from the Coroner's office this morning that they've opened and adjourned the inquest on Fred Appleyard pending further enquiries."

"Good. Let's hope we can clear all these up very quickly now."

"Yes, Sarge. See you later."

It was about ten to ten when John swung the Range Rover into the car park near the Coroner's court. He had not been to the Warrington court before and imagined a dark dingy Victorian building with all the foreboding that a coroner's court might imply. He was, along with his clients, very pleased to find a modern, light and airy building, part of the court complex in Warrington. John registered everyone with the clerk and they were asked to be seated until the court opened.

It was about ten fifteen when John saw DS Evans arrive. He acknowledged John but did not come over to speak to him. Evans registered with the clerk, and requested an audience with the Coroner, before the court sat.

"I will see what I can do for you sir."

The next to arrive was Roger Whiteside, closely followed by Frank Stringer. They acknowledged each other and gave a wave in the direction of the Walls and John England, but stood at the reception desk awaiting the return of the clerk.

"Sorry to keep you waiting, gentlemen. Are you here for the Peter Wall inquest?"

When the clerk received affirmative answers from both parties, he registered their attendance and asked them to be seated.

Roger went to shake Ann by the hand and acknowledged the girls – especially Sandra. Frank gave Ann a kiss, smiled broadly at the girls and shook John by the hand. Although nothing was said, the atmosphere was heavy despite the lightness of the building. There was a realisation amongst them all that, despite having had Peter's funeral and cremation, his final hours were about to be laid bare again and interrogated. The thought of Ann recalling the scene that met her on New Year's Day once again was clearly going to be very painful for her. Just as Frank was exercising his mind on these matters, a young PC arrived and registered. He was the PC who attended first and was so good throughout that day. He acknowledged everyone and took a seat two away from Roger Whiteside, leaving two empty chairs between them.

The clerk came over to speak to Evans, who had been standing at one side and chose not to sit.

"Can you follow me please sir?"

Evans and the clerk disappeared beyond some double doors at the opposite side of the reception, down a wide corridor to a door marked 'Coroner'.

The clerk knocked on the door.

"Come."

"DS Evans, sir."

Evans entered the Coroner's office and exchanged pleasantries with Dr Prescott, who advised Evans that he could not discuss evidential issues except in court, but apart from that he would be pleased to hear what Evans had to say.

"Sir, we are planning an arrest this afternoon of a person who we believe may well be responsible for a fraud on the Wall estate, as this person impersonated Peter Wall, used one of his properties to raise a mortgage of £100,000 and will defraud the Halifax of that money when he calls to collect the final payment at two thirty p.m. this afternoon. I have police officers ready to arrest him in the act. You will appreciate, therefore sir, that I cannot divulge this information in court this morning."

"I understand, but frankly what has this to do with the suicide of Peter Wall?"

"Well sir, you will appreciate that we will be arresting this individual because of the fraud he has committed and we are very sure of our ground on that. The property he used as security to raise the money is one Peter Wall owned. The property had the registration address of Peter Wall changed from Pater Wall's address in Tarporley to the property at 18 Squirrels Chase, which is where the fraudster is a tenant. He used a false passport to obtain a mortgage and open a bank account in the name of Peter Wall. We have further evidence that Peter Wall met with the fraudster, and they had an argument. We assume it was due to the change of registration address being notified to Peter Wall in Tarporley. We believe that because this fraudster felt his plot was about to unravel, he decided to murder Pater Wall. He has previous record for GBH, he is a known low-level drug dealer and we believe the funds he has raised by the fraud are to pay for a large consignment of drugs. Without the money he would be in very serious trouble, possibly fearing for his life. We consider the motive to be so strong that he chose to murder Peter Wall, before Wall had the opportunity to notify the land registry, which he was unable to do because of Christmas and the New Year holidays."

"I see. So it looks like we should at least adjourn today's hearing?"

"Yes, sir, I think that would be most appropriate. We have a requirement to carry out more forensic tests, particularly on the car of his in connection with the death of Fred Appleyard, whose inquest you have also opened and adjourned pending enquiries."

"Yes, that was yesterday. Is there a connection?"

"Yes, sir, we believe there is. We understand that Appleyard witnessed the car being used as the getaway car from Long Acre farm on the morning of New Year's Day. He believed he could identify the car used, if not the driver. This information was made available to us and was quite well known in the area and may have been disclosed to the fraudster unwittingly by one of the daughters of Mr Wall."

"Oh I see. How would she be in touch with the fraudster?"

"She is a chartered surveyor and works for Dents in Chester who let the property to the fraudster and subsequently manage the property. She met him following an inspection of the property after her father died and the conversation turned to the death. She let slip that their farm worker had seen the car."

"So you think the fraudster was involved in the death of Appleyard?"

"Yes, sir. We have an excellent witness who saw the car used and obtained a part of the index number of the car and the pieces fit, it all points to the fraudster."

"If that works out to be true, it will in some way be a relief to the relatives of Peter Wall, and of course enable them to claim on any insurance policies they had been denied from claiming against. It is perhaps as well we had this conversation DS Evans, as I am now satisfied an adjournment is appropriate and I shall await your further advice on this matter. Please do not disclose the contents of this conversation to anyone. You can, of course, be assured of my discretion."

"Thank you, sir."

"I will get the clerk to get everyone into court now as we are approaching eleven o'clock, and I will explain what will happen and deal with any questions that might arise. I would be grateful if you were in court, but I will not require you to say anything."

"Thank you, sir."

Evans left the Coroner's office and found his way to reception. As he was arriving at the reception desk, the clerk's phone rang.

"Yes, sir, straight away. Thank you."

"Ladies and gentlemen, the Coroner apologises for the delay but invites you all to go into court now. Please follow me."

The assembled company, together with reporters from the *Warrington Guardian* and the *Chester Chronicle* all filed into court. The press went to their special seating area, John England and DS Evans sat in the front row of the court whilst the rest sat behind them.

"All rise."

The Coroner, Dr Prescott, came in and sat in the large chair on a raised dais looking toward the assembled company.

The clerk announced: "This is the inquest into the death of Peter Wall. Dr Prescott, Cheshire Coroner presiding."

"Ladies and gentlemen, I am sorry you have been kept waiting. It has been necessary for me to be appraised of developments in this matter by the police. I regret at this time it is not possible to elaborate on the information I have received from the police, but I am sufficiently satisfied that it would be unsafe to proceed with the inquest today and therefore my decision is that this inquest is adjourned until further notice. Are there any questions?"

To the surprise of all, Roger Whiteside stood. "Could you please tell me when a death certificate will be issued?"

"Could you please introduce yourself and tell me your relationship with the deceased?"

"Yes sir, I am Roger Whiteside and I am the business partner of Peter Wall. I need a death certificate as soon as possible to affect a claim against the various insurance policies that are in place."

"I understand, Mr Whiteside, but until the outcome of this inquest I regret that it is impossible for a death certificate to be issued."

"Is there nothing that can be done, sir?"

"No, I am sorry. Are there any other questions?"

John England stood up and introduced himself and confirmed that the family were content to await the court's considerations in the interests of justice.

"Thank you, Mr England."

"All rise!" the clerk bellowed out and the Coroner got out of his chair and disappeared behind the screen, presumably to his office.

DS Evans, aware there would be questions, certainly from the press and possibly from Whiteside in view of his comments, scuttled off quickly and left the rest of the attendees standing in the body of the court, dumbstruck.

"Could you clear the court please?"

"What does all that mean, John?"

"Well Ann, I guess it means the police have other lines of enquiry all connected somehow with Peter's death, so until they have a full understanding of the case and have resolved what happened, then the inquest will stay adjourned. It's very unusual to get to court and for it then to be adjourned, there must have been some very last minute developments."

"How very upsetting. I just don't know what to think."

"It's a bloody mess if you ask me. How are we supposed to carry on running a business if we can't get the money from the insurance? The bank is on my back and I told them we would have the death certificate today."

"Mr Whiteside, please do not go on like that. It's nobody's fault, it's just as distressing for Mrs Wall, Sienna and Sandra as it is inconvenient for you."

"Inconvenient? You don't know the bloody half of it. You've obviously never run a business." Roger then stormed off out of the building, leaving John and the Walls looking after him as he departed.

"What do you make of that, Sandy?"

"On that display, we could have some interesting times. I would love to bring him down a peg or two."

"Let's all go back home, there's nothing more we can do here today."

"You're quite right, let's go. Mum, Sandy – John will get the car? We'll wait here as I see it has started to rain."

"Good idea Si, I will go and get wet! Hang on I won't be long."

"Tarrant, I'm on my way back, I'll be with you at the Halifax by half past one."

"Okay, Sarge."

The trap had been set. Two burly police officers with protective vests were waiting in the canteen at the back office of the Halifax. They were eating sandwiches and having cups of tea. Tarrant had been down the road for a Big Mac. The idea is that they would all reassemble at one thirty and brief the manager, on the way to handle this situation.

It was two twenty when Peter Wall entered the Halifax in Chester. He behaved as before and, after his initial enquiry at the reception desk, was ushered into the private interview room.

The manager dealt with the request in the same way as before and arranged for the cash to be brought into the interview room. Wall began to place the money into a duffle bag. At this moment a police constable entered the interview room and DC Tarrant and DS Evans came into the room. Wall looked up, as he had until that moment been concentrating on loading the money into his bag.

"Peter Wall?"

"Yes."

"I am Detective Sergeant Evans and this is Detective Constable Tarrant of Cheshire Police. Can you please tell me how you have come by this money?"

"Why do I have to tell you? This is a private matter between me and the Halifax?"

"Maybe if you were Peter Wall it would be, but you are not, you are not even Gary McCullock the tenant of 18 Squirrels Chase, Chester. You are in fact, Greg Mason."

"No. You've got the wrong man."

"I don't think so. Greg Mason, Gary McCullock or Peter Wall, I am arresting you for fraudulently obtaining money from the Halifax by deception, falsely using the identity of Peter Wall and being in possession of a false passport in the name of Peter Wall." Evans then said "You do not have to say anything, but it may harm your defence if you do not mention when questioned something which you later rely on in court. Anything you do say may be given in evidence."

"What have you got in your pockets?"

Evans commenced emptying the contents: a handkerchief, some change, a set of keys, a car key and two Yale keys.

"We will keep these keys. Where is your car?"

"You fucking well guess."

"Take him away."

The two police constables grabbed hold of him, bent his arms behind his back and placed handcuffs on him. Tarrant called on the radio to bring the van to the side door. When it arrived, Wall was taken to the van, locked in the back and driven away to police headquarters in Chester.

"I will take the money," remarked Evans as he picked up the bag containing fifty thousand pounds.

"That's the bank's money, Sergeant Evans."

"Sorry, sir, I appreciate the point you make but it is evidence. It will be returned to you in due course."

"Will you be able to get the other money back?"

"I would like to think so. It is possibly in the house he has been renting. We will not be able to let you have it back immediately but as soon as we find it, I will let you know."

"Thank you. I need to speak to head office and advise them what has happened. I don't suspect they will be too pleased that we don't have the money!"

"No, I understand but you are only temporarily without the money, you will get it back."

Evans then carried the bag of money to their car.

Tarrant took the car keys to SOCO who were waiting outside and they found the car in the multi-storey car park.

They were able to deliver it to their workshop for detailed examination.

"John, it's Lizzie."

"Hi, Lizzie, long time no speak."

"Yes, well you have been busy with other things haven't you, John."

"Now, Lizzie, don't be jealous, especially as we're all going on holiday together."

"No. I'm only kidding, I'm fine and having a great time, it's just that I have some news for you."

"Ah, my source of all news. What is it?"

"I've just had my reporter friend on the phone, he's on *The Chester Chronicle* and he says the police have just arrested a man in the Halifax branch in Chester and taken him away in handcuffs."

"Why would that interest me?"

"His name, he's called Peter Wall."

"What! It can't be true."

"It's one of the tellers on the counter who spoke to him before he went into an interview room to apparently collect some money. They took his name so he could be dealt with in the office. Apparently he came to collect a large sum of money."

"Well, Lizzie, you really do come up with the goods on occasions, thanks a lot. I may need to speak to the police."

"Great. I thought you would be interested. Bye."

"Bye, Lizzie."

"Si, it's John."

"Hello, darling, what can I do for you?"

"Lizzie's just been on the phone, she heard the police have arrested a guy at the Halifax who went to draw out some money. His name, Peter Wall."

"Oh no, how terrible! What's happening?"

"I don't know just now, but I think you have some evidence that will now be of interest to the police. You know the envelope from the Land Registry and the conversation you had with Fred before he was killed?"

"I see, yes. Well that all sounds a bit scary."

"Don't worry. I'll come with you to the police station, I'll phone Evans now. Can you remember to bring the envelope into Chester with you in the morning?"

"I will if I can find it. Oh my goodness, what a shock, what on earth will Mum say?"

"She doesn't have to know just yet, let me see what's going on. In the meantime you get the letter."

"Okay, but phone me back and tell me what's happening won't you, John?"

"Of course."

"Detective Sergeant Evans, please"

"Who's calling? He's rather busy at the moment."

"It's John England and you can tell him he has some important information about the man Sargent Evans arrested today."

"Mr England, it's Evans, how can I help you?"

"It's the other way round I think, Sargent Evans. I've heard you arrested a man today calling himself Peter Wall?"

"So?"

"Well, Miss Sienna Wall let the property at 18 Squirrel Chase to a man called McCullock."

"I know. I've already interviewed her on the matter."

"What you do not know is that when she was at the property, she found an envelope addressed to Peter Wall but at the Squirrel Chase address, franked from the Land Registry," said John England.

"Yes, I am aware of the Land Registry connection."

"Oh, well she also had a conversation with Fred Appleyard before he was killed. He told her that he did see a car coming out of the lane on New Year's Day. In fact, it nearly knocked him down then."

"That is interesting as Appleyard never made such a comment to us," replied Evans.

"No, I think he was frightened. He told Si, sorry, Sienna, that he recognised the driver as Roger Whiteside, but when he was told that Mr Whiteside was in Austria and it couldn't have been him, he was then unsure who it might have been."

"Well, thank you, that is useful, but we do know quite a lot already. Thank you for calling." Evans hung up.

"Tarrant. Let's start the interview with Mason. Has the brief arrived?"

"Yes, he's using the duty solicitor Alastair Murray."

"Okay, have they spoken yet?"

"Yes, they're meeting now."

"Okay, then we need to be making some moves as this man thinks he's up for fraud, whereas it may be two murder raps."

"Ian Birch, please, Roger Whiteside of Walls Civil Engineering."

"Mr Whiteside, good to hear from you. How can I help?"

"I desperately need to get some funds out of the insurers on the key man policy. The bank is hounding me and we're close to having an administrator appointed unless I can get some funds to them very soon."

"It's very difficult. Insurers like to see a death certificate, in this case there isn't one yet."

"No, but the man is dead! He's been cremated and I assume there will be papers involved in that process. Surely the insurers can be persuaded to part with some of the money? The fact he is dead is not going to change with the death certificate and as far as I'm aware, there are no issues with the insurer paying out under the policy. There are no restrictions relating to suicide."

"No. You are correct. I'll see what I can do for you."

"Thank you. Could you let me know later today if possible?"

"If I can get an answer, yes, I will."

A detailed interview started at four thirty p.m. in the rather austere surroundings of the secure interview suite. Present was Greg Mason and his solicitor Alastair Murray, DS Evans and DC Tarrant. The preliminaries had been completed by each party, introducing themselves for the tape.

"Mason, can you tell me what you were doing on the night of New Year's Eve and the morning of New Year's Day?"

Mason looked at his solicitor. Where had this question come from? It was totally unexpected.

"What do you want to know that for?"

"Just answer the question."

"I was in Liverpool with my partner. I went to the Three Feathers, a few doors from my house on Litherland Road in Toxteth and got pissed."

"You are quite sure?"

"Quite sure."

"Mm. What car were you driving at that time?"

"A Ford Focus."

"What colour?"

"Black. Why?"

"You were seen driving at high speed away from Long Acre farm in Tarporley on the morning of the first of January."

"No, not me."

"Yes, I think so."

"Okay, let's go back a bit, just before Christmas. Peter Wall, the real one came to see you, why?"

"He'd had a complaint about noise; his other tenant had complained, the silly bitch."

"Are you sure that's all that was discussed?"

"Yes, sure."

"This letter and its envelope are addressed to Peter Wall at 18 Squirrel Chase from the Land Registry, indicating that they had changed the address of the registrant to Squirrel Chase from Long Acre Farm. Peter Wall also received a letter from the Land Registry confirming the change, didn't he?"

"How would I know?"

"Because he came to see you, not about noise, but to see what the hell you were up to with his property."

"I don't know what you mean."

"What I mean, Mason, is that you were attempting to raise some money on a mortgage on the house you were renting and you impersonated Peter Wall to get that mortgage. It was essential that he never found out, so that all the papers came to you at the house. Isn't that right?"

"No."

"Yes. And you then, with the aid of a forged passport and a self-assessment form, managed to get a one thousand pound mortgage from the Halifax."

"No comment."

"Peter Wall rumbled what you were up to just before Christmas because he'd received a letter from the Land Registry confirming the new address for the registration. He came to confront you to find out what you were doing."

"No, he came about a noisy party."

"You realised that your game was up if you could not stop Wall from notifying the Land Registry of what you were doing. Luckily for you, because of the Christmas holidays, it was not possible for this to be dealt with by the Registry until the New Year."

"If you say so, Mr Evans. I have no recollection of any of this fairy story."

"It's no fairy story, Mason. You saw one hundred thousand pounds slipping out of your grasp, so you laid in wait for Wall on the night of New Year's Eve, and first thing in the morning you took your chance. Wall presented you with the perfect opportunity. You hit him on the head and then set about an elaborate arrangement to murder him."

"No, no, that was nothing to do with me. Mr Murray, this is all wrong, tell him!"

"We have a sighting of a black car in the lane in the early morning of the first of January. We have a witness who saw you leaving the lane to the farm early on that morning."

"No, sir, not me. You have the wrong man."

"I don't think so. You were about to lose £100,000 and were determined this would not happen, so you decided to kill Wall. What you didn't expect was that, early on New Year's Day, someone would see you, Fred Appleyard, the farm worker cycling to Tarporley. He got a good look at you and you were sure that he was a potential problem. You subsequently changed your car to the dark red Astra, lay in wait for him, and ran him over. We have a witness who saw you in the car when you did this. Not only that, you returned to Appleyard's body and ran him over again."

"No, no, no. This is nothing to do with me, it's all wrong!"

"You had the motive, you could easily have done these things, your cars are the same colours as the cars that witnesses saw. The forensic team are going over your car now with a fine toothcomb and they will confirm shortly that you killed Appleyard with the car, and a DNA match will link you to the Wall murder."

"No, no, Mr Evans. It wasn't me."

"We shall see."

"No. Go and ask my girlfriend and my mates in Liverpool, they'll all confirm where I was. I was nowhere near Tarporley."

"We shall see. In the meantime, this interview is ended at 17:30 hours."

Mason was returned to the cells and the duty solicitor told the custody sergeant where he could be found if further interviews were to be held.

"Tarrant, get on to the Liverpool police and get someone round to his house and The Three Feathers. Also, the keys on the car key ring are of interest. Get a search warrant and search the Squirrels Chase property. I guess one of the keys is for that and get the Liverpool boys to get a warrant to search the house on Litherland Road, the other key will be for that. It might be a good idea if you go to Liverpool to see what they find."

"Roger, can you spare a moment?"

"Yes, Christine, come in."

"I've had the bank on again about the overdraft and they need to speak to you most urgently, they're getting extremely agitated."

"Yes I know. I hope I've managed to sort something out with the insurers."

"Can you ring the bank and tell them what's happening. I don't want them to take any action that might put the brakes on the whole business."

"No, you are quite right."

"Are you okay, Roger?"

"Yes, why?"

"It's just that you look very pale and you have beads of perspiration on your forehead."

"No, I'm fine, it's just this insurance business that's getting to me, and the bank."

"Okay, can you call them now?"

"Yes, I will. I promise."

"Hi, Si, it's nearly the end of the week!" said John.

"Yes, thank goodness, it's been a bit of a roller coaster."

"What shall we do this weekend?"

"I want to go shopping for some skiing clothes."

"Where do you plan on going for those?"

"I thought I'd look around Chester and if there's nothing there, I'll go to the outlet mall off the M56."

"That's a good idea. I might be able to get something there as well, why don't you stay in Chester tonight and we can have an early start?"

"Yes, but I'll need to go home first. I've only got what I am standing up in and I don't want to go shopping in my work clothes."

"Okay, what time will you be over? Shall we go for a meal in town?"

"Yes, that would be great. I guess I could be with you at about seven to seven thirty."

"Great, see you then. Bye, darling."

"Bye."

28.01.2000 Friday

"Roger Whiteside, please?"

"Who's calling?"

"Ian Birch, insurance broker."

"Roger Whiteside."

"Sorry I couldn't get back to you yesterday, Roger, I had to wait for a senior manager to authorise any payment. If we can get a statement from the family doctor and a copy of the cremation certificate, they are prepared to advance two hundred and fifty thousand pounds on the understanding that if the circumstances change materially and there is a different perspective on the case which would call in to question the validity of the claim, then the money will become repayable. They'll need to get some paperwork on all this, and it might be best if I could perhaps speak to the Walls' solicitor for you to see what we can do. Your solicitor will also need to draw up an indemnity for the insurers in the way I've outlined and the insurers will need to see it and approve it before any payment can be made."

"Well I suppose that is progress, thank you. I'll contact my solicitor now. I'd be grateful if you could speak with John England who is acting for the Walls family."

"Yes I will. Let's talk later in the day."

"Sally Moulton, please."

"Who's calling?"

"Roger Whiteside from Walls Civil Engineering Limited."

"Hello, Roger, how can I help?"

Roger explained the predicament he was in: due to the delays in the inquest and no death certificate and that he was desperate to get some of the insurance money. He explained what the insurers were prepared to do, and requested Sally to draft the indemnity they needed.

"No problem, Roger, I'll speak to Birch & Co now and will get on with preparing the indemnity. As soon as I have it approved by the insurers, I'll let you know."

"Thanks, Sally, that's a great help."

Roger was getting very concerned at the delays in paying out. All his plans were on hold and he had hoped that by now he would be a personal millionaire, and the company would be solvent and that he could make a bid for the rest of the shares. This was not looking good. There must be some reason for the delay with the inquest. He just wished he could discover what it was.

"Sarge, can we have a chat?"

"Yes, Tarrant, what is it?"

"I've heard back from forensics. There's not a scratch on Mason's car and they cannot match the paint on the car to the samples taken from Appleyard's bike. Further, there are no DNA matches for Mason to any of the items in these cases."

"Oh shit, that's a bugger. Any other progress? Have you heard from Liverpool?"

"Yes, sir, they've completed the search of the house on Litherland Road, they were still at it when I left. You were right; the other key fitted the door there."

"Anything found during either of the searches of these premises? Have we found the other money?"

"Yes, sir, the bag containing the £50,000 was found at Litherland Road on to top of a wardrobe."

"That's a good bit of work in any event, we can nail him on the fraud charge but we're stuck with the murder theory."

"Yes, Sarge, I'll get the money transported here and I'll get forensics to check it over."

"Okay. Let's keep him under pressure on the murder charges just now, he may crack and of course he could be lying through his teeth."

"Yes, Sarge."

29 and 30.01.2000 Saturday and Sunday

John and Si spend an idyllic weekend just enjoying one another's company, shopping both in Chester and the outlet mall, where Si wanted to get some ski clothing and failed miserably, but John got fully kitted out in new gear.

"That's a bummer, I wanted to get new clothes and I get nothing and you get the whole works!"

"Well, it's just the luck of the draw."

"You wouldn't like to go to Manchester would you? There are one or two specialist ski shops and we just might strike lucky."

"Yes, let's go."

Fortunately, by the end of the day, Si did find what she was looking for although at a much greater price than John paid for his gear. She did look fantastic, however.

It was a quiet day at Long Acre Farm. Ann spent the day with Purdy and went for walks, but other than personal catering, looking after the dog and reading a book, Ann was on her own and lost in thought.

Sandra was in Chester and spent the day with Lizzie. They did some shopping, then went to the pictures and had dinner at home.

There was no excitement in any of the homes in which the Wall females resided this weekend. It was a non-event and a day when the weather didn't help either. By the end of Saturday, Ann was fed up with the peace and quiet. She was not used to this. She decided to throw caution to the wind and rang up her old friends Frank and Margaret Stringer and new friends George and Audrey England, to invite them to lunch tomorrow. She had unanimous success so she now had a project and set about her preparations for lunch the following day.

"So what's going on here then?"

"We've just got together and had a very pleasant lunch thanks, where have you two been?"

"Si and I have been shopping. We went out to the cinema last night and then went for a late dinner, and then drove back to Chester... sorry we were in Manchester."

"Very good. Did you get what you wanted, Si?"

"I did, but I had to go to Manchester to get it."

"She looks fantastic in the ski clothes she's bought."

"Good. Nice to see you, son."

"Thanks, Dad."

"Would you two like a cup of tea?"

"That would be great thanks."

"Pull up a chair. Si, can you grab a couple more cups from the kitchen?"

"Hi, Si, how's things?"

"Sandy, great, I'm fine. Will you have a cup of tea?"

"Yes please."

"We're all in the lounge." Si and Sandy went to the lounge and from a quiet house with just Ann it was now a full house.

"This is a great gathering. I'm delighted that everyone could come. I've decided that once the inquest is over, and the dust settles on all this, I'll sell the farm. I'd love to find a house in the village and take part in lots of local activities. I think this place is too big for me and I need to be surrounded by activity, otherwise I will stagnate."

"Well, Mum, I understand that you must do what you feel is best and we'll help you all we can."

"Si is quite right, Mum, she and I will do everything we can to help you achieve that."

"My only concern is what you two will do as it's your home as well."

"Don't worry about us, it's about time we had our own places anyway."

The group continued to debate the suggestion and they didn't break up until nearly five o'clock.

John decided by then that he needed to get going and sort his life out in Chester, beginning by unpacking the Porsche that was full of shopping, most of which was Si's.

31.1.2000 Monday

"Tarrant? I want to interview Mason again. Get hold of his solicitor and say that we shall interview his client again at two p.m. today."

"Yes, Sarge. You know he's in court this morning to answer the charges."

"Yes. Before you go, can we go over what we have on Mason?"

"Yes, Sarge."

The two of them sat for a good hour discussing how they might trap this man to make him admit to the murder charges. They looked at every angle they could. There were clearly some loose ends which they just couldn't get sorted out. Firstly there was the forensics issue. They had no DNA match, his car was clean and there was no match to his car's paint found on the bike of Fred Appleyard. Most importantly, they were unable to make the connection between Mason and Appleyard. They had been unable to establish any contact.

The death of Peter Wall was going to be difficult to pin on him despite the fact there was a clear motive. The issue was that he has a firm alibi borne out by about six witnesses either at his house or at the Three Feathers.

"The only way we can secure a conviction on the murder charges is for him to admit under cross examination and we're going to have to work hard at that. He has form and a motive. I'm sure he did them both."

"I agree, Sarge, it's just difficult to prove."

"Sergeant Evans?"

"Yes."

"It's the chief constable's office. Can you come up straight away please?"

"Yes, sir."

"Evans. I've been watching your progress on the Peter Wall and Fred Appleyard cases and I think you've managed to achieve a notable success with the apprehension of Greg Mason. It seems, however, there is no forensic evidence to back you up and from what I've read, little to connect him to Fred Appleyard, if not to Peter Wall."

"Yes, I agree, sir. We've been discussing it and we think the only way forward is to get a confession out of him."

"I think you'll be unlucky as it seems to me you have no evidence to back up your theory. It is evidence which wins cases, Evans."

"Yes, sir, I am aware of that."

"In view of the seriousness of the Appleyard case and the yet to be established connection with Peter Wall, which to all eyes looks like a suicide, I have decided that this whole thing needs looking at again. I've decided to put Detective Inspector Tom Sullivan on the case and you will report to him. I believe Mason is to answer charges this morning in the magistrate's court and it's probable that he'll be remanded for a week on the fraud and other connected charges. As to the murder theory, you can have one last go this afternoon with him on that, but I want no funny business. Do you understand me?"

"Yes, sir. Will DI Sullivan be taking over today?"

"No, he'll start work with a thorough case review tomorrow."

"Very good sir, thank you."

"Well that's a kick in the teeth and goodbye to promotion. I need a confession from that bastard Mason this afternoon," Evans mumbled to himself as he made his way downstairs to the CID suite.

Mason was remanded for a week and bail was not granted, due to his form and the seriousness of the crime. He had been caught virtually red-handed and it was going to be a piece of cake for the CPS to nail a conviction. He would probably get five years and serve no more than three.

"Christine, can you please get Sally Moulton of Frobisher's on the phone?

"Sally, Roger Whiteside. How are things coming along with the advance of the claim money?"

"Well, I've spoken with the solicitors and the insurers and they've laid down some terms. In fact I'm just re-drafting the document for them to consider."

"What are the terms?"

"They're prepared to advance two hundred thousand pounds from the key man policy taken out by the company, not the one you have in your name. I've been drafting a document to give them the right to have the whole two hundred thousand pounds returned in six months if a death certificate hasn't been issued to establish a legitimate claim under the policy terms. Also you will have to guarantee that personally and they want a second charge on the building."

"Mm, I see. The terms are a bit strict and I'll have to get approval to them from the estate of Peter Wall, as the premises are owned fifty fifty."

"I see. Well can you have a word with them and let me know who the solicitor is so I can advise him of the terms of the conditional release, and get approval to the second charge document? You will also need to advise the first mortgagee that there will be a second charge. Who is that?"

"It's our bank, HSBC in Chester."

"Okay, let's do things in order. You contact the Walls and the bank, I'll get approval of the documents from the insurers' solicitors and we'll touch base later in the week."

"Okay, thanks, Sally, I'll let you know how I get on."

"Can I speak with DS Evans please?"

"Who's calling?"

"Roger Whiteside of Walls Civil Engineering."

"Mr Whiteside, DS Evans, can I help you?"

"Yes, Sergeant. I'm very concerned that there's been a delay in the inquest of Peter Wall. I had expected that the inquest would be over and done with, as clearly the death is one of suicide."

"That's not something we can completely agree with. We have a suspect in custody on other charges and there could be a link."

"Can you tell me more?"

"No I'm afraid not, but there will be a further review of the case tomorrow by senior detective DI Sullivan, and he may wish to speak to you and others again before he can be satisfied as to the evidence the police will lay before the Coroner."

"I see. Well, thank you anyway."

Roger then thought about whom best to tackle next. The bank was applying the pressure and it should allow the temporary charge. After that he would tackle the Walls. Sandra was probably the best person to talk to. He made the calls and received an unexpected friendly reception and agreement from both parties. They could see the logic of the application for an advance payment and, further, they could see how failure to get some funds into the business would cause it harm. The one hundred thousand pound overdraft limit was regularly breached and the money from the insurance company would buy some breathing space. Roger conveyed this good news to Sally. She added to her list of jobs the draft second charge and the release from Peter Wall's estate of part of the equity for the second charge.

Evans and Tarrant spent three hours interviewing Mason. They put the murder charges to him again and again, firstly being pleasant, assuming he was frightened, and then frightening him, by being hard with the questioning.

"Sergeant Evans, if you insist on questioning my client in this aggressive manner I will have to lodge a formal complaint."

"Very well Mr Murray, but your client is not being very co-operative."

"My client does not have to co-operate. He only has to truthfully answer your questions. If you have some evidence that my client has been in any way involved with the deaths of these two men, please charge him now and we can all go home."

"The interview ended at seventeen twenty and Evans and Tarrant left the room."

"It looks as though he's either lying through his teeth and he has some very helpful friends to support his alibi, or he genuinely did have nothing to do with either of these deaths, in which case we cannot charge him."

"If he didn't do it, who did?"

"At this moment, Tarrant, I regret to say that I do not know."

1.02.2000 Tuesday

"Good morning. Tom Sullivan is my name but please call me Tom. I like to have an informal and hard-working atmosphere."

"Very well, sir."

"Now, Evans, you and Tarrant here have developed a theory that not only was Fred Appleyard murdered, but you now believe that Peter Wall was murdered too. Is that right?"

"Yes it is, but so far we've not been able to prove Peter Wall's death as murder. If you have that thought in your mind rather than the obvious choice of suicide then it's possible to work out how someone could have murdered him."

"But all this is on a hunch and not substantiated with fact."

"Yes. That's correct, sir."

"Tom, please."

"Sorry, Tom. Yes that's correct, we've been unable to get at any real facts to help us."

"Well, Evans, let's go back to basic principles of policing and work to find out if we've done everything we should. Let's look at possible motives and who would benefit from the death of one or both of these people."

The three men spent the next three hours going through a long list of events and possible scenarios in relation to the deaths, out of which came a considerable amount of extra work for Evans and Tarrant.

There was to be a full search of Appleyard's property. A detailed examination of his telephone account with a check on every number he telephoned in the last two months. He was to have his whole life examined in immense detail and a full and further examination of how he became a worker for Peter Wall. All the circumstances were to be cross-checked with staff.

Tarrant was to concentrate on finding the car that George England had seen and trying to establish its whereabouts. It would then undergo a full forensic examination.

In so far as Peter Wall was concerned, there were a number of details which had been overlooked. There was no copy of the will or any of the insurance policies and the beneficiaries of those policies needed to be understood. The fact that there was no suicide note needed to be examined and there had to be a full exposé of the financial position of Wall and who would be the main beneficiary if he died.

Finally, there needed to be a formal interview with everyone associated with Wall and his business. Their movements had to be recorded and witnesses checked for their alibis on New Year's Day.

"Blimey, Sarge. This is going to take forever."

"I agree, Tarrant, but this is what the DI wants so this is what he gets."

Tarrant started with the car search, whilst Evans started on the search of Appleyard's cottage. Before they left, Evans made contact with John England for copies of wills and insurance policies. John England was a little taken aback and started to indicate he needed consents and so on, but Evans reminded him that it was a murder enquiry they were involved in and if he did not co-operate, Evans would obtain a warrant and they would come and search his premises. This was not something John or any solicitor would want.

"Do you know how many cars in this part of the world have CC in the index number, Sarge?"

"No, but it must be a lot."

"It's thousands."

"There's bound to be far fewer when you look at the colour and if I were you, I'd look at Fords and Vauxhalls first."

"Good thinking, Sarge."

Along with a SOCO team, Evans started the fingerprint search of Appleyard's little cottage. There were certainly a large number of newspapers with the details of the case spelt out, mostly all over the front page. These were from the first week in January when the papers were speculating on the details of Peter Wall's death. Evans had forgotten how many speculations there were as to the cause of death. It was clear the papers were no nearer to finding the answer than the police were.

Taking the phone number down, Evans asked the office to obtain a full list of all calls for the previous two months so they could see if anyone had become a regular caller, and what the subject was.

"John, it's Lizzie. Did you catch up with the news from the court yesterday about 18 Squirrel Chase and the Halifax and Mr Mason?"

"No, Lizzie, I'm only interested in things that impact on what I deal with and I don't involve myself in speculation. There is just too much to do. What of the news from court?"

"The police have charged someone, a Greg Mason, for defrauding the Halifax of one hundred thousand pounds. He was remanded in custody for a week."

"Well, no doubt if I'm to deal with something to do with it, I'll hear more."

"Don't say I haven't told you."

"No, thanks, Lizzie. That's fine, bye."

"Bye."

"Si, Lizzie has just phoned." This in itself was enough to irritate Si, but she didn't let on and waited for what was to come. "Apparently the police have arrested and charged a man with fraud of the Halifax for one hundred thousand pounds. It looks as though it has something to do with 18 Squirrel Chase."

"No. I hadn't heard. What was his name?"

"Don't know, darling. I thought you should know as there may be some work to do."

"Yes okay. I'll make a few enquiries. See you later."

"Okay, see you later. Bye."

The police enquiries and searches continued and there was to be a further meeting of the police team at ten a.m. on Thursday, to review progress.

3.02.2000 Thursday

Tom Sullivan chaired the meeting at which representatives from SOCO, Forensics and Traffic were present as well as Evans and Tarrant.

"Where are we up to on this enquiry, gentlemen? Let's start with Appleyard. Any news about the car, Tarrant?"

"Yes, sir. There is and it's good and bad."

"Cough it out, lad."

"The vehicle in question was owned by Walls Civil Engineering and had come to the end of its useful life and so was sent for scrap. The appropriate documents and V5 had been sent to Cardiff together with the certificate of crushing. The vehicle is now a block of scrap metal."

"I see. Were we able to get a positive ID on the vehicle on the basis of the paperwork?"

"Yes, sir. Forensics has been able to match the paint on the bike with the specification of the paint for that car, a Ford Escort, sir."

"What have you done since this discovery?"

"Nothing, sir. I was waiting for this meeting."

"Very well. That's a note for further action please. I need to know where that car was from the first day of 2000 until it was scrapped. I need everyone who came into contact with it interviewed and the full history of who drove it, where and for how long, recorded and logged."

"What did you turn up at the house of Appleyard, Evans?"

"Not much, sir. Frankly, the guy was living a hand to mouth existence and he had very few possessions. He had retained copies of all the papers that covered the death of Wall."

"Any progress on the telephone?"

"Yes. This was far easier than expected. In fact, in the year 2000, he only made six calls. One was to Mrs Wall, the other to the vicar in Tarporley shortly after Peter Wall's death and then, strangely, after a week or so, there were four calls all at different times of the day or night to Roger Whiteside."

"And what did you make of that?"

"Well, sir, I'm not sure what to make of it. It does seem strange that he phoned his ex-employer so many times."

"Am I right in thinking that Appleyard had spoken to Sienna Wall and felt sure that the person driving the black car on New Year's Day was Roger Whiteside?"

"Yes, that is correct sir, although we only have her word for that and the evidence is, in fact, hearsay."

"Yes, but does the fact we know that cause you to think about Roger Whiteside and if he had a potential motive?"

"Yes possibly, but I cannot see a motive. We are still waiting for the insurance details and the will, sir."

"We need these quickly. Can you get them by tomorrow?"

"I don't see why not."

"Okay, let me know if you get it tomorrow and I'll then want to look at everything we've established so far. I want you, Tarrant, to get going on the life of the car and I would start at its end date, with Walls, and go and speak to anyone there who had contact with it."

"Very well, sir."

"Right, that's it. We'll meet at four tomorrow."

"Hi, Roger, Sally Moulton here."

"Hello, Sally. How's the indemnity going?"

"I've had various discussions with the bank and the insurers and there's now a section on paying interest to the insurers. They're looking at five per cent over base rate to be paid monthly. Were you aware of this?"

"No. That's a bit steep but I suppose it'll only be for a short time and we can cope with that. The important thing is to get the money across as soon as possible to get the bank off my back."

"I understand. I'll incorporate a section on interest and I'll email the draft to the insurers and the bank."

"Thanks Sally. Can you keep me posted?"

"Yes, of course. I've written to HSBC advising that consent is requested to create a second charge on the building and that will rank behind them, for a short period, whilst the claim is dealt with. I've yet to get an answer to that. Could you speak to the bank and see what you can do to hurry them up?"

"Yes, I will. Have you spoken to John England regarding the estate approving this facility?"

"No, but now I know all the terms I can email him today."

"Okay Sally, I'll let you know what the bank says and I'll let John England know what's going on."

"Thanks. Speak to you again soon."

The legal negotiations mean the bank was aware that there was to be a solution to the issue of the overdraft very soon, but everything seemed to take an age.

"John England? It's Roger Whiteside."

"Hello, Roger. What can I do to help you?"

Roger went on to explain the issue with the bank and the overdraft and how he needed the key man policy to pay out. He explained that the insurers wouldn't do this without a death certificate, but they had been agreeable to advancing half the money, and they also needed a second charge on the business premises. This would enable the overdraft to be cleared and allow the business to move forward.

"I see. I'll need to discuss this with the executors, but if they agree I'll get the document executed this weekend."

"Thank you. That would be a great help. Can you please let me know as soon as you have the document signed?"

"As soon as I have news, I'll phone you."

Roger turned his mind to sorting out the bank and advised the manager what was happening. He was amazingly co-operative, which surprised Roger, but he assumed the fact the bank were looking at the prospect of the overdraft being cleared helped the situation.

John England had the draft document on his computer within an hour of the conversation with Roger Whiteside. He decided that Si and Sandra were the best people to look at this first. He drafted a note by way of explanation and emailed the document to them both.

Unsurprisingly, Si was on the phone within half an hour.

"Hi, my darling, I've just read this agreement. I can't see what harm it can do."

"No, I think it's reasonable, but if something goes wrong then we could be looking at a further complication."

"What do you mean, if something goes wrong?"

"If for some reason the death certificate is not produced within six months."

"Surely that'll happen as Dad's death was clearly suicide."

"That's what we all think, but the inquest was adjourned at the last minute so there's something going on which has caused this, at the moment I really do not know what."

"I'm happy for Roger to get this advance. The business needs to be kept going."

"Yes I agree. I'll wait to hear from Sandy and then I'll speak to Ann."

"Okay, bye, darling."

"Bye."

Within the hour of the original email John had heard from both Si and Sandy and had spoken on the phone to Ann and explained the issue. All were in agreement. Roger emailed Sally in Manchester and requested that she supply an engrossment for signature. She agreed and said it would be in the post that evening.

4.02.2000 Friday

"Right, it's ten o'clock; let's get started. When Tarrant gets here he can join us."

Sullivan set to and reviewed where they were up to in the evidence gathering exercise on the Appleyard and Wall cases.

"Evans, where are we up to on this?"

"As previously reported, there seemed to be a number of calls from Appleyard's phone in the days before his death to Roger Whiteside's home. He is the MD of Walls."

"Yes, yes."

"There was the apparent identification of Whiteside driving a black car on the morning of New Year's Day by Appleyard. We only have Sienna Wall's account of this because there was no police interview of Appleyard before his death other than a DNA sample, taken by Tarrant, who also checked where he was on New Year's Day."

"It seems to me there needs to be a series of interviews of the Wall family."

"Yes, sir. Sorry, Tom."

"Ah, Tarrant, good of you to join us."

"Sorry I'm late, sir, I've been collecting some letters from the front desk and I've only just finished scanning the contents."

"I hope they were germane to these investigations."

"Yes, sir, they were."

Sullivan decided to let the informal approach drop. If they were all happy with the formalities, then he'd proceed on that basis.

"What were these letters you've received?"

"They were the will of Peter Wall and a schedule of all the insurances that would be triggered by his death."

"Please explain the contents."

"All the information has come from John England, solicitor at Bennett and Bennett, who are acting for the family and the estate of Peter Wall. It appears the legacies were to his children and the bulk of the estate to Mrs Wall. The insurances are all to the benefit of the family."

"Is that it? No insurance links with the business to underwrite loans and so on?"

"No. There's nothing here like that sir, there is a policy taken out in 1999 for one million pounds to cover a loan on some land but that, it seems, is nothing to do with Walls the company."

"That's quite unusual. You see gentlemen, there is normally cross insurance between business partners in small businesses, to protect the business in the event of one or the other dying or becoming incapable of work. Did they not have an insurance broker?"

"Don't know, sir."

"I suggest you find out when you visit Wall's today. Let's get going and review where we're up to on Monday. Court takes up the mornings on Mondays so let's say four o'clock Monday for a review meeting here?"

"Sir, I'd like to re-interview Mason on the subject of the fraud, as we need to get that case sorted out."

"Very well, report to me about that on Monday as well."

Evans and Tarrant had a brief meeting and decided that Evans would re-question Mason on the fraud charges and Tarrant would do a low-level enquiry at Wall's. Tarrant needed to discover who the insurance broker was, if there was one and also find out who drove the car they thought had killed Appleyard.

Evans notified Murray, Mason's solicitor that there would be a further interview at three thirty that day. Murray grumbled as he had hoped to be home early as it was Friday night.

"Can we make sure we're no longer than an hour, Mr Evans?"

"It all depends on how co-operative your client is, Murray." Evans hung up. He wasn't going to have his interrogation upset because of the social life of the accused's solicitor.

"Can I speak to someone about your vehicles, please?"

"Who are you?"

"DC Tarrant, Chester Police."

"Oh, I think the best person for you to speak to is Colin, he looks after all the vehicles."

"Very well, where do I find Colin?"

"He's in the workshop across the yard."

Tarrant made his way to the workshop and found Colin.

"I'm DC Tarrant, Chester Police. I understand that you have a dark red Ford Escort?"

"We did have, it's possibly a chunk of metal now."

"Why is that?"

"It's been sent to Wrexham, to the car crushers."

"Why did you send it there?"

"It had done more than one hundred and fifty thousand miles and was knackered. It needed an MOT and a lot of work, new tyres and so on, so it was best to get rid. It didn't owe us anything."

"Who drove the car?"

"Duggie, he's not here anymore, he's gone back to Ireland."

"Could anyone else have driven the car between Duggie and it going to the crushers?"

"No not really. I moved it around the yard, and I think Mr Whiteside had a test run in it, to confirm it wasn't worth spending money on."

"When was that?"

"Oh I don't rightly know. It was just before it went to the crushers."

"Can you find out exactly please?"

"I'll see what I can do."

"Who has the paperwork for the car?"

"That would be Christine, Christine Franks. She's Mr Whiteside's PA, and you'll find her in the office."

"Okay. Here's my card, give me a ring when you find out when the car was driven by Mr Whiteside."

"Okay."

"Can I speak to Christine Franks please?"

"I'll see if she's free."

"Hello, I'm Christine Franks," she said as she held out her hand to greet Tarrant.

"Can we have a private conversation, please?"

"Yes. Please come up to my office."

"Have you the papers for the dark red Ford Escort that has gone to the crushers?"

"Yes I have. I'll just get them from the filing cabinet."

It was all there including the official receipt from the car crushers, which was only two weeks old.

"Do you know if this car has actually been crushed?"

"No but I can phone to see."

"Yes please. I would like to know."

"Hi, it's Christine from Wall's. Do you recall the dark red Escort you collected a couple of weeks ago? I wondered if it had been crushed yet?"

"Hi, let me check, if it was only two weeks ago, it's unlikely as we do the stripping first and then we get a lot together and have a couple of days with the crusher. No, it's still here, and it hasn't been touched since we got it." Christine held her hand over the phone and advised Tarrant of the situation.

"Let me speak to them please?"

"Hello, this is detective Tarrant from Cheshire Police. We have an interest in that vehicle. Can you please ensure that no one touches it? I will try and get a forensic team to it today. It's very important as this vehicle is believed to have been involved in a serious crime. Do you understand?"

"Yes, sir. I will cone it off."

"Thank you."

"What serious crime? Do you need to speak to Duggie? He was the last person to drive it."

"No not at the moment. It's just part of our investigations."

Tarrant was kicking himself as he had nearly let the cat out the bag as to why they needed to find the car. He hoped that Christine would not make too much of the information she had received unintentionally.

No sooner had Tarrant left the office than he was on the phone to HQ requesting that a SOCO team left immediately to do a recovery of the Escort, so a full examination could be carried out back at police headquarters. He also requested that DNA sampling took place at the car crushers and at Walls for all employees. This was for elimination purposes.

Tarrant realised that he would need Duggie's DNA, so he returned to the office and recovered Duggie's address in Ireland from Christine.

Back at police headquarters, Tarrant phoned the Wrexham police out of courtesy to advise them what was happening on their patch. He also phoned the Irish Garda requesting that they take a DNA sample from Duggie and send it to them in Chester as soon as possible.

Tarrant hoped he would find the car in one piece and forensics could get lots of information from it.

"Hello, is that DC Tarrant?"

"Yes, who's that?"

"It's Colin from Wall's. You wanted to know when the Escort had been driven by Mr Whiteside?"

"Yes that's right, any clues?"

"Yes. He took the keys on the 20th January and the car was back in the workshop here the following morning. I'm not sure when it left the workshop or when it came back."

"Why is that?"

"Mr Whiteside took the car after I'd left for the day and it was back here before I got to work. I think he just took it home as when I got here the engine was still slightly warm."

"I may need a statement from you later, thank you for your help."

Wall's staff were surprised to find a police van entering the yard. The SOCO team were there to take DNA samples of everyone on site. The team leader met with Christine to get a list of all employees and to advise why they were taking DNA samples from everyone. They set to work getting samples and as it was a Friday afternoon, everyone was in place as they had all returned from the sites they were working on. The only person who was missing, and not on Christine's list, was Roger.

Roger was not classified as an employee by Christine, and anyway he was out. Christine thought he must have gone to a site. No one really knew where he was, but there seemed little point in advising him of the police activity as it didn't seem to be of any concern to Roger.

"Mason, for the tape, please confirm your identity and the same for you Mr Murray. DS Evans and DC Tarrant present."

"What do you want to speak to me about now?"

"I'm happy to discuss any of your activities, Mason, what would you like to say?"

"Fuck off."

"I see. We do at least know where we stand. The issue I need to talk to you about is the fraud you have perpetrated on the Halifax."

"I didn't commit a fraud, they granted me a mortgage."

"Yes, in the name of Peter Wall on a property you did not own."

Silence from Mason.

"I need to know how you set this up."

"If you're so clever, work it out for yourself."

"Where did you get the passport in the name of Peter Wall?"

"I found it."

"Who made it for you?"

"I assume the Government passport office."

"Mason, stop being so bloody clever. You're not helping your cause."

"Have you decided I'm no longer a murderer?"

"For the moment you seem to have an alibi; we're just checking all that now."

"It will help me when you say I'm not being held for murder as I have not done that."

"You're not behind the door when it comes to hitting people, as your record shows, so why wouldn't you take a swing at Wall and try to get his identity and get some money using that identity?"

"I didn't do that, Mr Evans. Just confirm that you accept that and I'll tell you all about the mortgage."

"We don't do deals, Mason."

"Yes, but you do charge people with murders they haven't done."

"All right, Mason, if you're not going to co-operate, we'll resume these discussions another day. In the meantime, you can stay banged up."

The interview ended after half an hour, which pleased Murray who scuttled off out of the station.

"Si, what are you doing later?"

"I was waiting for a call from my man with some suggestions."

John smiled to himself, and chuckled on the phone. "I have a document that needs the signature of all three of you. Can we get together?"

"You bet, but that is the most unromantic invitation I have ever had."

"Well, we can always go for a meal and then we can go to the farm and meet the others. I could stay if you like?"

"I like."

Later that evening, John's Porsche rattled the cattle grid immediately after Si's car had done the same. Ann peered out of the kitchen window to see who it was. She smiled to herself to see the convoy.

John and Si came into the farmhouse to see Ann and Sandra. They were having a glass of wine together having just finished supper.

"Hello, you two, glass of wine?"

"That would be good, thanks, Mum."

"John, you too?"

"Yes please." Ann poured out two more glasses of a rather delicious Rioja Reserva, which was a favourite of Peter's.

After catching up with the events of the week, John presented the indemnity document for them all to sign.

"Thanks, I'll get this back to Wall's solicitors on Monday so they can make progress. I think Roger is keen to get this money into the bank."

6.2.2000 Sunday

There had not been much activity by any of the Wall girls over the weekend other than a bit of shopping and spending the weekend, in Si's case, with John and, in Sandy's case, with

Lizzie. The weather was grey, cold and raining so there was little to persuade anyone to venture out.

On Sunday afternoon the girls and John visited Ann at the farm. There was a large fire with logs roaring in the lounge grate and Ann had plenty of tea, coffee and tea cakes. They all sat around and watched England at Twickenham take an early lead against Wales in the Six Nations Championship. The result was in favour of England and John nearly hit the ceiling with excitement. The girls showed excitement, but at a much lower volume than John.

"John England, what are you doing?"

"It's a rare event and one to savour!"

Roger Whiteside was also watching the rugby in his flat in Handbridge in Chester, although his emotions were not as exaggerated as those being displayed at Long Acre Farm. Halfway through the second half when both teams were in a position to win, the phone went. "Damn it," Roger muttered under his breath.

"Hello?"

"It's Duggie," said the now quite Irish voice on the other end of the line.

"Yes, Duggie, what do you want?"

"I want money, to put it simply?"

"Well you've phoned the wrong man."

"I don't think so, Roger. I know you were driving the Escort that killed Appleyard. That's a fact."

"You couldn't possibly know that."

"Yes I do and I can prove it. However, I would rather have money."

"I bet you would."

"Don't play games with me, Roger. I have friends over here that are keen to get some practice in with their baseball bats."

"What do you mean?"

"I mean, my friend, that if you don't have one hundred thousand available and brought over to Belfast then you will get a visit before I tell the police."

Duggie hung up. Roger by now, had no further interest in rugby, and became frightened. He double locked the back door and drew the curtains.

7.02.2000 Monday

Si and John spent the weekend with one another swapping between apartments. John called in to see his parents to say that he was going skiing the following weekend so they would not see him for a couple of weeks. The excitement was growing to fever pitch with Si. Sandy was excited too, but not to the same extent.

It had been agreed that the minibus would call and collect passengers from Tarporley on Saturday morning on its way to Manchester Airport. Si had suggested that it would be best if John stayed at her apartment on Friday night so they could leave together, with Sandy. John agreed that this was a workable plan.

As had been anticipated by DI Sullivan, Monday morning was a hectic round of court appearances to clear up the muggings, drunk and disorderly and drink driving offences over the weekend. Mason was pleased when the vans had arrived to move most of the occupants of adjoining cells to court. They were very noisy neighbours, and kept him awake all over the weekend. Being banged up in a police cell is no fun at all. There is no opportunity for recreation or socialising and he would be glad to be out of there and on remand, which he assumed would be the next step. The remand prison at Risley didn't have the greatest reputation, with a high suicide rate, but from experience, Mason knew it to be better than the cells in the nick.

Tarrant reported to Evans that the car had not been crushed and he had recovered it from Wrexham. It would take some time for the analysis of the car, the DNA checks and cross referencing to happen, possibly as long as a week.

"A week?"

"Yes, Sarge, it will take at least that and until we have the full picture, we are somewhat stuck on making progress against anyone who may have been involved in either of these deaths."

"There is no one we can identify at the moment that is potentially in the frame, other than Mason, and he seems to be in the clear if his alibis are to be believed."

"I agree. Any indication from Wall's insurance broker?"

"Oh bloody hell, Sarge, I forgot to ask who they were. I'll ring now and find out and try to get the details by this afternoon."

"Good afternoon, gentlemen. Please sit down as soon as possible, I want this to be a short meeting. What news Evans?"

"Well, sir, the good news is that the car involved in the hit and run incident with Appleyard appears to have been found and whilst it was sent away for crushing, it hasn't been crushed yet and is back at Forensics for a detailed examination. We've also taken DNA samples from all the staff and we've asked the

Garda in Ireland to get a DNA sample from the employee who used to drive the car."

"Good, that sounds like progress."

"Tarrant, anything to add?"

"Yes, sir, we've looked at the will of Peter Wall, as you know, and the schedule of insurances. There is also another insurance schedule we had not been given and that is for the Walls' firm. There are two policies which are of particular interest. There is one for five hundred thousand pounds known as a key man policy which is payable on the death of, or permanent injury of, one of the directors. This is to the benefit of the firm. There is a second one for one million pounds and that is to the benefit of the surviving director personally. The reason being, that the mortgage on the business premises is personal to the directors and this policy was in part to pay that off."

"Were there any other documents between the directors of Wall's that could in any way make it advantageous for one to outlive the other?"

"I don't know sir."

"Who is the solicitor acting for Wall's?"

"I think it's a firm in Manchester."

"Can you get me all the details and I'll go and see them. Clearly there may be some issues of a legal nature we need to know about. Following that we may then need to interview the surviving director, Roger Whiteside."

"There is an issue with Mr Whiteside in respect of the Appleyard case, in that he was potentially the last person to drive the car and that was on the night before the fatal hit and run."

"Can you place him at the scene at the time?"

"No, sir, we have Mr George England's statement but he was unable to identify the driver."

"There certainly seems to be good reason why we need to interview him. Let's get all the facts together and then we can talk to him, down here preferably."

"Very good, sir."

8.02.2000 Tuesday

Tarrant was at Wall's first thing and took a detailed statement from Colin. He advised Tarrant that the car was running before he sent it away and the keys had been held by Roger Whiteside. There wasn't a lot more for him to tell. He had decided it was not necessary to mention that the nearside headlamp had been broken whilst Roger had been driving. He could not see any reason why he should drop his boss in it.

"Sally Moulton, please?"

"It's DI Sullivan of Cheshire Police."

"Yes DI Sullivan, how can I help you?"

"I'm making some enquiries into the death of Peter Wall, you may be aware the inquest was adjourned?"

"Yes I was aware. What can I do to assist you, Inspector?"

"I'd like to know if there is any form of written agreement between Peter Wall and Roger Whiteside?"

"Yes there is."

"Can you please email me a copy?"

"Yes, I can, but I need to check that you are who you say you are so can you please email me and confirm your name, address, rank and number. Also, please give me the station phone number and your email address."

"No problem. May I call you again when I have had a chance to read the document?"

"No problem."

The arrangements were made to the satisfaction of Sally and the emailed shareholders agreement arrived. The DI spent the next hour reading every clause. It was clear that Peter Wall was the majority shareholder in the company but only by a small margin of two percent, but enough to make Peter the boss. The clauses that puzzled Sullivan were the clauses that referred to how on the death of one of them there was a right for the remaining shareholder to buy out the interest of the deceased. The double dealing of the clause intrigued Sullivan and the implications were not lost on him. The ninety-day timescale was also a significant issue. By Sullivan's calculations, the last day of March was going to be the deadline and how they would bid against one another would be significant.

Sullivan played a game at his desk to see what the implications of these clauses would be. He could see that the survivor of the two would have a significant advantage over the estate of the deceased. The half-million-pound key man insurance would make the survivor far more powerful in bidding for the remainder of the business than the estate of the deceased.

"Sally, it's DI Sullivan."

"Inspector Sullivan, have you received the shareholder agreement?"

"Yes I have and it's illuminating. I've been trying to access the implications of the option arrangements, can you enlighten me as to who it was that decided that these clauses should have been included in the agreement?"

"From recollection, I think it was Roger Whiteside who suggested it, but I would need to look at my file notes to answer that with any certainty."

"I would be grateful if you would kindly look at your file and let me know the answer."

"Yes, I can do that."

"Are you involved in preparing any offer in connection with the option clauses in the agreement?"

"If I were, I believe telling you would breach client confidentiality."

"Can I remind you that this is a police enquiry? We are not playing games here."

"Inspector, I am aware of your position and I have no reason to believe that the answer to your question can in any way have a bearing on your enquiries."

"As you are not aware of the nature of our enquiries, how could you know?"

"I assume you are investigating the death of Peter Wall?"

"Will you please find your file? I need to come and see you, and inspect the file. Please do not remove any items from it. I must remind you that this is a police investigation and the file is required by us in our enquiries. I will have a search warrant on me if necessary to take away the file, unless I have your co-operation."

"You have my co-operation, Inspector."

"Evans, who is the solicitor acting for the Wall family?"

Evans explained it was John England of Bennett and Bennett and he provided his phone number. Sullivan phoned the firm but England was out so he left a message for him to phone

Sullivan as soon as possible. The next call was to Sienna Wall, who the file told Sullivan could be found at Dents. She was out, too. Sullivan later discovered that they were out together, having lunch.

On receiving the call from John England, Sullivan asked if he would come to the station to be interviewed.

"I will not, DI Sullivan. I resent the implications of your question. My office is in Chester and if you wish to speak to me then I will be happy to meet you at my office."

"There is no hidden agenda, Mr England. We are investigating a murder and a suspicious death and it is important we get to the bottom of these matters. We also wish to interview a client of yours, Sienna Wall."

"If you would care to make an appointment, you can interview Miss Wall and myself at my offices."

"Would ten a.m. tomorrow be convenient?"

"Yes, Inspector, I shall see you at my office then, and Miss Wall will be here as well."

"Thank you."

What a supercilious man, thought John as he considered what he could possibly want from him. He also wondered what Si could tell the police that she hadn't already told them.

"Si, hi, can you get permission to come to my office for ten a.m. tomorrow? The police need to interview you again."

"Oh John, this all sounds very serious."

"It is but don't worry, I will be here."

"Okay, darling, I'll be there, see you tomorrow."

"Evans?"

"Yes, sir."

"I'm building up quite a picture here of an arrangement between the two men, both of whom had significant insurance policies in place, which could make the surviving party a millionaire when the other dies. This arrangement is in writing and possibly in the agreement at the request of Roger Whiteside."

"I see sir, that certainly would provide a motive; but Roger Whiteside was in Austria when Peter Wall died. Appleyard had certainly phoned Whiteside after Wall's death but that is not altogether surprising, as he was an employee of Wall's despite the fact he only worked at Wall's farm. He was possibly concerned about his job. I seem to recall someone telling me that Whiteside was not at all happy about the arrangement, so it would not be unusual for him to be concerned about his job as his main employer was now dead. He clearly couldn't call Whiteside before because Whiteside was on holiday."

"Yes, you may be right. It will be interesting to see who puts a bid in for the business, using the option scheme in the agreement."

"Yes, sir." Yet Evans was not at all sure what he was talking about.

Ann Wall was beginning to feel that she should consider making plans for her future. The loss of Fred has been a real blow as there was no one to keep the outside of the farm in good shape. She felt she should be finding someone else to help, but for the moment she had swept the yard, which took most of the afternoon. She was glad that the growing season was not yet upon her. When it starts, she thought to herself, she would have no chance of maintaining the place without some help.

She was secretly not looking forward to the weekend, when both her daughters were to go away for a week. It was the first time they would have been away from her since the death of their father. She knew that she must be strong and not show any emotion when they left for the airport. It was a challenge, and one she had to rise to.

9.02.2000 Wednesday

At just before ten o'clock Sienna Wall arrived at the offices of Bennett and Bennett and was invited to step into the meeting room, a room she had been in before. John joined her immediately and gave her a kiss by way of greeting, but not a loving embrace. John was in business mode and a deep embrace would not have been appropriate.

The intercom sounded and the receptionist advised that Inspector Sullivan had arrived.

"Show him in please."

"DI Sullivan. John England, and this is Sienna Wall."

"Hello, thank you for arranging this meeting."

"What has prompted further questioning, Inspector?"

"Mr England, I appreciate your question and if you would be good enough to answer my questions first, I will then be pleased to give you as much information as I can."

Sullivan then proceeded to go through all the notes on the interview Tarrant had conducted with Si. The main fact he wanted to establish was that Fred Appleyard had seen the driver of the black car on New Year's Day, speeding away from Long

Acre Farm. Fred had told Si that he was convinced that the driver was Roger Whiteside.

"When he told you that he was frightened, yet was sure that the driver was Roger Whiteside, what did he think Roger had been doing?"

"I really do not know Mr Sullivan. I did not have a detailed conversation with him as I knew that Roger Whiteside was in Austria. I'd spoken to him in Austria on the phone from his hotel when he called after my father's death. I also saw Roger when John and I went for a walk on the city walls during the Christmas break. We met Roger on the walls and we discussed the skiing in Seefeld as we are going there at the weekend."

"Oh I see, so you two are an item?"

"I wouldn't say that, Mr Sullivan, but we have become close, yes."

"This is a little unusual."

"Why do you say that, Mr Sullivan? I'm a single man and Si is a single girl. We met and it's fair to say that we get on very well together."

"I have no issue with any of that. It's just I had not been acquainted with the arrangement. Going back to Fred Appleyard, is there anything he said or did that gave you a feeling he was uncomfortable with the fact Whiteside was abroad at the time he saw him, or rather he thought he saw him?"

"No, I don't think so, but he was clearly taken aback that it couldn't have been Roger, because he was so sure and to have his assertion clearly rubbished, that I think deflated him somewhat."

"Did he say that he had contacted Roger to discuss his thoughts?"

"No, I don't think he did."

"Mr England, I have seen the shareholder agreement and the option arrangements in that agreement. Can you tell me if your clients, the executors and beneficiaries, are intending to make a bid to buy the shareholding of Roger Whiteside?"

"I cannot answer that."

"Cannot or will not?"

"I cannot answer that as I don't know at the moment."

"If they did make a bid, would they be pitching their bid to try and buy the business or making a bid to attract another bid to buy their share from Mr Whiteside?"

"I cannot answer as I don't know."

"Is there anything either of you can tell me that would assist our enquiries regarding the death of Fred Appleyard, or possibly the death of your father, Peter Wall?"

"You think someone might have killed my father?"

"I didn't say that, but there is always the possibility there may be foul play, there have been developments and that is why the inquest was adjourned."

"Does that mean you have someone in your sights or possibly in custody that could be responsible for the two deaths? Do you think the deaths are linked?"

"Yes, Mr England, I do think there is a link and yes we have someone in custody where there is a connection with Peter Wall. We are keeping an open mind about any connections and their consequences."

"That sounds like a politician's answer to me."

"We would appreciate your professional assistance with the individual we have in custody."

"Try me. I will do what I can."

"The man we have in custody was a tenant of 18 Squirrels Chase, Chester and was known to you, Miss Wall, as Gary McCullock. He is in fact Greg Mason, a known felon. He had chosen the property to rent, it would appear on purpose. He managed, with the use of a forged passport, to raise a mortgage of one hundred thousand pounds from the Halifax. Amazingly, the Halifax accepted his application for a mortgage on what they called a 'self-certification' basis. This cost half a percentage point extra but what it meant was the Bank accepted, without enquiry, everything that was written on the application form. What I am struggling to grasp is how it was possible for him to change the address of the owner."

"Well, Inspector, it is deceptively simple. All it takes is a ten-pound fee and a completed form signed by the owner. I don't actually think the Land Registry check signatures. So the moment the Registry is notified of a new address, the register is altered and all further communications go to the new address. If the register is searched, as it would be by the Halifax, they would find the owner living at the address of the property that is being used as security. There is nothing further to do, if there is no charge registered then the Halifax can proceed without any concern, they will get a first charge. As the property is already owned by the applicant there is no reason for a solicitor to be used as the bank can register a first charge and there are really no further issues. If the applicant is a single applicant he can sign the mortgage deed without any problem. He may have to get the deed sworn by a commissioner of oaths, and he would have to swear that the signature was his and that he was entering to the document truthfully. If he was not being truthful, well that possibly would not be any great safeguard. They would on completion of relatively simple and standard paperwork, and then on completion of the documentation they would release the funds."

"I see, it's that simple. Would the applicant have to give a reason for needing the money?"

"Possibly, but it is not a prerequisite of granting a loan."

"Thank you, this has clarified a lot for me. I gather no references were taken on Mason when he took the tenancy?"

"Yes, that is correct as the tenant had indicated he had just started a new job, and really couldn't offer satisfactory references so he offered to pay six months rent in advance."

"That was a neat way around the reference checks."

"Yes. As it seems he has tried to defraud Halifax, so getting the tenancy in the first place was not a problem to him."

"Is there anything else we can help you with Inspector?"

"No thank you. You have been helpful."

"Ann, this is George England. Sorry to bother you, how are you?"

"George, how good of you to phone. I am fine thanks, but I am finding the days are dragging by, I do not seem to have enough to occupy me, but frankly I cannot settle on any future plan until after the inquest."

"No, I understand. As John, Si and Sandra are all going on holiday together at the weekend, Audrey and I wondered if you would like to come over for dinner on Saturday night?"

"How very kind of you. That would be wonderful, yes please."

"That's excellent. Shall we say seven o'clock?"

"That's great. I look forward to seeing you then, thank you."

10.02.2000 Thursday

"Sally Moulton, please?"

"DI Sullivan," was the answer to the receptionist's question.

He was ushered into a meeting room just off reception, and shortly afterward Sally Moulton joined him in the meeting room.

"Inspector, I have the file you want," Sally Moulton advised the Inspector in a clipped way.

"Have you removed any documents from this file?"

"No, I have not."

"I will give you a receipt for it as I need to take this with me to Chester."

"Very well." Sally knew this was not the current file and the details of the new arrangements and the sums coming from the insurance company were all retained in the new file. The shareholder agreement was retained on her computer system, so she was not really deprived of any documentation.

"Can you please tell me who it was that requested the option clauses in the agreement?"

"Having read the file and my interview notes it would seem to have been Rogers' idea."

"Has he sought to make a claim on any of the insurance policies – the key man insurance as it is called?"

"I am not the company's insurance broker."

"That, with respect, is not what I asked."

"It would not be possible to make a claim until a death certificate had been issued and only the Coroner can do that after the inquest."

"Is there any other way Roger could get money from the policies in the meantime?"

This was a tricky one for Sally, how should she handle this one?

"There may be but you are now in the realms of client confidentiality, Inspector."

"I am in the realms of trying to solve a murder, if not two."

Sally felt trapped. On the one hand her training said she should protect her client, on the other she should not stand in the way of a police investigation.

I am not a criminal lawyer and I am not in court, she thought to herself.

"This is difficult for me, Inspector. You have to appreciate that my client is entitled to a degree of confidentiality, however yes, there is a move afoot to get some money from one of the policies."

"Please be frank with me – how much, when will it be paid, and to whom?"

"Okay, the sum is a quarter of a million as an advance and may have to be paid back if there is a change to the circumstances. The money should be in the bank of the firm on Monday next week."

"I see. I assume Roger Whiteside is the recipient of the money?"

"No, it is the key man policy of half a million, the beneficiary is the company."

"Very well. Thank you, that's very helpful."

"Christine, can you get me the bank? What's the manager's name again?"

Christine realised that dealing with the bank was a new experience for Roger, as this was entirely Peter's role. In fact, Roger had not even met the current bank manager. The bank changed managers, it seemed, on a five yearly cycle, so he had never had a need to meet the new one.

"It's Ted Beaton, at HSBC. Roger, would you like to speak with him?"

"Yes, thanks for that."

"Mr Whiteside, Ted Beaton. How can I help you?"

"Mr Beaton, I am sorry I have not been in touch before now other than speaking to a clerk regarding the overdraft, but as you can imagine life has not been easy since Peter died."

"Yes, I am sure. So how can I help you now?" he said this with the ominous feeling that he was about to be asked for a bigger overdraft.

"I am not sure if you are aware that there are key man insurances in place for the benefit of me personally in the sum of one million pounds, and half a million pounds for the benefit of the company. The issue has been the lack of a death certificate, as the inquest was adjourned at the request of the police. Without a death certificate, the insurers will not pay out, but in view of the overdraft I have negotiated an advance of quarter of a million pounds which should be in the account by Monday."

"That is good news, and I am sure as soon as the death certificate is issued you will get all the rest?"

"Yes, I have no doubt about that."

"I intend to leave one hundred and fifty thousand pounds in the current account which will leave a credit balance of fifty thousand having paid off the overdraft."

"That will be excellent. It will be a relief for you."

"Yes it will, but what I do want to do is to take out a substantial amount of cash. I have a need of the funds personally as I have undrawn dividends in the company and I would like to arrange to draw out ten thousand pounds in cash."

"Oh, well that is a substantial sum. Are you sure you want to draw out the cash? Would it not be better to have a banker's draft?"

"Thanks, but no. I need to have it in cash. Can I call on Tuesday morning and collect the money?"

"Yes, if you insist. You will have to bring your passport so we can check identities and so on. I must also advise you that this is such a large amount it falls within the money laundering requirements and we shall have to notify the authorities."

"Okay, if that has to happen. It is my money and I am entitled to withdraw it."

"Yes, sir, as you say."

Roger put the phone down and gave an involuntary whoop. For the first time since he became involved with Peter he was going to get his hands on some real money. He wondered how long he would have to wait for the big one.

"Evans, are you and Tarrant free for an update?"

"Yes, sir, we are. Tarrant will be back soon, he has been to Forensics to get their provisional report."

"I have had a good day; it seems Roger was the person behind the idea of the option agreements. Further, there will be two hundred and fifty thousand pounds going into Walls Civil Engineering's bank account next Monday. This is apparently an advance on the big insurance claim."

"That's interesting, sir. There will be some questions for Whiteside to answer."

"Have you made any progress with Mason?"

"No, sir, he is not very co-operative. He is demanding that he is assured he is not to be charged for murder."

"He is not really in a position to lay down terms, I would have thought."

"No, sir, but we do need to charge him on the murder count, or confirm the fraud charges and get him placed on remand."

"Yes, I agree. Tarrant, how are things going in forensics?"

"Extremely well, sir. They have identified the Escort as the car that killed Fred Appleyard."

"They have?"

"Yes, sir. They have been able to find traces of fabric and hair on the front nearside wing and there is a smear of blood on the nearside headlamp, which was broken. The DNA matched that of Fred Appleyard. The tread pattern of the tyres also matched the pattern of the tyres that ran over his torso. There seems little doubt that the car was the murder weapon."

"Have they managed to find any DNA match from the car to any employee at Walls?"

"Yes, they have found that Colin has matched the samples taken, but so far there is no other match. I have the report here."

"Thank you, Tarrant. I will have a read of that later."

"What do you think we should do with regard to the money Whiteside is going to get paid into the bank?"

"I have notified our interest to the authorities to ensure they advise us if any large amounts are to be withdrawn in cash."

"Why do you think Whiteside will need cash?"

"I have a hunch that he is known to Mason and it would not surprise me to find that they were involved with drugs."

"What makes you think that, sir? We have no evidence that they have ever met."

"No, that's true. It's just thinking outside the box and I just want to make sure we don't miss any angles. There is something we are missing in all this, there is a missing link. The more I find out about the potential for making serious money, the more I cannot help thinking there is the motive for the death of Peter Wall. Not how he was killed, but how it was executed and by whom, is the question. However, we must keep going, something will crop up soon."

Sullivan decided to leave the forensic report on his desk to look at tomorrow. There was a lot of detail, and it would need a clear head.

"Si, have you time to come round? I am going to make some pasta, how about supper?"

"Yes, please. I am just sweeping up at the office and I should be with you about seven if that's okay?"

"Fine, see you later."

"Hi darling, just in time. The spaghetti is just done al dente – it sticks to the wall."

"I hope not, I am a Wall!"

"Ha, how about a glass of pinot?"

"Yes please. What a day, I am not at all sure I enjoyed that interview with the police. The suggestion that Dad might have been killed still haunts me. I really do not know who might have done that, and why. Dad wouldn't hurt a fly."

"I know, darling. Don't let it prey on your mind. Let's look forward to our hols. And we shall have a wonderful week skiing and having fun."

"More wine?"

"Oooh yes please. The spag bol was great."

"Do you want a pud? I have some cheese or fruit?"

"No thanks, I am full."

"Let's throw this lot into the dishwasher, and snuggle up in front of the TV."

"Sounds good to me."

"Are you going to go home tonight or do you want to stay?"

"No, I need to go home. I still have things to do before we go away, and I need to see Mum as well, as I am concerned she may feel lonely when Sandy and I are away."

"Yes, I understand," John said in a somewhat disappointed voice.

"You sex-mad thing you! I know what you want, John England."

"How do you know what I want?"

"I know because it is the same thought going through my mind too."

"Just some practice for next week."

"John England, how dare you!"

They kissed embraced and gradually undressed one-another and enjoyed each other's naked bodies on the deep-pile woollen rug. They were as one for quite some time.

Si did not get home until gone eleven o'clock, so it was too late to see her mother, but Ann knew she was back when the cattle grid rattled its welcome.

I can go to sleep now content that my daughters are back safe and sound, thought Ann.

She was more concerned about their welfare now than she had been for years. They were all she had – her family, her future, and her past. She was determined not to smother them but equally she was keen to be sure they were safe and well looked after. Si's friendship with John was wonderful in Ann's eyes. She was concerned about Sandy, but was glad she was going skiing.

11.02.2000 Friday

"Tarrant! Tarrant!" barked Sullivan, "Have you really looked at this forensic report?"

"No, sir, I brought it straight down to you, but I was given the brief outline by the boys downstairs. Is there something wrong?"

"There certainly is."

"What is it, sir?"

"It's what isn't there that is the issue. There is no DNA sample from Roger Whiteside!"

"I don't believe it. Surely they got a sample from him."

"If they did he is not on the list. Can you go and check with them? If I am right, I think we need to go and see Mr Whiteside today."

"Christine?"

"Yes, Roger."

"I am thinking of going away for a few days. Can you cope with the admin of the jobs we have going at the moment?"

"Yes Roger, no problem. When are you thinking of going?"

"I will be going on Tuesday and will not be back until the following Monday."

"Yes, okay." Christine thought this was very strange and totally out of character.

"Where are you going to go?"

"I haven't decided yet, but not far."

"Okay." Christine decided not to pursue it. She really didn't care at this point. Clearly Roger had his own agenda.

Christine's phone rang. It was the receptionist downstairs.

"Yes?"

"There are two policemen down here to see Roger."

"Okay, I will tell him."

"Roger, there are two policemen downstairs to see you. Shall I ask them up?"

"Oh, right. Yes, bring them up."

"DI Sullivan and DS Evans, Mr Whiteside."

"Good morning, gentlemen, how can I help you?"

Despite his apparent cool demeanour, Roger was feeling somewhat uncomfortable and a bit hot.

"We are, as you are aware, investigating the murder of an employee of yours – Fred Appleyard."

"Yes, how can I help?"

"First things first. I believe you took the Escort that your employee Duggie used to drive?"

"Yes, but we've sent it to the crusher as it was beyond economic use, but am I right you have recovered it from the crushers?"

"Yes we have, and we have established that it was used to murder Fred Appleyard."

Roger was visibly shocked, and beads of sweat came out on his forehead.

"You look uncomfortable, Mr Whiteside."

"I am. I cannot believe that a company car has been involved with Fred's death. How could it have happened, and who could have done it?"

"That, Mr Whiteside, is what we are trying to discover. Have you ever driven the car, Mr Whiteside?"

"Yes, I have."

"And when was that?"

"It was shortly after the Christmas holiday. I will need to check."

"No worry, it was the 20th January."

"If you say so."

"Not just me. Colin confirmed it was then. How long did you have the car for and where did you go in it?"

"As I recall, I took it home overnight, parked it outside my home and brought it back in the morning."

"Are you sure you came straight here in the morning?"

"Yes I did."

"What time did you arrive?"

"I cannot recall, but probably about eight o'clock"

"Are you sure you brought it straight back?"

"Yes, absolutely."

"How then can you explain the car striking Fred Appleyard early in the morning of the 21st January?"

"I have no idea, Inspector."

"You are quite certain that you were not driving the car in Tarporley that morning?"

"No, I was not."

"In that case, Mr Whiteside, to enable us to exclude you from our enquiries we would like to take a DNA sample."

"Why, don't you believe me?" Roger was now very red in the face and sweating profusely.

"It is an insurance policy, we can exclude you from our enquiries, as it is quite possible we have collected your DNA from the car but have been unable to eliminate it."

"Very well, you may have my DNA."

Evans took a swab, and collected the DNA sample from Rogers's mouth.

"Thank you for your co-operation, Mr Whiteside. If you are planning to leave the country do not do so. If you plan to leave the area please let me know. Here is my card; we shall be in touch again shortly."

"Thank you." A very red-faced and heavily perspiring Roger Whiteside was left standing in his office, his mind racing and feeling quite disoriented.

"Are you all right, Roger?"

"Yes, Christine. I am fine."

"Would you like a coffee?"

"Yes, that would be kind."

"DI Sullivan, please."

"Sorry, sir, he is out of the office at the moment. DC Tarrant speaking, can I help?"

"Tarrant, this is SOCA," he meant the Serious Organised Crime Agency, "Are you involved with the investigation regarding a Mr Whiteside, Peter Wall, and Wall's Civil Engineers?"

"Yes, sir, in fact DI Sullivan is out visiting Mr Whiteside now."

"Good, then we have had a report from HSBC on the usual basis of customer confidentiality that the customer is to withdraw ten thousand pounds in cash on Tuesday next week."

"Is he now, I wonder why he needs that?"

"Sorry, that is all we have. I will register the fact you've been informed. Can you investigate and let us know? I will give you a report reference number."

"Yes I will pass this on." Tarrant took down the number, the name of the officer on the other end of the line, and their phone number.

On their return to the station, Tarrant advised Sullivan and Evans of the phone call he had received from SOCA.

"That's very interesting. It ties in with the fact that I know there is a deposit from the insurers into the Walls' account due on Monday of two hundred and fifty thousand pounds."

"Phew, that's very interesting."

"Yes, this is only the first bit. If suicide is proven then Whiteside will cop for a million and the firm will get half a million of which this quarter is a stage payment, pending the outcome of the inquest."

"Should we advise the bank that this transaction is of interest to us?"

"No I don't think so, Evans. We need to let Whiteside run to see what happens."

"Tarrant, I think it would be a good idea if you kept an eye on Whiteside on Tuesday. If he gets the money we may haul him in for further questioning."

"Very well, sir, I will get organised for that."

"Hello, is that Tony and Guy?"

"Yes."

"Can I make an appointment please? It's Ann Wall."

"Yes certainly, madam. When would you like to come in?"

"Tuesday would be good for me, say ten o'clock?"

"Yes we can fit you in on Tuesday morning. Shampoo and set, or do you want a cut as well?"

"A cut as well, I think. It is a while since I have been to the hairdressers and I need a good sort out."

"No problem, we shall look forward to seeing you then."

"Hello, can I speak to Sally Moulton, please?"

"Roger Whiteside."

"Roger, hope you are well?"

"Yes, thanks, Sally." Yet Roger's voice was strained and not at all confident.

"I wanted to check the insurers were transferring the funds to the bank on Monday?"

"No, they are not."

Roger nearly fainted.

"They have sent the money to us, and it is being transferred by CHAPS today."

"Sally, you nearly gave me heart failure."

"Sorry, I couldn't get the words out quickly enough."

"Thanks Sally, that's fine."

Roger went on to the Easy Jet website and booked a return ticket to Belfast on Wednesday. It was only twenty-four pounds each way. He decided to come back on Friday, which would give him more than enough time to carry out his business activities. He thought it best not to hang around too long. The reputation of a small minority of thugs in the North was legendry, and he had no intention of providing them with target practice.

"Si, I am leaving early tonight, and I will pack up and come over to you. What about eight?"

"Hi, darling, that would be great. Will you have eaten?"

"John England, that is a back-handed invitation to supper!"

"If you say so!"

"I do, but come over and we shall have supper before our first holiday together."

I see, thought John. It's good to think that there might be more.

"See you later, bye."

"Si, it's Mum."

"Hi, Mum, how are things?"

"Fine, darling, would you like to come over to the farm for supper tonight? Sandy is coming and it will make life easier for you by not having to cook just before you go away?"

"I would love to, but I have just asked John for supper."

"He is most welcome as well. So the two of you will come?"

"Yes, that would be lovely, but John will not be here until about eight."

"Okay, no problem. See you then."

"Thanks, Mum. Bye."

"Roger Whiteside?" asked an Irish voice on the other end of the phone.

"Yes, who wants to know?"

"Your ex-employee, Duggie."

"What do you want?"

"Where is the money, Roger?"

"It's in the bank. I get it on Tuesday and I am coming to Dublin on Wednesday morning."

"Fine, where are you going then?"

"I haven't planned that yet but a small hotel probably."

"Give me your mobile number and I will ring you on Wednesday evening and find out where you are and we can arrange to meet."

"Okay." Roger hung up.

"What a little bastard," he said to himself. "He can only be guessing and Fred really never saw him, how could he? I was in Austria."

"Hello, you two, come in."

"Hi, Mum. Sandy. How are you all?"

"Fine thanks. John, good to see you."

When the pleasantries had been exchanged, John and Si joined Sandy at the table in the kitchen whilst Ann started to serve up a starter. Vegetable soup, followed by lamb chops.

The minibus arrived at the farm just before eight o'clock on Saturday as arranged. Sandy, John and Si were waiting for it with their luggage stacked in the porch to the flats. There was much excitement in the group as everyone greeted one another. The driver loaded the luggage in the boot, one last kiss for Ann from Sandy, Si and now John, before they boarded the bus and then they were off. The cattle grid chattered its farewell as the bus swung out of the farm and into the lane.

The conversation on the bus was animated, especially from the female members. They didn't seem to stop chattering, although the M56 motorway drone calmed the conversation on their way to Manchester Airport.

"Well, Purdy, it's just you and me now for a whole week."

Purdy's tail wagged as if to acknowledge the situation. Ann settled down to breakfast, a cup of coffee and Radio Five Live.

"Shall we go for a walk?" The wagging tail and enthusiastic running around the kitchen indicated Purdy's desire to go for a walk.

On arrival at Terminal One there was a rush for the baggage trolleys to take the mountain of luggage from the back of the bus. The Monarch check-in was close, and after check-in the duty-free shopping attracted the female members of the group.

They spent ages sampling perfume, whilst the boys stocked up with gin or whisky.

The Monarch flight boarded on time but was held on the tarmac for twenty minutes by air traffic control. The one and a half hour flight was totally uneventful, save for the last minutes of the flight. None of the team had expected the landing. Innsbruck Airport lay at the head of a valley surrounded by mountains, with the runway running along the floor of the valley. To enable a landing into wind the plane had to bank around the mountain wall below the tops of the mountains and land on the runway into wind. It was certainly a dramatic entry into Austria.

On landing they were processed through the terminal quickly despite the fact there were two planes in ahead of them – a Lufthansa flight from Frankfurt, and Easy Jet from Liverpool. Within the hour they were at the reception of the hotel.

Sandy and Lizzie were the first to be given keys and given directions to their room. Helga, the hotel's hostess was on hand to welcome everyone and to invite them to a drinks reception for a free drink.

John and Si were the last to be given keys.

"We are sorry you are last but as you do have the best room in the hotel, we thought it would be best to leave you to the end once everyone else had gone to their room."

"No, that's just fine."

Keys were produced and John and Si were about to grab their cases when a bellhop moved in and insisted on taking them up in the lift to find their room on the top floor.

A two-euro tip was gratefully accepted and the porter left the room after leaving their suitcases.

"It's rather dark in here, John. Shall I open the curtains and shutters?"

"Wow, what a view."

The window revealed what could only be described as a winter wonderland. Snow right up to the door of the hotel, mountains in the background snow-covered fir trees – it was just fantastic. The sun was going down and the snow was turning pink and the crystals of ice glistened in the evening sun.

"Oh, John, how wonderful. What a beautiful room and such a big double bed. Do we have to go skiing?"

"Si, you are impossible. Let's unpack and get ready for the reception and dinner."

12.2.2000 Saturday

"Frank, Margaret, what a surprise. George and Audrey, you are all very kind."

"It is just a little something to allow you to relax and hopefully have an enjoyable evening."

"You are true friends. Thank you."

They all settled down to pre-dinner drinks and a chat.

At almost the same moment in Seefeld, Sandra, Sienna Wall, John England and their seven other friends were settling into drinks courtesy of the hotel hostess, Helga. They were given basic information about the facilities of the hotel, when the various party nights were and, of course, the Valentine's night on Monday. The hotel facilities also included a heated pool and sauna in the basement.

Helga was keen to take bookings for the various hotel events, including the gala dinner on Friday night, their last night at the hotel.

"Can we get a round table for ten for the gala night?" enquired John.

"Yes, I can arrange that."

"Listen up everyone, how about a big round table for us all for the gala dinner next Friday?"

"Yes."

"Yes."

"Good idea," were the answers fired back to John.

There, you have your answer, Helga. Ten with a round table for the gala dinner."

"That's great, John. The food is already included in your room price; it's just the drink you will need to pay for."

"That could add up to quite a bit!"

After the five had finished their drinks in front of a blazing fire in the lounge, Audrey invited everyone to come into the dining room of the Old Vicarage for dinner.

"I had quite forgotten what a luxury it was to have someone else to make dinner for me."

"Ann, it's been my pleasure. Let's look forward to doing it more often. More coffee, anyone?"

Seated at the bar after dinner, Helga was alone. Some of the team had strolled into Seefeld to sample the nightlife, and John and Si decided to have a drink at the bar and an early night.

"Hi, Helga, all on your own?"

"Yes, it happens sometimes, though it is also nice to be lost in thoughts."

"What would you like to drink, Si? Will you join us in a drink, Helga?"

"Yes please."

John got the drinks in and the three of them sat comfortably in squashy settees in the lounge area next to the bar.

"Where do you all come from?"

"England. Cheshire, in fact. It's in the north-west of the country."

"Oh yes, I know where that is. We had a single man on his own here over Christmas and the New Year and he came from Chester."

"That's where we all come from."

"Maybe you know Roger. Roger Whiteside?"

"Very well, he is a director of my dad's firm."

"That's amazing. Tell me, is he single or does he have a wife in Chester?"

"No, he is single as far as I know."

"Oh that's good. We really had a great time together, in fact a very good time together."

"I am glad to hear that. He was certainly here over the main party season. You two must have had a ball."

"Yes we did, we are not supposed to get it off with the guests but, as Roger was on his own, I think the management looked the other way!"

"That was very good of you. Poor Si had a terrible New Year as her father died in tragic circumstances on New Year's Day."

"Oh I am sorry to hear that. That's terrible."

"Yes, thank you. This week is special to me as John and I have recently met and looking forward to a relaxing week after all the pressures there have been over the New Year. It must have been good for you to have Roger to share that special night with?"

"Yes it would have been had he been here. He has some friends in Innsbruck, and he was invited to spend New Year's Eve with them, so no, he wasn't here then."

"That was a shame. When I see Roger when I get back I will tell him you are missing him, and ask him to make contact."

"Si, that would be great thanks."

"Shall we go up now, Si? I'm really tired."

"Oh, poor old you. Yes of course. See you tomorrow, Helga. Good night."

Si and John marvelled again at the view from their window. The starlit sky and the bright moon lighting up this Christmas card view was awesome.

"This is just wonderful, the view, the room, and you. Thank you so much, darling."

John turned to this beautiful creature alongside him and embraced her with a long and passionate kiss. Nothing was said as the pair just flopped into the squashy sofa with a view to the mountains beyond and just enjoyed one another's company.

"I really should be going now. It's been a wonderful evening, thank you so much."

Ann said her goodbyes and left with Frank and Margaret not far behind.

"What a wonderful woman she is. She has dealt with the death of her husband and a massive upheaval in her life. She has coped with it all with so much grace and dignity."

"I agree, George. She has a very strong personality and has coped very well so far. I think she is looking forward to the inquest and to get the matter settled once and for all so she can move on."

"Yes, I guess so. Everything is on hold for her until the death certificate is issued."

"That's right, the insurance money is on hold, and the whole business is on hold."

"Let's hope the inquest will be re-started soon and then she can move forward."

13.2.2000 Sunday

Day dawned brightly at Seefeld and the whole gang were assembled for breakfast at eight thirty.

Helga arrived to tell them about the ski school for those who felt they need it, and also to advise where skis could be hired and ski passes purchased. She also pointed out the best routes to go especially for the first day. She emphasised you don't want to be doing too much on day one as you wouldn't be able to walk, tomorrow.

"That all sounds just fine. Who is going to join Si and me on the blue easy run?"

"I will," said Lizzie and Sandy joined in.

Once they had collected skis and boots and bought their ski passes, they were off to the top of the easiest slope closest to the hotel.

"We can go on a more difficult run tomorrow. Let's just see how we go."

"Good morning, Mrs Wall. How nice to see you in church."

"Good morning, Vicar, I wonder if you could spare me a moment after the service?"

"Yes of course I can, if you would like to remain in the church after the service we can have a chat then."

"Thank you very much, yes, I will wait behind."

Walking into church Ann was aware that there were not that many people in the congregation, but nevertheless she had a feeling that she had become the centre of attention.

"Morning, Margaret. No Frank this morning?" Ann whispered.

"No, he's gone to play golf this morning."

"Oh I see. Good night last night?"

"Yes it was very good. What a very nice couple the Englands are."

"Yes."

The service began and the choir entered the church, a somewhat mixed bunch of choristers ranging from schoolboys and girls to retired men and women. The effect however was perfectly good and they all sang with gusto, although not all exactly on key.

"And the blessing of our Lord God Almighty be with you now and evermore."

With the much-practised blessing, the vicar brought the service to an end. After shaking hands with all the parishioners, he came back into church to have a chat with Ann.

"Mrs Wall, how good it is to see you in church today. I hope I can persuade you to become a regular attendee."

"You just might, Vicar. I need some extra inner strength just at the moment."

"I can imagine you must be very distressed."

"Yes, on occasions I can cry almost uncontrollably, and at other times I have deep remorse for what has happened. Then there are times I get very angry with Peter for apparently taking the easy way out and leaving all his problems for me and the girls to sort out."

"Oh yes, and how are the girls?"

"They are fine, thank you. They are so strong and a real support, I would not be able to cope without them. They are on holiday skiing in Austria for a week at the moment. I think a holiday will do them both the world of good."

"I am sure you are right. How can I be of help to you?"

"I really wanted a chat about the funeral for Fred Appleyard."

"Oh yes of course. He used to work for you, didn't he?"

"Yes, he used to work for my husband's firm for a good number of years and then he was involved in helping to convert our current house. He was a lovely man, so reliable and I cannot believe what has happened. I really do miss him."

"Yes, to be run over and killed when riding his bike on a journey he must have made a thousand times."

"It seems that it was deliberate. The police are investigating his death, they think it was murder."

"How awful. Whatever next?"

"As he has no relatives, I thought I would like to pay for and organise a funeral for him. I suspect there is no will and no money to talk of, and I wondered if it would be possible for him to be buried in the churchyard? It was, after all, a place he loved to work and he was your sexton."

"Yes I agree, and if you are prepared to foot the bill that would be a very generous gesture, thank you."

"I will and further, I will pay for the headstone."

"That is very kind of you, Mrs Wall."

"Oh, Vicar, please call me Ann."

"Very well, Ann. When had you in mind?"

"I need to check with the police tomorrow to see when the body can be released. I also need to check if I am permitted to make these arrangements."

"I am sure it will be allowed. I think it might need the consent of the official solicitor or the court of protection but I am sure the police will advise you."

"I will, thank you. I need to check the staff from Walls can come and I want to have my daughters at home because they loved Fred."

"Yes of course, as soon as you have a date in mind give me a ring and we shall see what we can fix up. I assume Mr Cartwright will be the undertaker?"

"Oh yes, I haven't spoken to him yet but I am sure he will agree."

"Ann, on another topic, we have a meeting here every week of the Townswomen's Guild. They have a coffee and try and work up a solution to a project either for the village or the wider community. It's very low key and really doesn't involve a lot of time but it might give you an opportunity to meet new people, what do you say?"

"I will certainly give it a try."

What was there to lose? Ann thought to herself.

"That's excellent; the next meeting is on Tuesday next week at ten thirty in the village hall. Usually there are about fifteen of us, and I am certain you will find it interesting."

"I am sure I will. You can count on me being there."

"I look forward to seeing you on Tuesday and please ring me if you get a possible date for Fred's funeral."

"I will."

"Wow, that was just fantastic. Just the one fall for you, otherwise you did very well, John."

"Cheek, just because you glide along like some ice goddess in your powder blue figure-hugging ski suit, making every man on the slopes ogle you as you go by so they forget what they are doing, get in my way and trip me up, you call me for falling over!"

"No, I am just pulling your leg. What wonderful skiing."

"You are wicked with that twinkle in your eye."

"No I'm not, I am just in seventh heaven and in love."

They embraced close to the edge of the piste and then fell over together into the deep soft snow.

"Come on, let's get these skis off and go for some lunch."

"Good idea, I am really hungry."

"After lunch we can have a good ski back to the hotel. Then how about having a swim, sauna and siesta before the others get back?"

"Sounds good to me. I will race you back, Si."

"John, you are incorrigible."

They ate lunch and skied as fast as they could back to the hotel. Shaking the snow from their boots they placed the skis in the rack and took the lift to their swanky room and changed into swimming costumes. They took the fluffy bathrobes provided by the hotel and a big towel each, before taking the lift to the basement pool area.

Three splashy lengths and a kiss in the shallow end, they decided that a sauna would be just the job.

As they were back at the hotel long before the others and the majority of the guests, the sauna was all theirs. They lay down on the pine-slatted seats. Si flipped a ladle of water on to the hot coals, which quickly pushed up the temperature. After about twenty minutes in the sauna they had a final dip in the pool.

Back in their room Si announced that she needed a shower to get rid of the chlorine smell of the pool. Dropping her revealing swimming costume on the bathroom floor she entered the shower followed by John.

They washed each other and embraced and then dried one another with the big fluffy towels. Flopping into bed warm and contented, they both fell fast asleep in minutes in each other's arms, despite Si's expectations of a romp.

14.2.2000 Monday

"Good morning, everyone. Tonight we have the Valentine's night gala dinner and disco. It's twenty euros extra. Shall I put you all down for it?"

"Yes please, Helga," rattled out the responses from the assembled group. They had all slept very well after their first full day skiing and were now very relaxed. After breakfast they put on their ski suits or salopets and headed out once more for a day in the sun-drenched ski slopes.

"Mr Beaton, it's Roger Whiteside of Wall's."

"Oh yes, good morning. I see the funds have arrived in your account. That is good news."

"Thanks. I just wanted to check that it had actually arrived as promised by my solicitor. I trust the arrangement for me to collect the money at ten thirty in the morning is still in order?"

"Yes, everything is fine, but I am still worried about you walking around with that sort of money in cash."

"Please don't. I regret I am unable to explain everything to you at the moment but if it is any reassurance to you, I will have a police officer with me when I leave the bank until I get to my final destination."

"I suppose that is a relief. You make it all sound very intriguing."

"Its complex but please, do not worry, everything is in order."

"Very well, I will see you tomorrow at ten thirty."

"Thank you. Goodbye."

"Hello, is that DI Sullivan?"

"Yes, who wants to know?"

"It's Roger Whiteside, of Walls Civil Engineering."

"Mr Whiteside, good morning. What can I do for you?"

"Mr Sullivan, I would like to come and see you, hopefully today, about a problem I have."

"Yes, that is possible. When did you have in mind?"

"Whatever suits you, but it needs to be today."

"Okay let's say twelve noon at the CID suite here at police headquarters."

"That's fine for me, I will see you at noon."

"Evans, I have just had Whiteside on the phone. He seems to have something on his mind and is coming here at noon to have a chat. I think you and I should see him and have a recorded interview. Can you make sure there is an interview room free?"

"Yes sir, that sounds very interesting."

"Is DS Evans available? It's Ann Wall."

"Mrs Wall, DS Evans. How can I help you?"

"I wondered if you could tell me if it would be possible for me to claim the body of Fred Appleyard and to arrange his funeral at my expense."

"Is he a relative of yours?"

"No, I don't believe he has any relatives. I have asked neighbours and people in the village. They all believe he had lived on his own for many years. No one had ever heard him make mention of a relative."

"I see. Well the inquest is due to be held next week and the Coroner's office have not requested the body be held until after the inquest. However, the Coroner will have to issue a burial order, and the local authority will have to authorise the release, as for persons without relatives the authority resides with them. If you are to bear all the costs then I feel sure they will be only too pleased to allow the body to be released to you. You need to speak to the Environmental Health Department at Chester. I will give you their number."

"Thank you very much, Mr Evans."

"It's a very nice gesture on your part, Mrs Wall. I am sure the authorities will be pleased to help."

"DI Sullivan, please."

"Yes, sir, who should I say is asking for him?"

"Roger Whiteside. He is expecting me."

"Have a seat please whilst I find him for you."

Roger sat down on the wooden chairs in the waiting area for visitors. The walls were plastered with official posters and notices warning of the effects of drugs, drink driving, details of rehabilitation schemes and so on. In fact, Roger thought there were so many they rather lost their impact. He mused to himself that people possibly didn't come to the police station to read the posters anyway.

"Mr Whiteside?"

Sullivan's call of Roger's name came as a bit of a shock and he looked up with a start.

"DI Sullivan, good of you to see me."

"Please follow me."

Sullivan led Roger down a long corridor to an interview room where DS Evans was already sitting at a table. As the pair entered the room Evans stood up.

"Mr Whiteside, DS Evans. We have met, please sit down." Evans gestured to a chair on the opposite side of the table.

"We will be recording this interview, Mr Whiteside, as it may be relevant to other enquiries. I hope you don't have any objection?"

"Err no. No, I don't think so."

This took Roger back a bit as his mind raced to think how what he was about to say could be linked by the police to any other matter.

"For the tape, Mr Whiteside, please introduce yourself giving your name and date of birth."

The detectives also introduced themselves to the tape and Sullivan started by stating Roger had come to the station of his own free will and wished to discuss an issue.

"Tell us what is on your mind, Mr Whiteside."

"Simply put gentlemen, I am being blackmailed."

Evans and Sullivan rocked back on their chairs at this revelation.

"How do you know?"

"Simply because I am being threatened by an ex-employee who is demanding ten thousand pounds from me in cash or I can expect to get beaten up."

"Very well," said Evans. "Let's start from the beginning and get everything in order."

"It was either the Sunday or the Monday after Fred Appleyard was knocked off his bike. Duggie who used to work for me phoned me to say that Fred Appleyard had told him that he had seen me driving away from Long Acre Farm on New Year's Day early in the morning. That was the day Peter Wall died. I explained to Fred before his death and again to Duggie that it couldn't possibly be me as I was in Austria, on holiday.

"Duggie didn't want to know this and was adamant that it was me that Fred had seen. He said unless I paid the money, he would let the police know. If I went to the police Duggie warned that he would get some of his friends from Northern Ireland who were always looking to do a bit extra to come and visit me, and it wouldn't be pleasant. I am, as you can imagine, extremely frightened. I had made arrangements to pay the money, but I have had had second thoughts and decided to come and see you."

"I see. We will need to go into the elements of the blackmail later, but what is the plan?"

"I take ten thousand pounds in cash to Belfast. Duggie will call me on Wednesday morning and tell me where to leave it."

"Does Duggie live in Belfast?"

"No he is from Dublin, but is coming to Belfast for the pickup. He said only euros would be of any use in Dublin, and he has business interests in Belfast so pounds will be fine."

"Can you explain to me why both Fred Appleyard and now Duggie are so sure it was you Fred saw on New Year's Day morning?"

"No I cannot, as I keep saying I was in Austria. All I can think of is that they know that Peter Wall's death means the company gets a large sum of money and, as I do too, they obviously want some."

"Okay, but why do you think Appleyard was killed? Do you have any idea who could have done this?"

"Firstly I can assure you it was not me. Yes, I took the car home and parked it up outside my house, but on the road as my own car was in the drive. It is possible that Duggie took the car and ran over Fred so he could continue the blackmail for the money."

"Did Appleyard seek to blackmail you for money then?"

"No, but he had phoned me to say it was me he saw leaving the farm on New Year's Day."

"He never asked for money?"

"No."

"If it wasn't you who killed Appleyard, it has to be Duggie or Colin."

"Yes I suppose so. My money would be on Duggie as he seems, by his current actions, to be a criminal."

"Yes, that would appear to be the case, but how would he have known where the car was and how did he have access to keys?"

"I have spoken to Colin on this. Seems that Duggie only returned one set of keys when he handed the car in. Colin didn't think too much about that as the car was going to be scrapped – what did an extra pair of keys matter?"

"Very well, we shall make some more enquiries. However, that leaves us with the issue of sorting out this blackmail business."

"Your help would be appreciated, otherwise I am going to lose ten thousand pounds."

"Have you got the money?"

"Yes, I am due to collect it from the bank tomorrow at ten thirty."

"Okay then, I will arrange for officers to escort you from the bank, and then to Ireland, with the money. Have you booked accommodation?"

"No, not yet but I had thought of booking into the central Travelodge in Belfast."

"Okay Evans, let's get organised. You will need to speak with the Royal Ulster Constabulary and make arrangements for armed response teams and back up so that Mr Whiteside can be protected and we can apprehend Duggie and any accomplices."

"Thank you, Mr Sullivan."

"You just go to the bank as arranged at ten thirty. You will not see anyone keeping an eye on you, but they will be there. DS Evans will travel to Ireland as well but he will be separate from you and it will not be obvious he is anything to do with you. We shall alert customs in Belfast that you are coming and to allow you and your money through without any search. Let us have your mobile phone number and we will call you shortly with a mobile number to call for contact. Thank you for coming, Mr Whiteside."

The skiing was as good as ever, they were becoming a little more adventurous in their routes and finding different cafes for lunch.

"I wonder what the Valentine's night gala dinner will be like."

"I really don't know, Si. I suspect it will be fine but I have no expectations of it being sensational."

"We shall have fun on our first Valentine's night together. Have you ordered some red roses?"

"Err, No! I really don't know where to get some red roses from around here. You will just have to imagine that I have bought you some."

"Well, I thought ahead." Unzipping her top Si produced an envelope which contained a Valentine's Day card, with a picture of red roses and a suitable mushy greeting.

"Is this for me?"

"Who else?"

"You are a one-off. I am sorry darling but I was not thinking about Valentine's Day before we left, or indeed today, as I was considering if I should phone Evans in Chester to tell him what we had discovered."

"Why, what have we discovered?"

"I was mulling over the fact that Helga, who was clearly having it off with Roger, was not able to see him over the New Year celebrations as he was with friends in Innsbruck."

"What was wrong with that?"

"If you recall, we met Roger walking on the walls before we came away and he said he'd had a wonderful holiday, and was delighted with the place, as he had never been there before."

"Maybe he met them in the hotel, or they were friends from way back he just hadn't seen for ages."

"I think it is very unlikely that someone living in Innsbruck would stay at this hotel which is only half an hour or more from their home, and it certainly would be a whirlwind friendship to get to be invited to their house. Surely the bigger attraction would be to spend New Year's Eve with Helga."

"Yes I see what you mean, it is strange."

"I'm maybe seeing things that aren't there, however I really don't want to spoil our holiday. I will make a few notes and phone Evans on our return."

"Yes that's better. Let's get going, I don't want any more lunch – more skiing and then sauna."

"I will go for that, let me pay then off we go."

15.2.2000 Tuesday

Evans received a call from the RUC confirming that they had made all the arrangements. He allocated a DS and some uniformed back-up troops and an armed response unit to be on standby for Wednesday morning.

Evans had booked his Ryanair flight, the same one that Roger Whiteside had booked – Liverpool to Belfast City Airport. He needed to pack a bag and be ready to go later in the day. He had already booked a room at the Belfast Travelodge.

"Mr Whiteside, DS Evans."

"Yes, hello."

"We are all fixed at our end. I am booked in at the Travelodge and I will be travelling on the same flight this afternoon from Liverpool to Belfast City Airport with Ryanair. Please note this mobile number and hold it in your mobile as this is the only way we can communicate."

"Very well, I am off to the bank shortly."

"Okay, you must let me know as soon as you get instructions on the drop and the time, and anything else that happens. DC Tarrant will be following you this morning, is all that clear?"

"Yes thank you, Mr Evans."

Tarrant was already in position by HSBC near the famous Chester clock, which sat on top of an ornate bridge over Foregate Street, close to the Grosvenor Hotel and HSBC. He spotted Whiteside coming up Foregate Street; he would need to cross the road to get to the bank.

Ann Wall was driving into Chester to make her hair appointment when she had a sudden realisation that she had made arrangements to be in two places at once. Suddenly her mind was filled with mild panic.

How stupid, could she be agreeing to go to the Townswomen's Guild Meeting and organising a hair appointment at the same time on the same day?

"Oh my God, what is he doing?"

Ann realised whilst thinking she should be in two places at once in that split second a man had walked across the road in front of her, she was screeching to a stop. She was sure she had hit him as he disappeared from view immediately. She was stopped now and trembling all over.

What have I done? she was asking herself.

Tarrant burst into a run and went to pick up Roger Whiteside from under the Range Rover. Fortunately he was all right, just a very slight bang. He had fallen over and cut his trouser knee and grazed the knee and a small amount of blood was visible. A small crowd had gathered.

Ann got out of the car, "Roger, it's you! I am so dreadfully sorry, my mind..."

She was interrupted by Roger saying, "Ann, it's all right. I am not really hurt. I was daydreaming and not thinking what I was doing."

Tarrant arranged for Roger to hobble to the pavement and for Ann to pull the Range Rover to the side of the road. After a brief exchange it was clear to Tarrant that no damage had been done and that Ann and Roger were unlikely to be taking action against one another, so he suggested everyone went on their way.

Ann carried on, shaken and in need of a coffee when she got to the hairdressers. She spent a good bit of the morning there explaining what had happened.

Roger continued on his way to HSBC.

"I am very sorry I'm late, Mr Beaton. I had a collision with a car on the way and managed to rip my trousers."

"Oh, Mr Whiteside, are you all right? Can I get you anything?"

"No I'm fine, just a graze and a bit of a shock. I think both the driver and I were thinking of other things rather than what we should have been doing and concentrating on the road."

"It's so easily done."

"Do you have the cash available for me?"

"Yes I do as promised. We just need to go through a few formalities."

After signing some forms and Beaton taking a copy of Roger's passport, the money was brought in from the back.

It was all in new fifty-pound notes and carefully wrapped in plastic. Roger was surprised how easily it all fitted into his holdall. After all, there were only two hundred notes with one hundred per bundle, so two bundles was not all that much really.

Tarrant was ready outside the bank and he followed Roger back over the road and back down to Handbridge over the river to Rogers's house. The arrangement was for Roger to be collected at about two p.m. in an unmarked car and taken to Liverpool Airport.

When he got home the post had arrived. Roger placed it to one side whilst he patched up his leg and started to cook himself brunch. A good fry-up should see him through to tonight when he hoped he might be able to get a meal out in Belfast.

He sat down to his brunch and started opening the three letters that had arrived. A letter from his solicitors sending him a bill for services provided to date.

They don't miss a trick, he thought to himself.

Along with the solicitors letter there was a water bill and a plain envelope with a Chester postmark. He stuck his fingers in to get the letter out and screamed with pain. He removed his badly cut figures and rushed to the bathroom to get a plaster and stop the bleeding.

What the hell was that? he thought to himself.

Very gingerly, he removed the contents to find a piece of cardboard folded over with a razor blade in the crease ready to do damage as soon as a finger was put into the envelope. On the card was a message in bold felt tip:

no police –
If you tell the police no legs!

That was clear enough to Roger, however it was too late now and he just hoped the police were up to the job of protecting him.

The unmarked car came on the dot of two p.m. He, along with his holdall containing another smaller bag with the money and some clothes, left his flat for a journey he was not looking forward to with a bound-up knee and two cut fingers.

Standing at the indicator board of the Liverpool John Lennon Airport, whose motto is *Above Us Only Sky* from a Beatles' song, Roger looked at the board waiting for the gate to be announced for the flight to Belfast. Roger and, separately, DS Evans could not help noticing that fifteen minutes after the flight to Belfast there was an Easy Jet flight to Innsbruck.

On landing in Belfast both men took separate taxis to the Travelodge in the centre of Belfast near the railway station, Roger to await instructions, Evans to check with his RUC counterparts that all was arranged for the following day.

Ann's hair appointment had gone well, after she had been fêted with coffee and biscuits and made to feel a million dollars, especially because of the trauma she had suffered on the way in.

On getting home, Ann had phoned the vicar to apologise for not attending the meeting in the village hall, but she had double booked. She also advised the vicar that the body of Fred Appleyard might be released to her and processes were under way.

Tarrant had received a note from the Coroner's office to enquire if they were ready to give evidence on the Appleyard inquest. He discussed the case briefly with DI Sullivan who had indicated a case conference would be necessary when Evans returned from Belfast.

Some tidying up was needed, not just of the Appleyard murder, but they also needed to be able to get a solution to the Peter Wall case. Was he a suicide, which looked most likely, or was it murder, which the blackmail of Whiteside would suggest? Or was that just a way of extorting money from someone they didn't like much and had now come into money?

"Hello, Mum, how are you doing?"

"I'm fine, darling, how good to hear from you. How is the holiday going?"

"We are having a fabulous time, the room John booked for us is just fabulous."

"Oh I am glad, you will never guess what happened this morning?"

"No, go on."

"I was on the way to the hairdressers when I nearly ran over Roger Whiteside."

"Heavens! Are you all right and is Roger okay?"

"Yes he was fine, a bit shaken. Fortunately that nice young detective was nearby and he came to help."

"That was lucky."

"Yes it was, in fact looking back, he was there in a flash as though he was expecting something."

"Oh well, you never know, Mum."

"Yes, I am fine darling, don't worry about me. Enjoy yourselves and thank you for calling."

"No probs. See you at the weekend, bye."

That's odd, thought Si as she recounted the conversation with her mother about Roger Whiteside with John. I wonder what else the police were doing? Were they keeping tabs on him and, if so why?

16.2.2000 Wednesday

Roger was startled at a quarter to seven when his mobile phone rang.

"Listen to me carefully and don't fuck this up."

"Okay."

"Leave the bag with the money in it in the waste bin on the river side of Oxford Street where it meets the Queens Bridge. Got that?"

"Yes, I think so."

"It has to be there at nine o'clock this morning, okay?"

The line went dead and Roger hoped he had heard everything properly. He immediately rang the mobile of DS Evans and told him of the instructions he had been given.

"Very well, get ready and do as you have been told. I will make the arrangements."

The mobile rang again almost the moment he switched off speaking to Evans.

"Who have you been talking to?"

"Err, what do you mean?"

"Immediately after I phoned you, you were on the phone to someone, who was it?"

"Err, it was just a voice mail message from my office from yesterday when I was flying here."

"No police, you bugger. Don't forget we have ways of making you pay if they get involved."

"Okay."

The phone went dead again. Roger was now very concerned and sweating profusely. He worried he might never leave Ireland. A shower and a breakfast were what he required. He just hoped Evans and his friends from the RUC were as good as they were cracked up to be. What should he do once he had made the drop?

Evans was already with the RUC and they were getting their unmarked cars and plain-clothes team assembled. How they were going to handle this had not been made clear to Roger and he was frightened that he was to be on his own when the pick-up took place. What if the wrong person got the money, what would happen then? So many thoughts were coursing through his brain and making him feel very uneasy.

It was five to nine when Roger crossed over Oxford Street to the river side and walked towards the Queens Bridge. He could see a large cast iron black litter bin with the Belfast coat of Arms embossed on the front. On the dot of nine he pushed the small holdall containing ten thousand pounds into the litter bin.

Roger retraced his steps and went into a Starbucks on the opposite side of Oxford Street. He didn't bother ordering a coffee and instead he sat at a window seat with a good view of the litter bin on the other side of the road. His eyes were fixed on the bin. The morning traffic was quite heavy and very slowly making its turn from the Queens Bridge south to Oxford Street. A whole line of cars and trucks was slowly coming around and in their midst, a white transit van. Roger took no particular notice of it as it was just part of the traffic. It was very slow going round the corner and created something of a gap between itself and the vehicle in front. It speeded up however, and then continued in the traffic.

Roger was getting fed up looking out of the window, so he ordered a coffee. It was half past nine now and nothing seemed to have happened. Suddenly his mobile rang.

"It's Evans, we have apprehended the team and the RUC have them in custody. We've recovered the money. That will have to remain here for a bit as evidence, you will get it back."

"I didn't see anything, what happened?"

"There was a white transit van that slowed for a moment in the traffic, a man got out of the side door and picked up the holdall and got back in the van and away."

"Wow that was a slick move."

"Yes, we thought there may be something like that involved in view of the location and the time of day which allowed them to slow up in the already slow traffic."

"How on earth did you find them then?"

"We had a helicopter monitoring the bin and he followed the van and pick-up. A marked police car picked them up on the road to Dublin."

"Very clever. I am booked on the noon plane back to Liverpool so I will go for that."

"I am too, so I will see you there."

Roger returned to the Travelodge and recovered his things and took a cab to the airport.

Evans and Whiteside met at Belfast City Airport and sat together on the Ryanair flight back to Liverpool. Evans had arranged a car to take them back to Chester. Roger was very upbeat as he felt he had helped the police secure an arrest of a man who looked the most likely, in Roger's eyes, to have murdered Fred Appleyard.

"When you were on holiday in Austria, did you at any time leave Austria either by road, rail or air, to go to a different country?"

"No I didn't. What a strange question."

"No, you have said that you were in Austria when Peter Wall died. I saw, and so did you when we were waiting for this plane in Liverpool, there is a daily service to and from Innsbruck, so I say again, did you fly home at any time?"

"No, not at all."

"Can I speak to DI Sullivan, please?"

"Who's calling?"

"It's John England, I am speaking from Austria, so I would be grateful if you would connect me as soon as possible."

"DI Sullivan."

"Ah Mr Sullivan, thank you for taking my call. By coincidence I am staying in the same hotel that Roger Whiteside stayed in when he was on holiday in Austria."

"Oh yes, is there something you have discovered?"

"Just some information I think you should have. Whilst he was here he got off with the hotel hostess and they spent most of his time here together."

"Yes."

"You would expect that he would have wished to spend the millennium New Year with her. In fact he spent, so he told her, the New Year's Eve with friends in Innsbruck."

"Okay, but that doesn't seem so exceptional."

"When Sienna Wall and I were having a walk on the Chester Walls before we came here we met Roger Whiteside walking the walls as well. During our conversation he told us he had never been to Austria before. In addition to that when we landed here we saw that there was an Easy Jet plane which flies back and forth to Liverpool."

"I see. I will note this, thank you for taking the trouble to phone me. Can I have your number in case I need to get back to you?" John provided the number.

Evans dropped Roger back at his house and then went on to Chester police headquarters.

"Evans, did it all go well?"

"Yes sir, I will let you have my report shortly. We need to get the CPS to arrange with the RUC to bring Duggie back to England for trial."

"I see. I would like to have a conference on this and the murder of Fred Appleyard, and the death of Peter Wall, so that we can get a clear strategy on how to clear up these two matters. How about three p.m.? Can you get Tarrant here as well?"

"Yes, sir."

"Is that EasyJet passenger services?"

"Yes can we help?"

"This is DI Sullivan of Cheshire police. We need to check that you carried a particular passenger on 31st December 1999, can I give you the details?"

"You can but I can tell you, sir, that we didn't fly him on the date you indicate."

"Oh, how can you be so certain?"

"Well, sir, due to the Millennium Bug which could have affected computers in aircraft and air traffic control, EasyJet, along with many other carriers, decided not to fly on New Year's Eve and into New Year's Day. We commenced flying for all flights scheduled to fly after noon on the first of January."

"I see. Thank you for that. I appreciate your help."

"Just one more thing however, even if we had flown I regret that we would no longer hold the data of passengers as we purge the system daily of details after a thirty-day gap under our data protection rules."

"That can't be, I get emails from you all the time offering cheap flights and deals."

"Yes that's correct sir. We keep email addresses if the customer has not checked the box to say they don't want them, we also keep details of account holders who have requested their details to be held."

"I see. Could you please just check to see if you have an account holder in the name of Roger Whiteside?" Sullivan went on to give Roger's details.

"Yes, but I will need a formal request. Can you please fax me on police official notepaper your request and I will look for you?"

"Very well," retorted a rather exasperated Sullivan. He made a note of the details and ended the call.

"Bloody data protection," he whispered to himself.

Roger was back at home having had a difficult twenty-four hours. He decided to have a sleep and then a shower before going out for a meal and a drink. He would walk back into Chester. It was a small city, so taking the car wasn't necessary.

"Right then, it's time we set about sorting these two cases out. Let's start from the beginning and deal with one at a time. Evans, what is your take on the Peter Wall death? By the way, where is Tarrant and why can't he be on time for a meeting?"

"He will be here shortly, sir. He had to go to Forensics to pick up a report that is appropriate to our discussion."

No sooner had the words left Evans's lips than Tarrant arrived into Sullivan's office.

"Sorry I am late sir. Forensic had a report on DNA that they thought we would find interesting and I have it here."

"What does it say?"

"Not sure yet, sir, I haven't even opened the cover."

"Let me have it." Tarrant handed the unopened report to Sullivan, who spent the next few minutes in silence looking at the findings it revealed. He then uttered a long low whistle on discovering a vital bit of evidence.

"Gentlemen, this discussion is going to take a very different turn to the one I had expected. This DNA report seems to suggest the blood found on the bumper of the Land Rover at Long Acre farm has an eighty per cent match to the DNA sample from Roger Whiteside. The reason they cannot be one hundred percent certain is that the sample from the Land Rover was contaminated with oil and very difficult to separate out. However the eighty per cent match does mean that it is one in one hundred thousand that the sample would match, which is to say the least a significant pointer."

"How did Whiteside commit the murder, if that's what it was, if he was still in Austria? Although I meant to mention sir that EasyJet have a daily service to Innsbruck, it was taking off fifteen minutes after the flight to Belfast."

"I know that. In fact, John England the solicitor rang and told me that Whiteside had not spent New Year's Eve in his hotel but with friends in Innsbruck. It just so happens he is staying in the same hotel Whiteside stayed in."

"I see, well that looks like a possibility. All we have to do is to prove he flew back here and back again and we have him banged to rights."

"Not so fast. My thinking exactly, but EasyJet didn't fly on New Year's Eve due to the Millennium Bug, so he couldn't have got back here. I also asked them to check other dates around then but helpfully under data protection they get rid of their data after thirty days and, before you ask, if you haven't checked the box they keep your email address so they can email you, but that signifies nothing, other than you flew with them once."

"No, I agree sir," interjected Tarrant who had been listening intently to the conversation. "It would seem that he was not in his hotel over the New Year period. Why couldn't he have flown back on the 30th December? That would give him all the time he needed."

"Yes I accept your thinking. Let's see, once we have finished this meeting if there is anything in that theory. Without evidence from EasyJet it's not so easy to track his movements but he must have hired a car, taken a taxi or stayed the night somewhere."

"Yes," said Evans. "A check with Travelodge might help. He seems to use them, that's where he stayed in Belfast."

"Bit of a long shot but we need to make those enquiries. Now, what about the murder of Fred Appleyard? Do you think your man from Belfast carried it out?"

"Well, sir, there is DNA evidence he had been in the car, but that in itself is not a surprise as it was his car to drive anyway and he drove it a lot before bringing it back. The car itself was the murder weapon. We have cast iron forensics to back that up, the motive is the difficult one to come to terms with."

"I see, the thinking is that Fred Appleyard was the only witness to a car leaving Long Acre farm on New Year's Day and he was able to positively identify Roger Whiteside as the driver. Whiteside's answer to this has always been that it was not him as he was in Austria. If our thinking is that Whiteside was not in fact in Austria and is borne out by our enquiries, then Fred Appleyard was possibly correct and there was every reason for Whiteside to eliminate him as the only witness that could put him in the frame."

"Yes, I agree, sir. Duggie had heard from his mate Colin at Walls that Fred knew he had seen Whiteside leave the farm. Apparently Fred knew and maintained contact with them all at Walls. Furthermore it was a very fast drive to get from Handbridge to Tarporley and back in time for Whiteside to take the car to his office. He would surely have been suspicious that the car was warm. Also how would Duggie know exactly when Fred would be riding his bike? It would have been a complete gamble to try and get there, find Fred and be back again before the car was noticed to be missing."

"Yes, sir, and if Whiteside did do it he had a much wider time frame with which to stalk and kill Appleyard and still be back at his office in good time for the start of the day."

"No, I don't disagree with this theory Evans, Tarrant. I think you may have the key to both these deaths in the flights back from Innsbruck. I suggest we leave it here and you get going on making some enquiries."

It was about seven o'clock when Roger had finished preparing himself for going out. He left his flat and walked into Chester city centre by way of the bridge over the River Dee. He was suddenly full of optimism; he could see that all his troubles were at an end. It wouldn't be too long before the inquest re-opened on the death of Peter Wall and he would then be in a position to claim not only the balance of the monies on the company's key man policy but also the million pounds on the life policy written in trust for his benefit on the death of Peter. There was, of course, the policy on his life in favour of Peter, but that was now irrelevant. He would be rich, own the Walls Civil Engineering business outright and have a bright future to look forward to without any hindrance from the Walls. Where should he, this new wealthy business man, go for dinner? There could only be one place, the Arkle restaurant in the Grosvenor Hotel. He would be waited on hand and foot, and drink good wines and eat exceptional food. He hadn't booked but usually one on your own could get in most places.

"Is it a table for one sir? Are you staying in the hotel?"

"Yes to the first question and no to the second. I live in Chester and run a business here."

"Very well, sir, you are most welcome. I have a very nice table here in the corner, please follow me."

Roger liked being pampered and looked after. This was a treat and he would enjoy fine dining despite the cuts on his fingers which were very sore.

"Has sir decided on what he would like to eat?"

"Yes I have. I would like some Scotch smoked salmon with blinis, followed by a medium rare fillet steak with a side salad and some thin cut French fries."

"Very well sir, and what would you like to drink?"

"I would like a bottle of the Penfolds Cabernet Sauvignon and a half litre of sparkling spring water."

"That will be our pleasure. Would you like a newspaper to read, sir?"

"Yes, that would be a good idea."

The maître d' was well aware that people dining on their own usually eat too quickly as they have no other distractions and need to be slowed down a bit, otherwise it can upset the kitchen and the client thinks he is getting slow service. He delivered Roger the latest edition of *The Chester Chronicle*. Imagine Roger's surprise when he turned to page two to find a picture of himself being nearly run over by Ann Wall. It seemed, on reading the totally inaccurate article, that a passer-by had a mobile phone with a camera and they had taken a series of photographs and emailed them to the newspaper. Some bright spark had made a few enquiries and discovered the parties involved and, with the death of Peter Wall and Fred Appleyard, concocted a story with the headline: DEATH STALKS WALLS

"Whatever next?" Roger asked himself.

"Would you like a sweet, sir?"

"No thank you. I will just have a coffee."

Following the payment of the bill, Roger left this plush restaurant and walked out into Chester's cool evening air.

Where now? He thought. Half past nine, far too early to go home.

He thought a pub would be a good place to go, but which one? Chester was full of beautiful old pubs, modern bars and wine bars. So where to go? The Pied Bull dating from 1155, thought to be the oldest pub in town, seemed a good choice.

Roger was not a regular but his face fitted and was recognised. It was also the pub of choice for many of the employees from Wall's.

"Pint of bitter, please," was his request as he found a space at the bar. He looked around to see if he could see anyone he knew or if there was a seat in a corner that he could occupy. To spend time in a pub on your own was slightly more daunting than eating in a restaurant on your own. Having been single for a large number of years he had become used to it and found ways of enjoying a visit to a pub by engaging strangers in conversation.

"Roger, what are you doing here?"

"Well I never! Christine, Colin. Fancy seeing you here."

"I thought you had gone away?"

"I had. I will tell you all about it if you like. Can I get you both a drink?"

"That's very good of you. I would like a gin and tonic."

"Colin?"

"Just a pint of bitter, please."

Roger got the drinks in and passed them round. The three of them sat down near the old fireplace with splendid coats of arms, believed to have been painted in the sixteenth century, over the mantle.

After some small talk, Roger explained where he had been and what had happened. He was shocked to have been blackmailed first by Fred Appleyard and secondly by Duggie. He explained the police operation and how he had to take the money to Ireland.

"I only got back this afternoon, and I have had quite enough of this intrigue."

"Why did you think Fred started to blackmail you? Surely he only told the police what he had seen. Was it you?"

"No it couldn't have been. I was in Austria."

"So what now, Roger?"

"The firm can go from strength to strength. It has plenty of money now thanks to the insurance company."

"Another drink? Same again?" Colin went to the bar and topped everyone up.

After about an hour and a half of chatting, Roger was getting rather drunk and was not holding back on his conversation.

"Yes I made the company. I made sure what we did was the best, Wall just fannied about pretending that he was all important but a monkey with a briefcase could have got those jobs because I made sure we did such a good job."

"Were you not friends with Peter then, Roger?"

"Yes Christine, in the sense we didn't come to blows and we had built the business, but I was very unhappy when he bought that bloody farm and spent the company's money on doing it up. He was a bloody crook in that respect."

"Clearly that got to you, then?"

"Yes it did, Colin. I could have strangled the man."

"Did you?"

Roger nearly choked on his beer. "What do you think? The fact he is dead has made me a millionaire. That's only fair as I have done all the work."

"So what you are saying is that given half a chance you would have strangled him?"

"Yes, I suppose so."

"How did you do it?"

"Ah, that's my secret as I was in Austria at the time, clever trick eh! No, it was suicide, everyone says so."

Colin and Christine looked at one another and both had the same thoughts – were they in the presence of a murderer?

"When you took Duggie's car home, Roger, where did you go in it? When you brought it back it had a broken nearside headlight."

"Did it? How do you know?"

"I am the vehicle maintenance engineer. It's what you pay me for!"

Christine went to get another round in, and it was clear to both Christine and Colin that Roger was well pissed and had slipped into the area of loose-tongued chatter.

"Colin, can I tell you something in confidence?"

"Of course, Roger."

"When I took the Escort home I did in fact go to find Fred, but he was not at home and I decided to go and see him in Tarporley. As I recall he worked at the Church on Fridays and Mondays, because I was getting fed up with Fred talking about me and suggesting I had something to do with Peter Wall's death."

"Yes, and what happened then?"

"I was driving to Tarporley and I passed the lane to long Acre Farm and shortly afterward there was Fred on his bike."

"Yes?"

"I needed to speak to him and I thought if I got in front of him I could stop him and have it out. I was about to overtake him when he wobbled out in front of me and fell off, there was nothing I could do. I ran over him."

"Oh my God! You have to tell the police!"

"No, it will cause me all sorts of problems. Look, if I give you a share of my insurance money, say ten thousand, just keep your mouth shut on this, but tell the police it was about nine or just after when I got back to the office."

"You want me to lie for you?"

"No, but it doesn't matter about Duggie. He is going down anyway for blackmail so he could take the rap for this as well, and as it was an accident, he wouldn't serve much longer."

"What did you do for Fred after you had hit him?"

"I panicked and drove on and then turned round in the first driveway I came to. The guy was opening the gate and got a shock when I backed into his drive to turn round and then I drove back to the office as fast as I could."

Christine brought another pint for Colin, another whisky for Roger and a gin and tonic for herself.

"Ssh! Colin, this is just between you and me. Do this and the money is yours."

"What's all this about?"

"Oh, it's nothing, Christine. It's just a little arrangement I have made with Colin."

Roger was really drunk now and was slurring his words and finding it hard to string a sentence together. The bell sounded behind the bar.

"Time, ladies and gentlemen please. Your time's up."

Colin, Roger and Christine downed the residue of their drinks, Roger downing his large whisky in one.

"It was good to see you both. I must go." Roger got up and staggered out of the door.

"What a bastard. He has just confessed to me he killed Fred and tried to bribe me to keep quiet."

"I don't believe it, Colin. This is outrageous, you must tell the police."

"Yes I will, but I need to reflect on what he has told me. I need a night's sleep, first. Tonight has developed into more than I had expected."

"Yes I agree." They both got up and left.

At the door, they found the weather had taken on a totally different complexion to when they arrived. It was very windy and blowing torrential rain almost horizontally.

"I think we are going to get wet!"

"Yes, mind how you go. See you tomorrow, Christine."

Christine walked and half ran to her car, which she knew she shouldn't drive. She was not going to get a taxi as they had all disappeared.

Colin seemed to follow the route towards Handbridge. Christine thought that strange as his car was at the back of the shops on Lower Bridge Street.

Roger was ahead but not walking very quickly, he was wearing a long brown mac, and was getting soaked. Every step he took made him feel very queasy. As he reached the centre of the bridge to Handbridge he stopped and looked down at the River Dee which was swollen. The rain had been falling hard in the Welsh hills and the river was now a fast-flowing torrent. If Roger was able to see the colour of the water he would have seen it was the same colour as his mac. His head was swimming and he had to lean over the parapet and was violently sick into the river.

17.2.2000 Thursday

Tarrant started the job of trying to check the movements of Roger Whiteside and to see if there were any records with anyone regarding a possible visit to the UK on the 30th December 1999. He phoned airlines, Liverpool airport, car hire companies, hotels, boarding houses and motels. He had a huge list of establishments to check. As usual the people with the authority to speak to you were never available so he had to phone back and, in many cases, fax a letter to get through the data protection barrier.

"How's your head this morning?"

"Not as good as it should be, Colin, I have to say. I am not sure I should have driven home last night but there were no taxis."

"I agree, I am not sure I should have either, but I did."

"Oh, I thought you might be walking as you seemed to be going to follow Roger and not to your car."

"No, there is a short cut to the car park off Lower Bridge Street up some steps, not everyone knows that."

"Oh I see. I say, whilst you are here I have just opened a letter addressed to Roger."

"Oh, why are you doing that? Shouldn't he be opening his own post?"

"Normally yes, but he is away until Monday."

"Oh, well what does it say?"

"It's from Mrs Wall, what a nice lady. She says that she has been given consent to arrange a funeral for Fred and it will be on Thursday the 24th February, a week today, at St Helen's Church. It's at eleven in the morning and afterwards at The Swan."

"Is she doing that for Fred?"

"Yes it would seem so. She goes on to ask that all employees of Walls attend and the company allows that at no loss of pay."

"Roger won't like that."

"No, but he should agree to it."

"I agree after what he told me last night, even though he was pissed."

"Are you going to tell the police?"

"I don't know. I feel he may have been making some of it up as bravado. If the police come here again I will mention it, but

I really don't see how telling them will change anything. It won't bring Fred back."

"True, have a good day."

"Okay, bye."

Ann was busying herself with arrangements for Fred's funeral, and she had already had Mr Cartwright collect the body. She needed to go to The Swan and arrange a funeral lunch, choose some flowers for the coffin, and have a word about the order of service and the choice of hymns for the printers, but she needed advice from the vicar. What a busy day.

"Come on, Purdy. Let's go for a walk in this wet and windy weather."

Purdy didn't seem so keen but followed her out into the still-raging storm. They walked as usual up to the old oak tree and Purdy saw a couple of rabbits and was off, her concern about the weather had immediately evaporated. They were soaked and covered in mud when they got back to the farm.

"We need a hot drink now, Purdy."

Her tail wagged as if she understood every word. Just as Ann was drying herself off and plugging in the kettle, the cattle grid rattled its greeting. Into the yard came Frank.

"Come in, Frank. The kettle's on, perfect timing."

"How are you, Ann? I was just passing the end of the road so I thought I would just pop in and see how you are."

"How kind. Do you take sugar?"

"No, just as it comes please."

"I am very grateful, Frank. It has been a bit lonely this week with the girls being on holiday. I must tell you of the excitements in Chester, I even made *The Chester Chronicle*!"

"Good Lord, what have you been up to?"

Ann then recounted the incident with Roger Whiteside, and the running over incident. Ann also went on to tell Frank all about the arrangements she has made for Fred's funeral.

"You must come, Frank. He was such a lovely man."

"Yes I will. In fact, Margaret and I will both come."

Back at police headquarters, Tarrant was wading through phone call after phone call of contacts trying to find out the movements of Roger Whiteside. DI Sullivan came into the office.

"Any progress, Tarrant?"

"Not yet, sir, I had no idea how many people I would need to contact. It may well be tomorrow before this is done unless I get lucky with a contact today."

"Okay, well keep at it. I have a feeling about this and you could be on the right track."

In Seefeld, the skiing was going well. John and Si were even more in love with one another. As the week progressed, they spent more and more time alone and together, whilst the rest of the team were as a group, and were having a ball.

Sandra was having just a wonderful time. She had met a ski instructor and he was a god on skis. She soon realised the fling with Lizzie was just that – an interesting interlude in life but not her life.

"Hi, Mum, how are you?"

"Sandy, how great to hear from you. Is everything all right?"

"Yes, Mum it's just great. I was just calling to see how you are."

"I have been for a walk with Purdy and Uncle Frank popped in for a coffee, and I have arranged Fred's funeral next Thursday. I hope you and Si will be able to come."

"Yes of course. That's very good of you, Mum."

"He was a great worker and friend so I thought it was the least we could do."

"Si and I will definitely come. I will ask John when I see him if he would come."

"How are those two doing?"

"They are in love, Mum. There is no doubt about that. We don't see much of them, as they spend a lot of time together. I am so pleased for them."

"That's great. How are you doing?"

"There is a ski instructor I would like to bring home but I guess he won't come!"

"Ah, that's good."

"Anyway, Mum, we have just stopped at a lovely alpine café for lunch before we go on. So I just wanted to check you were okay. All my love."

"Yes same to you and Si. Have fun see you on Saturday."

"Yes, bye, Mum."

"Bye."

In Belfast the RUC had charged Duggie with blackmail and extortion and they also charged the driver of the white van with aiding and abetting a crime. Duggie was incandescent with rage. He was swearing and threatening to get Roger for bringing in the police.

The police had heard all this sort of thing before from criminals, it was the usual thing.

The local magistrates had made an order that Duggie should be transported under guard to Chester to face the charges and be sent for trial there. The order also made a demand that should he be found guilty and a custodial sentence handed down that he should serve that sentence in Northern Ireland.

The Good Friday Agreement had meant that the co-operation between the authorities in the North and South of Ireland were working closely together, and it enabled the authorities to transport criminals to the mainland in the event of a crime being committed in England. This was such a case and Duggie was to be transported back to England on Friday 18th February.

19.02.2000 Friday

It was the last day of the holiday in Seefeld, so John and Si decided to go on the longest possible ski run they could. They were up early and had already finished breakfast before the rest of the gang had arrived.

"So where are you two going so early?" enquired Lizzie as she entered the dining room for breakfast.

"We are going on the longest route we can so that we can have the maximum amount of skiing and then come back for the gala dinner tonight."

"Very well, have a good day. See you later."

The skiing and the weather were as good as they had been all week.

"Aren't we lucky, John, the weather has been so fantastic. I really have had such a wonderful week."

"Yes, Si, we have been very lucky. Let's hope it holds until we have flown back tomorrow."

"It might, I saw on the reception TV that they are expecting gales over the weekend which were travelling in from the west and that the weather had been really bad in the UK."

"Let's get going and enjoy it whilst we can."

"How are things progressing, Tarrant?"

"Slowly, sir. I hope I am on the right track with the Travelodge in Widnes but I have to wait until four p.m. when the night receptionist comes in as she may well recall who stayed. Again, they delete all records thirty days after the event and just keep the email address if so requested. The Data Protection Act is really causing me a problem here."

"Yes I know. Have you tried Whiteside's mobile phone records?"

"No, because I don't have his mobile phone number."

"Try his secretary at work."

"Thanks, sir, I will."

Tarrant continued with his chores, but he was determined to track down the connections if they existed.

Evans had to go with some uniformed police to meet the Ryanair flight from Belfast to welcome Duggie back to the UK. The formal handover didn't take long and Duggie, who was handcuffed all the time, was met on the tarmac by a police van and two police officers and DS Evans. Evans signed the receipt for the prisoner, and he was loaded into the police van and taken off to Chester. Evans had to be there as he was able to identify Duggie. The escorts from Belfast headed for the arrivals hall to await the plane home, and maybe to have some refreshment whilst waiting.

It didn't take long to get Duggie back to Chester, and it had been arranged to put him up before a magistrate that afternoon. He was, of course, entitled to a solicitor and the duty solicitor attended, which was Murray. The interview with his client didn't last long as the charge was straightforward enough and it seemed an open and shut case to Murray, but what the heck, it was money and paid by the state eventually!

The magistrate, after hearing the charge and getting Duggie to confirm his name and date of birth, remanded him in custody for seven days, to appear before the magistrates again, for directions as to what should happen next.

John and Si had had lunch and were on their way back to the hotel, as the afternoon wore on. They handed back their skis and boots, and sauntered back to the hotel for a Glüwein and warmth, before heading back to their room to pack.

"Thank goodness!" shouted Tarrant, "a break through at last!" The receptionist at the Widnes Travelodge phoned him back to confirm that she recalled a Mr Whiteside had stayed at the lodge on the nights of the 30th and 31st of December. She recalled him vividly as there were very few people staying but all of them were parties or families who were visiting friends in the area. Whiteside was the only man on his own and he stood out as a result. Further, she was prepared to give a statement to this, so Tarrant despatched a PC from the Widnes station with the approval of the sergeant on duty at Widnes, and the PC went to take a statement.

Everything seemed to be coming together. It was a matter of minutes after that the representative of Alamo car hire at Liverpool came back to him, confirming that they had rented a black Vauxhall Astra to a Mr Roger Whiteside on the 30th of December 1999 to 1st January 2000.

"Great, now we're getting somewhere," Tarrant mused out loud to himself. "So we are able to confirm that he was in fact staying in Widnes over the holiday and that he hired a car at Liverpool Airport and returned it there on the 1st January."

What they couldn't confirm is that he was actually on the EasyJet flight from Innsbruck, but how else could he be in Cheshire if he hadn't been on that flight?

"Could I have a word, sir?"

"Yes, Tarrant, have you made progress?"

Tarrant then recounted all the evidence he had acquired and he was getting statements from the Travelodge receptionist and the agent at Alamo car hire at Liverpool Airport confirming Whiteside's presence in the area at the time Peter Wall died. He was now placed in the area, and had a motive to murder Peter Wall.

"Why did he stay in a Travelodge rather than go to his flat?"

"I assume he was making as sure as he could that no one saw him. Staying at his own flat was too much of a risk."

"Now you have all this you had better go and arrest him and get him in for questioning, he has a lot to explain."

"Very good, sir."

Tarrant along with DS Evans and two uniformed officers in a separate marked car set off to Wall's on the Sealand Industrial Estate. They screamed into the yard, but there were no blue lights or sirens. They parked the marked police car across the entrance to avoid anyone making an escape.

Entering the office, Evans requested to speak with Whiteside.

"Sorry sir, but he is away at the moment."

"Can I speak to his secretary, please?"

Christine came down to reception and met with the officers. She explained that both she and Colin had met with Roger on Wednesday night in the Pied Bull.

"He was dressed up and very happy. He left very drunk, but he did say he would be away until Monday next week."

"Did he say anything to you I should know about?"

"No not to me, but it might be useful if you had a word with Colin."

"Where do I find Colin?"

"Follow me." Christine led the two detectives in to the machine shop and into Colin's office. After the introductions Colin explained what Roger had told him on Wednesday and how he had offered Colin ten thousand pounds not to tell the police.

"Is that why you failed to report this?"

"No, I just felt what he was saying to me was not really credible. He was very drunk, and I didn't want to cause my boss a problem over some fantasy he had made up whilst drunk and in a pub."

"I see. Colin, I am arresting you for conspiracy to pervert the course of justice," he then went on to give Colin the formal warning that all police officers give. Colin was handcuffed and taken out to the marked police car.

The marked car with Colin in the back returned to police headquarters for Colin to be processed. Christine, who was now very upset and crying, went back to her office with Tarrant and Evans in tow.

"Christine, I need Whiteside's home address or any other address you have for him. Further, one of us will be back either later today or we will come to your home over the weekend to take a statement from you."

Christine provided all the information the police officers requested, and continued to sob as they left.

"Right let's go and see if Whiteside is at home. Call in for back-up, Tarrant."

"Yes, Sarge."

They hammered on the door but got no reply. As soon as two burly PCs arrived, they instructed them to force entry. It didn't take long for them to search the flat and it was clear no one was at home nor had anyone slept there, certainly not last night.

"Look what I have found in here, Sarge."

"Let's have a look, Tarrant."

"Mmm that's interesting, a bottle of diazepam here in the bathroom."

"Interesting. The name on the bottle is Judy Whiteside, dated 1989!"

"That must have been his wife?"

"Yes, but there is only one pill in the bottle. Do you suppose he has taken the rest?"

"No, I doubt it. It's strange however just to keep one pill."

"It's just another thing to note and ask him about."

"Yes, Sarge."

"Thanks, guys. Can you try and secure the door, or one of you stay on duty here until we arrange a locksmith to fix it?"

Back at the station Colin was being processed and charged formally and held in a cell. A full report was delivered within the hour to Sullivan.

"Tarrant, Evans, you have done well. We need to clarify the position of Colin and we need to arrest Whiteside. Where do you think he has gone?"

"I have no clue on this at all sir, but he has clearly considered his position and if the information he had given to Colin on Wednesday night is true then he had compromised his carefully worked out plan."

"Yes, I agree sir. Shall we issue a warrant for his arrest?"

"Yes and I think if one of you is free, you should go and see Mrs Wall and advise her of the developments. We don't want her reading about all this in the papers."

"Mrs Wall? It's DS Evans. I wonder if I could come and see you, please?"

"Oh well, my daughters are away, and not back until tomorrow. I would prefer it if you could come when they are at home tomorrow."

"When do you expect them?"

"About noon I think."

"Very well, Mrs Wall. May I come over about twelve thirty?"

"Yes, of course."

There was much excitement in Seefeld at the gala dinner for their final night. New friendships were soon to break up. Sandy's ski instructor would have to go back to the slopes and Sandy back to Chester.

John was thinking to himself that the ski instructor would be really lonely until the next plane load of tourists from wherever in Europe landed. It was a perk of the job.

John and Si had a perfect night. They didn't stay long at the disco after the dinner. They retired to their wonderful room at the top of the hotel and embraced one another whilst looking at the view. They spent the rest of the night in one another's arms, until the early morning call rang and they had to get up at six a.m.

20.2.2000 Saturday

In Seefeld, the whole gang were up early and, after breakfast, the bus took them to Innsbruck airport ready for the Monarch flight home. The flight was called on time and they boarded the plane at nine thirty for the flight. However, due to the fact they were heading west, the flight time was an hour shorter than on the way out, simply because of the time zone change. They landed at Manchester at eleven o'clock.

The baggage was off quickly and their minibus was waiting for them. The journey was quiet, and reflective, perhaps in some part due to an excess of alcohol the night before. Friendships made and now lost were reflected upon. The thought of back to work on Monday was also a downer on the excitement that had accompanied the outward journey.

As they approached Tarporley, the goodbyes started and the noise level increased as the two girls and John were deposited in the farmyard at Long Acre farm. Ann came out of the farmhouse to greet them home. The conversation was all over the place, everyone talking at once. John was busy with the driver getting the luggage out of the back.

"Hello, Ann, how good to see you again."

"Hello, John, have you managed to survive with these two for a week?"

"Yes, no problem at all."

The minibus turned round in the yard accompanied with much waving from the rest of the gang as they left the yard, the cattle grid confirming their departure.

"Phew," said Sandy. "Let's get our stuff into the flats, and then we will come and have a chat, Mum."

"Okay, darling, see you in a minute."

The cattle grid rattled again and, low and behold, Frank Stringer's car came into the yard.

"Hello, Frank, Margaret, how good of you to come. I wanted some support just in case the girls were not back in time."

"Yes that's okay. Are the girls back?"

"Yes, they are just putting their stuff in their flats. They will be over in a minute."

Sandy, Si and John walked briskly with a skip and hop across the yard, and into the kitchen. Much hugging and kissing ensued between the girls, Frank and Margaret. As all this was going on, the cattle grid rattled again.

"Just listen one moment, girls. Hang on, I must tell you that DS Evans will be in here in a minute. I wasn't sure what he wanted but in case you were not home in time I asked Frank and Margaret to come and give me some support."

"Oh, Mum, what is going on?"

"We shall find out in a minute."

Ann went outside to welcome DS Evans and explain to him who he was going to meet. He enquired if Ann had any objection to Evans speaking to everyone, and of course, Ann had said that she would wish him to speak to everyone as they were effectively all family.

"This is DS Evans, everyone. Shall we go into the lounge? There is room for us all to sit down there."

"Mrs Wall, everyone, we have had a number of developments in the last three days and I wanted to bring you up to speed so that should anything appear in the papers you understood what was happening."

"How intriguing," said Si.

"Si, hang on darling, let's find out what this is all about."

"Thank you. The position is that Roger Whiteside had been the subject of a blackmail attempt by Duggie who used to work for Walls. The basis of this was that Fred Appleyard had witnessed Roger Whiteside leaving Long Acre Farm in the early morning of New Year's Day. Fred was adamant that it was Roger. The issue was that Roger was on holiday in Austria for two weeks which covered Christmas and New Year. Now apparently Fred tried to get money from Roger, or so the story goes, because Fred recognised him. Fred had also told Duggie that he had seen him. As we all know, Fred was murdered and run over by the red Ford Escort that used to be driven by Duggie at work. The car was in fact witnessed turning round in your father's gateway, Mr England."

"Yes, I recall my father saying so."

"Duggie continued with the blackmail and tried to collect ten thousand pounds from Roger and got him to take the money to Belfast. Duggie lives in Dublin. You will recall earlier this week, Mrs Wall, when you had a slight coming together with Roger as he was on his way to the bank to collect the money."

"Yes I do. Gosh, that is what he was doing."

"When Roger returned to the UK after Duggie had been arrested in Ireland at the pick-up of the money, he apparently went to the Pied Bull, got very drunk and confessed to Colin, the head mechanic at Walls, that it was he who had knocked Fred off his bike, not Duggie, as Roger had maintained all along. Colin failed to pass this information to us and he is currently in custody for perverting the course of justice."

"Oh heavens, what a thing! So Roger ran over Fred?"

"It would seem so. However, further to this we have been investigating the whereabouts of Mr Whiteside over the New Year period, following the call from Austria from you, Mr England. We are very grateful to you for the information."

"No problem, Sergeant."

"We have established that indeed Mr Whiteside was in this area on New Year's Eve and New Year's Day. We have traced the car that he hired, a black Vauxhall Astra."

"That's the car I had to swerve around on our way back from the golf club."

"Yes I am sure it was, Mrs Wall. We have also been able to make a match of blood traces on Jumbo, the Land Rover's bumper with the DNA of Roger Whiteside."

"So, what does all this mean Sergeant?" enquired Ann in a rather weak and trembling voice.

"It means, Mrs Wall, that we are of the firm opinion that your husband was murdered by Roger Whiteside and we have an arrest warrant out for him now for murder. Murder on two counts, one for your husband Peter Wall and one for Fred Appleyard."

"Oh good lord!" screamed Ann, "So poor Peter didn't commit suicide after all?"

"No, we believe not."

Si and Sandra comforted their mother as the whole horror of the events of New Year's Day flooded back into her memory.

"DS Evans, there are just a few things that puzzle me. If someone had wanted to kill Peter in the way they did they would not have been able to walk one step into this yard without Purdy sounding the alarm."

"That is a puzzle we have yet to explain, Dr Stringer."

"If you recall, Purdy was not well and she hardly moved. Don't you recall I had to take her to the vets? They said she had had been given an excessive dose of diazepam, whatever that is."

"It's a tranquiliser used to calm down humans and in small doses given to animals to calm them down. It is used a lot around Guy Fawkes night for the animals."

"Very interesting, thank you, Doctor, because we have found a nearly empty bottle of diazepam in Whiteside's bathroom. It seems that he has used this drug to feed to Purdy whilst you were out at the golf club, and that ensured she would not make a sound in the morning."

"Very successful it was. He nearly killed her as well."

"So, what do you think happened, Sergeant?" enquired John.

"It seems as though Whiteside prepared the Land Rover knowing Mr Wall's habits and undid the cable whilst you were out, having fed the drug to Purdy. He then put the cable in the back, but whilst undoing the cable the sharp bits of wire sticking out of the cable cut his fingers and dripped a little bit of blood on the bumper, and mixed with a lot of oil and grease that Fred had applied to the winch not many days before. The sharpening stone for Fred's scythe seemed to be the ideal implement to knock Mr Wall out as it would not hold any fingerprints. Once he had made Mr Wall unconscious he drove the Land Rover up to the field and rigged the noose and we all know what happened then. We are fairly sure that when Whiteside walked down the field to the gate, the engine was still running with the wheels spinning in the mud. He just switched the ignition switch to stop the engine. He then left the farm in a bit of a hurry and nearly knocked Fred off his bike as he came out of the lane, turning right in front of Fred to drive back to Liverpool Airport."

"Blimey, what an audacious plot! But why?"

Ann sat motionless as she took in the full horror of what had happened and tears once again began to trickle down her cheeks.

"The answer is jealousy and money, he was consumed with jealousy at your success and the lovely home you had built, and he wanted to become a millionaire by claiming on the insurance."

"Well," said John, "on a purely mercenary note, murder changes everything and allows the insurances to be paid out, even the April 1999 million pound policy. That will be a huge help. The key man insurance is of course no longer payable to Whiteside, because he caused the death."

Evans was listening with interest to the various reactions and the professional advice available to the family.

"What a terrible set of circumstances, this man has destroyed two lives and our family," sobbed Ann.

Just at that moment Evans' mobile rang.

"Yes, Tarrant, what do you want? I am in the middle of speaking to the Wall family... Okay, I will."

Evans excused himself and went out to the kitchen. Purdy was wagging her tail and nuzzling up to his legs.

"I see, are you quite sure?"

"Yes, Sarge, I am here now. There can be no doubt."

"Okay, I will tell them."

"Ladies and gentlemen, I am sorry for that interruption but I can tell you that we have found Roger Whiteside."

"Oh my word, that was quick. Will you be questioning him today?"

"No we won't. He was spotted by a dog walker first thing this morning, he has been pulled out of the River Dee and is dead. He has been identified by DC Tarrant."

The result of Roger's death meant that the key man insurance on Roger could be claimed by the estate of Peter Wall, and the family could move on.

The End

The next novel in the series continues the story of the Wall family – "England's Wall"